徐薇

教你背 新多益
單字 (上)

NEW TOEIC

10種
多益必考情境

1000個
多益必背單字

2000組
單字詞組搭配

4 小時徐薇老師精華單字教學

5 小時美籍、英籍雙口音朗讀 MP3

記單字也學用法，多益單字再難都不怕！

U0085204

《徐薇教你背新多益單字》序

從事英文教學二十多年，我深刻了解學習者在學英文和參加英文考試時會遇到的困難。尤其是年齡愈大的學習者，想要學好英文或是應考備戰，最需要的就是「快速而有效的方法」，這正是我們推出《徐薇教你背新多益單字》套書的目的，期望透過我一直推動的「徐薇UP學」，幫助眾多想挑戰多益測驗及加強英文能力的學習者，以最有效的方式學好英文，英文成績不斷UP、UP、UP！

《徐薇教你背新多益單字》套書，參考多益測驗官方所列出的主題情境及多益測驗常用字詞，同時對照全民英檢分級字表，套書分為(上)、(下)兩冊，共二十個單元，每單元皆有100個與多益測驗情境最相關的單字，並列出單字結構與記憶口訣方便理解，重點單字更有我的教學MP3，徐薇老師會透過英文部首、小故事及聯想記憶法，教你用最快的方式把單字牢牢刻進腦海裡哦！

針對多益測驗中一定會出現的不同口音，我們也聘請了專業美籍與英籍外師，為每個單字與例句錄製了朗讀音檔，透過聆聽不同口音，更能加深印象、增進聽力應考實力。

每單元結束前皆附有精選實力進階區，內容包括：易混字比較、與主題相關的補充字彙、實用片語、常用字根等，增強英文應用能力必不可少；而隨堂測驗區則可讓您在學習完一個單元後，還能自我檢測對單字的理解程度與學習成效。

《徐薇教你背新多益單字》不只是一套教你有效背單字的寶典，同時也是集結了多益考試、商用情境、日常生活溝通必備的英文學習秘笈。跟著徐薇老師學多益單字，收穫的不只是更漂亮的測驗成績，還有更扎實的語文實力喔！

預祝各位學習者

征戰考場，無往不利！

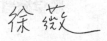

目錄

目錄

徐薇教你背新多益單字（上）

目錄

Unit 6 買賣交易.....................**168**

實力進階.........................196

隨堂練習.........................198

Unit 7 採購與物流.....................199

實力進階.........................226

隨堂練習.........................228

Unit 8 廣告與宣傳.....................229

實力進階.........................257

隨堂練習.........................259

Unit 9 業務協調.....................260

實力進階.........................288

隨堂練習.........................290

Unit 10 企業經營.....................291

實力進階.........................319

隨堂練習.........................320

附錄 1：職場必學實用詞彙.............321

附錄 2：字彙索引.......................323

5

頁面說明

頁面說明

對照全民英檢單字分級作為難易度參考。

中高
92. tardy
['tardɪ]
adj. 遲到的；延遲的

tardily adv. 遲緩地
tardiness n. 遲緩
同 late / sluggish
反 punctual adj. 準時的
  prompt adj. 及時的

⇨ -tard-「緩慢的」+ -y「有…性質的」
Anyone who is tardy for meetings gets the evil eye from the boss.
任何開會遲到的人會被老闆惡狠狠地瞪著。

補充 be tardy in doing sth. 做某事拖拖拉拉地

補充例句內特殊用語，一次學會好幾個實用單字！

中級
93. tray
[tre]
n.（辦公桌上的）文件盒；托盤

Always completely fill the paper tray with two reams of paper.
送紙匣裡要一直放滿兩令的紙張。

★ ream「令」是紙張的計數單位，一令 = 500 張。

典故 tray 源自古英文 treow「樹木、木頭」，也表示木製器皿。

單字起源典故幫助記憶也增長知識喔！

補充 tray 泛指各種淺薄的托盤，辦公室內最常見的就是 filing tray「公文架」和 paper tray「影印機的送紙匣」；或是招待客人喝茶時會用到 tea tray。另外，in tray 是指放置待處理文件的收文格；而 out tray 則是放置已處理文件的發文格。

94. turn in
[tɝn][ɪn]
phr. 歸還；繳交，上交
同 hand in

I expect each employee to turn in a self-evaluation by next Monday.
我希望每一位員工在下週一之前交出自我評量表。

補充符合多益情境的常用詞組、片語、句型。

中高
95. underneath
[ˌʌndɚˋniθ]
prep. 在…底下
adv. 在…底下；本質上
n. 底部

同 prep. = under / beneath / below

⇨ under「在下面」+ beneath「在下面」
Emily muttered underneath her breath as the boss blathered on and on.
老闆持續在滔滔不絕的同時，Emily 暗暗地在底下嘀咕。

補充 mutter underneath one's breath
用別人聽不到的聲音說話

長字記憶有訣竅：字根、字首、字尾，見招拆招最有效！

.00

每單元精選實力進階課程，難字不混淆，實力更上一層樓！

01
實力進階

Part 1. 比一比：bill, invoice 和 receipt

bill
一般統稱為帳單，為對出售的商品或提供的服務所列出的請款單據，內含各項商品或服務項目、單價及應付總金額等資訊，並註明應付款日期，功能與 invoice 相似，只是 invoice 較 bill 更為正式。

invoice
一般稱為發票，但實際功能為出貨請款單，上面載明貨品或服務細項及單價和總金額等資訊，也會註明應付款日期，買方收到 invoice 後要在應付款日期前支付款項給賣方，賣方收到款項後則會再開立收款憑證 receipt。

頁面說明

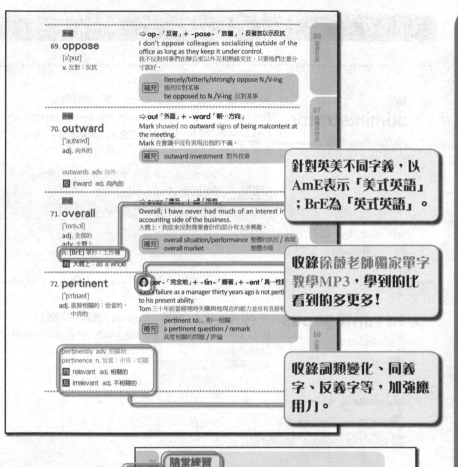

69. oppose
[əˋpoz]
v. 反對；反抗

⇨ op-「反著」+ -pose-「放置」，反著放以示反抗

I don't oppose colleagues socializing outside of the office as long as they keep it under control.
我不反對同事們在辦公室以外互相熱絡交往，只要他們注意分寸就好。

補充
fiercely/bitterly/strongly oppose N./V-ing
強烈反對某事
be opposed to N./V-ing 反對某事

70. outward
[ˋautwəd]
adj. 向外的

⇨ out「外面」+ -ward「朝…方向」

Mark showed no outward signs of being malcontent at the meeting.
Mark 在會議中沒有表現出他的不滿。

補充 outward investment 對外投資

outwards adv. 向外
反 inward adj. 向內的

針對英美不同字義，以 AmE表示「美式英語」；BrE為「英式英語」。

71. overall
[ˋovərˌɔl]
adj. 全部的
adv. 大體上
n. (BrE) 罩衫；工作褲
同 大體上：as a whole

⇨ over「遍及」+ all「所有」

Overall, I have never had much of an interest in accounting side of the business.
大體上，我從來沒對商業會計的部分有太多興趣。

補充
overall situation/performance 整體的狀況 / 表現
overall market 整體市場

收錄徐薇老師獨家單字教學MP3，學到的比看到的多更多！

72. pertinent
[ˋpɜtnənt]
adj. 直接相關的；恰當的，中肯的

⇨ per-「完全地」+ -tin-「握著」+ -ent「具…性質」

Tom's failure as a manager thirty years ago is not pertinent to his present ability.
Tom 三十年前當經理時失職與他現在的能力並沒有直接相關。

補充
pertinent to... 和…相關
a pertinent question / remark
高度相關的問題 / 評論

pertinently adv. 相關地
pertinence n. 恰當；中肯；切題
同 relevant adj. 相關的
反 irrelevant adj. 不相關的

收錄詞類變化、同義字、反義字等，加強應用力。

隨堂練習

請選出最適合的單字

( ) 1. Mr. Benton was _____ from the committee and replaced by Mr. Smith because of the infamous affair with his secretary.
(A) dispatched　　(B) reimbursed
(C) discharged　　(D) estimated

( ) 2. Since Beth is a workaholic, it's not easy for her to _____ from working full-time to retirement.
(A) erect　　(B) transition
(C) solicit　　(D) quote

( ) 3. It's common to _____ over the price when you make a purchase at a night market.
(A) haggle　　(B) assure
(C) linger　　(D) misdirect

每單元附隨堂練習，學完做檢測、記憶更深刻！

01 職稱職務／聘僱面試

02 人事／薪資／福利

03 辦公室／電話傳真

04 文書作業

05 會議

Unit 1 職稱職務／聘僱面試

中高

1. administrator

[əd`mɪnə͵stretə]
n. 管理人；行政官員

⇨ administer「管理」+ -or「做…動作的人」

You must have a minimum of ten years' experience to be considered for the **administrator** position.
你必須有最少十年的工作經驗才能擔任主管職。

補充
data administrator [電腦用語] 資料管理員
administrative work/duties 管理職責
business administration　企業管理

administrative adj. 行政的；管理的
administration n. 管理，經營；管理部門，行政部門

2. advantageous

[͵ædvən`tedʒəs]
adj. 有利的

⇨ advantage「優點」+ -ous「充滿…特質的」

It is **advantageous** to be able to speak multiple languages.
會說多國語言是很有利的。

advantage n. 優點

同 beneficial / helpful

反 disadvantageous adj. 不利的

中級

3. ambitious

[æm`bɪʃəs]
adj. 有抱負的，野心勃勃的

⇨ ambi-「到處」+ -it-「走」+ -ious「充滿…特質的」，四處走動以求名望的樣子

Overly **ambitious** people tend to be promoted quickly.
極度有野心的人較容易很快升遷。

補充　an ambitious plan 難度很高的計畫

ambition n. 野心，企圖
ambitiously adv. 勁頭十足地；熱切地

4. application

[ˌæpləˈkeʃən]

n. 申請、請求；申請書；
應用程式

apply「申請」+ -ion「名詞字尾」

Just fill out our online **application** and someone will get back to you in a short while.
只要填寫我們的線上申請書，很快就會有人給您回覆。

補充		
application form	申請表格
job application	工作申請
make/submit an application	提交申請書

apply v. 申請
applicant n. 申請人

初級

5. assistant

[əˈsɪstənt]

n. 助理；(BrE) 店員
adj. 助理的 (用於職稱以表示位階)

assist「協助」+ -ant「表動作執行者」

You've got to have a few years of experience as an **assistant** before we can promote you to department head.
你必須具備幾年助理經驗我們才能把你升為部門主管。

補充		
administrative assistant	行政助理
executive assistant	執行助理
assistant manager	副理；協理
sales assistant = sales clerk	店員

assist v. 協助

中高

6. attribute

[ˈætrɪˌbjut]
n. 特性；特質
[əˈtrɪbjut]
v. 歸因於

at-「to」+ -tribut-「給予」，上天給予人不同的特質

Some **attributes** necessary for this position are: high intelligence, diligence, and creativity.
這個職位須具備的特質是：高智商、勤奮，以及有創造力。
He **attributed** his failure to misfortune.
他認為他會失敗是因為不幸。

補充		
personal attribute	人格特質
essential attribute	本質屬性
attribute A to B	把 A 歸因於 B

attribution n. 歸因

同 n. = trait / characteristic

中級

7. **autobiography**
[ˌɔtəbaɪˈɑgrəfɪ]
n. 自傳

biography n. 傳記

⇨ **auto-**「自己的」 + **-bio-**「生命」 + **-graphy**「紀錄」
Most famous entrepreneurs confess their flaws in their **autobiographies**.
大多數有名的企業家都在他們的自傳中坦承自己的缺失。

中級

8. **background**
[ˈbækˌgraʊnd]
n. 出身，個人背景

⇨ **back**「後面的」 + **ground**「地面」
Please discuss your specific **background** in the field of website design.
請詳細介紹您在網頁設計領域的專業背景。

補充
educational background 教育背景，學歷
background information/details/data 背景資料
a background in + 專業領域 有某領域的背景

初級

9. **board**
[bord]
n. 委員會；董事會；（政府的）部，局，會

We have to run this idea by the **board** before we can present it to the employees.
在我們讓員工知道這項計畫之前，我們必須先上呈董事會。

補充
board of directors 董事會
on board 到職

中級

10. **candidate**
[ˈkændədet]
n. 候選人；求職應徵者

candid adj. 白的；純潔的

⇨ **candid**「白的；純潔的」 + **-ate**「表人」
There are so many **candidates** for this job that we need five staff members to sort the applications.
這個職務的應徵者多到我們需要動用五名員工來整理求職信。

典故
古羅馬時代，找公職的男人和官員都是穿著白色的 (candid) 托加長袍；因此只要看到穿著白袍，散發白色光芒的人就知道那是想當官的人。

中級

11. capable
['kepəbl]
adj. 有能力的；能力好的

⇨ **-cap-**「抓」＋ **-able**「能夠…的」，能抓很多就表示是有能力的

Alice only has two weeks of training, so I don't think she is **capable** of going solo yet.
Alice 才受訓兩週，因此我不認為她已經可以獨立作業了。

補充 be capable of + N./V-ing 有…的能力

capability n. 能力
同 competent / skilled
反 incapable adj. 不能勝任的

中級

12. certificate
[sə'tɪfəkɪt]
n. 憑證；證書；執照
v. 發證書給…；用證書證明

⇨ **certify**「證明」＋ **-ate**「名詞字尾」，證明能力的東西

You'll need to bring original copies of your Microsoft **certificates** so we can validate their authenticity.
你需要帶你的微軟證照正本來，這樣我們才能驗證其可靠性。

補充
have/hold a certificate in sth.	具備某專業的證照
gift certificate	禮券
medical certificate	診斷書；醫師證明
certificate of deposit	銀行存款單
certificate of insurance	保險單

certify v. 證明；證實
certificated adj. 持有合格證書的

初級

13. chief
[tʃif]
n. 主任；長官；領袖
adj. 主要的

We should consult the **chief** architect for this project before proceeding any further.
在有下一步動作之前，我們應該先請教首席設計師關於這份企劃案的事。

 典故 chief 源於拉丁文 caput，意思是「頭」，用來描述一群人裡面的老大。

 補充
Chief Executive Officer (CEO)	首席執行長；總裁
Chief Financial Officer (CFO)	首席財務長
editor in chief	主編

易混 chef n. 主廚

11

初級

14. **clerk**

[klɜk]

n. 職員；店員

The **clerks** at this chain store constantly work overtime to make ends meet.

這間連鎖店的店員長期超時工作以求溫飽。

典故 古代只有神職人員 (cleric) 有閱讀和書寫的能力，所以 cleric 形容有讀寫能力的人。 衍生的 clerk 則指執行文書作業的人。

補充 office clerk 職員
desk clerk (AmE) 飯店櫃檯人員
sales clerk (AmE) 商店店員

cleric n. 教會神職人員
clerical adj. 文書的；事務的

中級

15. **committee**

[kəˈmɪtɪ]

n. 委員會

⇨ commit「委託」＋ -ee「被…的人」，被委託任務的人組成委員會

The CEO has just organized a **committee** to look into the discrepancies between reported and actual revenues.

執行長剛剛組織了委員會來調查報告收入和實際收入的不一致處。

補充 be on the committee 屬於委員會的成員

commit v. 委託

中高

16. **competent**

[ˈkɑmpətənt]

adj. 有能力的，勝任的

⇨ compete「競爭」＋ -ent「具…性質的」，能同場競技的就是有能力的

Sally seems **competent** enough to be promoted, but she doesn't mesh well with the team.

雖然 Sally 的能力足以被提拔升職，但是她卻沒辦法好好配合團隊。

competence n. 能力；技能

同 capable

中級

17. **consideration**

[kənˌsɪdəˋreʃən]

n. 考慮

⇨ **consider**「考慮，認為」+ **-ation**「名詞字尾」

After careful **consideration**, we have decided not to pursue a merger at this time.

經過審慎考慮，我們決定了這次先不要合併。

 take sth. into consideration 將某事物列入考慮
in consideration of sth. 考慮到某事物

consider v. 考慮
considerate adj. 體貼的

初級

18. **contact**

[ˋkɑntækt]

v./n. 聯繫，聯絡

⇨ **con-**「一起」+ **-tact-**「接觸」

I'll have someone in my office **contact** you within one hour about when to schedule our next meeting.

我會請我辦公室的同仁在一小時內聯繫你關於我們下次會面的行程。

 in contact with sb. 與某人有聯繫

中級

19. **contribute**

[kənˋtrɪbjut]

v. 貢獻，提供，出力；捐獻

⇨ **con-**「一起」+ **-tribut-**「贈與」

Employees are encouraged to **contribute** any ideas at staff meetings.

我們鼓勵員工在員工會議中提出各種想法。

 contribute to sth. 捐獻給某單位；促使某事發生
contribute sth. to sth./sb. 將某物貢獻給…

contribution n. 貢獻

初級

20. **degree**

[dɪˋgri]

n. 學位；程度；度數

Having a simple BA **degree** doesn't even get you an interview at the biggest engineering firms.

只擁有一個學士學位根本無法得到最大工程公司的面試機會。

 get a degree in + 學科 取得某學科的學位
bachelor's degree 學士學位
master's degree 碩士學位

初級

21. department
[dɪ`pɑrtmənt]
n. 部門

departmental adj. 部門的

⇨ **depart**「分離」+ **-ment**「名詞字尾」，不同部門都是分開的

The phone system has kicked me around to the wrong **department** several times.
電話系統好幾次將我轉接到錯誤的部門去。

中級

22. dependable
[dɪ`pɛndəbl]
adj. 可靠的

dependability n. 可靠性

同 reliable

⇨ **depend**「依靠」+ **-able**「能夠…的」

I need someone **dependable** to take charge of this project and make it a success.
我需要可靠的人來負責這個企劃讓它成功。

中高

23. desirable
[dɪ`zaɪrəbl]
adj. 合乎希望的；令人滿意的

desire v./n. 渴望
desired adj. 被渴望的；受喜歡的

⇨ **desire**「渴望」+ **-able**「能夠…的」，會被渴望的表示是令人滿意的

Your experience in the area of finance makes you a **desirable** candidate.
你在金融圈的經驗使你成為一個理想的候選人。

中級

24. devote
[dɪ`vot]
v. 奉獻；致力

Mr. Blake has been **devoted** to the career training program for years.
Blake 先生致力於職訓計畫行之有年。

補充
devote A to B	將 A 奉獻於 B 上
devote oneself to sth.	獻身於某事
be devoted to sth.	致力於某事

devoted adj. 全心投入的；忠實的
devotion n. 奉獻

同 commit / dedicate

中級

25. **diploma**

[dɪˋplomə]

n. 文憑

 di-「兩倍」＋-plo-「摺」＋-ma「名詞字尾」

Sandy received her **diploma** from a prestigious private high school, but without a degree, we still can't hire her.

Sandy 取得一所極富盛名的私立中學文憑，但是沒有大學學位，我們還是不能僱用她。

補充　a diploma in sth. 某專業科目的文憑

初級

26. **director**

[dəˋrɛktɚ]

n. 主管；主任；董事

⇨ direct「指導」＋-or「做…動作的人」

We need to speak to the **director** of this department about the recent mass layoffs that have been occurring.

我們需要和部門主任討論關於最近持續在進行的大量裁員。

補充
Managing Director (MD)　常務董事；總經理
Executive Director (ED)　執行總監；執行長

direct v. 指導

初級

27. **division**

[dəˋvɪʒən]

n. 部門

⇨ divide「分割」＋-ion「名詞字尾」

Each floor of this building is comprised of a different **division** within the sales department.

這棟大樓每一層樓都包含了業務部旗下的不同處室。

divide v. 分割

同 department / section

---

28. **dress code**

[drɛs] [kod]

n. 穿衣法則，著裝標準

The company **dress code** states that all men have to wear buttoned shirts and pants.

公司穿著規定所有男性員工必須穿著鈕扣襯衫和長褲上班。

補充
business casual (smart casual)　商務休閒裝
dress-down Friday (casual Friday)　便裝日

code n. 規範；密碼

中級
29. employment
[ɪmˋplɔɪmənt]
n. 僱用

⇨ **employ**「僱用」＋ **-ment**「名詞字尾」
We need to watch the government **employment** report to get an accurate gauge of how healthy the economy is.
我們需要觀察政府就業報告來精確判斷經濟健全的程度。

 in employment　　在職，有工作
employment agency 人力銀行，職業介紹所

employ v. 僱用
employer n. 雇主
employee n. 受僱者，員工
反 unemployment n. 失業

中級
30. essential
[ɪˋsɛnʃəl]
adj. 必要的；基礎的

⇨ **essence**「本質」＋ **-al**「關於⋯的」
Your **essential** job duties include but are not limited to answering emails and investigating all order discrepancies.
你的基本工作職責包含，但也不限於，回覆電子郵件以及調查所有訂單差異。

essence n. 本質，要素
同 crucial

中高
31. ethic
[ˋɛθɪk]
n. 道德

⇨ **ethos**「精神特質」＋**-ic**「名詞字尾，表學術用語」
Bob's strong work **ethic** is evident since he has the highest sales figures of all our staff.
Bob 強烈的工作使命感是顯而易見的，因為他是全體員工中達到最高銷售額的人。

 work ethic　　　　 工作使命感
professional ethics 職業道德

ethics n. 倫理學

中級

32. executive

[ɪgˈzɛkjʊtɪv]

n. (高階) 行政主管；經理
adj. 行政的；主管級的；
　　經營管理的

execute v. 執行；實現

⇨ **execute**「執行；實現」+ **-ive**「有…性質的」

Bryan was hired as an **executive** for the firm immediately after getting his Ph.D.
Bryan 拿到博士學位後就立刻被這間公司聘為經理了。

 補充
an executive position	行政職務
a business executive	企業主管
the executive	政府的行政部門

中級

33. expectation

[ˌɛkspɛkˈteʃən]

n. 期待

expect v. 期待

⇨ **expect**「期待」+ **-ation**「名詞字尾」

It was my **expectation** that you would learn the operating system on your own.
我期望你能獨自學會這個操作系統。

 補充　live up to one's expectations　符合某人的期待

中高

34. expertise

[ˌɛkspɚˈtiz]

n. 專門技術；專業知識

expert n. 專家

⇨ **expert**「專家」+ **-ise**「名詞字尾」

Frank's **expertise** in managing the company's data in the cloud is unquestioned.
Frank 管理公司雲端資料的專業是無庸置疑的。

中高

35. familiarity

[fəˌmɪlɪˈærətɪ]

n. 精通，通曉；熟悉

familiar adj. 熟悉的

⇨ **familiar**「熟悉的」+ **-ity**「名詞字尾」

Do you have any **familiarity** with our newest line of products?
你熟悉我們最新的產品線嗎？

 補充　familiarity with + N.　精通某領域

初級

36. fill

[fɪl]

v. 遞補；填滿

Rebecca quit suddenly, so we have to rush to **fill** her position.

Rebecca 突然辭職了，所以我們必須趕快遞補她的職缺。

補充	fill the position/job vacancy	遞補職缺
	fill in (for sb.)	幫某人代班
	fill in/out a form	填寫表格

中級

37. flexible

[ˈflɛksəbl̩]

adj. 有彈性的；可變通的

flexibility n. 彈性；適應性
flextime n. 彈性工作時間

⇨ flex「彎曲的」+ -ible「能夠⋯的」

We need a more **flexible** break policy; sometimes I work six hours continuously.

我們需要一個更有彈性的休息時間；有時候我得連續工作六個小時。

中高

38. fluency

[ˈfluənsɪ]

n. 流利度；流暢

fluent adj. 流利的

⇨ fluent「流利的」+ -cy「名詞字尾」

Once you have achieved **fluency** in Japanese, we can put you in the call center.

只要你能說流利的日文，我們就可以派你去客服中心。

---

39. freelance

[ˈfriˈlæns]

n. 自由工作者
adj. 自由（獨立）工作的
adv. 自由（獨立）工作地

 free「自由的」+ lance「長矛騎兵」

Martha works for us **freelance**, so she does not qualify for the company health care plan.

Martha 是我們的自由工作者，所以她沒有參與公司醫療保健計畫的資格。

| 典故 | freelance 最早用來指中世紀的僱傭兵，後來演變成沒有固定雇主的自由工作者。 |

| 補充 | freelance writer | 自由作家 |
| | freelance journalist | 自由記者 |

同 n. = freelance worker / freelancer

中級

40. guidance

[ˋgaɪdəns]

n. 指導

 ⇨ guide「指導」+ -ance「名詞字尾」

It would be best to seek the **guidance** of your trainer on this matter.

關於這件事，你最好向你的訓練員尋求指導。

補充　under the guidance of... 在…的帶領之下

guide v. 指導；帶領

---

41. headhunt

[ˋhɛdˌhʌnt]

v. 獵頭；獵才，挖角

⇨ head「頭」+ hunt「打獵」

I never grow tired of **headhunting** for that perfect employee.

爲了找到完美理想的員工，我從來不會感到疲倦。

headhunter n. 獵才者
headhunting n. 替公司物色人才挖角

---

42. hear from

[hɪr] [frɑm]

phr. 收到消息

We haven't **heard from** you for days, so we've offered the job to another candidate.

因爲我們有好多天沒收到你的消息，所以我們將工作給了另一位應徵者。

初級

43. hire

[haɪr]

v. 僱用；租用

We only need to **hire** 30 people from this pool of 2,000 applicants.

我們只需要從這兩千名申請者中僱用其中三十人。

典故　hire 源自古英文 hyrian，是給人工錢的意思。

補充　美式英語中 hire 是僱用的意思；英式英語中 hire 是指短期的僱用某人，如：hire a private detective；如果要表示公司僱用員工，employ 是比較常用的字。

中級

44. ideal

[aɪˋdiəl]

adj. 理想的

  ⇨ idea「意見、想法」+ -al「具…性質的」

Everyone wants an **ideal** environment to work in, but few companies can provide it.

人人都想要一個理想的工作環境，不過幾乎沒有公司可以提供。

idea n. 想法

01 職稱職務／聘僱面試

02 人事／薪資／福利

03 辦公室／電話傳真

04 文書作業

05 會議

中級

45. identity

[aɪˋdɛntətɪ]

n. 身分

⇨ **ident**「拉丁文，一樣」+ **-ity**「名詞字尾」，和你一樣的東西就是你的身分

Our firm deals with preventing **identity** theft, which is on the rise.

我們公司負責防止身分盜用的業務，這類業務正在增加中。

補充	identity card/ ID card	身分證
	confirm/prove one's identity	證明身分
	identity theft	身分盜竊

identify v. 認出，識別

中級

46. impress

[ɪmˋprɛs]

v. 使⋯印象深刻

⇨ **im-**「進入」+ **press**「按、壓」

Your professional answers to each question really have **impressed** me.

你對每個問題的專業答覆真的使我印象很深刻。

impressive adj. 令人印象深刻的
impression n. 印象

47. in charge

[ɪn] [tʃɑrdʒ]

phr. 管理；負責

Fred is our agent **in charge** of sales at this facility.

Fred 是負責我們在這裡的銷售代理人。

| 補充 | in charge of + N. | 管理某事 |
| | take charge of + N. | 管理某事 |

charge n. 責任

初級

48. industry

[ˋɪndəstrɪ]

n. 企業；產業；行業

We are responsible for the majority of research in the energy **industry**, exploring possible new sources.

我們負責多數的能源產業研究，並探索可能的新能源。

| 典故 | **industry** 源自拉丁文 **industria**，表示「為達到目的而進行的勞力活動」。工業革命之後，人力逐漸以投入工業生產為主，因此 **industry** 也有了工業的意思。 |

| 補充 | service industry 服務業 |

industrial adj. 工業的
industrious adj. 勤勉的

中級

49. **intermediate**
[ˌɪntəˈmidɪət]
adj. 中等程度的，中級的

⇨ **inter**-「在…之間」+ **-medi**-「中間」+ **-ate**「有…性質的」

The internship posting requires that applicants have at least an **intermediate** level of knowledge about computer programming.

這個實習生招聘公告上要求應徵者要有至少中等程度的電腦程式設計能力。

| advanced | adj. 進階的、精通的 |
| basic | adj. 基礎的 |

50. **intern**
[ˈɪntɝn]
n. 實習生

 inter-「在裡面；往內」+ **-nus**「拉丁形容詞字尾」

Ted is just an unpaid **intern** right now; he's waiting for his chance to start as a salaried employee.

Ted 目前只是個不支薪的實習生；他正在等待能成為正式員工的機會。

| trainee | n. 受訓者，練習生 |
| apprentice | n. 學徒 |

internship n. 實習期間

初級

51. **interview**
[ˈɪntɚˌvju]
n./v. 會面；面談

⇨ **inter**-「在…之間，互相」+ **view**「觀看」

We were impressed enough to ask you to a second **interview** this Friday.

我們對你印象很深刻，請你這週五來參加第二次的面談。

panel interview	主管共同面試
group interview	集體面試
lunch interview	餐敘面試
phone interview	電話面試

中級

52. junior

[`dʒunjɚ]

adj. 資淺的

n. 晚輩

反 senior adj. 資深的

Thomas is the **junior** salesman of the group, with only one year of experience.

Thomas 是這一組裡較資淺的業務，他只有一年的工作經驗。

中級

53. location

[lo`keʃən]

n. 地點

locate v. 使…座落於

 locate「使…座落於」+ **-ion**「名詞字尾」

In the restaurant business, **location** can mean everything since people don't want to go out of their way to eat.

在餐飲業，地點決定了一切，因為一般人不會為了吃東西給自己找麻煩。

補充 prime location 黃金地段

---

54. look forward to

[luk] [`fɔrwəd] [tu]

phr. 期待

I'm **looking forward to** overseeing the rapid expansion of our company in this area.

我很期待能負責我們公司在這一區的快速業務擴展。

補充 look forward to + N./V-ing 期待…

初級

55. major

[`medʒɚ]

v./n. 主修

adj. 主要的

majority n. 多數

反 minor v./n. 副修

Barbara's **major** for her BA was Literature, but she ended up becoming a police officer instead.

Barbara 大學主修文學，不過她最後反而成為一名警察。

The server crash was a **major** test of our IT Department's ability to repair everything quickly.

這次伺服器當機對我們公司資訊部的快速維修能力是一次重大考驗。

初級

56. manager
[ˋmænɪdʒɚ]
n. 經理；負責人

 manage「管理」＋ **-er**「做…動作的人」

All of our **managers** undergo at least three months of serious customer service training.

我們所有的經理都要接受為期至少三個月的嚴格客服訓練。

補充
a bank/hotel manager　銀行 / 飯店經理
the sales/marketing/personnel manager
銷售部 / 行銷部 / 人事部經理

中級

57. motivated
[ˋmotɪvetɪd]
adj. 有動機的；有積極性的

 motivate「給…動機；激勵」＋ **-ed**「形容詞字尾」

Rob is our best **self-motivated** salesman, and doesn't let rejection get him down.

Rob 是我們業務員中最會自我激勵的，並且他不會讓自己被拒絕打倒。

補充
highly-motivated　adj. 非常積極的

motivation n. 動機；動力

中高

58. novice
[ˋnɑvɪs]
n. 新手；初學者

 -nov-「新的」＋ **-ice**「名詞字尾」

Luckily, when I was a **novice**, I was matched up with a veteran to learn the ropes of the business.

幸運地，在我還是新人的時候，我和一位前輩搭檔跟他學了很多做生意的竅門。

★ learn the ropes：表示掌握竅門。

補充
形容新手常用字：
beginner, rookie, newbie, new-comer

中級

59. occupation
[͵ɑkjəˋpeʃən]
n. 職業

 occupy「佔用」＋ **-ion**「名詞字尾」，職業佔了大部分的人生

Choosing the right **occupation** is the key to a balanced life.

選擇一份適合自己的職業是生活平衡的關鍵。

補充
current/previous occupation　現職 / 曾任職業
occupational disease　　　　職業病
occupational hazard　　　　職業上的風險

occupy v. 佔據
occupational adj. 職業的

初級

60. **opportunity**

[ˌɑpɚˈtjunətɪ]

n. 機會

 opportune「時間恰好的」+ **-ity**「名詞字尾」

Having the chance to be a project leader is an **opportunity** that I can't let pass me by.

這個成為專案領導人的機會是我絕不能錯過的。

| 補充 | job opportunity | 工作機會 |
| | equal opportunities | 平等就業機會 |

同 chance

中高

61. **orientation**

[ˌorɪɛnˈteʃən]

n. 培訓，準備；傾向

 orient「東方」+ **-ation**「名詞字尾」

I spent the entire **orientation** day filling out paperwork and reading about company policies.

新人培訓日當天我一整天都在填寫資料和閱讀公司規定。

| 補充 | political/religious/sexual orientation |
| | 政治／宗教／性傾向 |

orient n. 東方 v. 定位；以…為方向，面向

---

62. **overtime**

[ˈovɚˌtaɪm]

adv. 超時地

n. 加班

over「超過」+ **time**「時間」

Mr. Davies was looking into why so many staff members were forced to work **overtime** last month.

Davies 先生正在調查為什麼上個月有那麼多員工被迫超時工作。

| 補充 | work overtime | 超時工作 |
| | overtime pay | 加班費 |

---

63. **overview**

[ˈovɚˌvju]

n. 概觀；概要；綜述

⇨ **over**「遍及；從頭到尾」+ **view**「觀看」

To get an accurate **overview** of the budget, we need to look more closely at where we are wasting money.

為了得到精確的預算綜述，我們需要更仔細看看我們是在哪裡把錢浪費掉了。

| 補充 | company overview 公司概述 |

中高

64. **part-time**

[`part`taɪm]

adj. 兼任的，兼職的

adv. 兼職地

 part「部分」+ time「時間」

It is cheaper for us to hire loads of **part-time** workers because they don't receive benefits.

對我們來說，僱用大量兼職員工比較便宜是因為他們並不享有員工福利。

補充　work part-time　做兼職工作

part-timer n. 兼職者

反 full-time　adj. 全職的

中級

65. **permanent**

[`pɜmənənt]

adj. 固定的；永久的

 per-「完全的」+ -man-「維持」+ -ent「具…性質的」，完全維持住的就是固定的

We must find a **permanent** solution to the slowdown in our manufacturing plant.

我們必須找到解決製造工廠怠工的永久方法。

補充　a permanent job　固定工作

permanent employees (regular employees)

一般 / 正式員工；終身制員工

反 temporary　adj. 臨時的；暫時的

---

66. **permatemp**

[`pɜmətɛmp]

n. 約聘員工；派遣員工

 perma(nent)「固定的」+ temp(orary)「暫時的」

More and more companies use **permatemps** to avoid constant training of new employees.

越來越多公司僱用約聘員工以避免不斷在訓練新進員工。

補充　常見的臨時員工種類有：

1. temporary employees 通常指代理原來休假的正職員工而另聘的約聘人員，或是正式員工人數不足時聘請的約聘人員。

2. seasonal employees 指在一段限定的時間才會特別僱用的短期臨時工。

中級

67. personality

[ˌpɝsn̩ˈælətɪ]

n. 個性

personal adj. 個人的

同 character

⇨ **personal**「個人的」**+ -ity**「表性格」

We are now requiring that each new employee complete a **personality** survey to find out which section might be the best fit.

我們目前要求每位新進員工完成一份性格調查以便找出最適合每位員工的所屬部門。

中高

68. personnel

[ˌpɝsn̩ˈɛl]

n. 全體人員；人事部門

person n. 人

We have just the right **personnel** to implement the new customer-friendly policy.

我們有最理想的人選來執行新客戶友善制度。

補充　six personnel 六名員工

中高

69. portfolio

[portˈfolɪˌo]

n. 作品集；紙夾，公事包

 -port-「攜帶，包含」**+ folio**「對開紙」，包含多張對開紙的紙夾

The interview **portfolio** is required since you are applying as a website designer.

既然你是應徵網站設計師，你就必須帶你的作品集去面試。

補充　interview portfolio / career portfolio
面試檔案 / 職涯檔案
investment portfolio [金融用語] 投資組合

初級

70. position

[pəˈzɪʃən]

n. 職位，工作；位置

⇨ **-pos-**「擺放」**+ -tion**「名詞字尾」

There are not enough **positions** available after the merger, so we'll need to let some people go.

公司合併之後就沒有足夠的職缺了，所以我們將需要讓一些人離開。

補充　apply for/take up/fill the position
應徵 / 從事 / 遞補某職務
hold a position 擔任某職位

中級

71. possess
[pəˈzɛs]
v. 具有，擁有

➡ pos「拉丁文，能夠」+ -sess-「坐」，擁有者才能坐這兒

We now **possess** an inventory of about 3,000 cars at our suburban dealership.
我們現在在郊區的經銷商那裏還有庫存約三千輛車。

possessions n. 所有物；財產

中級

72. potential
[pəˈtɛnʃəl]
n. 潛力
adj. 潛在的，可能的

➡ potent「有力的」+ -ial「有…性質的」

We have the **potential** to open five new offices abroad this year if our sales are up ten percent.
如果銷售額成長百分之十，我們今年有可能會在海外開設五間新的辦公室。

 補充

a potential employee/employer
有機會成為員工 / 老闆的人
potential customer 潛在客戶

---

73. preferred
[prɪˈfɜːd]
adj. 優先的

➡ prefer「較喜愛」+ -ed「形容詞字尾」

A BA degree is required for this job, but an MA degree is **preferred**.
這份工作需具備大學學歷，但有碩士學位則會優先考慮。

prefer v. 較喜愛
preference n. 優先權

初級

74. president
[ˈprɛzədənt]
n. 總裁；董事

➡ pre-「在前面」+ -sid-「坐」+ -ent「動作執行者」，坐最前面的就是總裁

At forty, he is the youngest **president** ever at Deco Corporation due to his diligence and intelligence.
現年四十歲，他因勤奮與聰明才智成為 Deco 股份有限公司有史以來最年輕的總裁。

vice president n. 副總裁；副社長

75. probation

[proˈbeʃən]

n. 試用期；緩刑；
(AmE) 留任察看期

 probate「驗證（合法性）」+ **-ion**「名詞字尾」

Margaret is on **probation** since she has been late five times this last month.

Margaret 正在試用觀察期，因爲她過去這個月已經遲到五次了。

補充	probation period 試用期 pass probation 通過試用期 on probation 在試用期；在觀察期；在緩刑期間

probate v. 驗證（遺囑）的合法性
probationary adj. 試用的；緩刑的

中級

76. profession

[prəˈfɛʃən]

n. 專業；職業

⇨ **profess**「公開聲明」+ **-ion**「名詞字尾」，公開宣布的強項就是專業

What made you choose accounting as a **profession**?
你爲什麼選擇以會計作爲職業？

補充	enter a profession 從事某職業 the... profession 某職業的全體人員；同業

professional adj. 專業的

中高

77. proficiency

[prəˈfɪʃənsɪ]

n. 熟練，精通

⇨ **proficient**「精通的」+ **-ency**「名詞字尾」

Once I am confident enough in your **proficiency** with this software, I can turn you loose on your own.

一旦我對你使用這套軟體的熟練度夠有信心了，我就可以放你自己一個人獨立作業了。

補充	表示 language proficiency level 的常用字彙： novice adj. 初階的 intermediate adj. 中階的 advanced adj. 進階的 superior adj. 優秀的

proficient adj. 精通的

中高

78. profile

[ˋprofaɪl]

n. 人物簡介；輪廓

⇨ **pro-**「向前」+ **-fil-**「畫線」，向前畫出事物的輪廓

Our clients prefer to keep a low **profile**, so we never share their personal information.

我們的客戶比較喜歡保持低調，所以我們從不會對外透露他們的個人資料。

補充　keep a low profile 保持低調

中級

79. promising

[ˋprɑmɪsɪŋ]

adj. 有前途的；有希望的

⇨ **promise**「給人希望」+ **-ing**「形容詞字尾」

After touring their factory, I would say that the acquisition of this company looks **promising**.

在參觀過他們的工廠後，我可以說收購這間公司看來是很有希望的。

補充　a promising career/man 有前途的工作 / 人

promise v. 承諾；給人希望
promised adj. 應許的

---

80. punch in

[pʌntʃ] [ɪn]

phr. 打卡上班

We were told not to punch in by the boss because the card machine was broken.

老闆吩咐我們不要打卡，因為打卡機壞掉了。

補充　clock in/out (BrE) 打卡上下班

反 punch out 打卡下班

中級

81. qualification

[͵kwɑləfəˋkeʃən]

n. 資格；合格證明；工作資歷

⇨ **qualify**「使合格」+ **-ation**「名詞字尾」

You possess the minimum **qualifications** for the position, but other candidates are quite overqualified.

雖然你具備這個職位的最低資格，不過其他應徵者的條件卻是相當好。

補充　paper qualifications 書面資格證明

qualify v. 使合格
qualified adj. 合格的；具備必要條件的

同 credentials

中高

82. recommendation

[ˌrɛkəmɛnˈdeʃən]

n. 推薦；推薦書

 recommend「推薦」+ -ation「名詞字尾」

Our online application requires five letters of **recommendation** instead of the usual three.

我們線上申請需要五封推薦信，而不是一般的三封。

補充　letter of recommendation 推薦信

recommend v. 推薦；介紹

中高

83. recruit

[rɪˈkrut]

n. 新招募的人員
v. 招募；吸收

 re-「再次」+ -cru-「生長」，招募新人使人數再次成長

None of the new **recruits** is older than twenty four, so we may need them to spend more time with their mentors.

新招募進來的員工沒有一個超過二十四歲，所以我們可能要讓他們多花點時間向他們的指導者學習。

補充	recruitment agency	人事顧問公司
	recruitment consultant	招聘顧問
	annual recruitment	年度招聘
	campus recruitment	校園徵才

recruitment n. 招募，招收
recruiter n. 招聘人員

中級

84. reference

[ˈrɛfərəns]

n. 介紹信；介紹人

 refer「參考；提及」+ -ence「名詞字尾」

May I ask your permission to write your name as a **reference** on my CV?

我可以在我的簡歷上將您列為推薦人嗎？

補充　FYR = For Your Reference 供你參考

refer v. 參考；提及

06 買賣交易

中級

85. related

[rɪˈletɪd]

adj. 相關的

⇨ **relate**「與⋯有關」+ **-ed**「形容詞字尾」

Our divisions are not **related** at all, but we share the same floor.

我們的部門一點都不相關，不過我們都在同一層樓。

補充 a related field/experience 相關領域 / 經驗

relate v. 與⋯有關

同 connected / associated

07 採購與物流

08 廣告與宣傳

中級

86. reliable

[rɪˈlaɪəbl]

adj. 可靠的

⇨ **rely**「依靠」+ **-able**「能夠⋯的」

My strong point is that I am a **reliable** worker.

我的優點是我是個可靠的員工。

Only those with **reliable transportation** are encouraged to apply in the USA.

在美國只有具備功能正常的車子的人是有機會應徵工作的。

補充 reliable transportation/vehicles 指功能正常不會拋錨的交通工具。在美國擁有功能正常的交通工具是求職的必要條件，以免員工因為交通因素無法正常上班。

reliability n. 可靠，可信賴性

同 dependable

09 業務協調

10 企業經營

中級

87. requirement

[rɪˈkwaɪrmənt]

n. 必要條件

⇨ **require**「需要」+ **-ment**「名詞字尾」

A Master's Degree is a **requirement** to be considered for management jobs here, but a Ph.D. is preferred.

碩士學位是這裡應徵管理職的必要條件，不過有博士學位則是優先錄取。

require v. 需要
required adj. 必要的

中級

88. responsibility

[rɪˌspɑnsəˈbɪlətɪ]
n. 職責；負責

responsible adj. 負責的

⇨ **responsible「負責的」 + -ity「名詞字尾」**
It is Tom's **responsibility** to double check each and every order before it ships out.
Tom 的職責是在訂單出貨前再次檢查每一筆訂單。

補充 system of job responsibility 工作責任制

中高

89. résumé

[ˈrɛzəme] / [ˌrɛzuˈme]
n. 履歷表

同 CV = curriculum vitae

Any candidate who does not include a complete work history on his or her **résumé** will have it thrown out.
履歷表裡面沒有包含完整工作簡歷的任何應徵者是連一點面試機會都沒有的。

補充 cover letter 應徵函；求職自薦信

初級

90. section

[ˈsɛkʃən]
n. 課，股，科；部門

⇨ **-sect-「切」 + -ion「名詞字尾」，公司切割成不同部門**
It's a big step up from being a **section** leader to being a division manager, so get ready to work hard!
從一個科長變成一個部門經理是往上的一大步，所以準備好要努力工作囉！

初級

91. seek

[sik]
v. 尋找

Now that we are downsizing, it's not an ideal time to **seek** a promotion.
既然我們正在縮編，現在就不是尋求升職的理想時機。

補充 jobseeker 求職者

中級

92. **senior**

[ˈsinjɚ]

adj. 資深的

n. 前輩

反 junior adj. 資淺的

➪ **-sen-**「老的」+ **-ior**「更…的」

For that kind of complicated question, I suggest consulting with a **senior** programmer.

對於那一類複雜的問題，我建議去請教資深的程式設計師。

補充 an old hand 老手；有經驗者

93. **shortlist**

[ˈʃɔrtˌlɪst]

n. 候選名單

v. 列入候選名單

➪ **short**「短的」+ **list**「名單」

We've compiled a **shortlist** of names from over 2,000 applications that have been sent in.

我們已從寄來的兩千多份應徵資料中整理出一份候選名單了。

補充 be on the shortlist 在候選名單中
finalist 決賽選手

中高

94. **specify**

[ˈspɛsəˌfaɪ]

v. 具體指定；詳細指明；明確說明

specific adj. 特定的

➪ **specific**「特定的」+ **-fy**「使…化」

You did not **specify** which team you preferred to be part of, so we assigned you randomly.

你並沒有具體說明你比較想參與哪一組，所以我們就將你隨意指派了。

中級

95. **staff**

[stæf]

n. 員工

易混 stuff n. 東西

We typically don't have a high turnover in **staff**; the average person stays here 10.3 years.

我們一般員工流動率不高；員工平均待在這裡十年三個月。

補充 staff member 職員
senior staff 資深員工
temporary staff 臨時工；約聘人員

初級

96. suited

[ˋsutɪd]
adj. 適合的

⇨ suit「適合」+ -ed「形容詞字尾」

Your MBA makes you well-suited for entry level management, but becoming an executive will take you some time.

你的企管碩士學位使你適合做入門級管理，不過要成爲主管還要再花一些時間。

補充　be suited for　適合

suit v. 使⋯相稱，適合

同 suitable

中級

97. summary

[ˋsʌmərɪ]
n. 總結，摘要
adj. 概括的；立即的

⇨ sum「總數；整體」+ -ary「關於⋯的」

A good CV will list a short summary of your best qualities rather than writing everything down.

一份好的簡歷會列出你最佳優勢的簡短摘要，而不是把每樣東西都寫出來。

補充　in summary　總結而言

sum n. 總數 v. 總結
summarize v. 做總結

中級

98. supervisor

[ˌsupɚˋvaɪzɚ]
n. 監督人，管理人，指導者

⇨ supervise「監督」+ -or「做⋯動作的人」

We must report all serious customer complaints to the supervisor on duty.

我們必須向値班的管理者報告所有重大的顧客投訴。

補充　immediate supervisor　直屬主管

supervise v. 監督，管理，指導
supervision n. 管理；監督

99. **temporary**

[ˈtɛmpəˌrɛrɪ]

adj. 暫時的

n. 臨時工

⇨ **-tempor-**「時間，季節」+ **-ary**「關於…的」

I can only offer you **temporary**, seasonal work during the summer for now, but we will see how business is going in the fall.

我現在只能提供你夏季的臨時季節性工作，不過我們會看看秋季的生意如何。

補充
temporary employee/worker	臨時雇員
temporary work	勞動派遣
temporary work agency	人力派遣公司

temporarily adv. 暫時地

中高

100. **vacancy**

[ˈvekənsɪ]

n. 空缺；空職；空房

 -vac-「空的」+ **-ancy**「名詞字尾」

You have seven days from the date on the **vacancy** posting to submit your application and letter of interest.

職缺公布當天算起，你有七天的時間可以提交你的求職申請書以及詢問信函。

補充
a vacancy for...	有某職務的職缺
job vacancy	職缺（口語也可說 job opening）

vacant adj. 空的

實力進階

Part 1. 各種表達 degree 的方式

degree 是正式學位，包含學士、碩士、博士學位。

常見學位 (degree) 表達方式有：B.A. / M.A. / B.B.A. / M.B.A. / B.S. / M.S. / Ph.D.

縮寫	全名	意思
B.A.	Bachelor of Arts	大部分的學士，尤其是文學院。通常會用加註方式表示其專業學科，寫成「Bachelor of Arts in 專業學科」。例如：Bachelor of Arts in Economics 就是經濟學學士
M.A.	Master of Arts	大部分的碩士
B.B.A.	Bachelor of Business Administration	工商管理學士
M.B.A.	Master of Business Administration	工商管理碩士
B.S.	Bachelor of Science	理工科的學士
M.S.	Master of Science	理工科的碩士
Ph.D.	Doctor of Philosophy	博士

Part 2. department/ section/ division

division/department/sector 三字都可翻譯成「部門」，因為每間公司慣用的字不盡相同，現在已經越來越難區分三者在組織規模上的大小之分。不過普遍來說，**department** 一字使用最廣泛。

常見公司部門名稱如下：

Human Resources Department (HR)	人力資源部
Personnel Department	人事部
Sales Department	業務部
Marketing Department	行銷部
Finance Department	財務部
Accounting Department	會計部
Research and Development Department (R&D)	研發部
Manufacturing Department	製造部
Purchasing Department	採購部
Public Relations Department (PR)	公關部
Customer Service Center / Call Center	客服中心
Information Technology Department (IT)	資訊部

Part 3. administrator / director / manager / executive / supervisor

常用來表示管理者的英文單字有：administrator/director/manager/executive/supervisor。這些字也常用在英文職稱 (title) 中，但因為各產業或公司使用職稱時的用字不一致，光看名片上的職稱也很難區分此人在公司中屬於哪一個管理階層；因此學習時不須刻意區分這些字代表的職權大小，重點在於去熟悉每個單字慣用的搭配語。

01 職稱職務／聘僱面試

02 人事／薪資／福利

03 辦公室／電話傳真

04 文書作業

05 會議

隨堂練習

★ 請根據句意，選出最適合的單字

( ) 1. The interviewer asked me to show any relevant _____ to prove that I possess the necessary qualifications to work in this company.
(A) certificate
(B) expectation
(C) responsibility
(D) summary

( ) 2. A powerful letter of _____ can help you to get a job or get admitted to a prestigious college.
(A) diploma
(B) recommendation
(C) profession
(D) orientation

( ) 3. A good manager should possess such _____ as leadership, the ability to make good decisions and patience.
(A) sections
(B) profiles
(C) divisions
(D) attributes

( ) 4. This company is having difficulty _____ knowledgeable and competent staff to keep its business successful and to get ahead.
(A) devoting
(B) recruiting
(D) impressing
(D) contributing

( ) 5. His _____ in the area of computer programming is the reason why he was appointed as project leader.
(A) ethic
(B) occupation
(C) expertise
(D) fluency

解答：1. A   2. B   3. D   4. B   5. C

Unit 2 人事 / 薪資 / 福利

中級

1. achievement

[əˈtʃivmənt]
n. 成就

➪ achieve「完成；達到」+ -ment「名詞字尾」

Landing 50 new accounts in just your first 50 days on the job is quite an **achievement**.
你上班才五十天就得到五十個新客戶著實是個成就。
★ land an account 表示得到新客戶

補充 sense of achievement 成就感

achieve v. 完成；達到

中級

2. additional

[əˈdɪʃənl]
adj. 額外的；附加的

➪ addition「附加」+ -al「有⋯性質的」

All staff members will receive **additional** bonuses for finishing the project on schedule.
全體員工會因如期完成這專案而得到額外的獎金。

補充 additional charge 額外收費

add v. 添加
additionally adv. 額外地
同 supplementary

初級

3. advance

[ədˈvæns]
v./n. 前進；進步

Martin decided to earn an MBA so he can **advance** up the corporate ladder in the future.
Martin 決定要取得工商管理碩士學位以便未來能在公司裡一路往上爬。

補充 in advance 預先

advanced adj. 先進的，高級的
advancement n. 晉升；進展

中級

4. allowance

[əˋlaʊəns]
n. 津貼；零用錢

allow v. 允許；給予

⇨ **allow**「允許；給予」+ **-ance**「名詞字尾」，老闆給的東西就是錢

The company gives an **allowance** of one hundred dollars to each employee each month exclusively for supplies.
這家公司每個月給每位員工一百元津貼專供補給物資使用。

補充
travel allowance　旅行津貼
clothing allowance　服裝津貼
housing allowance　住房津貼

中級

5. announce

[əˋnaʊns]
v. 宣佈；公告

announcement n. 宣佈；通知

Mr. James is expected to **announce** who the new head of the department will be during the weekly conference call tomorrow.
James 先生預計在明天的每週電話會議上宣布部門的新主管是誰。

中級

6. appoint

[əˋpɔɪnt]
v. 任命，委派；安排時間

appointed adj. 任命的，委派的
appointment n. 任命；約會

 a-「to」+ **point**「指著」，指著要指派的人

As the president of the company, it is Mr. Craig's right to **appoint** who he likes, but the board still must approve of his decision.
身為公司總裁，Craig 先生是有權利任命他喜歡的人，但是還是要得到董事會的同意才行。

補充
appoint sb. (as) + 職位　指派某人擔任某職位
appoint sb. to + 工作單位　指派某人到某單位任職
appoint sb. to do sth.　委派某人去做某事
take up an appointment　就職

中高

7. **appraisal**

[ə`prezl]

n. 評價，鑑定；估價

⇒ appraise「鑑定」+ -al「名詞字尾」

We will decide who to promote according to the performance **appraisal**.

我們會根據績效考核來決定誰可以晉升。

| 補充 | self-appraisal　自我評估 |
| | appraisal fee　房屋鑑價費 |

appraise v. 鑑定；估價

同 assessment / evaluation / estimation / review

中級

8. **assign**

[ə`saɪn]

v. 指派，分配

⇒ as-「to」+ -sign-「做記號」，做了記號表示要被指派

I've been meaning to tell you to **assign** some of your mundane duties to one of our entry-level employees.

我的意思是要你把你手上一些不那麼重要的工作分配給我們的一名初階員工去做。

| 補充 | assign sb. a job/duty/task　指派某人去做工作 |
| | assign sb. to + 工作單位　　指派某人到某單位 |

assignment n. 工作，任務；功課

reassign v. 重新指派

初級

9. **assume**

[ə`sjum]

v. 承擔；接任；認為，以為

⇒ as-「to」+ -sume-「拿取」，把責任拿來承擔

The manager should **assume** responsibility for the plummeting business sales.

該名經理應該為業績滑落承擔責任。

I **assumed** that Tom had prepared all the necessary documents, but when the presentation rolled around, he didn't have anything.

我以為 Tom 已經準備好所有需要的文件了，但是當報告開始的時候他卻什麼也拿不出來。

| 補充 | assume responsibility for sth.　承擔某事的責任 |
| | assume a role　擔任某個角色或職位 |

assumption n. 承擔；就任；假定，設想

中高

10. authorize
[ˋɔθəˏraɪz]
v. 授權；委託

⇨ **author**「作者」+ **-ize**「使…化」，使東西與原作相同要經過授權

I never **authorized** any of the transactions listed on this monthly statement!
這份每月對帳單裡列出的任何一筆交易都沒有經過我的授權！

補充　authorize sb. to V　授權某人去做…

unauthorized adj. 未授權的
authorization n. 授權；批准；認可

中級

11. benefit
[ˋbɛnəfɪt]
n. 利益；福利
v. 有益於；受益

⇨ **bene-**「好的」+ **-fit**「做」，做好事會帶來利益

New employees are not eligible to receive **benefits** until after the 90-day probationary period.
新進員工要在過了 90 天試用期之後才有資格享有公司福利。

補充	unemployment benefit	失業救濟金
	company benefits	公司福利
	for sb's benefit	為了幫助某人；對某人有益

beneficial adj. 有益的

中高

12. bonus
[ˋbonəs]
n. 紅利，獎金；額外收穫

Thomas will receive a hefty **bonus** if sales are up over ten percent for the quarter.
如果這一季的業績成長超過百分之十，Thomas 就會得到一筆優渥的獎金。

補充	added bonus	額外的好處
	annual bonus	年終獎金
	performance bonus	績效獎金

中高

13. compensation
[͵kɑmpən`seʃən]
n. 補貼金；(AmE) 報酬

 compensate「補償，賠償」+ -ion「名詞字尾」

Although his salary is not high, the CEO's total **compensation** package adds up to over two million dollars a year.

雖然他的基本薪資不算高，執行長的總體薪酬一年還是可以累計到超過兩百萬元。

補充		
	unemployment compensation	失業補償金
	compensation for injuries at work	工傷補償金
	total compensation package	總體薪酬

compensate v. 補償，賠償；酬報

中級

14. consequence
[`kɑnsə͵kwɛns]
n. 後果

⇨ **consequent**「隨之發生的」+ **-ence**「名詞字尾」

You have to take the **consequences** of making such an improper statement at the meeting.

你必須承擔在會議中說出不當言論的後果。

補充		
	take the consequences	承擔後果
	in consequence	結果，所以

consequent adj. 因…的結果而起的，隨之發生的
consequently adv. 結果，因此，必然地

初級

15. consider
[kən`sɪdə]
v. 考慮；認為

⇨ **con-**「一起」+ **sidus**「拉丁文，星象」

I beg that you **consider** the effect that your new policy will have on our workers.

我懇請你認真考量這項新政策會給我們員工造成的影響。

典故	consider 最早是表示觀察研究星象，故衍生出認真思索的意思。

補充	consider + V-ing 考慮做某事 consider sb. for + a job/position 考慮讓某人做某工作或職位

considered adj. 考慮過的
consideration n. 考慮

中高

16. **contestant**

[kənˈtɛstənt]

n. 競爭者

⇨ contest「競爭」＋ -ant「做…動作的人」

To compete for the best employee award, each **contestant** will be required to submit a self-introduction video.

角逐最佳員工獎的每位參賽者必須提交自我介紹短片。

contest [kənˈtɛst] v. 競爭
contest [ˈkɑntɛst] n. 競賽

中高

17. **counsel**

[ˈkaʊnsl̩]

n. 忠告；律師

v. 建議，勸告；與…商議；輔導

counselor n. 顧問

You should listen to your superior's wise **counsel**.
你應該聽從你長官的明智忠告。

補充 general counsel
(AmE) 公司的法律總顧問；大律師

中高

18. **crucial**

[ˈkruʃəl]

adj. 重要的

crucially adv. 至關重要地；關鍵地

 -cruc-「十字」＋ -ial「有…性質的」

Taking accurate minutes during the meeting is **crucial** to our record keeping.

開會時做好精確的會議紀錄對我們保存紀錄非常重要。

中級

19. **cultivate**

[ˈkʌltəˌvet]

v. 培養；培育；耕種

⇨ -cult-「耕種」＋ -ate「動詞字尾」

It's your duty as our contact person to establish and then **cultivate** a strong relationship with each client.

你的職責是做爲我們的聯絡窗口去跟每一位客戶建立並培養深厚的關係。

補充 cultivate a positive attitude/relationship
培養正向的態度／關係

06 買賣交易
07 採購與物流
08 廣告與宣傳
09 業務協調
10 企業經營

20. deputy

中級

[ˈdɛpjəti]

n. 代表，代理人
adj. 代理的；副的

🙂 de-「往下」+ -put-「思考」+ -y「名詞字尾」

The **deputy** mayor had to make an appearance at the fundraiser since the mayor was out of town.
副市長必須出席這場募款活動，因爲市長出城了。

depute v. 指定⋯爲代理人；委任；授權給

---

21. deserve

中級

[dɪˈzɝv]

v. 應得；該得

⇨ de-「完全地」+ serve「服務」，完全地服務是因為你「值得」

Brady truly **deserves** this promotion after dedicating so much of his extra time to improving the business.
在投入如此多額外時間改善業績之後，Brady 確實配得上這次晉升。

補充
deserve to do sth. 值得去做某事
deserve consideration/attention
（建議、觀點、計劃）值得考慮 / 注意

---

22. designate

中高

[ˈdɛzɪɡ‚net]

v. 指定；指派
adj. 指定的；候任的

🙂 de-「往下」+ -sign-「做記號」+ -ate「動詞字尾」

Our paper files are **designated** only for clients who have not done business with us for ten years or more.
我們的紙本檔案被劃定爲超過十年沒和我們有生意往來的客戶資料。

補充
designate sb. to do sth.
指派某人去做某工作或職位
the ambassador designate 候任大使
chairman designate 指定主席

designation n. 任命，委派；指定事物；正式稱號

初級

23. **diligent**

[ˈdɪlədʒənt]

adj. 勤勉的，勤奮的

⇨ **di**-「分開」+ **-lig**-「選擇」+ **-ent**「與…有關的」，仔細挑選的動作是認真努力的

Our employees must be **diligent** because all our bonuses are based on performance only.

我們的員工必須很勤奮因爲我們所有的獎金都只會根據表現來給。

補充　be diligent in sth. 對某事很勤奮

diligently adv. 勤奮地
diligence n. 勤勉

同 industrious

中高

24. **disable**

[dɪsˈebl]

v. 使失去能力；使無資格

⇨ **dis**-「除去」+ **able**「有能力的」

I want you to go into your control panel and **disable** all the applications that are currently running.

我要你進到你的控制台裡面把現在正在運作的應用程式都關掉。

補充　be disabled from sth. 失去做某事的能力或資格

disabled adj. 殘障的，殘疾的

中級

25. **discipline**

[ˈdɪsəplɪn]

n. 紀律

v. 使有紀律；訓練，管教

⇨ **disciple**「信徒」+ **-ine**「名詞字尾」，信徒接受教誨而有紀律

You must have the **discipline** to set aside three thousand NT dollars each paycheck for your retirement account.

你必須養成紀律每個月從薪水裡另存台幣三千元到你的退休戶頭。

disciplined adj. 受過訓練的；遵守紀律的
self-discipline n. 自我約束、自制力

中高

26. **discretion**

[dɪˋskrɛʃən]

n. 決斷能力；處理權；謹慎

 discreet「謹慎的」+ **-ion**「名詞字尾」

The funds for the special project have been released at the **discretion** of the board.

這項專案的資金已經根據董事會的決定撥下來了。

> 補充
>
> at one's discretion/at the discretion of sb.
> 根據某人的決定或意願
> age of discretion 成年，解事年齡，責任年齡
> Discretion is the better part of valor.
> [諺語] 不知進退非真勇。(謹慎要比無謂冒險強得多。)

discreet adj. 謹慎的

中級

27. **dismiss**

[dɪsˋmɪs]

v. 解聘

⇨ **dis-**「離開」+ **-miss-**「送走」

It is my duty to inform you that you have been **dismissed** from your duties as supervisor due to the poor performance of the department.

我負責通知你由於部門表現欠佳的緣故，你的主管職務被解除了。

> 補充
>
> dismiss sb. from + 職位 某人從某職位被解僱
> dismiss sb. for + V-ing 某人因某原因被解僱

dismissal n. 免職

中高

28. **drawback**

[ˋdrɔˏbæk]

n. 缺點；退款

⇨ **draw**「拉」+ **back**「往後」，缺點使你往後退

There are several **drawbacks** to the plan being considered, but it's still better than our current policy.

雖然現在討論的計劃有些缺點，但它仍然比現行的政策好。

> 補充
>
> 金融情境中，drawback 也指退款或是退稅。
> draw back 退縮；閃躲

同 缺點：disadvantage

初級

29. **effective**

[ɪˈfɛktɪv]

adj. 有效的；生效的

⇨ **effect**「效果」+ **-ive**「具…性質的」

An **effective** salesman must have the ability to close the deal within 24 hours.

一名工作能力好的業務員必須有能力在二十四小時內完成交易。

補充	be effective in + V-ing	有效地做某事
	be effective against N.	對抗某物是有效的
	highly effective	極為有效的
	cost-effective	adj. 符合成本效益的

effectively adv. 有效果地

反 ineffective adj. 不起作用的，無效果的

中高

30. **eligible**

[ˈɛlɪdʒəbl]

adj. 符合資格的；有資格當
選的；法律上合格的

 e-「出去」+ **-lig-**「= -leg- ，選擇」+ **-ible**「能夠
…的」

Only current employees are **eligible** to enter the raffle to win a new Toyota car.

只有現任員工有資格參加對獎活動贏得一台全新的 Toyota 汽車。

| 補充 | be eligible for sth. | 有做某事的資格 |
| | be eligible to V. | 有做某事的資格 |

eligibility n. 被選舉資格

反 ineligible adj. 無被選資格的；不適任的

中高

31. **elite**

[ɪˈlit]

n. 精英、優秀分子

Only a small, **elite** group of company representatives will be chosen to attend the conference.

公司代表中只有少數優秀菁英會被選中參加會議。

| 補充 | the corporate/financial/media elite |
| | 企業 / 金融 / 媒體菁英 |

06
買賣交易

07
採購與物流

08
廣告與宣傳

09
業務協調

10
企業經營

32. **emolument**

[ɪˈmɑljʊmənt]

n. 薪水；酬勞

 e -「出去」**+ molere**「拉丁文，磨碎」**+ -ment**「名詞字尾」

The **emolument** of our executive-level employees is a more complicated formula, and each has slightly different language in his or her contract.

我們主管級員工的薪資採用比較複雜的準則，每一位主管的薪資合約上都會有細微的不同。

同 earnings

中級

33. **engage**

[ɪnˈgedʒ]

v. 僱用；從事；訂婚

⇨ **en -**「使成為」**+ gage**「古法文，保證」，保證會去做就可以定下契約

Once he gets **engaged** in the development of a new game, he is very focused.

一旦他從事新遊戲的開發，他就會全神貫注。

補充		
engage sb. to do sth.	聘用某人來做…
engage sb. as...	聘用某人擔任…
engage sb. in + N./V-ing	使某人參與…
be engaged in + N./V-ing	從事…；忙著…

engaged adj. 從事…的；忙於…的
engagement n. 約定；婚約

中級

34. **evaluate**

[ɪˈvæljuˌet]

v. 評價；估價

⇨ **e -**「出來」**+ value**「計算價值」**+ -ate**「動詞字尾」

We have a set of guidelines which are used to **evaluate** each employee, and the standard must be met in each category.

我們有一套用來評估每位員工的準則，而每個類別的標準都必須要達到。

 assess 是估價，強調對金額數量的評估。
evaluate 則強調對人事物品質的評估。

evaluation n. 評價；估價
reevaluate v. 重新評估

中高

35. **exclude**

[ɪk`sklud]

v. 開除；排除

⇨ **ex -**「外面」**+ -dud -**「關閉」，關到外面就是排除掉了

When the board's final vote took place, Stacy was **excluded** due to her inexperience.

董事會進行最終投票時，Stacy 因爲缺乏經驗的緣故被淘汰掉了。

 exclude sb./sth. from sth.　將…排除在…外
exclude the possibility of...　排除…的可能性

excluding　prep. 除…之外
exclusive　adj. 除外的；獨有的

反 include　v. 包含

初級

36. **experience**

[ɪk`spɪrɪəns]

n. 經驗
v. 體驗

⇨ **ex -**「出去」**+ peritus**「拉丁文，試驗」**+ - ence**「名詞字尾」，試驗後就得到經驗

The position requires five years of **experience** or more in human resources along with advanced knowledge of all of the state's hiring laws.

這個職位需要有五年以上的人資相關經驗，並對所有與這州有關的聘僱法有深厚的了解。

 have experience in sth.　有某領域的經驗
work experience　　　工作經驗
previous experience　先前的經驗

experienced　adj. 有經驗的；老練的

初級

37. **former**

[`fɔrmɚ]

adj. 前任的；從前的；在前的

⇨ **forme**「古英文，表第一」**+ - er**「比較…的」，比第一更好表示更前面的

We will need to file for bankruptcy due to the disgraceful actions of our **former** CFO.

因爲前任財務長不光彩的行爲，我們將會需要申請破產。

 the former　前者

formerly　adv. 以前，從前

反 latter　adj. 後者的

中高

38. fringe

[frɪndʒ]

n. 次要部分，流蘇；邊緣；額外的

Our company is staffed with those who are considered to be on the **fringes** of society, which explains why our videos are so controversial.

我們公司僱用了被認定是社會邊緣人的員工，這也說明了爲什麼我們的影片如此具爭議性。

補充
fringe benefit 額外福利
fringe market 附加市場

中級

39. gratitude

[ˋɡrætəˏtjud]

n. 感激，謝意

 - **grat** - 「滿意；感謝」 ＋ -**itude** 「法文名詞字尾」

I would like to express my **gratitude** to Rebecca for her willingness to take a leadership role when no one else was stepping up to the plate.

我想要感謝 Rebecca 願意在沒有人可以承擔責任的時候接下領導的職責。

補充
deepest gratitude 萬分的感激
with gratitude 充滿感激地

grateful adj. 感謝的

同 thanks / appreciation

中高

40. incentive

[ɪnˋsɛntɪv]

n. 刺激，鼓勵；獎勵金
adj. 獎勵的

 in - 「裡面」 ＋ - **cent** - 「唱歌」 ＋ - **ive** 「形容詞兼名詞字尾」

Our company-wide rewards program provides a great **incentive** for workers to always make their best effort.

我們全公司獎勵計畫提供豐厚的獎勵金鼓勵員工在工作上全力以赴。

補充
incentive tour 員工旅遊
incentive payments 獎金
tax incentives 減稅優惠

01
職棲職務／聘僱面試

02
人事／薪資／福利

03
辦公室／電話傳真

04
文書作業

05
會議

41. **independently**

[ˌɪndɪˋpɛndəntlɪ]
adv. 獨立地

⇨ **in-**「不」＋ **depend**「依賴」＋ **-ent**「有…性質的」
＋ **-ly**「副詞字尾」

Craig accomplishes quite a lot **independently**, but he doesn't work well with a group.
雖然 Craig 獨自達成了相當多成就，但是他卻無法與團隊好好合作。

 | work independently　獨立工作
work on a team　　團隊工作

independent adj. 獨立的
independence n. 獨立自主

中級

42. **inferior**

[ɪnˋfɪrɪɚ]
adj. 較差的；下級的
n. 部屬

⇨ **inferus**「拉丁文，低的」＋ **-ior**「更…的」

Frankly speaking, we believe your company uses **inferior** quality materials and, therefore, we will be changing suppliers.
坦白說，我們覺得你們公司使用品質低劣的材料，因此我們將會更換供應商。

　inferior product 次級品

同 n. = subordinate
反 superior　adj. 較優的，較高的
　　　　　　　n. 上司，主管

---

43. **inherit**

[ɪnˋhɛrɪt]
v. 繼承；延續

I **inherited** a small amount from my parents, but much of what I have is due to my own efforts.
我從我爸媽那裏繼承了一小筆財產，不過我大多數擁有的都是靠我自己努力得來的。

　inherit sth. from sb. 從某人那繼承某物

inheritance n. 遺產；繼承權

06 買賣交易

07 採購與物流

08 廣告與宣傳

09 業務協調

10 企業經營

44. inspire

[ɪnˈspaɪr]

v. 鼓舞；激發；給予靈感

⇨ in-「進入」＋ -spir-「呼吸」，氣吹入體內人就甦醒，就有靈感，就被激發了

The tireless efforts of cancer researchers at this hospital **inspire** all of us to pledge to donate more.

這間醫院的癌症研究人員堅持不懈的努力激勵我們承諾捐更多錢。

inspiring adj. 激勵人心的
inspiration n. 靈感

45. labor

[ˈlebɚ]

n. 勞動；勞工；工作；分娩
v. 努力、費力工作

We hire very few full-time employees to keep our **labor** costs low.

我們僱用非常少的全職員工好讓我們維持低人工成本。

 labor 原來是指身體的勞動。

labor cost	人工成本
labor dispute	勞資糾紛
labor hour	工時
labor union	工會

labor-saving adj. 節省勞力的，省力的
labor-intensive adj. 勞力密集的

46. lay off

[le] [ɔf]

phr. 解僱；資遣

Laying off employees can still be quite expensive, as we need to compensate them legally with severance pay.

資遣員工可是相當昂貴的，因為我們必須依法補償資遣費給他們。

 get fired 通常是因為員工自身的因素（如：犯大錯）被炒魷魚。**lay off** 是指因公司本身有狀況，不得不進行人員縮編而產生的狀況。

47. leadership

['lidəʃɪp]

n. 領導地位；領導權；領導力

⇨ **leader**「領導者」+ **-ship**「名詞字尾，表狀態或權限」

In all my years of recruiting, I often found great **leadership** in students who went to public universities.
在我進行人才招募的這些年，我常常在公立大學學生身上發現很棒的領袖特質。

補充 leadership qualities/skills 領導品質／技巧
under one's leadership 在某人的領導下

lead v./n. 領導

初級

48. leave

[liv]

n. 休假

The school official was placed on paid **leave** while an investigation of fraud was conducted.
這名學校行政人員被要求在調查詐騙行為的期間放帶薪假。

補充 sb. be on leave 在休假中
sb. be absent without leave 曠課；曠職；不假外出
ask for a leave 請求准假
take French leave 擅離職守

中級

49. lifetime

['laɪf.taɪm]

n. 一生，終身；(事物的)使用期

adj. 一生的，終身的

⇨ **life**「生命」+ **time**「時間」

The days of working at the same place for a **lifetime** are over as workers jump around the job market looking to get ahead faster.
一輩子在同一個地方工作的日子已經結束了，現今員工在求職市場裡到處跳槽期望能快一點領先他人。

補充 the lifetime employment system 終身僱用制

 adj. = lifelong

中高

50. longevity
[lɑn`dʒɛvətɪ]
n. 壽命；長壽；年資

The **longevity** of cars has increased greatly in the past thirty years as technology continues to advance.
在過去三十年間，隨著科技不斷進步，汽車的壽命也大大地增加了。

補充 longevity pay 年資加給；年功俸

---

51. managerial
[ˌmænə`dʒɪrɪəl]
adj. 經理的；管理的

⇨ **manager**「經理」＋ **-ial**「有關的」
Thanks to **managerial** savvy, Frank was still able to save our branch office money this month, even in this terrible economy.
幸虧有精明的管理，即便是在這麼糟糕的經濟狀況下，Frank 這個月還能夠幫我們的分公司省下錢。

補充 a managerial position 經理職位；管理職位

中級

52. merit
[`mɛrɪt]
n. 功績，功勞；優點，長處

Your argument has **merit**, but the project has already been green-lighted by the boss.
你的論點雖然有可取之處，不過這個企劃已經被老闆批准通過了。

補充
merit system 考績制度
certificate of merit 獎狀

中高

53. morale
[mə`ræl]
n. 士氣

I have noticed an increase in **morale** around the office since we introduced our new flexible work schedule.
自從我們引進新的彈性工時之後，我注意到整間辦公室的士氣提升了。

補充
a pep talk 打氣，精神喊話
keep up morale 保持士氣
boost morale 鼓舞士氣

易混 moral [`mɔrəl] n. 道德；品行

中高

54. **nominate**

[ˈnɑməˌnet]

v. 提名；任命

⇨ **-nomin-** 「名字」 + **-ate** 「動詞字尾」，叫出名字就是提名

Of the five individuals who are **nominated** to become partner, the one who is chosen always has more seniority.
五位被提名爲合夥人的人選中，永遠是較資深的會被選中。

 補充
nominate sb. for sth.	提名某人爲…
nominate sb. as + 職位	提名某人擔任…
nominate sb. to do sth.	提名某人去做…

nomination n. 提名；任命
nominator n. 提名者；任命者；推薦者
nominee n. 被提名人

中高

55. **optional**

[ˈɑpʃənl̩]

adj. 可選擇的，非必需的

⇨ **option** 「選擇」 + **-al** 「有…性質的」

In the final year of my contract, I get an **optional** performance-based salary.
我在工作合同到期的最後一年選擇了用績效待遇來計薪。

option n. 選擇
optionally adv. 隨意地

反 compulsory adj. 必須做的；義務的

中高

56. **oust**

[aʊst]

v. 攆走

The board voted unanimously to **oust** Chairman Frank due to the insider trading investigation.
因內線交易調查案，董事會一致通過投票開除 Frank 主席。

補充 oust sb. from... 將某人從…攆走

中高

57. **outdo**

[ˌaʊtˈdu]

v. 超越

⇨ **out-** 「向外」 + **do** 「做」

Different teams try to **outdo** one another to win the coveted commercial contract.
各團隊努力超越彼此爲的是要贏得夢寐以求的廣告合約。

補充 outdo sb. in... 在某方面超越某人

同 excel / beat / surpass

中高

58. overwork
[`ovɚ`wɝk]
n. 過於繁重的工作；過分勞累
v. 使工作過量；過度使用

⇨ over -「超過」+ work「工作」

Overwork is the number one cause of fatigue in this office, so management is cutting everyone's hours back.
工作量過大是疲勞的首要原因，因此管理層正在縮減每個人的工作時數。

 death from overwork 過勞死

overworked adj. 操勞過度的；工作過度的

---

59. particularly
[pɚ`tɪkjələlɪ]
adv. 特別地；尤其

⇨ particular「特別的」+ -ly「副詞字尾」

I was **particularly** impressed with the professional and informative report by the shipping department.
我對於出貨部門專業又資訊齊全的報告印象特別深刻。

particular adj. 特別的

圓 in particular

---

60. payroll
[`pe,rol]
n. 發薪名冊，在職人員名冊；薪金總額

⇨ pay「付錢」+ roll「名單，名冊」

The **payroll** department has informed me that your first paycheck will be delayed two weeks so they can process your new hire information.
薪資部門告知我說你的第一筆薪水會延遲兩週發，以便他們處理你的新聘資料。

 be on/off the payroll 被僱用 / 被解僱

paycheck n. 付薪水的支票；薪津

中高

61. pension
[`pɛnʃən]
n. 養老金；退休金
v. 給養老金

 -pens -「衡量，秤重」+ -ion「名詞字尾」

Forced into early retirement, he withdrew funds from his **pension** to make ends meet.
因為被迫提早退休的關係，他從他的退休金裡提取資金以打平開銷。

|補充| occupational pension 職業退休金
draw a pension 領取退休金
live on a pension 靠退休金維生
pension sb. off 發給某人養老金使其退休

pensioner n. 領養老金者

中級

62. **performance**

[pɚˋfɔrməns]
n. 表現，成果

⇨ **perform**「行動，表現」+ **-ance**「名詞字尾」

Most sales representatives in this company take lower base salaries along with more **performance**-based pay.
這間公司大部分業務員的底薪低，績效獎金高。

補充	job performance	工作表現
	performance management	績效管理
	performance appraisal	績效考核

perform v. 行動，表現

---

63. **perk**

[ˋpɝk]
n. 額外補貼

One **perk** of the position is that health care premiums for your entire family are 100% paid by the company.
這個職務的額外補貼之一就是你們全家的醫療保險費由公司全額負擔。

補充
1. perk 是簡寫，原來是 perquisite [ˋpɝkwəzɪt]。
2. bonus, fringe, perk 都是指額外所得，不過 perk 專指因工作而享有的額外補貼。

中高

64. **predecessor**

[ˋprɛdɪˌsɛsɚ]
n. 前任

⇨ **pre-**「先前」+ **de-**「離開」+ **-cess-**「走」+ **-or**「做⋯動作的人」，先前走掉的人就是前任

My **predecessor** depended too much on technology to do the work for us, but I believe the future of this company lies in manpower.
我的前任同仁太過倚賴科技來為我們工作，但是我相信這間公司的未來是在於人力。

 previous job holder
反 successor n. 繼任者

中級

65. **promote**

[prəˋmot]
v. 升遷；促銷

⇨ **pro-**「向前」+ **-mot-**「移動」

After years of waiting to be **promoted** to management, Tom left the company to start his own.
經過了數年等待升遷為主管的日子，Tom 離開了這間公司自己去創業了。

補充　promote sb. to + 職位　將某人升至某職位

promotion n. 升遷；促銷
反 demote v. 降職；降級

初級

66. raise

[rez]

n. 加薪；提高

Clara is scheduled to receive a one-dollar **raise** per hour each year, but this year there was a salary freeze due to the terrible economy.

Clara 原定每年可以每小時加薪一美元，但是今年因為經濟不景氣而薪資凍結了。

pay raise	加薪
ask for a pay raise	要求加薪
give sb. a pay raise	給予某人加薪
get a pay raise	得到加薪

初級

67. range

[rendʒ]

n. 範圍；系列商品

v. 處於某範圍內

I'm hoping for a salary within the **range** of $30,000 to $34,000.

我希望薪水是在三萬元到三萬四千元的範圍內。

Be sure to offer our entire **range** of products to customers, and try to quickly gauge how much they are willing to spend.

務必給顧客看我們全系列產品並試著快速判斷他們願意花多少錢。

典故 range 最早指一排軍人，表示佔了一個固定的範圍。

age/price range	年紀 / 價格範圍
within/beyond the range	在範圍之內 / 之外

中級

68. recognition

[ˌrɛkəgˈnɪʃən]

n. 認識；承認；表彰

⇨ re-「再次」+ co-「一起」+ -gnit-「知道」+ -ion「名詞字尾」，再次得知表示你認識、承認

Our architects rarely receive the **recognition** they deserve for designing such marvelous structures.

我們的建築師很少因為設計出如此宏偉的建築物而得到應得的表揚。

in recognition of 表彰…

recognize v. 認識

69. relocate

[ri`loket]

v. 調職；搬遷

⇨ re-「再次」+ locate「設置地點」

We will pay your expenses to **relocate**, but we urgently need you at our branch office in Texas.

我們會支付你調職的費用，不過我們緊急需要你到德州分公司去。

補充　relocate sb. to 地方　將某人調至某處
公司 relocate to 地方　公司遷至某處

relocation n. 調職；搬遷

70. remuneration

[rɪˌmjunə`reʃən]

n. 酬金，酬報

⇨ remunerate「酬報」+ -ion「名詞字尾」

Remuneration at this company is not commensurate with experience.

這間公司的工資與經驗並不對等。

補充　remuneration package 整套薪資福利方案
remuneration 單指因工作得到的報酬，意思與 reward 相近；compensation 則強調補償和賠償的用途。

remunerate v. 給酬勞

中級

71. renew

[rɪ`nju]

v. 續約，續期，更換

⇨ re-「再次」+ new「新的」，合約再更新表示續約

Your job is to get 100% of our customers to **renew** their memberships while offering them discounts for referring new members.

你的工作是讓我們所有的客戶續期會員資格，同時提供他們推薦新會員的折扣。

補充　renew a contract　續約
renew a license　換證

renewal n. 更新；續約

中高

72. **replacement**

[rɪˋplɛsmənt]

n. 代替者

⇨ **replace**「代替」+ **-ment**「名詞字尾」

Finding and then training Phil's **replacement** may take several months, so his departure puts us in a bind.

要找到並訓練 Phil 的代理人可能要花上好幾個月，所以他的離職使我們陷入困境。

 補充

a replacement for sb./sth.
某人或某物的代替者或代替品
a permanent/temporary replacement
永久／暫時代理人

replace v. 代替

中級

73. **resign**

[rɪˋzaɪn]

v. 辭職

⇨ **re-**「再次」+ **sign**「簽名」，第一次簽名是就職，第二次簽名是辭職

It would be mutually beneficial to you and the company if you **resigned** quietly so we can put this embarrassing episode behind us.

如果你秘密離職，這一切的不愉快我們會當作沒發生，這對你和公司都是有好處的。

 補充

resign from + 組織機構　從某組織機構辭職
resign as + 職位　　　辭去某職位

resignation n. 辭職；辭呈

中高

74. **restructuring**

[riˋstrʌktʃərɪŋ]

n. 重建；改組

⇨ **re-**「再次」+ **structure**「組織；建造」+ **-ing**「名詞字尾」

After the acquisition, all our branches went through a massive **restructuring**, with over 800 people getting laid off.

在併購之後，我們所有的分公司都經歷了大規模的改組重整，資遣了超過八百人。

restructure v. 改組；重建；調整

01 職稱職務／聘僱面試

02 人事／薪資／福利

03 辦公室／電話傳真

04 文書作業

05 會議

中級

75. **retire**

[rɪˋtaɪr]

v. 退休

⇨ re-「回去」+ tirer「法文，拉走」，把人從公司拉回家就是退休了

Due to not accumulating enough savings, I will probably never be able to **retire**.

因為沒有累積足夠的存款，我想我大概永遠無法退休了。

補充 retire from + 組織機構　從某組織機構退休
retire as + 職位　　　以某身份退休

retired adj. 退休的

retirement n. 退休；退休生活

中級

76. **reward**

[rɪˋwɔrd]

n. 報酬

v. 獎勵

Often there is no **reward** for being a loyal, responsible employee.

當一個忠心盡責的員工通常是不會有報酬的。

典故 reward 源自 regard，表示注視、關注的意思。

補充 reward system 獎勵制度

中級

77. **sack**

[sæk]

v. 開除

n. 麻袋

Sam was **sacked** for repeatedly skewing his financial reports to hide his embezzling.

Sam 因為一再地竄改財務報表來隱藏他挪用公款的事情被開除了。

補充 get the sack 被解僱

中級

78. **salary**

[ˋsælərɪ]

n. 薪水

 -sal-「鹽」+ -ary「名詞字尾」

While our upper-level management receives a set yearly **salary**, most workers under this level are paid hourly.

我們高層主管領的是固定的年薪，而大部分在這階層以下的員工是領時薪。

典故 古羅馬政府發鹽巴給士兵作為薪餉。

補充 starting salary 起薪

79. seniority

[sin`ɔrətɪ]

n. 年資，資歷；年長

⇨ **senior**「年長的、資深的」＋ **-ity**「名詞字尾」

We take many different factors into account when determining who is worthy of a promotion, not just **seniority**.

我們在決定誰有資格升遷的時候會考量各種不同因素，不會只考量年資。

補充　seniority system 年資制度

senior adj. 年長的　n. 前輩

80. severance

[`sɛvərəns]

n. 分離，隔離

⇨ **sever**「切斷」＋ **-ance**「名詞字尾」

My **severance** pay only sustained me for one month, and then I had to file for unemployment benefits.

我的遣散費只夠讓我維持生活一個月，之後我必須要申請失業補助金。

補充　severance pay 遣散費

sever v. 切斷；斷絕關係

中級

81. shift

[ʃɪft]

n. 輪班；轉移

v. 轉換，轉移

We need volunteers to work the graveyard **shift** at our factory to keep our operation running around the clock.

我們需要有人自願在工廠輪大夜班讓機器維持不停運作。

補充

take sb's shift = cover for sb.	為某人代班
work a shift	做輪班工作
be on the day/night shift	值早／晚班
graveyard shift	大夜班

中級

82. shortly

[`ʃɔrtlɪ]

adv. 不久後

⇨ **short**「短的」＋ **-ly**「副詞字尾」

The boss will be along **shortly**, so you'd better have the reports laid out for him.

老闆不久後就會到，所以你最好把報告展示給他看。

補充　shortly before/after ... 在…不久前／後

同 soon

中級

83. **status**
[ˋstetəs] / [ˋstætəs]
n. 狀態；地位，身分

I demand to know our **status** of the bridge construction project. Will we make the deadline?
我要知道我們橋樑建設案的狀況。我們來得及在截止日期之前完工嗎？

補充
the status quo	現狀
track the status	追蹤配送狀況
employment status	就業狀況，工作情況
marital status	婚姻狀況

中級

84. **stimulate**
[ˋstɪmjəˌlet]
v. 激勵

 stimulus「刺激物」+ **-ate**「動詞字尾」
The workshop **stimulated** our team members to work harder.
這個研討會激勵了我們團隊成員更加努力工作。

補充
stimulate the economy 刺激經濟發展
stimulate sb. to do sth. 激勵某人去做某事

stimulus n. 刺激；刺激物
stimulation n. 刺激；激勵

中級

85. **strength**
[strɛnθ]
n. 優勢；力量

strong adj. 強的

 strong「強的」+ **-th**「名詞字尾」
Although innovation is one of our company's **strengths**, we need more operating capital.
雖然創新是我們公司的強項之一，我們還是需要有更多的營運資金才行。

中高

86. **subordinate**
[səˋbɔrdɪnɪt]
n. 部屬
adj. 下級的；次要的；隸屬的

 sub-「在…之下」+ **-ordin-**「順序」+ **-ate**「有…性質的」，排序在你之下的就是部屬
Although Tom is my **subordinate**, I believe he will leapfrog me and be promoted quickly within the company.
雖然 Tom 是我的屬下，不過我相信他很快就會超越我，並且在公司裡快速升遷。

補充
be subordinate to sb. 階級在某人之下
a subordinate employee/position/role 屬下

中級

87. substitute

[ˈsʌbstətjut]

n. 代理人；代用品

v. 代替

 sub -「在…之下」**+ -stitute -**「站立」，站在下方準備替代

Ben **substituted** for Ian, who was off sick.

Ian 因病沒有上班，Ben 就來代班。

補充　substitute for sb.　幫某人代班
　　　substitute teacher　代課老師

substitution n. 代替；代用

初級

88. succeed

[səkˈsid]

v. 繼任；成功

⇨ **suc -**「在下面」**+ -ceed -**「走」，從下方走上台順利繼位就表示成功了

Claude will **succeed** Hilary as president of the organization.

Claude 將會接替 Hilary 成為這個組織的總裁。

補充　succeed to N.　　　　繼承…
　　　succeed sb. as sth. 接替某人擔任某職位
　　　succeed in/at N.　　在某方面取得成功

succession n. 繼任，繼承
success n. 成功

中級

89. superior

[səˈpɪrɪəˌ]

adj. 優秀的

n. 上司

⇨ **super -**「上方」**+ -ior**「更…的」

Although your product delivers **superior** performance, it is way over our approved budget.

雖然你們的產品有卓越的性能，但是它超出我們的核定預算太多了。

補充　immediate superior　頂頭上司，直屬上司

superiority n. 優越；上等

中高

90. **terminate**

['tɜːmənet]

v. 終止，結束

⇨ **-termin-**「盡頭，終點」+ **-ate**「使成為…」

Your contract of employment will be **terminated** immediately.

你的僱用契約將會立刻終止。

> **補充** 美式用語中 terminate a worker 也有解僱員工的意思。

termination n. 終止
terminal adj. 終端的；n. 終點

中級

91. **thorough**

['θɝo]

adj. 徹底的，完全的

After the fraudulent documents were discovered, our department underwent a **thorough** house cleaning.

在發現了偽造文件之後，我們部門經歷了徹底的人事大搬風。

thoroughly adv. 徹底地

易混 through prep. 穿越

中高

92. **timely**

['taɪmlɪ]

adj. 及時的
adv. 及時地

⇨ **time**「時間」+ **-ly**「形容詞字尾」

The auditors paid our office a **timely** visit, just after we had organized all our books.

稽核人員及時來到我們公司，剛好就在我們整理好所有帳本之後。

> **補充** timely reminder 讓人及時想起某事的東西

中級

93. **transfer**
[trænsˋfɝ]
v. 調職；轉移
[ˋtrænsfɝ]
n. 調動；轉移

⇨ **trans -**「橫跨，越過」+ **-fer -**「搬運」，把東西搬過去

A number of employees have requested to be **transferred** to another branch office due to the horrible manager.
有一些員工因為該名惡劣經理的緣故請求轉調到另一間分公司。

補充　transfer sb. (from...) to... 把某人 (從⋯) 調到⋯

---

94. **understaffed**
[͵ʌndɚˋstæft]
adj. 人手不足的

⇨ **under -**「在下方；不足的」+ **staff**「員工」+ **-ed**「形容詞字尾」

Most firms are perfectly content to be **understaffed** so that they can rake in the profits.
大多數公司對於人手不足的狀態是很滿意的，這樣他們可以撈進一大把錢。

反 overstaffed　adj. 人員過剩的

中級

95. **undertake**
[͵ʌndɚˋtek]
v. 承擔，接受

⇨ **under -**「在下面」+ **take**「拿取」，拿了就表示接受了

Rob **undertook** the challenge of a lifetime when he attempted to win one hundred new business accounts in one hundred days.
Rob 接受了一個千載難逢的挑戰，要在一百天內得到一百個新客戶。

★ **N. + of a lifetime**：千載難逢的⋯

　undertake a job/task/duty/project
承擔工作 / 任務 / 責任 / 企畫

understaking n. 任務

中高

96. **validity**

[vəˋlɪdətɪ]

n. 正當；確實性；效力

⇨ **valid**「有效的；正當的」+ **-ity**「名詞字尾」

There was a major question about the **validity** of the company's claim to be the patent holder.

這間公司聲稱他們擁有這項專利，這件事的合法性受到很大的質疑。

補充
legal validity 法律效力
validity and reliability 信度與效度
question/challenge/confirm the validity of sth.
質疑／挑戰／確認某事物的正當性

valid adj. 有效的；正當的
validate v. 確認；使有法律效力

中級

97. **wage**

[wedʒ]

n. 薪資；工資

The school board is having continued negotiations with the teachers' union regarding the **wage** increases for the next ten years.

學校董事會正持續與教師工會協商關於未來十年工資調漲的事情。

補充
hourly/daily/weekly wage 時薪／日薪／週薪
minimum wage 最低工資
wage packet 薪資袋
wage freeze 工資凍結

---

98. **weed out**

[wid] [aʊt]

phr. 除去，淘汰

weed n. 雜草 v. 除草

同 get rid of

Giving new job candidates a test is an attempt to **weed out** the undesirable ones.

給這些新的應徵者做測驗是一個將不適合者剔除的方法。

初級

99. **willing**

[ˈwɪlɪŋ]

adj. 有意願的

⇨ will「意志」+ -ing「形容詞字尾」

Since he is **willing** to take on more responsibility, Ron will be given a raise and his own corner office.

因為 Ron 願意承擔更多職責，所以他會被加薪並且有自己在角落的一間辦公室。

補充　be willing to... 願意做…

will n. 意志

反 unwilling adj. 不願意的

100. **workload**

[ˈwɝkˌlod]

n. 工作量

⇨ **work**「工作」+ **load**「裝載量」

Since Tom quit, I now have twice the **workload** until we can find a suitable replacement.

因為 Tom 辭職了，一直到我們能找到適合的人遞補之前我都會有兩倍的工作量。

補充　have a heavy/light workload 工作量大 / 少

load n. 裝載量；工作量

實力進階

Part 1. benefit vs. welfare

benefit 原來是指「利益」。benefit 一字意思表示福利的時候，常用複數形態。在描述公司內部的福利時會用 benefits 一字，不是 welfare。因此公司福利一詞在英文是 company benefits。welfare 指社會性的福利，尤指政府機構提供的福利，如社會救濟制度。所以描述社會福利我們會說 social welfare。

Part 2. leave vs. off

leave 和 off 都有不上班的意思。差別在於 off 純粹指不用上班，休息的日子或一段時間。而 leave 通常必須是自己申請的休假。因此 off 前面通常只會加上一段時間來表示休息時間有多久，但是 leave 前面可能會加上時間或是假別。

例：
{ 請兩天假：take two days' leave ➡ take two days' off 是指休兩天假
{ 請病假：take a sick leave ➡ 這裡的 leave 就不能用 off 一字取代

常見假別的說法：

leave of absence	休假 (尤指較長時間的假期)
paid leave	帶薪休假
sick leave	病假
annual leave	年假
maternity leave	產假、育嬰假
official leave	公假
compensatory leave	補休
unpaid leave	無薪假；留職停薪
personal leave	事假
marital leave	婚假
paternity leave	男性陪產、育嬰假
bereavement leave	喪假

Part 3. reward / emolument / remuneration

reward	報酬 （最常見）	泛指因爲所做的事而得的回報，可能以金錢或是其他形式（如：休假）出現。
emolument	酬勞 （正式用語）	強調是以金錢的形式給予的報酬，通常是指員工領的薪資。
remuneration	報酬 （英語術語）	意思與 reward 幾乎相同，但 remuneration 是人力資源領域的專業術語，一定是針對公司內部所用。

※ 各類報酬的說法整理：

表示薪資	earnings	salary	wages
表示獎金	allowance	benefit	bonus
	incentive	perk	
表示補償金	compensation	reimbursement	

隨堂練習

★ 請根據句意，選出最適合的單字

( ) 1. In our company, all overtime payments must be _____ by the manager. Without the manager's permission, you will get nothing.
(A) announced　　　　　　(B) authorized
(C) dismissed　　　　　　(D) substituted

( ) 2. If you insist on _____ the contract, there will be some damages charged to you; therefore, you had better give it a second thought.
(A) appointing　　　　　　(B) undertaking
(C) promoting　　　　　　(D) terminating

( ) 3. When the time comes to promote an employee, a department head needs to thoroughly _____ each candidate before making the choice.
(A) evaluate　　　　　　(B) relocate
(C) inherit　　　　　　(D) transfer

( ) 4. Since Mark was just recently promoted to a new position higher up in the company, he does everything he can to win the respect of his _____.
(A) merits　　　　　　(B) drawbacks
(C) subordinates　　　　　　(D) disciplines

( ) 5. If you sustain an injury at work due to an employer's negligence, by law you have the right to seek _____.
(A) compensation　　　　　　(B) pension
(C) reward　　　　　　(D) payroll

解答：1. B　2. D　3. A　4. C　5. A

Unit 3 辦公室 / 電話傳真

中高

1. **accessory**

[æk`sɛsərɪ]

n. 附件，配件（常用複數）

adj. 附加的，附屬的

 access「進入」+ -ory「名詞字尾」

Thanks to the deals we get with our vendors, our office **accessories** are almost free since we buy in bulk.

幸好我們跟業者達成交易，我們的辦公用品因為大批購買幾乎是免費的。

補充	office accessories	辦公用品
	desk accessories	桌上辦公用品
	fashion accessories	時尚飾品

access n. 進入；接近的方法

中級

2. **apparent**

[ə`pærənt]

adj. 顯而易見的

apparently adv. 顯然地

同 obvious

It is **apparent** that your video won't play because it's the wrong file type.

顯然你的影片因為檔案格式錯誤而無法播放。

| 補充 | for no apparent reason 沒有明確的理由 |

中級

3. **ascend**

[ə`sɛnd]

v. 上升

反 descend v. 下降

⇨ a-「to」+ -scend-「登；爬」

With her talent, it's no surprise that she is **ascending** fast up the corporate ladder.

她很有才幹，所以她能很快在公司裡往上爬也沒什麼好驚訝的。

| 補充 | in ascending order 按升序排列 |

01 職稱職務／聘僱面試

02 人事／薪資／福利

03 辦公室／電話傳真

04 文書作業

05 會議

4. **attire**

[əˋtaɪr]

n. 服裝

The proper **attire** for this office is business casual, but we do dress formally for big meetings with clients.
這裡上班是穿商務便裝，不過我們跟客戶開重要會議時就會穿著正式服裝。

補充
| formal attire | 正式服裝 |
| business attire | 正式商務服裝 |

同 apparel / garment / outfit

5. **badge**

中高

[bædʒ]

n. 識別證；徽章；標誌

You'll need a temporary ID card at the security desk because you don't have an official ID **badge** yet.
你需要拿警衛室的臨時識別卡因為你還沒有拿到正式的員工識別證。

補充
identification badge/name badge/Staff ID
員工識別證
visitor badge 訪客識別證

6. **binder**

[ˋbaɪndɚ]

n. 活頁夾

⇨ **bind**「捆，綁；裝訂」＋ **-er**「做…動作的物品」
Files from over ten years ago are all kept in large **binders** in our storage room in the basement.
超過十年以上的檔案都用大的活頁夾收著放在地下室的儲藏室裡。

補充
| ring binder | 活頁夾 |
| binder clip | 長尾夾 |

bind v. 捆，綁；裝訂

7. **bulletin**

中級

[ˋbʊlətɪn]

n. 公告，告示；會刊；新聞簡報

Don't tack everything to the company **bulletin** board. It looks so messy.
不要什麼東西都往公司佈告欄上面釘。它看起來一團亂。

典故
bulletin 來自拉丁文 bulla，原來是指教堂的公告或是教皇的詔書。

補充
bulletin board　(AmE) 告示牌
noticeboard　(BrE) 告示牌，佈告欄
message board 留言板

初級

8. cabinet

[ˈkæbənɪt]

n. 櫃子，貯藏櫃

⇨ **cabin**「小屋」 + **-et**「表小東西」，比小屋還更小的東西

I can't find the file you requested in any of these file **cabinets**.

我在這些檔案櫃裡面都找不到你要的檔案。

補充 file/filing cabinet 檔案櫃

cabin n. 小屋

中級

9. calculate

[ˈkælkjəˌlet]

v. 計算

⇨ **-calc-**「石灰」 + **-ul**「表小東西」 + **-ate**「動詞字尾」

The hours for each employee must be carefully **calculated** and then verified to ensure accurate payment.

每一個員工的時數都必須仔細計算並確保支付正確數目的薪水。

典故 古代是用小石頭來計數。

calculation n. 計算
calculator n. 計算機

中級

10. carbon

[ˈkɑrbən]

n. 碳；複寫紙；複寫的副本

You'll find that the **carbon** footprint of this company is less than half of that of other companies.

你會發現這間公司的碳足跡比其他公司碳足跡的一半還要少。

補充 carbon paper 複寫紙
carbon copy 複寫的副本 (縮寫成 CC)

中高

11. cardboard

[ˈkɑrdˌbord]

n. 硬紙板
adj. 硬紙板製的

⇨ **card**「卡片；硬紙板」 + **board**「板子」

All of the accessories must be packed separately in individual **cardboard** boxes.

所有的配件都必須分開包裝在不同的厚紙箱裡。

補充 cardboard paper 厚紙板
cardboard box 硬紙板盒；紙箱

12. cartridge

[ˈkɑrtrɪdʒ]

n. 碳粉匣；彈藥包

When the toner **cartridge** is low on ink, you can take it out and shake it to get a few more days of use from it.
墨水匣快要沒有墨水的時候，你可以把它拿出來搖一搖，這樣還可以多用幾天。

 cartridge 源自拉丁文 carta「紙張」，cartridge 最早是指做彈藥或炸彈的紙捲。

 toner cartridge / ink cartridge 墨水匣

13. catch up on

[kætʃ][ʌp][ɑn]

phr. 趕完，彌補；得到…消息

Since you've been on leave for a week, stop by my office so I can **catch** you **up on** the latest developments.
因為你已經請假一週了，到我的辦公室來跟我更新最新的進度。

補充 catch up 追上，趕上

中高

14. category

[ˈkætəˌgorɪ]

n. 種類

Our website is currently organized by product **category**, but we're thinking about just using a search box instead.
我們的網站目前是以產品分類組成，不過我們正在考慮只用搜尋列來代替。

 category 源自希臘文，原來表示「宣告」。亞里斯多德以 category 一字表示「範疇」之後，category 才產生「種類」的意思。

補充 a category of sth. 一類…
product category 產品分類

categorize v. 進行分類
categorization n. 分類

中級

15. chore

[tʃɔr]

n. 例行工作，雜務；令人厭煩的工作

It's quite a **chore** trying to type out all the minutes from last week's shareholder meeting.
要把上週股東會議的紀錄通通打出來真的是件繁瑣的事。

 do the chores 做雜務
household chores 家庭雜務
routine chore 例行工作

同 task

中級

16. **code**

[kod]

n. 代碼；密碼

v. 把…編碼；編成密碼

Randy's only job duty is to sit in the back room on a small laptop and **code** since he is the only programmer.
Randy唯一的工作就是坐在後面房間裡的電腦前面進行編碼，因為他是唯一的程式設計師。

典故	code 來自拉丁文 codex「法條、法典」，也指書寫文字的木板。因此 code 代表了文字或符號，也引申成代碼的意思。

補充	code name	代號
	bar code	條碼
	area code	電話區域號碼
	QR code	QR 碼，快速反應碼
	= Quick Response code	

coded adj. (編成) 密碼的
encode v. 譯成密碼
decode v. 解碼

中級

17. **colleague**

[ˋkɑlig]

n. 同事

回 co-worker

⇨ col -「一起」+ league「聯盟」，在同一聯盟工作的就是同事

Several of my **colleagues** got mixed up and picked up the wrong documents at the printer.
我的一些同事搞混了，而且拿錯了印表機的文件。

初級

18. **complete**

[kəmˋplit]

adj. 完成的；完整的

v. 完成；使完整

completely adv. 完全地
completion n. 完成，結束

反 incomplete adj. 未完成的；不完整的

⇨ com -「完全地」+ plere「拉丁文，充滿」，完全地充滿就是完整的

Give Chairman Davis a **complete** summary of our negotiations with Jet Corporation.
把我們和 Jet 公司協商的內容完整摘錄給 Davis 主席看。

中級

19. **concentrate**

[ˈkɑnsɛnˌtret]

v. 集中，集結；專注

⇨ con-「一起」+ -centr-「中心」+ -ate「動詞字尾」，所有心思都放在一個中心點上便是專注

As a senior editor, Rick must **concentrate** when he proofreads articles.

作爲一位資深編輯，Rick 必須在他校對文章時集中注意力。

 補充

concentrate on sth. 專注於某事物
concentrate on doing sth. 專注於做某事
concentrate your efforts/attention on sth.
投入力氣／精力在某事物上

concentration n. 專心，專注
concentrated adj. 集中的

20. **congenial**

[kənˈdʒinjəl]

adj. 友善舒適的，宜人的

 con-「共同」+ -gen-「種族」+ -ial「具…性質的」，同鄉令人感到親切安心

The success of our company has more to do with our **congenial** work environment than anything else.

我們公司的成功與舒適的工作環境大有相關。

補充 a congenial working environment
舒適的工作環境

congenially adv. 意氣相投地
congeniality n. 同性質；意氣相投

中級

21. **container**

[kənˈtenɚ]

n. 容器

⇨ contain「容納」+ -er「做…動作的物品」

Just throw all the loose computer hardware into this **container** and I will deal with it later.

把這些散落的電腦硬體設備通通丟進這個容器裡面，我等一下會處理。

contain v. 容納，包含

中級

22. **content**

[ˈkɑntɛnt]

n. 內容，要旨；含量；容納
的東西，具體內容

⇨ con-「一起」+ -tent-「握」，握在一起的東西就是內
容物

The online **content** of this magazine does not match
the newsstand edition.
這本雜誌的線上版和紙本的內容不一致。

> 補充　content 表示文章的內容要旨及表示物質的含量容
> 量時，為不可數名詞；要表示容納的物品或是書信
> 的具體內容時要用複數形 contents。
> 例：table of contents 目錄，目次
> 　　 contents page 目錄頁

初級

23. **crash**

[kræʃ]

v./n. 電腦當機；股票狂跌

Too many customers were bidding on our online items
at the same time, so our server **crashed**.
有太多顧客同時在競標我們的線上商品，所以我們的伺服器就
當機了。

> 補充　crash 與電腦連用時就是指電腦當機；用在金融情
> 境則指經濟狀況突然惡化的意思，尤其是指股票狂
> 跌。

---

24. **cubicle**

[ˈkjubɪkl̩]

n. 小隔間

I have heard that Glenn Bank is getting rid of all their
cubicles and going with an open-office floor plan.
我聽說 Glenn 銀行要淘汰他們所有的小隔間，採用開放式辦
公室。

易混　cubical [ˈkjubəkl̩] adj. 立方體的；體積的

---

25. **cursor**

[ˈkɝsɚ]

n. 游標

⇨ -cur-「跑」+ -sor-「做…動作的物品」，在螢幕上跑
來跑去的就是游標

You need to wait until the **cursor** is blinking again
before you try to type anything.
你要等到游標再次閃爍時才能打東西。

中級

26. deadline

[ˋdɛdˏlaɪn]

n. 截止日期，期限

⇨ **dead**「死亡的」+ **line**「線」

With the **deadline** looming, Barb stayed in the office until morning to put the finishing touches on her report.

因為截止期限要到了，Barb 在辦公室待到早上將她的報告做最後的潤飾。

補充		
	a tight/strict deadline	時間緊促
	meet a deadline	如期完成
	work to a deadline	計劃如期完成
	work under a deadline	在時間壓力下工作

中高

27. definitely

[ˋdɛfənɪtlɪ]

adv. 絕對；必定

⇨ **definite**「一定的，肯定的」+ **-ly**「副詞字尾」

Being a business analyst is **definitely** more relaxing than being a programmer!

當商業分析師一定比當程式設計師更輕鬆！

definite adj. 一定的，肯定的

同 absolutely / certainly

初級

28. deny

[dɪˋnaɪ]

v. 否認；拒絕

It's hard to **deny** that our competitors have designed a superior product.

不可否認我們競爭對手設計的產品比較優秀。

補充	
	deny + V-ing 否認做了某事
	deny sb. sth. = deny sth. to sb.
	拒絕給某人某物 (常用被動態)
	There's no denying (that)... 不可否認…是真的。

denial n. 否認；拒絕

29. **desktop**

[ˈdɛsktɑp]

adj. 桌上型的

n. 桌上型電腦；電腦桌面

⇨ **desk**「書桌」＋ **top**「上方」

For optimum performance, it's ideal to have very few icons on your **desktop**.

為了達到最佳效果，你的電腦桌面上最好不要有太多圖示。

補充		
	desktop computer	桌上型電腦
	tablet computer	平板電腦
	laptop computer	筆記型電腦

中高

30. **diagram**

[ˈdaɪəˌgræm]

n. 圖表，圖解，示意圖

 dia-「穿過」＋ **-gram**「書寫」，透過書寫使意思清楚就是圖解

Make a rough sketch of the **diagram** you have in mind on the whiteboard over there.

將你記得的圖表畫一張草圖在那邊的白板上。

補充		
	chart	圖表（指用圖形或表格呈現資料的圖表）
	graph	圖表，曲線圖（指用線條說明數字變化關係的圖表）
	table	表格

diagrammatic adj. 圖表的

diagrammatically adv. 圖表似地；概略地

中高

31. **directory**

[dəˈrɛktərɪ]

n. 名冊；工商名錄；電話簿

⇨ **direct**「指引」＋ **-ory**「名詞字尾」，指引你找到人的東西就是名冊、電話簿

I didn't know Tamara's last name, so I made a quick inquiry in our company **directory**.

我不知道 Tamara 姓什麼，所以我很快地查了一下我們公司的通訊錄。

補充		
	business/trade directory	工商名錄
	telephone directory	電話簿
	classified directory	分類電話號碼簿
	directory enquiries/directory assistance	電話查號臺

direct v. 指示，指導

中高

32. distraction

[dɪˋstrækʃən]

n. 分心；使人分心的事物；
消遣娛樂

⇨ **dis -**「離開」**+ -tract -**「拉」**+ -ion**「名詞字尾」，
把你的心拉離開就是分心

The air conditioning unit is right next to my desk, so the noise is a constant **distraction**.
空調設備就在我的桌子旁邊，所以噪音一直使我分心。

補充　drive sb. to distraction
讓某人煩得要命，把某人逼瘋

distract v. 分心
distracted adj. 分心的

反 attention n. 注意力
concentration n. 專注
focus n. 焦點

初級

33. document

[ˋdɑkjəmɛnt]

v. 記錄，記載

[ˋdɑkjəmənt]

n. 文件；證件

⇨ **-doc -**「教導」**+ -ment**「名詞字尾」，教學內容記載
在文件上

Make sure to **document** all evidence of harassment that you see in this office.
務必將你在這間辦公室裡見到的騷擾行為的證據記錄下來。

補充　original document 原始文件檔案
portable document format (PDF)
可攜式文件格式

documentation n. (總稱) 文件；紀錄
well-documented adj. 有大量記載的；證據充分的

中級

34. efficient

[ɪˋfɪʃənt]

adj. 有效率的

 ef -「出來」**+ -fici -**「做」**+ -ent**「具…性質的」，
能做出來的就是有效率的

Be **efficient** when processing applications and discard those which are deemed unsuitable.
處理求職信的時候要有效率，把那些不適合的淘汰掉。

efficiently adv. 有效率地
efficiency n. 效率

反 inefficient adj. 無效率的；效能差的；不稱職的

易混 effective adj. 有效果的

中級

35. errand

[ˈɛrənd]

n. 任務；差事

Tom hates running **errands** for the boss all over town, but at least he gets to use the company car.

Tom 雖然很討厭幫老闆在城內四處跑腿，不過他至少還可以開公司車。

補充		
	do/go on/run an errand	跑腿，處理雜務
	send sb. on an errand	叫某人去辦事

 中級

36. extension

[ɪkˈstɛnʃən]

n. 延長；(電話)分機

⇨ **extend**「延伸；延長」+ **-ion**「名詞字尾」

We need an audio **extension** cord to reach the microphone at the podium.

我們需要一條音頻延長線連接到講台的麥克風。

補充		
	extension cord	延長線
	brand extension	品牌延伸
	extension number	分機號碼 (縮寫為 ext.)

extend v. 延伸；延長
extensive adj. 廣泛的

⇨ **fold**「摺疊」+ **-er**「做…動作的物品」

Drop a copy of the Excel file into my share **folder** and I will review it as soon as possible.

複製一份 Excel 檔案到我的共用資料夾，我會盡快校閱。

I demand that employees at the very least have a **folder** at their desk with the workplace policies inside.

我要求員工的桌上至少要有一個文件夾，裡面要放工作守則。

37. folder

[ˈfoldɚ]

n. 文件夾

補充	文件夾的說法有 file, folder, file folder 等。美式英語中，文件夾可以用 file 或是 file folder 稱呼；例如 expanding file 是指文件袋或風琴夾。而在英式英語中會只用 folder 一字來表示文件夾。但是要注意在電腦用語中，file 和 folder 各自有不同意思。file 指檔案；而 folder 是指資料夾。

fold v. 摺疊；交疊 n. 褶痕
foldable adj. 可摺疊的

同 file folder

中高

38. foremost

['forˌmost]
adj. 首要的，最重要的
adv. 首先；最重要地

同 adj. = first / leading

⇨ **fore-**「前面」＋ **-most**「表形容詞最高級」

The customer insisted on speaking to the **foremost** supervisor in our department.

那名顧客堅持要和我們部門最重要的主管談話。

 first and foremost 比什麼都重要，首要的

中高

39. hinder

['hɪndɚ]
v. 阻礙

hindrance n. 妨礙，障礙

同 prevent / hamper

反 facilitate v. 使便利
help v. 有助於

The computer's slow processor did not **hinder** Mr. Andrews from researching all the information.

這台電腦的龜速處理器並沒有妨礙 Andrews 先生搜尋所有的資料。

 hinder...from... 阻礙某事發生，阻礙某人去做某事

40. hold on

[hold][ɑn]
phr. 保持通話

反 hang up 掛斷電話

I was asked to **hold on** twenty minutes ago, but I haven't heard from anyone since.

二十分鐘前對方要我不要掛斷電話，但是我從那之後就再也沒聽到任何人接聽電話了。

 其他常見電話用語：
1. transfer/put ... through to 轉接
2. dial/call at +... 撥打（某號碼）
3. call back 回電

41. integral

[ˈɪntəgrəl]
adj. 不可或缺的，構成整體
　　所必需的；整體的

⇨ integer「整體；整數」+ -al「有關…的」，與構成整體
　有關的就是不可或缺的

Replacing the ancient copy machines is an **integral** part
of our office improvement plan.
更換老舊影印機是我們辦公室改進計畫中不可或缺的一部份。

同 essential

---

42. intercom

[ˈɪntɚˌkɑm]
n. 對講機

⇨ inter -「在…之間，互相」+ com(munication)「溝通」，
　可互相溝通的東西就是對講機

We use an **intercom** system instead of the loudspeakers
in our warehouse to promote faster communication.
我們在倉庫使用對講機系統而非擴音喇叭好讓溝通更加快速。

intercommunication n. 內部通訊

---

43. interface

[ˈɪntɚˌfes]
n. 介面

⇨ inter -「在…之間，互相」+ face「表面」，相互連結接
　觸的面就是介面

The user **interface** of our new software is not as easy
to navigate as our old versions.
我們新軟體的使用者介面沒有像舊版本一樣容易瀏覽。

 a user/computer/software interface
使用者介面 / 電腦介面 / 軟體介面

中級

44. jam

[dʒæm]
v. 塞滿；卡住
n. 堵塞；果醬

Rebecca opened the copier while it was still running
and created a massive paper **jam**.
Rebecca 在影印機還在運作的時候把它打開了，結果造成大
量卡紙。

 paper jam 卡紙
traffic jam 塞車

中級

45. label

[ˈlebl̩]

n. 標籤
v. 貼標籤

Margaret did not align the text of her **labels** properly, so they all needed to be thrown out.
Margaret 沒有對齊標籤上的文字，所以它們全部都得要丟掉了。

補充
address label 地址標籤
care label （繫在衣物上的）清洗說明單
food label 食品標示
warning label 警告標示

46. laminate

[ˈlæməˌnɪt] / [ˈlæməˌnet]

v. 把⋯製成薄板；護貝

⇨ lamina「薄板」＋ -ate「動詞字尾」
Every sheet of the user manual must be printed and then **laminated** before you place it in the binder.
使用說明書的每一單張都要印出來護貝好，再放進資料夾。

補充 laminator film 護貝膜

laminated adj. 層壓的
laminator n. 護貝機

47. laptop

[ˈlæptɑp]

n. 膝上型電腦，手提電腦，
筆記型電腦

⇨ lap「大腿」＋ top「上面」
Since she's constantly out visiting clients, Melissa just takes her small **laptop** with her to present to them.
因為要一直外出拜訪客戶，Melissa 只帶著她的小筆電給客戶做簡報。

補充
筆記型電腦也有人稱呼 notebook computer 或 notebook。不過在歐美國家要表示筆記型電腦時大部分還是會用 laptop 一字。notebook 則通常用來指真正的筆記本。

lap n.（人坐著時）腰以下到膝為止的大腿部

中級

48. literacy
[ˈlɪtərəsɪ]
n. 識字，讀寫能力；某領域的知識能力

⇨ **literate「能讀寫的」＋ -cy「名詞字尾」**

Lack of financial **literacy** leads to many people getting swindled by slick salesmen.

缺乏財金知識使很多人被油嘴滑舌的推銷員欺騙。

literacy skills/levels 讀寫能力 / 程度
literacy rates 識字率
computer literacy 電腦知識，使用電腦的能力
economic/financial literacy 經濟 / 財金知識

literate adj. 能讀寫的

中級

49. locker
[ˈlɑkɚ]
n. 置物櫃，鎖櫃

⇨ **lock「鎖上」＋ -er「做…動作的物品」**

My smart phone was stolen from my **locker** when I was working out at the gym.

我在健身房運動的時候，我放在置物櫃裡的智慧型手機被偷了。

locker room 更衣室

lock v. 鎖上

中級

50. magnet
[ˈmæɡnɪt]
n. 磁鐵

We always distribute **magnets** with our company logo on them at city festivals.

我們總是會在節慶時發送上面有我們公司商標的磁鐵。

最早的磁石是在希臘的美格尼西亞 (Magnesia) 發現的。

magnetic adj. 有磁性的；深具吸引力的

中級

51. manual

[ˋmænjʊəl]

n. 手冊

adj. 手的；手工的

⇨ **-manu-**「手」+ **-al**「有關…的」

We need to make sure that our manual is intuitive and simple to follow for customers.

我們要確保我們的使用手冊是可以靠直覺理解並且對顧客來說是容易操作的。

補充　an instruction manual　說明手冊
manual job/labor/work　手工（體力）活
on manual（機器）手工操作的，手動的

同 n. = handbook

中級

52. memorandum

[ˌmɛməˋrændəm]

n. 便條；便箋；備忘錄

An official memorandum was sent out to all employees regarding the new printing policy.

關於新的列印規則的正式備忘錄已經寄給全體員工了。

補充　memo = memorandum 的簡寫
memos = memoranda / memorandums

初級

53. message

[ˋmɛsɪdʒ]

n. 消息；口信，信息

⇨ **-miss-**「傳送」+ **-age**「名詞字尾」

Why are there still twenty messages sitting in the voice mailbox?

為什麼語音信箱裡頭還有二十封訊息？

補充　leave a message for sb.　留訊息給別人
take a message　留下對方的訊息
voice-mail message　語音留言
text message　簡訊

messenger　n. 信差；使者

06 買賣交易

07 採購與物流

08 廣告與宣傳

09 業務協調

10 企業經營

54. miscellaneous

[ˌmɪsɪˈlenjəs]

adj. 混雜的，五花八門的

⇨ **miscellany**「混雜」+ **-eous**「具…性質的」

I complained about the **miscellaneous** fees on my bank statement and some of them were dropped.

我向銀行抱怨了銀行對帳單上的雜費，然後其中有一些就被取消了。

 miscellaneous charges/costs/expenses
雜費，雜項開支

miscellany n. 混雜；(作品) 雜集

中級

55. monitor

[ˈmɑnətɚ]

v. 監視；監督；監控

n. 監視器；電腦顯示器

⇨ **-moni-**「提醒，警示」+ **-tor**「做…動作的人或物」

We need at least five employees to **monitor** the office phone at all times.

我們需要至少五名員工隨時監控辦公室的電話。

---

56. multifunctional

[ˌmʌltɪˈfʌŋkʃənl]

adj. 多功能的

⇨ **multiple**「多樣的」+ **functional**「有功能的」

My dashboard stereo is **multifunctional**, and has a voice-activated phone feature.

我的汽車音響具有多重功能，還有聲控電話的特色。

 multifunction printer 多功能事務機

multifunction n. 多功能

---

57. newsletter

[ˈnjuzˌlɛtɚ]

n. 商務通訊，公司新聞，會訊

⇨ **news**「新聞」+ **letter**「信件」

Our company **newsletter** keeps employees abreast of upcoming events.

我們的公司新聞讓員工能掌握即將要發生的事件。

 相對於 newspaper，newsletter 報導的內容較少，規模也比較小。newsletter 是公司內部業務通訊用的新聞；也指給特定讀者定期寄發的快訊。

初級

58. **notice**

[ˋnotɪs]

v. 注意

n. 公告，通知，貼示

Sharon **noticed** how some of the profits were being diverted into a secret account.

Sharon 注意到一部分的利潤是如何被轉移到一個秘密帳戶去的。

補充
take notice (of)	注意，在意
give sb. notice	向某人發出解僱通知
until further notice	直至另行通知

noticeboard n. 公告欄

中高

59. **overlap**

[ˏovɚˋlæp]

v. 與…部分重疊

[ˋovɚˏlæp]

n. 部分重疊的範圍

 over -「超過」**+ lap**「疊上，重疊」

The job duties of Mary and Jack **overlap**, so they occasionally step on each other's toes.

Mary 和 Jack 的工作內容有部分重疊，所以他們有時候會踩到彼此的界線。

補充 overlap with... 與…重疊

lap v. 使部分重疊 n.（兩物）重疊部分

overlapping adj. 重疊的

---

60. **oversight**

[ˋovɚˏsaɪt]

n. 監督；疏忽出錯

 over -「上面；超過」**+ sight**「看見」，在上面看就是監督；看過頭就是疏忽

Our financial **oversight** committee did nothing as corrupt traders ran wild.

我們的財政監督委員會在那些貪腐的交易員亂來的時候什麼也沒做。

補充 have oversight of... 監管，監督…

中高

61. **partition**

[parˋtɪʃən]

n. 分割；分隔物；隔牆；隔板

v. 分割；（用隔板等）隔開

 part「分開」**+ -ition**「名詞字尾」

We need to at least install **partitions** to separate the work areas to make the office look more organized.

我們必須至少設置隔板把工作區域分出來好讓辦公室看起來更整齊。

補充 partition sth. off from sth.
從某處將某物分隔出來

62. peripheral

[pəˋrɪfərəl]

adj. 次要的，非主要的；外圍的

n. 電腦周邊設備

🎧 **periphery**「周圍，外圍」+ **-al**「有…性質的」

My **peripherals** were not packed inside my desk, so when we moved offices, they were all lost.

我的電腦周邊沒有裝在辦公桌裡，所以我們辦公室搬家時它們都不見了。

補充　peripheral device　周邊設備

periphery n. 周圍，外圍

63. photocopier

[ˋfotəˌkɑpɪə]

n. 影印機；複印機

⇨ **photocopy**「影印」+ **-er**「做…動作的物品」

The **photocopier** is smearing ink all over every page and it needs to be serviced.

影印機墨水把每一頁都弄髒了，它該送修了。

同 copier / copy machine

初級

64. pile

[paɪl]

v. 堆積

n. 一堆，一疊

Her desk was so disorganized that she simply had papers **piled** high in no particular order.

她的書桌非常不整齊以致於她只能亂七八糟地將文件往上堆。

補充
pile up	堆積；累積
a pile of... (= piles of...)	一堆的…，大量的…
Pile it high, sell it cheap.	大批購進，低價銷售。

同 stack

中級

65. postage

[ˋpostɪdʒ]

n. 郵費

⇨ **post**「郵件」+ **-age**「名詞字尾，表費用」

I would rather just send this to you as an email attachment to avoid the high cost of **postage** on such a thick document.

為了避免寄這麼厚重的文件要花費的巨額郵資，我寧願把它用電子郵件附檔寄給你。

補充
postage free (post free)	免郵資
postage paid (postpaid)	郵資已付
postage and packing	包裝加郵寄費

post n. 郵件

中級

66. **preparation**

[ˌprɛpəˈreʃən]

n. 準備

 prepare「準備」+ -ation「名詞字尾」

Please allow five business days for the **preparation** of your tax documents.

請預留五個工作天讓我們準備您的稅務文件。

補充	make preparations	做準備
	be in preparation	在準備中
	in preparation for	為…作準備 (強調目的)
	in preparation of...	準備…

prepare v. 準備

初級

67. **project**

[ˈprɑdʒɛkt]

n. 計畫，企劃

[prəˈdʒɛkt]

v. 預計；投射；計畫

 pro-「向前」+ -ject-「投擲」

I need to assign Ken to another **project** since he does not mesh well with the group.

我必須讓 Ken 去做別的案子，因為他和這一組的人無法合作。

補充	project management professional (PMP) 專案管理專業人員
	be projected to do sth. 計畫，預定去做某事
	sales projections 銷售預測

projector n. 投影機

projection n. 預測，估算，規劃；投射

---

68. **protocol**

[ˈprotəˌkɔl]

n. 禮儀；協定

 proto-「最初的」+ -col-「膠，用膠黏」

Frank did not follow proper security **protocol** in checking the bank's transactions.

Frank 在檢查銀行交易的時候沒有遵守正確的安全規範。

補充	office protocol	辦公室禮儀
	protocol for sth.	做某事的規矩
	a breach of protocol	違反禮節

同 禮儀： etiquette / courtesies / p's and q's

06 買賣交易

07 採購與物流

08 廣告與宣傳

09 業務協調

10 企業經營

中級

69. **punctual**

[ˈpʌŋktʃʊəl]

adj. 準時的

 -punct- 「刺穿」+ -ual 「有…性質的」

If employees can't be **punctual**, then I can't trust them to be team leaders.

如果員工無法準時上班，那麼我也無法信任他們能當團隊領導。

補充　be punctual for sth. 準時做某事
punctual payment/delivery
準時支付 / 及時交貨

punctuality n. 守時
punctually adv. 準時地

初級

70. **rapid**

[ˈræpɪd]

adj. 迅速的

⇨ -rap- 「搶奪」+ -id 「形容詞字尾」，搶奪的動作很迅速

Anytime we see that stocks have a **rapid** rise, we tell customers to be on the lookout for a steep drop.

每次我們看到股市快速上漲時，我們都會告訴顧客要密切注意會有猛跌。

rapidly adv. 迅速地
rapidity n. 迅速

同 swift / speedy

71. **rationale**

[ˌræʃəˈnæl]

n. 理念原則；根本原因

What is your **rationale** for putting off work on the Walker project in favor of smaller projects?

你延後 Walker 計畫去做較小型的案子是為了什麼原因？

補充　the rationale for (doing) sth. 做某事的理念

中級

72. **reception**

[rɪˋsɛpʃən]

n. 接待；接待處；接收效果

⇨ re-「返回」+ -cept-「拿」+ -ion「名詞字尾」，把訊號拿回來就表示接收

The **reception** for our newest smart phone model is far more positive than I would have imagined.

我們最新型的智慧型手機的接收效果比我想像的要好得多。

	a wedding reception	婚宴
	reception room	接待室
	reception desk	接待處／接待櫃檯

receptionist n. 接待員
receive v. 接受，接收

中高

73. **rectangular**

[rɛkˋtæŋgjələ]

adj. 長方形的

⇨ -rect-「直的」+ -angul-「角度」+ -ar「具…性質的」

Our **rectangular** conference room is only big enough to fit our conference table, but nothing else.

我們長方形的會議室只夠放我們的會議桌，放不下其他東西了。

	其他常見形狀說法：
補充	1. triangle 三角形
	2. square 正方形
	3. oval 橢圓形
	4. cone 圓錐形

rectangle n. 長方形

中級

74. **refresh**

[rɪˋfrɛʃ]

v. 更新；重新整理

⇨ re-「再次」+ fresh「新鮮的」

I want to **refresh** your memory about what happened when we presented an extreme idea to the CEO- he flipped out.

我來幫你回顧我們向執行長提出那個激進想法時發生的事 --- 他大發雷霆。

 refresh the page [電腦用語] 重新整理頁面

refreshment n. 點心飲料

同 renew v. 更新

06 買賣交易

07 採購與物流

08 廣告與宣傳

09 業務協調

10 企業經營

中級

75. **reminder**

[rɪˋmaɪndɚ]

n. 提示；提醒物；催單

⇨ re -「再次」+ mind「注意」+ -er「做…動作的人或物」，讓你再次注意的東西就是提示、提醒

This is a **reminder** that there is still space available for those who want to sign up for the company retreat this weekend.

這是要提醒那些想報名這週末公司出遊的人目前還有空位。

補充　final reminder　最後提醒

remind v. 提醒

中級

76. **remove**

[rɪˋmuv]

v. 移除；免職

⇨ re -「返回」+ move「移動」，移動回去表示解除了原來的動作

We need to **remove** all the customers on this list from our database.

我們需要把這張表上面的所有客戶資料從資料庫裡移除。

補充
remove sth./sb. from sth.	從…移除…
remove barriers/obstacles	清除障礙
remove restrictions	解除限制

removal n. 移動；排除
removable adj. 可移動的，可拆裝的

初級

77. **repair**

[rɪˋpɛr]

v. 維修；糾正，補救

n. 修理；修補工作

⇨ re -「再次」+ -par -「準備」，再次準備好使東西能被使用就表示經過維修

There is no need to renovate the entire office when there are only certain things that need to be **repaired**.

只有一些東西需要維修就不需要翻修整間辦公室了。

補充
be in need of repair	需要修理
under repair	修理中
beyond repair	無法修理
in good repair	維修良好
repair service	維修服務

repairable adj. 可修理的
irreparable adj. 無法修理的

同 v. = mend / fix

初級

78. **reply**

[rɪˋplaɪ]

v./n. 回答，回覆，回應

⇨ re-「往回」+ -ply-「摺疊」，寫上答案摺好寄回

Have you gotten a **reply** from our client?
你已經收到我們客戶的回覆了嗎？

 補充

reply to sb./sth.	回覆某人或某物
reply that...	回覆說…
make no reply	不回答
in reply to	答覆（正式用法）

初級

79. **review**

[rɪˋvju]

v. 仔細檢閱；修正；寫書評；
複習

n. 檢查，檢討；評論

⇨ re-「再次」+ view「看」，再看一次就是要檢查

I suggest that you **review** your notes again before stepping into the meeting with the bigwigs.
我建議你去跟那些大人物開會之前再檢查一次你的筆記。

 補充

under review	在審查中
conduct/carry out a review (of sth.)	執行審查
peer review	同儕評鑑；同業審查
be well reviewed	受到好評

中高

80. **rotate**

[ˋrotet]

v. 轉動；輪流做…

⇨ -rot-「輪子；旋轉」+ -ate「動詞字尾」

Our team has a schedule so we can **rotate** job duties.
我們團隊有排班表，所以我們的工作可以輪替。

 補充

rotate between sb.	在某些人之中輪流
rotate shifts	輪流換班

rotation n. 旋轉；輪流，交替

中級

81. **routine**

[ruˋtin]

adj. 日常的，例行的

n. 例行公事；慣例

⇨ route「途徑，方法」+ -ine「名詞字尾」，常用的方法
就是慣例、例行公事

During a **routine** check of procedures, my manager found several severe violations committed by my colleagues.
進行例行流程檢查的時候，我的經理發現了我同事犯下的一些嚴重違規事項。

 補充

a fixed/set routine	固定流程
a break in the routine	打破常規
routine jobs/tasks	平淡無奇的工作

route n. 路徑
routinely adv. 固定地

82. run out of

[rʌn][aut][əf]

phr. 用完

We have **run out of** funding sources, so we will need to finish the project with what we already have.

我們已經沒有資金來源了，所以我們必須用現有的資源來完成這項計畫。

run out of time	沒時間
run out of steam	精疲力竭；沒有精力
run out	（某物）用完了

中級

83. scan

[skæn]

v./n. 審視；掃描

scanner n. 掃描機

易混 skim v. 略讀

I just want you to **scan** through the document to find any mention of a deadline.

我只要你看過這份文件找出有提到關於截止期限的資訊。

補充 scan through 粗略地看；瀏覽

中級

84. schedule

[ˋskɛdʒul]

n. 時間表；計畫表

v. 安排時程

 sched「拉丁文，紙張」＋ -ule「表小東西」

We are on a very tight **schedule**, so we can't afford to start the meeting even one minute late.

我們的行程很緊湊，因此我們會議晚一分鐘開始都不行。

典故 schedule 最早是指附在文件後面，上面寫了字的小紙張。

補充
full/hectic/tight schedule
排的很滿 / 時間很緊的時程表
ahead of/on/behind schedule
先於 / 按照 / 遲於預定時間
be scheduled to do sth. 被預定去做某事
schedule sth. for +特定時間 定於某時間安排某事

reschedule v. 重新排程

中級

85. seal

[sil]

v. 密封；蓋章；決定

n. 印章，圖章；蠟封

Some of the contents of the envelope were missing because it had not been **sealed** properly.
這信封裡的一些東西不見了，因爲它沒有密封好。

 典故　古代寄信時會用蠟封住信件後再蓋上表示身分的特製印章。

補充
seal a(n) friendship/promise/agreement
締交／鄭重承諾／正式達成協議
seal of approval　正式批准
self-seal envelope　自黏信封
company seal　公司章
official seal　公章，單位印章

sealed adj. 密封的

反 unseal v. 開啟；拆掉封條

中級

86. security

[sɪˈkjʊrətɪ]

n. 安全；保障；保全人員

⇨ secure「安全的」+ -ity「表狀態，性質」
The building was closed for an hour because of a **security** alert.
由於有安全警報，大樓封閉了一小時。

 補充
security guard 警衛
security firm　保安公司
security measures/checks/procedures 保安措施
job/financial security 工作／經濟保障

secure adj. 安全的

中高

87. shredder

[ˈʃrɛdɚ]

n. 碎紙機

⇨ shred「切條，切絲」+ - er「做…動作的物品」
Put all these agenda sheets into a **shredder**.
把這些議程表全部放進碎紙機。

 補充　paper shredder 碎紙機

shred v. 切條，切絲；用碎紙機撕毀 (文件)

88. **sort**

[sɔrt]

v. 將…分類；整理

n. 類型

同 類型：kind / type

I want all the applications **sorted** by last name and education level.

我想要所有的申請書用姓氏和教育程度來分類。

補充
sort through　查看並整理
sort out　　　選出

---

89. **spontaneous**

[spɑnˋtenɪəs]

adj. 即興的；自發的

spontaneously adv. 自發地，不由自主地
spontaneity n. 自發性

They had the **spontaneous** idea to just take an extended lunch break and eat out.

他們靈機一動想要延長午休時間去外面吃飯。

補充　a spontaneous offer of help 自願提供幫助

---

90. **spreadsheet**

[ˋsprɛdˌʃit]

n. 電子製表軟體；試算表

⇨ **spread**「伸展，延伸」＋ **sheet**「紙張」

It's your duty to check every number on that **spreadsheet** before we deem the data to be official.

你的職責是在正式公開這些資料前先檢查試算表上的每筆數字。

補充　原始的紙張試算表因為要記錄很多筆數據會做得非常大張，因此包含 spread 一字。

---

91. **stationery**

[ˋsteʃənˌɛrɪ]

n. 文具；信紙

stationer n. 文具店；文具商

易混 stationary adj. 不動的

🌀 **stationer**「文具店；賣紙筆的地方」＋ **- y**「名詞字尾」

The boss limited our supply of **stationery**, so I started bringing some from home.

因為老闆限制我們文具的供給量，所以我開始從家裡帶一些來。

中高

92. tardy

['tardɪ]

adj. 遲到的；延遲的

tardily adv. 遲緩地
tardiness n. 遲緩
同 late / sluggish
反 punctual adj. 準時的
prompt adj. 及時的

⇨ -tard- 「緩慢的」+ -y 「有…性質的」

Anyone who is **tardy** for meetings gets the evil eye from the boss.

任何開會遲到的人會被老闆惡狠狠地瞪著。

補充 be tardy in doing sth. 做某事拖拖拉拉地

中級

93. tray

[tre]

n. (辦公桌上的) 文件盒；
托盤

Always completely fill the paper **tray** with two reams of paper.

送紙匣要一直放滿兩令的紙張。

★ ream「令」是紙張的計數單位，一令 = 500 張。

典故 tray 源自古英文 treow「樹木、木頭」，也表示木製器皿。

補充 tray 泛指各種淺薄的托盤，辦公室內最常見的就是 filing tray「公文架」和 paper tray「影印機的送紙匣」；或是招待客人喝茶時會用到 tea tray。另外，in tray 是指放置待處理文件的收文格；而 out tray 則是放置已處理文件的發文格。

94. turn in

[tɜn][ɪn]

phr. 歸還；繳交，上交

同 hand in

I expect each employee to **turn in** a self-evaluation by next Monday.

我希望每一位員工在下週一之前交出自我評量表。

中高

95. underneath

[ˌʌndɚ`niθ]

prep. 在…底下
adv. 在…底下；本質上
n. 底部

同 prep. = under / beneath / below

⇨ under「在下面」+ beneath「在下面」

Emily muttered **underneath** her breath as the boss blathered on and on.

老闆持續在滔滔不絕的同時，Emily 暗暗地在底下嘀咕。

補充 mutter underneath one's breath
用別人聽不到的聲調說話

中級

96. unexpected
[ˌʌnɪkˈspɛktɪd]
adj. 預料之外的，意外的

⇨ un-「不」＋ expect「預期」＋ -ed「形容詞字尾」
Steve's abrupt exit from the board meeting was totally **unexpected**.
Steve 突然從董事會議離開完全在預料之外。

unexpectedly adv. 意外地

同 accidental / unanticipated

反 expected adj. 預期的
usual adj. 通常的，常見的

97. upcoming
[ˈʌpˌkʌmɪŋ]
adj. 即將來臨的（僅用於名詞前）

The **upcoming** review from a major magazine will either make or break us.
即將在主流雜誌刊登的評論報導不是會幫助我們就是會毀了我們。

 come up 發生；出現

中級

98. urgent
[ˈɝdʒənt]
adj. 緊急的；急迫的

⇨ urge「催促；驅策」＋ -ent「具…性質的」
I have an **urgent** need for an executive secretary with a myriad of office skills.
我急需一位具備多種辦公技能的執行秘書。

 be in urgent need of... 急需…

urgently adv. 緊急地
urgency n. 緊急；急事

99. workplace
[ˈwɝkˌples]
n. 職場；工作場所

⇨ work「工作」＋ place「地方」
Our **workplace** is in chaos due to the upcoming rollout of a new line of products.
我們的工作場所因為新產品線即將開始營運而處於混亂的狀態。

in the workplace	在職場中
workplace bullying	職場霸凌
workplace injuries	職業傷害

中級

100. **wrap**

[ræp]

v. 包，裹；纏繞，盤繞

n. 包裝用品；披肩

wrapping n. 包裝材料
wrapper n. 包裝紙

In this department, our workers carefully **wrap up** fragile china in bubble wrap.

在這個部門，我們的員工用泡泡袋仔細地包裝易碎的瓷器。

補充	wrap up	包起來，包裝；完成、結束工作
	gift wrap	禮物包裝紙
	bubble wrap	（防衝擊的）泡泡袋
	plastic wrap	保鮮膜

實力進階

Part 1. Describe the peripherals 常見電腦周邊設備：

disk drive	磁碟機
keyboard	鍵盤
modem	數據機
mouse	滑鼠
mouse pad	滑鼠墊
printer	印表機
scanner	掃描機
USB flash drive	隨身碟
webcam	網路攝影機
speaker	喇叭

Part 2. Describe the stationery 常見辦公室文具：

paper clip	迴紋針
binder clip	長尾夾
thumbtack / pushpin	圖釘
adhesive tape	膠帶
twin adhesive (tape)	雙面膠
stapler	釘書機
staple	釘書針
notepad	便條簿
notepaper	便條紙
Post-it note	便利貼
rubber band	橡皮筋
correction tape	立可帶
scissors	剪刀
cutter knife / box cutter / paper cutter	刀片，美工刀

Part 3. label vs. tag

label 與 **tag** 都表示標籤或是貼標籤的動作，但是兩者慣用的搭配語是不同的。

tag 是標籤或吊牌，常指不是原來就標示在產品上面，而是另外掛上去的標籤。通常是為了與其他東西區分而放上標籤。如：**name tag** 名牌、**price tag** 價格標籤。

label 相對來說，則強調是產品本身就有的識別標示，如 **food label** 食品標示。**label** 甚至衍生出能代表品牌或公司名稱的意思，如 **record label** 最初是指貼在唱片上的標籤紙，後來衍生出指唱片公司的意思。

Part 4. schedule vs. timetable

timetable 主要用在英式英語，表示交通工具時刻表或課程表；而且常以表格形式呈現。**timetable** 可以說是 schedule 的一種。

schedule 主要用在美式英語，除了表示交通工具時刻表或課程表，還表示行程或計畫，如：**daily schedule** 每日行程、**work schedule** 工作時間表。

隨堂練習

★ 請根據句意，選出最適合的單字

( ) 1. A table of _____, which is a list of the parts of a book organized in the order in which the parts appear, helps readers to get a general idea about a book.
(A) categories
(B) accessories
(C) contents
(D) magnets

( ) 2. If you have a problem with the computer and the printer, consult the _____ without delay.
(A) manual
(B) shredder
(C) monitor
(D) reminder

( ) 3. Sincerity is a(n) _____ element of his success in landing so many new clients within just three days.
(A) routine
(B) punctual
(C) miscellaneous
(D) integral

( ) 4. In our company, employees are encouraged to _____ job duties so that they can get a wider variety of experience.
(A) sort
(B) rotate
(C) hinder
(D) scan

( ) 5. Marvin was eliminated after the first interview for lack of computer _____ since this company wants its workers to have basic computer skills.
(A) extension
(B) diagram
(C) rationale
(D) literacy

解答：1. C 2. A 3. D 4. B 5. D

Unit 4 文書作業

中級

1. abstract

[ˈæbstrækt]
n. 摘要
[æbˈstrækt]
v. 做摘要，寫梗概

 abs - 「從…分離」+ -tract - 「拉曳」，從內容拉出大意

Hand in your abstract of this report by tomorrow.
明天以前交出你讀完這報告所作出的摘要。

補充　make an abstract of sth. 做某物的摘要
abstract sth. from sth.　從某資料中做出摘要

中高

2. acknowledge

[əkˈnɑlɪdʒ]
v. 承認；告知收到（信件等）；
表示感謝

 ac - 「表加強語氣」+ know「知道」+ -ledge「名詞字尾」

I have to acknowledge the fact that Ted actually did a better job programming the software than I did.
我必須承認 Ted 在軟體程式設計方面表現比我要好。

補充
acknowledge sb. as...　公認某人是…
sb. be acknowledged as...　某人被認爲是…
acknowledge receipt of sth. 告知收到某物
in acknowledgment of N.　作爲對 N. 的答謝

acknowledged adj. 公認的
acknowledgement n. 承認；確認通知；致謝

同 承認：admit

初級

3. advise

[ədˈvaɪz]
v. 勸告；建議；告知，通知

⇨ ad - 「to」+ -vis - 「看見」，去看一看才能給通知或建議

I advise that you slowly move through the PowerPoint presentation one slide at a time.
我建議你 PowerPoint 簡報要走慢一點，一次放一張投影片。
We will advise you of the delivery date by email later.
我們稍後會寄電子郵件通知您交貨的日期。

補充
advise (sb.) to V. / advise (sb.) against V-ing
建議某人去做 / 不要做…
advise sb. of sth./ advise sb. that...
通知某人關於某訊息
keep sb. advised 讓某人了解變化的情況

advice n. 忠告（不可數名詞）；通知（可數名詞）
adviser n. 顧問

同 通知：inform / notify

中高

4. affirm
[əˋfɝm]

v. 堅稱，斷言，確認，鄭重
聲明；肯定

⇨ ad-「to」+ firm「使堅固」

I can **affirm** that Mike spent most of his normal working hours on this project.
我可以證實 Mike 大部分的正常工作時間都花在這個企劃上面。

affirmative adj. 肯定的；表示贊成的
affirmation n. 斷言；證實

---

5. annul
[əˋnʌl]

v. 取消，廢止，宣告…無效

⇨ an-「to」+ -nul-「無，沒有」，使變成沒有的動作就
是取消、廢止

The contract was **annulled** because the company didn't pass inspection.
這份契約廢止是因為發現這間公司沒有通過檢驗。

annulment n. 廢除，取消；失效

同 abolish

中高

6. appendix
[əˋpɛndɪks]

n. 附錄；附加物
v. 加附錄於

⇨ append「附加」+ -ix「名詞字尾」

Just quickly flip to the **appendix** and scan for the name of the policy you are describing.
快翻到附錄頁找到你所說的規定名稱。

 an appendix to sth. 某物的附錄
append sth. to sth. 將某物增附在某物上面

append v. 附加，增補

初級

7. appreciate
[əˋpriʃɪˏet]

v. 感激；欣賞；理解；增值

⇨ ap-「to」+ -preci-「= -preti-，表價值」+ -ate
「使有…」

I **appreciate** the efforts of everyone in this department to have our new order-taking system ready before the deadline.
我要感謝這個部門每位同仁努力讓我們新的訂單接收系統在期限內完成。

 I would appreciate it if you...
如果你…，我將不勝感激。
show appreciation for sb. 對某人表達感激

appreciation n. 感激；欣賞；理解；增值
appreciative adj. 表示讚賞的，感謝的

中級

8. **approve**

[ə`pruv]

v. 批准，認可；贊成，同意

⇨ ap -「to」+ -prov -「試驗」，通過試驗才能認可

The new policy has to be **approved** by the board of directors before it can be implemented.

這項新政策得獲得董事會批准才可實行。

補充　approve the bill/deal/settlement
批准法案／交易／協議
approve of 批准；贊許

approval n. 批准，認可；贊成，同意
approved adj. 被認可的；眾所公認的

同 endorse

反 disapprove v. 反對

中級

9. **attach**

[ə`tætʃ]

v. 貼上；附上；附加

⇨ at -「to」+ -tach -「栓，繫上」

Be sure to **attach** a business card to the inside of each folder.

記得要在每個資料夾裡面貼上一張名片。

補充　attach A to B　　將 A 貼附到 B 上
strings attached　附加條件，限制條款
email attachment 附加檔案

attached adj. 附屬的
attachment n. 附件，附屬物，附加裝置

中高

10. **autograph**

[`ɔtəˌgræf]

n. (名人) 親筆簽名
v. 親筆簽名於…

⇨ auto -「自己」+ -graph -「書寫」

The football superstar **autographed** my replica jersey and I had it framed and hung in my office.

那名足球巨星親自在我的燙印球衣上面簽名，我就把它裱了框掛在我的辦公室裡。

autography n. 親筆；筆跡
autographic adj. 親筆寫的

初級

11. **aware**

[əˈwɛr]

adj. 察覺的

⇨ a-「表加強語氣」+ ware「留心的，知道的」

I am not **aware** of any existing policy about the number of bathroom breaks that employees are allowed to have.
我沒有注意到現行的公司規定中有規範員工使用洗手間的次數。

補充
aware of/that...　察覺到…
awareness of sth. 察覺某事

awareness n. 察覺；意識

中高

12. **breach**

[britʃ]

n./v. 違反

The **breach** of accounting policy must be reported to my superiors at once.
這件違反會計規定的事情一定要立刻向我的上司報告。

補充
breach of contract　　違約
breach of trust　　　　失信
breach of confidence　洩密
breach of etiquette　　違反禮節

同 n. = violation

中級

13. **circular**

[ˈsɝkjələ]

n. 通知，公告；傳單
adj. 環形的；循環的；供流
　　傳的，供傳閱的

We're going to need our weekly **circulars** to advertise even better discounts with huge font.
我們要在每週公告上使用大型字體做廣告宣傳有更好的折扣優惠。

補充　circular letter　宣傳信（如公司用的通函或傳單）

circulate v. 循環；流通，發行
circulation n. 循環；（報刊等的）發行量，銷售量

中高

14. **cite**

[saɪt]

v. 引用；引證

You did not **cite** your sources for any of the quotes or charts presented in your report.
你沒有在你報告中的任何引言或圖表上標明引用出處。

補充　be cited as sth. 被引用、引證為某物

above-cited adj. 上面所引的
citation n. 引用；引證

易混 site n. 地點，場所

初級

15. **claim**

[klem]

n./v. 聲稱；要求；索賠

Helen was unable to back up her **claim** that she had written dozens of successful grants.
Helen 無法證實自己曾經寫過很多成功的經費補助計畫書的聲明。

補充	claim to V.../ claim that...	宣稱…
	claim responsibility	聲稱有責任
	claim damages	要求賠償
	claim sb's life	奪去某人的生命

中高

16. **clause**

[klɔz]

n. 條款；子句

There is a **clause** in your contract stating that you must be physically in the office for at least fifty hours a week.
你的合約裡有一項條款載明你一週必須至少有五十個小時人要待在辦公室。

補充	add/remove/include a clause	增加／刪除／含有條款
	confidentiality clause	保密條款

clausal adj. 條款性的；子句的

中高

17. **coherent**

[ko'hɪrənt]

adj. 協調的，一致的；連貫的，有條理的

➪ **co -**「一起」**+ -here -**「黏著」**+ -ent**「具…性質的」，有條理的黏在一起就是連貫的

The management team did not present a **coherent** plan about how they will handle the sudden surge of sales.
關於要如何處理突然激增的銷售量，管理團隊並沒有提出一個協調的計畫。

cohere v. 黏著；附著
coherence n. 一致；連貫
coherently adv. 連貫地

---

18. **cohesive**

[ko'hisɪv]

adj. 有粘著力的；有結合力的；凝聚性的

➪ **cohesion**「結合；凝聚」**+ -ive**「具…性質的」

Mr. Anderson expects our division to function as a more **cohesive** group, so increased communication will be necessary.
Anderson 先生期望我們部門成為更有凝聚力的團隊，所以更多的溝通會是必要的。

cohesion n. 結合，凝聚力；(句子、文章等的)緊湊

中高

19. **comparative**
[kəm`pærətɪv]
adj. 比較而言的，相對的

⇨ compare「比較」+ -ive「具…性質的」
I would like a **comparative** analysis regarding our two most popular phone models on my desk by Thursday.
星期四之前我要在我的桌上看到一份關於我們兩款最受歡迎的電話型號的比較分析。

 comparative advantage in sth. 相對優勢

compare v. 比較
comparison n. 比較
comparatively adv. 相對地；比較地

易混 comparable adj. 可比較的；比得上的

中高

20. **compile**
[kəm`paɪl]
v. 匯編；編製

compiler n. 編輯者；電腦編譯程序
compilation n. 匯編

⇨ com-「一起」+ pile「堆疊」，把資料堆在一起做彙整
I want you to **compile** as much evidence as possible.
我要你盡可能彙整越多證據越好。

中級

21. **composition**
[ˌkɑmpə`zɪʃən]
n. 構成；作品，作文；作曲，創作

compose v. 構成；寫作；作曲
composer n. 作曲人
composite adj. 混合的 n. 合成物

⇨ compose「構成，寫作」+ -ition「名詞字尾」
Your **composition**, which introduces our company, should include our mission statement.
你介紹我們公司的文章應該要包含我們的企業宗旨。

 be composed of... 由…組成

中高

22. **comprehend**
[ˌkɑmprɪ`hɛnd]
v. 理解

comprehension n. 理解
comprehensive adj. 有理解力的
comprehensible adj. 能理解的

⇨ com-「完全」+ -prehend-「抓住」，完全抓到重點就懂了
I realize that it's difficult to **comprehend** why I would suddenly resign without warning.
我明白要理解我為什麼會突然無預警離職是很困難的。

初級

23. concern

[kənˈsɝn]

v. 涉及，關係到；影響到

n. 關注；關心的事；企業，公司

 con-「一起」+ -cern-「篩選，詳查」，放一起檢查的彼此都相關

The policy changes will **concern** thousands of workers in the power plant.
政策改變會影響到在發電廠工作的上千名工人。

補充
To whom it may concern
敬啓者 (用於正式信件開頭)
To the authorities concerned 致有關人士 / 單位

concerned adj. 有關的
concerning prep. 關於

中高

24. concise

[kənˈsaɪs]

adj. 簡潔的，簡要的

concisely adv. 簡潔地
concision n. 簡明，簡潔

⇨ con-「一起，全部」+ -cis-「切」，內容越切越簡潔
I need you to make your PowerPoint slide descriptions very **concise** and to the point.
我要你製作內容簡潔且切中要點的 PowerPoint 投影片。

同 succinct / terse / brief

反 lengthy adj. 冗長的

中高

25. condense

[kənˈdɛns]

v. 壓縮；濃縮

⇨ con-「一起，全部」+ -dens-「濃厚的」
Your job is to **condense** these classic novels to make them simpler to read for non-native speakers.
你的工作是濃縮這些經典小說，讓非母語人士更容易讀懂它們。

補充 condense sth. into sth. 將某物壓縮成某個狀態

condensed adj. 扼要的；濃縮的
condensable adj. 可壓縮的；可簡約的

中高

26. condition
[kənˋdɪʃən]
n. 合約的條件，條款

 con-「一起」+ -dit-「說」+ -ion「名詞字尾」

Make sure you read the **conditions** carefully before signing any agreements.
簽署任何合約之前要仔細閱讀條款。

I will only approve the contract on the **condition** that your team meets certain targets to show progress.
只有在你們團隊達到既定目標表示成長的條件下我才會批准這份合約。

補充	terms and conditions	條款及條件
	conditions of sale	銷售條件
	under the conditions of sth.	按照某條款
	on the condition that...	只有在某條件下

中高

27. continuity
[ˌkɑntəˋnjʊətɪ]
n. 連續性；持續性；連貫性

continue v. 繼續
continuous adj. 不間斷的，連續的

⇨ continue「繼續，持續」+ -ity「名詞字尾」

There is no sense of **continuity** between this management team and the last one.
這個管理團隊和上一個管理團隊的管理並不一致。

28. contract
[kənˋtrækt]
v. 訂契約
[ˋkɑntrækt]
n. 合約

 con-「一起」+ -tract-「拉」，雙方一起拉來簽合約

We were so loaded down with work that we began to **contract** out part of it.
我們的工作量太大大了以致我們開始將一部分的工作外包出去。

補充	put sth. out to contract/contract sth. out	
	請人承包工作	
	sign a contract	簽署合約
	enter into a contract	訂立契約
	draw up a contract	擬定合約
	be under contract	受合約約束

中高

29. **correspondence**

[ˌkɔrə`spandəns]

n. 通信；信件

⇨ **correspond**「通信」+ **-ence**「名詞字尾」

We need to appoint someone to keep in **correspondence** with the design firm.

我們需要派人與這間設計公司保持信件往來。

 補充

be in correspondence with sb. 與某人通信
correspondence from/to sb.
來自 / 給某人的信件
correspondence between sb. and sb.
某人與某人之間往來的信件
by correspondence 經由通信的方式

correspond v. 通信
correspondent n. 通信者；通訊記者；特派員

中高

30. **counterpart**

[`kaʊntəˌpart]

n. 合約複本；相對應者

⇨ **counter -**「相對應的」**+ part**「部分」

This agreement is made in two **counterparts** with each party holding one copy.

本協議一式兩份，雙方各執一份。

My **counterpart**, Jessica, will show you around and introduce you to the whole team.

跟我同級的同事 Jessica 會帶你到處看看並把你介紹給整個團隊認識。

 補充

counterpart 原指文件的多份正本；現在常指職務相當的人。

中高

31. **description**

[dɪ`skrɪpʃən]

n. 描寫；描述

⇨ **describe**「描述」+ **-ion**「名詞字尾」

Please give me a detailed **description** of your plan.

請向我詳細描述你的計劃。

補充

job description　　工作說明，職務說明
be beyond description　難以形容

describe v. 描述

中級

32. despite

[dɪ`spaɪt]
prep. 儘管，無論，不管

⇨ de-「往下」+ -spite-「同 -spic- ，看」，往下看
就是輕視、不管它

Despite the setbacks recently, we expect to successfully negotiate an agreement.
儘管最近遭遇挫折，我們還是期待能夠成功地透過談判達成協議。

同 in spite of

中級

33. detail

[`ditel]
n. 細節
v. 詳述

⇨ de-「分開」+ -tail-「切割」，切開的小塊就是細節

The following illustrations will provide more **details** about this gadget's functions.
以下的說明會有更多關於這個機械功能的細節。

in detail	詳細地
go into detail/details	敘述詳情
for further details	欲知詳情

detailed adj. 詳細的

中級

34. dictate

[`dɪktet]
v. 口述，使聽寫

⇨ -dict-「說」+ -ate「動詞字尾」

Peter was **dictating** a letter to his secretary when I called.
我打電話去的時候，Peter 正在請他的秘書寫下他口述的信件。

dictate a letter/memo/reply to sb.
口述信件 / 便條 / 回覆給某人聽
take dictation 做聽寫

dictation n. 口述；聽寫；聽寫的文章

中高

35. documentary

[ˌdɑkjə`mɛntərɪ]
adj. 書面的，文件形式的；
紀錄的
n. 紀錄影片

⇨ document「文件」+ -ary「與…有關的」

Please attach relevant **documentary** evidence to support your explanation.
請附上相關的書面證據資料證明你的論述。

documentary proof	書面證據
documentary film	紀錄片，文獻片

document n. 文件；證件

中級

36. draft
[dræft]
n. 草稿；(BrE) 匯票
v. 起草

Could you do me a favor and proofread my first **draft** of our company's five-year plan?
你可以幫我校對我寫的關於我們公司五年計畫的初稿嗎？

補充
first/final draft	初稿／最後草案
original draft	原稿
draft plan/proposal	計劃草案／建議草案
cash a draft	兌現匯票
draft beer (draught beer)	桶裝啤酒

draftsman n. 起草者；立案者；製圖者

37. due to
[dju] [tu]
phr. 由於

Due to the sluggish economy, we will need to cut costs and even eliminate some positions.
由於經濟蕭條，我們將必須減低成本甚至淘汰掉一些職位。

中高

38. duplicate
[ˋdjupləkɪt]
adj. 複製的
n. 合約副本
v. 複製

 du-「二」+ -plic-「摺疊」+ -ate「動詞字尾」，摺疊使成兩份就是複製

Sort this entire file and delete any **duplicate** names.
把整份檔案分類並刪除任何重複的名稱。

補充
| in duplicate | 一式兩份 |
| duplicate copy | 副本，複製本 |

duplication n. 複製；副本
duplicable adj. 可複製的

39. elaborate
[ɪˋlæbəˌret]
v. 詳盡說明；闡述
[ɪˋlæbərɪt]
adj. 精心製作的；詳盡的

 e-「出來」+ labor「勞動」+ -ate「動詞字尾」，以勞力做出來就表示是精心製作的

I do not care to **elaborate** on the company-wide policy changes that may be put into place.
我不想要對於可能會實行在全公司規定上的改變再多做解釋了。

補充
elaborate on sth. 詳述某事物
elaborate plan/notes/excuses
詳盡的計劃／詳細的筆記／精心編造的藉口

elaboration n. 詳細闡述；精巧
elaborately adv. 詳盡地

40. enclose

[ɪnˋkloz]

v. 封入；隨信附上，裝入

 en - 「使成為…狀態」+ close 「關閉」

Be sure to **enclose** a business card in each envelope of the mass mailing.

這一大批郵件的每個信封裡一定要隨信附上名片。

補充 please find enclosed... 茲附上…

enclosed adj. 隨函附上的
enclosure n. (信函或包裹的) 附件

---

41. exact

[ɪgˋzækt]

adj. 確切的，精確的

⇨ **ex -**「出去」+ **act**「行動」，**實際做出來才精確**

Although our design is not an **exact** match, it is too similar to the famous company's logo.

雖然我們的設計不完全一樣，不過它和該知名公司的商標真的太相似了。

補充 to be exact 確切地說
not exactly 不完全如此

exactly adv. 精確地

---

42. except

[ɪkˋsɛpt]

prep. 除外

v. 把…除外，不計

⇨ **ex -**「出去」+ **-cept -**「拿，取」，拿出去的就是除外的

Everything has been prepared for the conference **except** printing the handouts.

除了列印講義之外，這個會議所有要的東西都準備好了。

補充 except for... 除了…以外
be excepted from sth. 從某處被刪除掉了

excepted adj. 除外的
excepting prep. 除…之外
exception n. 除外；例外

易混 besides prep. 除此以外還…

---

43. excerpt

[ˋɛksəpt]

n. 摘錄；引用；節錄

[ɪkˋsɝpt]

v. 摘錄；引用

⇨ **ex -**「出去」+ **-cerpt -**「挑，摘」，挑出來的東西就是摘錄、引用

I prefer to start my speeches with an **excerpt** from Homer's *The Odyssey*.

我比較喜歡引用荷馬的奧德賽來開始我的演講。

補充 excerpt from... 節錄自…

44. expire

[ɪk'spaɪr]
v. 到期

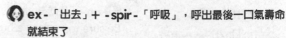 **ex -「出去」+ - spir -「呼吸」，呼出最後一口氣壽命就結束了**

Our restaurant's liquor license is about to expire, so go downtown and renew it.
我們餐廳的售酒執照要到期了，去市中心申請續期吧。

補充
be set/scheduled/due to expire 到期
expiration date (EXP) 到期日，截止日，保存期限

expired adj. 到期的；過期的
expiration n. (AmE) 到期
expiry n. (BrE) 到期

---

45. feel free to

[fil] [fri] [tu]
phr. 隨意，隨時

Feel free to roam the banquet hall and introduce yourself to your fellow attendees.
請隨意在宴會廳四處走走向其他與會者介紹自己。

補充
feel free to do sth. 請隨意…

---

46. fine print

[faɪn] [prɪnt]
phr. 附屬細則；小號字體印刷品

Franklin never reads the fine print, so he violated policy without knowing it.
Franklin 從來不閱讀附屬細則，所以他在不知情的狀況下違反了規定。

補充
Read the fine print. / Beware of the small print.
注意附屬細則。

fine adj. 細微的
同 (BrE) small print

中高
47. format

['fɔrmæt]
n. 格式；方式，樣式
v. 編排格式；格式化

Please look over the template I sent you, so you will send reports in the proper format from now on.
請看一看我寄給你的範本並從現在起用正確的格式寄送報告。

補充
in a ... format 以…的格式

form n. 形式，方式；形狀

初級

48. **forward**
[`fɔrwəd]
v. 轉寄；發送（縮寫 FW）
adv. 向前

This email was sent to you by mistake, so please **forward** it to the appropriate party.
這封電子郵件被寄錯給你了，所以請將它轉寄給對的群組。

補充	forward sth. to sb. 轉寄某物給某人 forwarding address 轉寄地址 store-and-forward adj. 儲存並轉發的

 中級

49. **hassle**
[`hæsl]
n. 麻煩，困難；爭吵
v. 找麻煩；爭吵

Having my pay sent to me via direct deposit saves me the **hassle** of going to the bank.
將我的薪資直接存入帳戶省去了跑銀行的麻煩。

補充	it's a hassle + V-ing 做某事很麻煩 hassle sb. to do sth. 煩擾某人使他去做某事

中級

50. **hence**
[hɛns]
adv. 因此；從這時起，從此

The store was closed; **hence**, I have none of the supplies you asked for.
那家店打烊了；因此，我沒有你要的東西。
The project will be completed two years **hence**.
這項專案會在從現在算起兩年內完成。

同 因此：therefore / as a result

51. **immensely**
[ɪ`mɛnslɪ]
adv. 非常，極度地

⇨ **im-**「表否定」+ **-mense-**「測量」+ **-ly**「副詞字尾」，無法測量地就是極度地

Kate was **immensely** disappointed to find that Rob had taken credit for her work.
Kate 非常失望的發現 Rob 搶了她的功勞。

immense adj. 極大的，無邊無際的，無限的

同 extremely

中級

52. implement

[ˋɪmpləmɛnt]
v. 履行，執行
[ˋɪmpləmɛnt]
n. (大且不用馬達的)工具，
用具

 im-「裡面」+ -ple-「填滿」+ -ment「名詞字尾」，
把東西填滿就執行完工作了

If you're going to **implement** our new production process,
I suggest doing a test run first.
如果你要執行我們新的生產程序，我建議要先做運行測試。

補充 implement a plan/policy/proposal
執行計劃／政策／建議

implementation n. 實施，執行

中級

53. imply

[ɪmˋplaɪ]
v. 意味著；暗示

⇨ im-「裡面」+ -ply-「摺疊」，摺進去不顯露就是暗示

I did not mean to **imply** that you hadn't followed policy.
我沒有要暗示說你沒有遵守規定的意思。

補充 imply (that) + S + V... 意味著…
as the name implies 顧名思義

implied adj. 含蓄的

---

54. inaccuracy

[ɪnˋækjərəsɪ]
n. 錯誤，差錯；不精確；
不準確的說法

⇨ in-「表否定」+ accuracy「準確性」

Your report is rife with **inaccuracies**, so you'll have to
start over from scratch.
你的報告錯誤百出，所以你必須從頭開始重寫。

inaccurate adj. 不正確的；不精確的
accurate adj. 準確的；精確的

中高

55. inclusive

[ɪnˋklusɪv]
adj. 包含在內的

⇨ in-「裡面」+ -clus-「關閉」+ -ive「具…性質的」，
關在裡面的就是包含在內的

Our ad campaign is not very **inclusive** of adults, so I'd
like a new commercial made for a broader demographic.
我們的平面廣告活動並沒有涵蓋到所有的成人，所以我想要一
個針對更多族群的新的電視廣告。

補充 inclusive of sth. 包含某事物
all-inclusive holiday/package/resort
全包式假期／套裝行程／渡假勝地
socially inclusive 社會包容的

include v. 包括
including prep. 包括
inclusively adv. 包含地；在內地

中高

56. index

[ˋɪndɛks]

n. 索引；指數；標誌
v. 編為索引

Just flip to the **index** and look for the 1994 law that pertains to this topic.
快翻到索引去找與這個主題有關的 1994 年法規。

 典故 index 來自拉丁文 index，原表「食指」，後衍生出「指引、標示」的意思。

 補充

index card	索引卡
card index	卡片索引
price index	物價指數
Body Mass Index (BMI)	身體質量指數

中級

57. inform

[ɪnˋfɔrm]

v. 通知；告知

⇨ in-「往裡面」+ form「形成」，告知就是在你心裡形成訊息

I'm elated to **inform** you that we will be promoting you to a regional management position.
我很高興通知你我們將會升你去做區經理。

補充
inform sb. of sth. / inform sb. that...
將某事通知某人
keep sb. informed 讓某人知道
for information only 僅供參考（寫在信件和文件的副本上，發給需要知道的人，但對方不用處理）
for your information (FYI) 提供資料讓你參考；讓你知道一下（用於提供給對方的資料是可以參考，有資訊價值的東西時）

information n. 資訊
informational adj. 提供消息的
informative adj. 資料豐富的；增進知識的

中級

58. inquire

[ɪnˋkwaɪr]

v. 詢問；調查

⇨ in-「往裡面」+ -quire-「尋求」，向內找答案就要不斷詢問

I'm calling to **inquire** about the price of the ticket.
我打電話是要詢問票價。

 補充
inquire about sth. 詢問某事
inquire into sth. 調查某事
inquire within
入內詢問（張貼在店外，表示可入店內詢問相關資訊）

inquiry n. 詢問；調查；問題

01 職稱職務／聘僱面試

02 人事／薪資／福利

03 辦公室／電話傳真

04 文書作業

05 會議

59. jot down
[dʒɑt] [daʊn]
phr. 匆匆記下

jot v. 草草記下

Just **jot down** all the details that the customer tells you as we might need to reference them later.
把顧客告訴你的所有細節記下來，因爲我們之後可能會需要用來參考。

中高

60. layout
['leˌaʊt]
n. 佈局，設計；版面編排

I want our magazine's **layout** to be similar to that of Vogue.
我想要我們的雜誌版面跟 Vogue 的類似。

 page layout 頁面設計
lay out   展開，展示；設計，計畫；詳細說明

---

61. legible
['lɛdʒəbḷ]
adj. (字跡) 可以辨認的；易讀的

⇨ -leg- 「讀」 + -ible 「能夠的」
The font you chose for the company logo is hardly **legible**.
你幫公司商標選的字型太難辨識了。

 barely legible 看不清楚

legibly adv. 易辨認地

反 illegible adj. 難讀的；難認的

---

62. letterhead
['lɛtɚˌhɛd]
n. 信頭

⇨ **letter** 「信」 + **head** 「頭」
Every customer email must be sent on company **letterhead**, no matter how informal it is.
每一封給顧客的電子郵件都必須要有公司信頭，不論信件有多麼不正式都一樣。

 letterhead 是指寄件人印於信紙上端的公司或個人名稱和地址，也稱爲信箋抬頭或箋頭。

初級

63. mail

[mel]

n. 郵件
v. 寄信

Unfortunately, this document must be sent back to me via certified **mail** since I need your actual signature.
很遺憾地，這份文件必須用掛號寄回來給我，因為我需要你的親筆簽名。

snail mail	透過郵局寄的信（相對於 email）
mail drop	通信地址（非收件人居住地址）
interoffice mail	公司內部信件

---

64. mandatory

[ˈmændəˌtorɪ]

adj. 義務的；強制性的，依法必須做的

⇨ **mandate**「命令」+ **-tory**「具…性質的」，命令就是一定要做的

Five years of HR experience is **mandatory** for this position.
五年的人資相關經驗是擔任這個職位的必要條件。

 mandatory for sb. to do sth. 某人有義務去做某事

mandate n./v. 命令；授權；委任

同 obligatory / compulsory

中高

65. manuscript

[ˈmænjəˌskrɪpt]

n. 原稿；手寫本
adj. 手寫的

⇨ **-manu-**「手」+ **-script-**「寫」

I sent **manuscripts** to every major publisher before I finally decided to publish my novel online on my own.
在我最後決定要自己在網路上出版我的小說之前我曾經把原稿寄給每一間主流出版社。

中高

66. margin

[ˈmɑrdʒɪn]

n. 頁邊空白；邊緣；差數

My supervisor always writes comments in the **margin**.
我主管總是在頁邊寫評語。

in the margin	在頁邊上
by a wide/narrow margin	以極大 / 些微的差距
marginal notes	邊註，旁註

marginal adj. 邊緣的

中高

67. modify

[ˈmɑdəˌfaɪ]
v. 修改，修飾

⇨ -mod-「形式，風格」+ -ify「做成…」，修改成特定形式

We have **modified** our design for this car model several times to make it look more sleek.
我們修正了這台汽車模型的設計好幾次，要讓它看起來造型更優美。

補充
modified car　　　　　　改裝車
slight/minor modification　些微修正

modified adj. 更改過的
modification n. 修改；修改的行為或過程

中高

68. norm

[nɔrm]
n. 基準；規範

Having a smart phone with all the bells and whistles is the **norm**.
有一台具備所有附加功能的智慧型手機是常態。

補充　be the norm …是習慣做法，常態

normal adj. 正常的

中高

69. obligation

[ˌɑbləˈgeʃən]
n. 義務

 ob-「表加強語氣」+ -lig-「綁住」+ -ate「動詞字尾」+ -ion「名詞字尾」，義務就是一種約束

You need to meet all of your regular office **obligations** before you get involved in training to learn extra skills.
你需要盡到所有的辦公室例行職責，才能去參加受訓，學習額外的技能。

補充
be under obligation to do sth. 有義務去做某事
meet/fulfil an obligation　　　履行義務職責
impose/place obligations on sb.
使某人有義務做某事

obligate v. 使負義務
obligatory adj.（因法律規定）必須履行的，有義務的；習慣上的
同 duty / responsibility / liability

中級

70. original

[əˈrɪdʒənl]

adj. 最初的，原本的；原版的；有獨創性的

n. 原物，原著

originally adv. 起初，原來
origin n. 起源

⇨ **origin**「起源」＋ **-al**「具…屬性的」

I believe that we need a really **original** catch phrase to make our ad campaign come alive.

我認為我們需要一個真正原創的宣傳標語使我們的廣告變得活靈活現。

中高

71. pact

[pækt]

n. 條約

Although we didn't sign anything, Tom and I made a verbal **pact** to continue doing business in the near future.

雖然我們沒有簽屬任何條約，我和 Tom 達成了口頭協議要在未來繼續一起做生意。

 make/sign a pact 簽署條約
a pact to do sth. 為某事而訂的條約

中級

72. parcel

[ˈpɑrsl]

n. 包裹

v. 分配；把…包起來，捆紮

同 package n. 包裹

⇨ **part**「部分」＋ **-cel**「名詞字尾，表小東西」，包一小部分在包裹裡

Our front desk was given a notice that you have an oversized **parcel** waiting for you at the post office.

我們櫃台收到通知說你有一件超大的包裹在郵局等你去領。

 parcel out 分配
parcel up 包起來

初級

73. party

[ˈpɑrtɪ]

n. 合約的當事人；一組人

Both **parties** were happy with the result of the negotiations.

雙方當事人都對談判的結果很滿意。

 a party of... 一群…人

中級

74. **permit**
[pəˋmɪt]
v. 允許；容許
[ˋpɝmɪt]
n. 許可證

➥ **per -**「通過」**＋ -mit -**「送出」，可送過去就是允許了
It's doubtful that the boss will **permit** you to take three vacation days with all our important meetings coming up next week.
在下週有重要會議要開的狀況下，老闆會允許你請三天假是不大可能的。

work permit	工作許可證
parking permit	停車證
residence permit	居住許可證

apply for/grant/issue a permit
申請／批准／核發許可證
weather permitting
如果天氣允許的話，假如天氣好的話

permission n. 許可，同意
permissible adj.（依法律或規定）許可的，准許的

中級

75. **phrase**
[frez]
v. 以某種方式表達，以…措辭表達
n. 詞彙

Your introduction was **phrased** particularly well, and helped to break the ice.
你的開場白說得特別好而且能幫助破冰。

 a politely phrased refusal 婉言拒絕

比較 phrase「詞彙」指一串有意義且通常不成句的詞組。
expression「措辭；詞句」可以指一個字或一個詞彙，甚至是一個完整的句子。
idiom「慣用語；成語」常以詞組的形式出現，多半是用字面意思比喻其真正詞義。

初級

76. **policy**
[ˋpɑləsɪ]
n. 政策方針；處事原則；保險單

🧑 **-poli -**「國家」**＋ -cy**「名詞字尾」
Craig is obviously unaware of the **policy** requiring employees to give two weeks' notice for vacation requests.
Craig 顯然不知道員工需要提前兩週請假的規定。

company policy	公司政策，公司規定
privacy policy	隱私政策
insurance policy	保險契約，保單
policymaker	n. 決策者
policyholder	n. 保單持有者

中高

77. **primarily**

[praɪˋmɛrəlɪ]

adv. 主要地；起初

⇨ -prim- 「第一個」＋ -ary「關於…的」＋ -ily「副詞字尾」

Our new design concept is **primarily** the idea of Frank, but we all assisted with the development.
我們新的設計概念主要是來自 Frank 的想法，不過我們都有協助開發。

primary adj. 主要的；原先的

同 主要地：mainly / essentially / mostly / chiefly
　　起初：at first / originally / initially

78. **problematic**

[ˌprɑbləˋmætɪk]

adj. 有很多問題的，麻煩的

⇨ problem「麻煩，問題」＋ -ic「關於…的」

The lawsuit that has been filed against us is **problematic** for our public image.
那件告我們的案子對我們的公眾形象造成很多麻煩。

補充　problematic 也可寫成 problematical

problematically adv. 有問題地

79. **proofread**

[ˋpruf⸴rid]

v. 校正，校對

⇨ proof「檢驗」＋ read「讀」，用讀的方式來驗證就是在校對

The article was so rushed that no one **proofread** it; thus, big errors were found.
這篇文章寫得太倉促沒有人校對，因此就發現了嚴重的錯誤。

補充　proofreading stage 校對階段

proofreader n. 校對者
proof n. 檢驗；證據 v. 試驗；校對

初級

80. **purpose**

[ˋpɝpəs]

n. 目的；用途

⇨ pur-「向前」＋ -pos-「放；表述」，向前提出我的目的

When I come by your desk, I want to see you working with a **purpose**!
當我經過你的桌子的時候，我想要看到你有認真在工作！

with/for the purposes of	出於…目的，為了…
sb's purpose in doing sth.	某人做某事的目的
serve a purpose	起到作用
on purpose	故意地，有意地

01
職稱職務／應徵面試

02
人事／薪資／福利

03
辦公室／電話傳真

04
文書作業

05
會議

中高

81. recipient
[rɪ`sɪpɪənt]
n. 接受者，領受者；收信人

⇨ re -「回來」+ -cip -「拿」+ -ent「表動作執行者」
The **recipient** of these funds must sign for them and show proof of ID.
領取這些資金的人必須簽名並出示身分證明。

補充
recipient「接受者」通常指的是人。
receiver「接受者」可以指人或者物品、設備等，因此也有話筒的意思。

receive v. 接受

初級

82. regard
[rɪ`gard]
n. 關注；問候；尊敬
v. 認為；注意重視

In **regard** to your inquiry, we don't have that style of sweatshirt in stock.
關於您的詢問，我們那一款式的運動衫已經沒有存貨了。

補充
with kind/best/warm regards
謹致問候（友善並相當正式的問候，用於信的末尾）
in regard to/with regard to/as regards/regarding
關於
regard... as sth. 將…視為某事物
highly regarded 高度重視

regarding prep. 關於

中級

83. remark
[rɪ`mark]
v./n. 評論

⇨ re -「再次」+ -mark -「做記號」，一再做記號就是在評論、評註
After Cheryl's **remarks** about her supervisor, it's no surprise that she was dismissed.
在 Cheryl 那樣子評論她的主管之後，她會被解僱也不令人意外。

補充
remark that... 評論說…
remark on sth. 評論某事物
make a remark (on sth.) 給予評論
personal remark (personal comment) 人身攻擊

remarkable adj. 值得注意的；非凡卓越的

中級

84. response
[rɪˈspɑns]
n. 回覆；反應

⇨ re-「返回」+ -spons-「承諾」，將承諾送回就是回應

It usually takes three business days to get a response from the accounting department.
要得到會計部的回覆通常要花上三個工作天。

補充
response to sth.	對某事物的回應
in response to	作為…的回應
a written/positive response	書面回應 / 正面回應

respond v. 回覆；反應
responsive adj. 積極回應的；反應快的，靈敏的

---

85. restate
[rɪˈstet]
v. 再聲明；重新敘述；（換一種方式）重說

⇨ re-「再次」+ state「說明」

Sum up the points so far and restate the question under debate.
總結目前的重點並重申有爭議的問題。

補充　restate earnings 重申財報

state v. 陳述，說明
restatement n. 再聲明；重申

初級

86. revise
[rɪˈvaɪz]
v. 修訂，校訂；修正

⇨ re-「再次」+ -vis-「看」，再看一次才能做修訂

Obviously, we need to revise the contract since we couldn't agree on anything today.
既然我們今天無法取得任何一致的意見，顯然我們需要修訂這份合約。

補充
revised edition	修訂版
be subject to revision	可能會做修改
be under revision	在修訂中

revision n. 校訂；修正；修訂本

129

01 職稱職務／聘僱面試

02 人事／薪資／福利

03 辦公室／電話傳真

04 文書作業

05 會議

中高

87. script

[skrɪpt]
n. 腳本，原稿；筆跡
v. 把…改編為劇本

scripted adj. 使用稿子的；照稿子念的
scripture n. 經典，經文

Your job is to write a speech **script** for the CEO.
你的工作是幫執行長寫演講稿。

補充 script 一字本身就是字根，表示書寫的意思。

中級

88. signature

[ˈsɪɡnətʃɚ]
n. 簽字，簽名

⇨ **sign**「做記號」+ **-ture**「表結果」
We will send you a copy of the contract for **signature**.
我們將把一份合約送交給您簽字。

補充
put your signature to/on...	在…上簽字（表示同意）
forge one's signature	偽造簽名
specimen signature	簽名樣本
signature file	簽名檔

sign v. 簽字

中高

89. signify

[ˈsɪɡnəˌfaɪ]
v. 表明；意味著

⇨ **sign**「記號」+ **-ify**「做成…」，做記號就標明出來了
I tried to figure out whether the boss's memo **signified** that business was slowing down or picking up.
我試著要搞清楚老闆的備忘錄意思是指業績下滑還是提升。

補充
sb. signify that... 某人表明說…
sth. signify that... 某物的意思是…

signification n.（詞的）意義
significance n. 涵義；重要性
significant adj. 有意義的；表示…的；重大的

06 買賣交易

07 採購與物流

08 廣告與宣傳

09 業務協調

10 企業經營

中級

90. **sincerely**

[sɪnˋsɪrlɪ]
adv. 誠摯地

 sincere「誠摯的」＋ -ly「副詞字尾」

Although Amy jokes around a lot, this time I think she is **sincerely** praising my hard work.
雖然 Amy 常常開玩笑，我想她這次是很真誠地在稱讚我的努力。

> 補充　Sincerely yours = (Yours) sincerely
> 敬上，謹啓 (寫在正式信件末尾的客套話)

sincere adj. 誠摯的
sincerity n. 真摯，誠實

中級

91. **skim**

[skɪm]
v. 瀏覽；掠過

I **skimmed** through your article in just a few minutes and I was impressed.
我花了幾分鐘瀏覽你的文章而且我感到印象深刻。

> 補充　skim through/leaf through/flick through/ browse
> 粗略地看一遍

初級

92. **subject**

[ˋsʌbdʒɪkt]
n. 主題，題材；話題
adj. 易受影響的
[səbˋdʒɛkt]
v. 使隸屬；征服

 sub-「在底下」＋ -ject-「投擲」

Whether Mr. Williams will sell his company or not is the **subject** of intense speculation.
Williams 先生是否會賣掉他的公司是大家熱切揣測的話題。

> 補充　email subject line　電子郵件標題
> get onto/off the subject (of)
> 開始談論…話題 / 離開…話題
> be subject to sth.　會受到某事物影響
> Prices are subject to change.　價格可能會改變。

中高

93. submit

[səb`mɪt]
v. 提交，呈上；服從

 sub - 「在下面」＋ -mit - 「送」，從下方恭敬地向上呈送

Submit your proposal to Charles as soon as possible.
盡快把你的提案呈送給 Charles。
I refuse to **submit** to my strong anxiety about public speaking.
我拒絕屈服於我對於公開演說的強烈焦慮。

補充　submit a bid/plan/proposal 提交投標／計畫
submit your resignation　　遞辭呈

submission n. 屈服；提交，呈遞
submissive adj. 順服的

94. terms

[tɝmz]
n. 合約的條款；條件 (只用複數型)

The two sides need to come to **terms** sometime in the next two days to avoid a strike.
雙方需要在未來兩天內達成協議以避免罷工。

補充
come to terms 達成協議
under the terms of an agreement
根據協議的條款
in terms of sth. (= in... terms; with regard to; concerning) 在某方面，從某方面來說
be on good terms with sb. 和某人關係友好

term n. 措辭；術語；期間

中高

95. transcript

[`træn͵skrɪpt]
n. 抄本，副本；錄音的文字紀錄

 trans - 「橫跨，越過」＋ -script - 「寫」

Let's check the podcast **transcript** to make sure Alicia did not make any false claims.
我們來檢查播客錄音稿確認 Alicia 沒有說假話。

補充　a transcript of sth. 某事物的文字紀錄

transcribe v. 謄寫；逐字逐句記錄
transcription n. 抄寫，記錄；抄本；文字記錄

初級

96. underline

[ˈʌndɚˌlaɪn]

v. 強調；在…的下面劃線

n. 底線

⇨ **under**「在下面」＋**line**「畫線」

I want to **underline** the fact that I never take shortcuts when it comes to making a quality product.

我要強調我在製作有品質的產品時從來沒有偷工減料。

同 emphasize / stress / highlight　v. 強調

中高

97. undoubtedly

[ʌnˈdaʊtɪdlɪ]

adv. 肯定地，毫無疑問地

⇨ **un-**「不」＋**doubted**「被懷疑的」＋**-ly**「副詞字尾」

Mr. Gregory's investment is **undoubtedly** the biggest reason I was able to build a thriving business.

Gregory 先生的投資毫無疑問是我生意能夠興隆的最重要原因。

undoubted　adj. 毋庸置疑的；肯定的

同 definitely / surely / indeed

中高

98. versus

[ˈvɝsəs]

prep. 以…為對手，對抗；相對

If you're looking for a chance to grow and develop skills **versus** just collecting a salary, we are the best place for you to work.

如果你正在尋找機會成長與培養技能而不是只有領到薪水，我們這兒就是最適合你工作的地方。

 versus 源自字根 -vers-，表示轉向的意思。versus 常略作 v. 或 vs.。

99. write up

[raɪt] [ʌp]

phr. 詳細描寫

Since this is the fifth time you have been late to work this month, I am forced to **write** you **up**.

因為這是你這個月第五次上班遲到了，我必須要寫成報告。

 write up 可以指寫出好的評論或是向上級告狀，因此要注意上下文情境才能知道 write up 的內容是好的還是壞的喔。

write-up　n. 報導，評論（尤指捧場文章）

中高

100. **ZIP code**

[zip] [kod]

phr. 郵遞區號

The corporate headquarters is so huge that it almost has its own **ZIP code.**

這間公司的總部規模大到它快要有自己的郵遞區號了。

典故 ZIP 是縮寫，原來是指 zone improvement plan 「地區改進計劃」。ZIP code 是使郵件可以更有效率及快捷地送到目的地而設的代碼系統，就是郵遞區號。

補充 zip 小寫是指拉鍊。

實力進階

Part 1. 常見的郵寄信件用語

airmail	航空郵件
surface mail	平信
registered mail/ prompt registered letter	掛號信 / 限時掛號信
certified mail	掛號信 (保證寄到，但無金錢保險)
prompt delivery	限時專送
business reply mail	廣告回函
direct mail	直接向廣大群眾投寄的直效廣告郵件
printed matter	印刷品
bulk mail	大宗郵件
express	快遞

06 買賣交易

07 採購與物流

08 廣告與宣傳

09 業務協調

10 企業經營

Part 2. 書信的結尾敬辭

注意結尾敬辭中只有第一個字的起首字母要大寫，且在末尾要有一個逗點。

常見結尾敬辭 (complimentary close)	使用時機
Yours faithfully	收件者是不知道姓名的人，或是整個部門。是商業書信最常用、最正規的結尾敬辭。
Yours truly	基本上與 yours faithfully 相同，只是使用頻率較少。
Yours sincerely	知道收件者的姓名時使用。是相識者之間最適宜的結尾敬辭，在商業書信中也越來越流行。
Respectfully yours	用在收件者是長官、長輩時，是非常正式的用語。
Best wishes/Best regards	收件者是關係親近的朋友、平輩。

隨堂練習

★ 請根據句意，選出最適合的單字

( ) 1. The software company was in _____ of contract, as they did not bother to finish the project they had started.
(A) breach
(B) remark
(C) draft
(D) hassle

( ) 2. It is _____ for all the members of the committee to attend this annual meeting. You are no exception.
(A) marginal
(B) circular
(C) legible
(D) mandatory

( ) 3. Your driving license is going to _____ next week; you had better renew it as soon as possible.
(A) except
(B) expect
(C) expire
(D) excerpt

( ) 4. The magazine's new page _____ is the reason for the increased sales. It has appealed to more young adults.
(A) layout
(B) term
(C) norm
(D) composition

( ) 5. Management found it cheaper to _____ existing equipment rather than buy new.
(A) skim
(B) underline
(C) modify
(D) cite

解答：1. A   2. D   3. C   4. A   5. C

Unit 5 會議

1. **abrupt**
[əˋbrʌpt]
adj. 突然的

⇨ **ab-**「分離」 + **-rupt-**「打破，切斷」，話說一半被打斷就是突然的

The event came to an **abrupt** end after the speaker was asked to leave for his insulting comments.
在主講人因辱罵評論被要求離場後，活動就突然終止了。

補充 an abrupt departure/end 突然的離開 / 結束

同 sudden

中高

2. **agenda**
[əˋdʒɛndə]
n. 議程，待議事項

If you all refer to your **agenda**, you'll notice that at 5:15 we are scheduled to break into smaller focus groups.
若你有參閱議程，你會注意到在 5 點 15 分時我們預定要分成焦點小組討論。

補充 set the agenda 設定議程
N. be placed high on the agenda
N. 為議程中的首要議題

中級

3. **alternative**
[ɔlˋtɝnətɪv]
n. 選擇；二擇一
adj. 二擇一的；替代的

 alternate「供選擇的」 + -ive「名詞字尾」

You leave me with no other **alternative** but to send Cindy to the conference in your place.
你讓我沒其它選擇，只能派 Cindy 代替你去開會。

補充 alternate route 替代路線
work on alternate days 隔日上班，做一休一

alter v. 變更
alternate v. 輪流、交替 adj. 輪流的、交替的
alternatively adv. 二擇一地

中高

4. **amend**

[əˋmɛnd]

v. 修訂；修正

⇨ a-「= ex-，出去」+ -mend-「錯誤」，修正就是把錯誤丟出去

We don't have time to **amend** our slide show because we are presenting to the board in five minutes!

我們沒時間修正幻燈片了，因爲再五分鐘我們就要對董事會報告了！

 A be amended to B 將 A 修正爲 B
review the amendments to N.
檢視對 N. 的修訂事項

amendment n. 修正；修正案

中級

5. **approval**

[əˋpruvl]

n. 贊成，同意；批准

⇨ ap-「to」+ prove「驗證」+ -al「表狀況」，驗證為真品就通過核准

I, for one, want to voice my **approval** for moving ahead with the V-series product rollout as fast as possible.

我，一票，聲明支持以最快的速度推動 V 系列產品問世。

 meet sb's approval 符合某人的喜好
win sb's approval   贏得某人的贊同
buy sth. on approval
可免費試用某物，適用滿意再購買

approve v. 贊成，同意；批准

反 disapproval n. 不贊成，不同意；不准

中級

6. **arrangement**

[əˋrendʒmənt]

n. 籌備，安排

⇨ arrange「安排」+ -ment「名詞字尾」

The **arrangement** to buy out the manufacturing division of my company was never agreed to by all parties.

各方對於買下本公司製造部門的安排一直沒有共識。

 make an arrangement for... 爲…做安排
come to an arrangement   達成協議

arrange v. 籌備，安排

中級

7. aspect

[ˋæspɛkt]

n. 方向；觀點、（對事物所持的）看法、角度

⇨ a-「to」＋ -spect-「看，觀察」

The adaptability of your company is one **aspect** of your business that my colleagues cannot imitate.

貴公司的應變力是我們同業仿效不來的一個面向。

補充　cover all aspects of the issue
涵蓋這個議題的所有面向

同 side

中高

8. assumption

[əˋsʌmpʃən]

n. 假設

⇨ as-「to」＋ -sumpt-「拿」＋ -ion「名詞字尾」，拿他人的想法來做假設

I am under the **assumption** that we will only be staying for the first two days of the convention.

我以為我們只會在會議的頭兩天待在這裡。

補充　It's one's assumption that... 某人的假設是…
N. be based on the assumption that...
N. 是以假設…為前提而來的

assume v. 假設

初級

9. attend

[əˋtɛnd]

vt. 出席；參加
vi. 注意；傾聽

 at-「to」＋ -tend-「伸出」

I have never had the pleasure to **attend** a trade show in the brand new convention center downtown.

我一直都不怎麼喜歡去市中心那個全新的會議中心參加商展。

補充　attend 指「出席」，participate 強調「參與」，join 則是「加入」：
attend + N.　　出席 N.
participate in + N.　參加 N.
join + N.　　加入 N.

attendance n. 到場；出席
attendee n. 出席者；在場者
well-attended adj. 出席者眾多的

10. **attentive**

[əˋtɛntɪv]
adj. 注意的；留心的；專心的

⇨ attend「注意」+ -ive「形容詞字尾」

So much of the audience was not **attentive** to the speaker, and many were even chatting on their cell phones.
好多觀眾都沒在注意演講者，很多人甚至還在講手機。

 be attentive to N. 對 N. 很關心

attention n. 注意力

中高

11. **attorney**

[əˋtɝnɪ]
n. 律師

⇨ at-「to」+ -torn-「轉向」+ -ey「被…的人」，轉身來向律師求助

It's best to have the company **attorneys** present at the next board meeting to give us a clear direction of where we are headed.
下次董事會最好請公司的律師出席，以提供我們清楚的未來方向。

 district attorney = D.A.　檢察官
a defense attorney　　　辯方律師

回 lawyer / legal counsel

初級

12. **audience**

[ˋɔdɪəns]
n. 聽眾；觀眾

⇨ -audi-「聽」+ -ence「名詞字尾」

He rushed through the conference doors as they were closing and was forced to sit at the back of the large **audience**.
他衝過正要關起來的會議廳大門，然後被迫坐在一大群觀眾的後面。

 an audience of + 數字　為數…的觀眾
target audience　　　　目標客群

中高

13. **ballot**

[ˋbælət]
n. 選票
v. 選舉，投票

Barb's name does not appear on the **ballot** as a nominee to be a board member- she was passed over again.
Barb 的名字沒有出現在董事會成員候選人的選票上，她又被略過了。

 hold a ballot　　　　　　舉行投票
secret ballot　　　　　　無記名投票
win 10% of the ballot 得到總投票數的百分之十

回 vote

初級
14. basic
[ˈbesɪk]
adj. 基本的
n. 基本原則（複數型）

⇨ base「基本」+ -ic「形容詞字尾」
We have come to a **basic** understanding that you will continue in your present position for the foreseeable future.
我們已經有個基本認知，就是在可預見的未來你會繼續留在你現任的職位上。

basic price	基本價格；未稅價格
basic wage	基本薪資
back to basics	回歸基本面

basis n. 基礎

---

15. brainstorm
[ˈbrenˌstɔrm]
n./v. 腦力激盪；集思廣益

⇨ brain「腦力」+ storm「風暴」
This newest smart phone model is the result of months and months of heavy **brainstorming** by our creative team.
這款最新的智慧型手機樣式是我們創意小組大量腦力激盪好幾個月的結果。

 brainchild n. 原創；獨創的概念

初級
16. breakthrough
[ˈbrekˌθru]
n. 突破；重大進展

⇨ break「打破」+ through「穿過」
The **breakthrough** finally came when we were playing around with low cost materials, just hoping to get something malleable, but attractive.
就在我們反覆嘗試低成本材料、希望它既具延展性又能吸引人時，這個突破點終於出現。

a breakthrough in + N.	在 N. 上的突破
a significant breakthrough	顯著的突破

---

17. cancellation
[ˌkænsəˈleʃən]
n. 取消

⇨ cancel「取消」+ -ation「名詞字尾」
The last minute **cancellation** of the celebrity guest speaker has the event organizers scrambling to fill the void.
那位受邀演講的名人在最後一分鐘取消出席，活動主辦單位只好急忙填補空缺。

 the cancellation charge / fee 取消費；註銷費

cancel v. 取消（ = call off）

06 貿易交易

中高

18. **certify**

['sɝtəˌfaɪ]

v. 證明；保證

⇨ **certain**「確定」+ **-fy**「使…」

Turn in your paperwork before the deadline to give us ample time to **certify** your credentials.

請在截止期限內繳交書面資料，好讓我們有充裕的時間確認你的證明文件。

 This is to certify that... 茲證明…（證書用語）
A be certified by B　　A 獲得 B 的認證

同 confirm / approve

07 採購與物流

中高

19. **chairperson**

['tʃɛrˌpɝsn]

n. 主席

⇨ **chair**「椅子；主持會議」+ **person**「人」

As the **chairperson** for AGT Tech, there are certain perks to go along with the stress of working 80-hour weeks.

身為 AGT 科技的主席，擔負一週工作 80 小時的壓力當然會有額外的補助津貼。

同 chairman / chairwoman / president

08 廣告與宣傳

中級

20. **clarify**

['klærəˌfaɪ]

v. 澄清；闡明

⇨ **-clar-**「清楚的」+ **-ify**「使…」

Please **clarify** what you mean by "malfunction" with the hardware.

請清楚說明你指的硬體「失常」是什麼意思。

 clarify the misconception 澄清誤會
clarify the issue　　　　闡明議題

clarification n. 澄清；闡明、說明

09 業務協調

中高

21. **colloquial**

[kə'lokwɪəl]

adj. 口語的

⇨ **co-**「一起」+ **-loqui-**「說」+ **-al**「形容詞字尾」

The **colloquial** meaning of the song's lyrics can really spice up this commercial, so I think we should stick with it.

這首歌的歌詞很通俗，可為這支廣告添增趣味，所以我認為我們要堅持下去。

同 conversational

10 企業經營

22. come up with
[kʌm] [ʌp] [wɪθ]
phr. 想出

I can't **come up with** any good reason why we should stick with our old slogan anymore.
我再也想不出爲什麼我們要守著舊標語的理由了。

 come up with N. 想出 N.

同 figure out

初級
23. comment
[ˈkɑmɛnt]
n. 評論
v. 發表評論；議論

⇨ com-「一起，共同」＋ -ment-「心意，意見」
Your **comments** would be welcome at this point, only a month before the rollout.
在離發表只剩一個月的這個時間點，我們需要你的評論。

 No comment. 不予置評。
comment on/about sb. or sth. 評論某人或某事物

易混 comment 是「發表評論；議論」，可記結尾 t 是 talk，大家說出自己的評論；commend 是「稱讚；推薦」，可記結尾 d 是 hand，大家舉手 (hand) 推薦人選。

中高
24. commentary
[ˈkɑmənˌtɛrɪ]
n. 評論；實況報導

⇨ comment「評論」＋ -ary「與…有關」
The TV **commentary** on the football match was very bad.
電視上的足球賽播報很糟。

 a running commentary on the game
有關比賽的實況報導
political commentary 政治評論

同 annotation

中高
25. commentator
[ˈkɑmənˌtetə]
n. 評註者；時事評論者；實況播音員

⇨ commentary「評論」＋ -or「做…動作的人」
There are plenty of **commentators** out there, but we need some unbiased news anchors to host our shows.
已經有許多時事評論者了，但我們需要一些公正的新聞主播來主持節目。

 a news commentator 新聞評論員

同 reviewer / annotator

中高

26. **complexity**

[kəm`plɛksɪtɪ]

n. 錯綜複雜，複雜性

⇨ com-「一起」+ -plex-「編織」+ -ity「名詞字尾」，編在一起就很複雜

Due to the **complexity** of our financial picture, we need a qualified CPA to look into our books.

由於我們的財務資料的複雜性，我們需要一位合格的特許會計師來檢查我們的帳。

★ CPA = Certified Public Accountant 特許會計師

complex adj. 錯綜複雜的
　　　　 n. 情結，錯綜複雜的心理狀態

同 complication

中高

27. **compromise**

[`kɑmprə‚maɪz]

v./n. 妥協；折衷；和解

 com-「一起」+ promise「承諾」

The union is not willing to **compromise** with management, so there won't be any deal.

工會拒絕和管理階層妥協，所以不會有任何協議。

補充　arrive at/come to/reach a compromise 達成和解
the compromise between A and B
A 與 B 之間的折衷方案

中高

28. **concede**

[kən`sid]

v. 容忍；容許；讓步

⇨ con-「一起」+ -cede-「退讓」

I won't **concede** a victory to you on the Carrish Project, as we haven't shown the CEO yet.

在 Carrish 計劃上我不會退讓，因爲我們還沒給執行長看過。

補充　concede to N. = yield to N. = give in to + N.
對 N. 讓步；對 N. 退讓

同 yield

中高

29. **conception**

[kən`sɛpʃən]

n. 觀念，想法

⇨ con-「一起」+ -cept-「抓」+ -ion「名詞字尾」，一起抓進心裡形成觀念

I originally had a **conception** of our organization when I was still operating everything out of my garage.

當我還在車庫裡創業時，我原本就有一個對我們組織的想法。

concept n. 概念

中級

30. **conclusion**

[kənˋkluʒən]

n. 結論；決定；結尾

⇨ con - 「一起」 + -clus - 「關閉」 + -ion 「名詞字尾」，嘴巴一起閉上不爭吵就能做結論

At the **conclusion** of the conference, each exhibitor will hand out courtesy sample packets.

在會議結尾，每家參展廠商都會分發贊助的免費樣品組。

補充	in conclusion	總之
	come to/reach a conclusion	達成結論
	jump to conclusion	遽下結論

conclude v. 做結論

中高

31. **condemn**

[kənˋdɛm]

v. 責難；譴責

 con - 「一起」 + -demn - 「傷害」

The accountant was arrested for embezzlement of company funds, and was **condemned** for his lack of integrity.

該名會計師因為挪用公款被捕，且被譴責缺乏誠信。

| 補充 | condemn sb. for sth. | 為某事責難某人 |
| | condemn sb. as sth. | 怪罪某人是… |

 blame

中級

32. **conference**

[ˋkɑnfərəns]

n. 會議；協商；討論會

⇨ con - 「一起」 + -fer - 「攜帶」 + -ence 「名詞字尾」，東西一起帶來做討論

I don't want our video **conference** delayed again by technical difficulties.

我不希望我們的視訊會議因技術問題再度被延後。

補充	press conference	記者會
	video conference	視訊會議
	hold a conference on N.	
	舉行一個有關 N. 的會議	

 meeting

中高

33. **consensus**

[kən`sɛnsəs]

n. 共識

⇨ con-「一起，共同」+ -sens-「感知」+ -us「名詞字尾」，一起共有的感受就是共識

The **consensus** is that the new employee benefit package has not yet been adjusted accordingly.

我們的共識是新進員工福利配套還沒跟著做調整。

 補充

general consensus	普遍共識
reach a consensus on + N.	對 N. 達成共識
fail to reach a consensus	無法達成共識

同 agreement / unanimity

中高

34. **contradict**

[ˌkɑntrə`dɪkt]

v. 反駁；與…矛盾、抵觸

⇨ contra-「反對」+ -dict-「說」，說出反對的話就是反駁

Our sample data seems to **contradict** the traditional thinking that only women are concerned with the price of groceries.

我們的樣本數據似乎和傳統認為女性較關心日常用品價格的想法相反。

contradiction n. 反駁；矛盾

同 oppose

中高

35. **convene**

[kən`vin]

v. 集合；聚集；開會

⇨ con-「一起」+ -vene-「來」，來聚集在一起開會

Let's take a two-hour respite and **convene** again at seven o'clock.

我們休息兩個小時然後七點再集合。

補充 convene a meeting 召開會議

同 call together / gather / convoke

中級

36. **convention**

[kən`vɛnʃən]

n. 大會；公約；慣例，常規

⇨ convene「開會」+ -tion「名詞字尾」

Only thirty vendors attended the **convention** this year, primarily because so many could not afford the booth fee.

今年只有 30 個廠商來參加大會，主要是因為許多人連攤位的費用都付不起。

 補充 a social convention 社會慣例

conventional adj. 習慣上的；傳統上的

01
職稱職務／聘僱面試

02
人事／薪資／福利

03
辦公室／電話傳真

04
文書作業

05
會議

中級

37. **convey**

[kən`ve]

v. 傳達；運送

 con-「一起」**+ -vey-**「取道，來自」

The problem with Brian's presentation is that he doesn't **convey** his ideas to his audience well.

Brian 的簡報問題出在他沒有完整地對觀眾傳達他的想法。

> 典故　convey 原本指走同一條路的護衛、護花使者，後來引申為傳送、傳達。

> 補充　convey N. to sb. 將 N. 傳達給某人知道

conveyer/conveyor n. 傳送者；(貨物的) 輸送帶

同 express

中級

38. **convince**

[kən`vɪns]

v. 使信服

⇨ **con-**「一起，完全地」**+ -vince-**「克服」，一起克服困難就能說服別人

Convincing your colleagues to sign up is one thing, but **convincing** the boss to enroll is quite another.

說服你同事加入是一回事，但說服老闆加入則是另一回事。

> 補充　convince/persuade sb. of sth. 說服某人相信某事
> be convinced of + N. 相信 N.

convincing adj. 有說服力的、令人信服的

同 persuade

初級

39. **decision**

[dɪ`sɪʒən]

n. 決定

⇨ **decide**「決定」**+ -ion**「名詞字尾」

Rebecca's **decision** to proceed with the venture herself highlights the glaring issues she has with Rick.

Rebecca 要獨自進行那項投資的決定突顯她和 Rick 之間有明顯的問題。

> 補充　a decision-maker 決策者
> come to/reach a decision (終於) 做出決定

decide v. 決定
decisive adj. 果斷的；決定性的

反 indecision n. 優柔寡斷

中級

40. decline

[dɪˋklaɪn]

n. 下降

vi. 衰落；衰退

vt. 婉拒

⇨ de-「向下」+ -cline-「傾斜」

Our **decline** in sales can be attributed to the particularly harsh winter we have just had.

我們的銷售衰退肇因於才剛過去的嚴寒冬季。

補充

be in decline	在下降中
a declining market	一個衰退中的市場
decline sharply/rapidly	急劇下滑
decline gradually/steadily	緩慢下滑

 decrease v./n. 下降減少

反 increase v. 增加

rise v. 升起，高漲

中級

41. delegate

[ˋdɛləˌget]

v. 委派給⋯

[ˋdɛləget]

n. 代表

⇨ de-「分離」+ -leg-「派送」+ -ate「動詞字尾」，把任務送出去就是委派

If you need to get more work done, I would suggest **delegating** your less important duties to your secretary.

如果你想要做完更多事，我建議你要分派一些較不重要的任務給你的祕書做。

補充

a delegate to a meeting	出席會議的代表
a delegation to...	派至⋯的代表團

delegation n. 代表團

 representative n. 代表

初級

42. describe

[dɪˋskraɪb]

v. 描繪形容；描述

⇨ de-「往下」+ -scribe-「書寫」，寫下來就是在描述

Since we are on a conference call, I'll have to **describe** the appearance of our office's interior.

由於我們是進行電話會議，我得要向你們描述一下我們辦公室內部的樣子。

補充

describe A as B	將 A 描述成 B
describe N. to sb.	為某人介紹 N.

description n. 描繪；敘述

 depict / portray

中高

43. diplomacy

[dɪˈploməsɪ]

n. 交際手腕；外交

 di -「兩次」**+ -plo -**「摺」**+ -macy**「名詞字尾」

When there was a polarizing disagreement in the board room, Bill stepped in and provided some much-needed **diplomacy**.

當董事會議呈現意見分歧時，Bill 介入並使出了些我們極需的交際手腕來打圓場。

典故 古時官方文件都要對摺以確保機密，diplomat 就是負責遞送官方文件的外交官員，而 diplomacy 就是外交官員處理事務的手法、手腕。

補充 tact and diplomacy　　手段，計謀
international diplomacy　國際外交

diploma n. 文憑
diplomat n. 外交官
同 tact n. 外交手腕

中級

44. disagree

[ˌdɪsəˈgri]

v. 意見不一致；不同意

 dis -「不」**+ agree**「同意」

I couldn't **disagree** with you more about this project; I think it's going to be a total waste of money.

關於這項計劃，我完全不同意你的看法；我認為這根本就是在浪費錢。

補充 disagree about/on sth.　　對某事意見不一
disagree with sb.　　　　和某人意見不同
couldn't agree/disagree more 完全同意／不同意

disagreement n. 意見不合、不一致
反 agree v. 同意，贊同；意見一致

中級

45. disapprove

[ˌdɪsəˈpruv]

v. 不贊成；不同意

 dis -「不」**+ approve**「贊同」

The conference organizers **disapprove** of the images you have displayed at your table, and we suggest that you remove them.

會議組織人員不贊同你在桌子上放的圖像，我們建議你把它們移掉。

補充 disapprove of sb. / sth. 不贊同某人／某事

disapproval n. 不贊同
同 disagree
反 approve v. 同意，贊同

中高

46. discriminate
[dɪˋskrɪməˌnet]
v. 區別，辨別；歧視

 dis -「分開」+ crime「犯罪」+ -ate「使變成」

We don't **discriminate** against any candidate due to their religion, gender, or race.
我們不會因為候選人的宗教、性別或種族而有所歧視。

補充　discriminate A from B　將 A 和 B 區別開來
　　　discriminate against N.　歧視 N.

discrimination n. 歧視

初級

47. discussion
[dɪˋskʌʃən]
n. 討論

⇨ discuss「討論」+ -ion「名詞字尾」

Whether to proceed with the annexation of land in Cobbersfield for our mall is not for **discussion** at this point.
要不要處理在 Cobbersfield 的土地合併事宜以建造購物中心，在這個時間點上並不是我們的討論重點。

補充　have a discussion with sb.　和某人做討論
　　　a discussion of N.　　　針對 N. 的討論
　　　be under discussion　　　正在討論中

discuss v. 討論

中高

48. dissuade
[dɪˋswed]
v. 勸阻

⇨ dis -「不」+ -suad -「驅策，力勸」

Let's not **dissuade** our clients from making decisions that will be beneficial to our business.
客人做對我們公司有利的決定，我們就不要去勸阻他們吧。

補充　dissuade sb. from doing sth.　勸阻某人不要做某事

反 persuade v. 說服

中級

49. distribute
[dɪˋstrɪbjut]
v. 分發；散佈

 dis -「分開，離開」+ tribute「贈禮，貢品」

First, I want to **distribute** pamphlets all over the city to hype up the new science museum.
首先，我要在全市分送小手冊來炒作我們的新科學博物館。

補充　distribute sth. to sb.　發送某物給某人

同 hand out

中級

50. disturb
[dɪˋstɝb]
v. 打擾

disturbance n. 擾亂；混亂

⇨ dis -「完全地」+ -turb -「混亂」

It's better not to **disturb** the monthly meeting.
最好不要打斷月會。

補充　DND = Do Not Disturb. （標誌）請勿打擾。

中級

51. dominate
[ˋdɑmə͵net]
v. 支配；主導

domination n. 主導權，支配權；優勢

⇨ -domin -「主人」+ -ate「動詞字尾」，主人可以支配一切

Every time we get together, labor costs seem to **dominate** the conversation.
每次我們聚在一起討論，勞動成本總是主導了我們的對話。

補充　dominate the market for N. 主導 N. 的市場
a male-dominated/female-dominated market
由男性 / 女性主導的市場

---

52. enactment
[ɪnˋæktmənt]
n. 法律的制定，法規

enact v. 制定法律；實施

⇨ enact「實施」+ -ment「名詞字尾」

This **enactment** of our new policies includes a provision about employees not being allowed to check their personal email at work.
新的政策制定包括了員工不可在工作時查看個人 email 的條款。

中高

53. execute
[ˋɛksɪ͵kjut]
v. 實施；施行；將…處死

execution n. 實行；實施
executive n. 執行者；業務主管

We need to **execute** the new policy as soon as possible to get things running smoothly.
我們要儘快施行這個新政策以使事情能順利進行。

補充　execute a plan/an agreement 執行計劃 / 協議

54. follow up

['falo] [ʌp]

phr. 跟進；在…後採取進一步行動

If you don't **follow up** with the clients about their experience at our web site, how will we know what to improve?

如果你對客戶在我們網站上的體驗沒做後續追蹤，我們要如何知道改進什麼？

 | follow sth. up | 對某事物做進一步追蹤
| a follow-up call/interview | 後續追蹤電話／訪談

follow-up n. 後續行動 adj. 後續的，接續的

中高

55. graph

[græf]

n. 圖像；圖表

If you all focus your attention on the **graph** on the screen, you'll notice that our stationery sales increased by ten percent last quarter.

如果你們注意看螢幕上的圖表，你們可以注意到我們的文具銷售在上一季增加了百分之十。

 | circle graph = pie chart | 圓餅圖
| bar graph = bar chart | 長條圖
| line graph | 曲線圖
| broken-line graph | 折線圖

graphic adj. 圖解的；寫實的

 chart

---

56. hand out

[hænd] [aut]

phr. 分發

Take out the flow chart that I **handed out** at yesterday's meeting, and it will show you the next step in the process of handling a data user issue.

請拿出昨天會議中分發給各位的流程圖，可以看到在處理資料使用者問題的過程中下一步驟是什麼。

handout n. 講義；會議或演講的書面資料

 pass out

中高

57. highlight

['haɪlaɪt]

v. 用強光照射；使顯著、突出，強調

n. 最重要的部分，要強調的東西

⇨ **high**「高」+ **light**「光線；用光照」

It would be best to start by **highlighting** the flaws in the order-taking software before we discuss the advantages.

最好一開始時先將訂單處理軟體中的瑕疵標明出來，然後再來討論它的優點。

 to highlight the concerns/problems
使議題／問題更加突顯

highlighter n. 螢光筆

中級

58. instructor

[ɪnˈstrʌktə]
n. 指導者；教練；(AmE) 講師

> **instruct**「教，講授」+ -or「做⋯動作的人」

How fast you progress with your proficiency depends a lot on your course **instructor**, as some are better organized than others.
你的能力可以進步得多快，大部分取決於你的課程講師，因為有些人比其他人的組織能力更好。

| 補充 | a fitness/diving/ski instructor
健身 / 潛水 / 滑雪教練 |

同 coach

中高

59. legitimate

[lɪˈdʒɪtəmɪt]
adj. 合法的，正當的
[lɪˈdʒɪtəmet]
v. 使合法

legislation n. 制定法律；立法

同 adj. = legal / lawful

> **legitimus**「拉丁文，表合法」+ -ate「形容詞字尾」

We need to have **legitimate** ownership of the software to continue our business venture.
我們必須有合法的軟體所有權以繼續進行我們的商業投資。

| 補充 | a legitimate business | 合法的生意 |
| | legitimate fees | 法律費用 |

初級

60. meeting

[ˈmitɪŋ]
n. 會議

> **meet**「會面」+ -ing「名詞字尾」

The boss called a last-minute **meeting** this morning, which put everyone behind in their daily work.
老闆今早召開了一個緊急會議，每個人的日常工作都被延後了。

補充	a board meeting	董事會議
	a virtual meeting	網路會議
	hold a meeting	舉辦會議
	call a meeting	召集會議
	attend a meeting	參與會議

同 conference

中級

61. minute

[`mɪnɪt]

n. 會議記錄；分鐘

v. 做記錄

On reviewing the **minutes** from our monthly convention, I came across some contradictions in policy that you should be aware of.

在檢視我們月會的會議記錄時，我發現政策上有一些相互矛盾的地方，你們要特別注意。

補充
take the minutes　做會議記錄
approve the minutes　同意決議事項

 中級

62. moderate

[`mɑdəret]

adj. 穩健的，溫和的；節制的

v. 使和緩；克制；調停

同 temperate adj. 溫和的

反 extreme adj. 極度的

Although I did notice **moderate** improvement, the sales techs still have a long way to go.

雖然我有看到緩慢的進步，但銷售技巧仍有待改善。

補充　moderate growth　溫和的成長

中級

63. negotiate

[nɪ`goʃɪet]

v. 協商；洽談

negotiation n. 協商；談判

同 bargain

⇨ neg-「表不」+ otium「拉丁文，表悠閒」+ -ate「使…」，做生意洽商一點都不悠閒

The executives are **negotiating** the conditions of their retirement packages today.

主管們今天正在協商他們退休配套的條件。

補充
negotiate with sb. for sth.　和某人針對某事進行協商
negotiate a contract/a deal　協商合約 / 交易
negotiate a discount/a price　協商折扣 / 價格

中高

64. notion

[`noʃən]

n. 想法；見解

同 idea / opinion

The **notion** that we have not yet reached the minimum standards set forth by management is a matter that is up for debate.

對於我們未達管理階層設定的最低標準這件事的看法，其實仍有待討論。

補充　have a notion to V.　突然想做…

中級

65. **objective**

[əb`dʒɛktɪv]

n. 目標；目的

adj. 客觀的

⇨ **ob-**「對著」+ **-ject-**「投射」+ **-ive**「形容詞字尾」，對著投過去的就是目標物

The **objective** of our orientation video is to have you prepared to work the phones the very next day.

我們培訓影片的目的是要讓你們能準備好隔天就能處理電話應對事宜。

補充	set objectives	設定目標
	meet/reach objectives	達成目標
	short-term objectives	短期目標
	long-term objectives	長期目標

object [`ɑbdʒɪkt] n. 物體
 [əb`dʒɛkt] v. 反對

反 subjective adj. 主觀的

中高

66. **ongoing**

[`ɑn,goɪŋ]

adj. 進行中的

⇨ **on**「正在…中」+ **going**「向前進的」

Our involvement with the Monroeville factory is **ongoing**, as it has lacked proper supervision in the past.

我們對 Monroeville 工廠的介入仍持續進行，因為過去它們缺乏適當的監督。

| 補充 | the ongoing restructuring | 持續進行的改組 |
| | sb. be on the go | 某人很忙碌 |

中級

67. **panel**

[`pænl]

n. (一群人的) 小組

Our advisory **panel** has concluded that an expansion of the park is necessary to hold the interest of the public.

我們的諮詢小組認為要確保大眾的利益，擴大公園是必要的。

補充	panel discussion	小組會談
	a panel of experts	專家小組
	advisory panel	建議諮詢小組

中級

68. **participant**

[pɑr`tɪsəpənt]

n. 參與者；與會者

⇨ **part**「部分」+ **-cip-**「拿」+ **-ant**「人」，你拿了一份就表示你參與了

How many **participants** were involved with the test run of our new web page design?

有多少參加者會加入我們新網頁設計的測試？

| 補充 | a participant in N. | …的與會者 |

participate v. 參與、參加
participation n. 參與；參加

同 attendee

中級

69. **persist**

[pɚˋsɪst]

v. 持續；堅持

⇨ **per -**「徹底的」+ **- sist -**「站立」，持續站著要靠堅持

If these server crashes **persist**, we may be forced to let some of our database administrators go.

如果這些伺服器持續當機，我們可能得被迫得請一些資料庫主管走路。

 persist in V-ing 堅持、持續做…
persist with N. 堅持在 N. 上

persistence n. 持續；堅持

中高

70. **perspective**

[pɚˋspɛktɪv]

n. 觀點；前景

adj. 透視的

⇨ **per -**「穿過」+ **- spect -**「看」+ **-ive**「形容詞字尾」，可看穿的就是透視的；可透視就能看到前景

From the **perspective** of our ground-level employees, management just doesn't consider family time to be important.

就我們基層員工的觀點來看，管理階層一點都不認爲家庭時間是重要的。

 keep sth. in perspective 樂觀看待某事

中級

71. **persuade**

[pɚˋswed]

v. 說服；勸服

⇨ **per -**「徹底的」+ **- suade -**「驅策，力勸」

I've **persuaded** Jenny to work the second shift schedule every other week so we can get more phone coverage in the evening.

我已經說服 Jenny 隔週輪第二段的班，以便我們可以接聽更多夜間時段的來電。

 persuade sb. of sth. 說服某人相信某事
persuade sb. to V. 說服某人去做某事

反 dissuade v. 勸阻

中高

72. **plea**

[pli]

n. 懇求；請求

Our department head listened to our **pleas** for new phone headsets, but in the end she only decided to buy one for herself!

我們的部門主管聽了我們要新的電話耳機的請求，但最後她只決定買一個給她自己。

 make a plea for N. 懇請…

中高

73. plead

[plid]

v. 懇求為；（案件）做辯護；
認罪

★ 動詞變化：plead, pleaded, pleaded, pleading /
plead, pled, pled, pleading

I have already **pleaded** for someone to rearrange the file cabinets for two months, so I'll just do it myself.

我已經找人重新整理資料櫃求了兩個月了，所以我乾脆自己來做。

補充　plead for sth. 懇求某事物

中高

74. pledge

[plɛdʒ]

v. 發誓，保證
n. 誓言

The key is to get most employees to **pledge** their support for the blood drive by asking them to make an appointment well in advance.

要訣是透過請員工們先事前預約，以讓大部份的人都能保證支持這個捐血活動。

補充	pledge sth to sth./sb.	向某人或某事物宣誓…
	pledge to V	承諾會做…
	pledge A for B	承諾為 B 提供 A

同 promise / vow

中級

75. postpone

[post`pon]

v. 延遲；延期

 post-「在…後」+ -pone-「放置」

I'm afraid that we can't **postpone** the board elections any longer for fear that business operations will come to a halt.

我想我們不能再延後董事會選舉，以免公司運作會停止。

補充　postpone A until B 將 A 延期至 B

同 adjourn / put off

中級

76. presentation

[ˌprɪzən`teʃən]

n. 呈現、提出的內容；簡報；
贈予禮物

⇨ present「呈現，提出」+ -ation「動作的結果」

The goal of this **presentation** is to show our new idea of how to pump up the sales.

這個簡報的目的在展示我們對提振銷售的新點子。

補充	make/give a presentation to sb.
	向某人做簡報
	a sales presentation 業務簡報

present v. 呈現，簡報

同 brief n. 簡報

77. prospect

中高

prospect

['prɑspɛkt]

n. 前景；成功的可能性；有希望的人選

⇨ **pro -**「向前」**+ - spect -**「看」

I met quite a few excellent **prospects** at the job fair this past Thursday, and I would suggest that we hire some of them.

這個週四的就業博覽會我碰到不少優秀的人選，我建議僱用他們之中的一些人。

補充
prospect for N. N. 的前景
There is little/no prospect of sth.
某事的成功機率很小 / 無望

prospective adj. 可能的

---

78. protest

中級

protest

['protɛst]

n. 抗議；異議

[prə`tɛst]

v. 抗議，反對

⇨ **pro -**「向前」**+ - test -**「見證，主張」

Due to widespread **protests** by the subway workers against unfair wages, many people were forced to drive their own cars to work today.

由於地鐵員工針對薪資不公舉行大規模抗議，今天許多人被迫得自己開車上班。

補充 protest against + N. 抗議 N.

---

79. provision

中高

provision

[prə`vɪʒən]

n. (法規中的) 條款；預備措施；供應；供給

⇨ **provide**「提供」**+ - ion**「名詞字尾」

There is a **provision** in the clause about paid time off which grants two mental health days for each employee per year.

法規中有一個條款是關於每年提供每位員工兩天的心理健康給薪假。

補充
make provision for N.　　為 N. 預做準備
service/pension provision 提供服務 / 賠償

provide v. 提供

---

80. recess

recess

['rɪsɛs]

n./v. 休息；休假；休會

⇨ **re -**「回來」**+ - cess -**「走」，走回來是為了休息

Several changes were made to the draft while the board was in **recess**, and it looked nothing like the original.

董事會休會期間，草稿做了一些修改，看起來就不像原稿了。

補充 in recess 休會中、休息中

recession n. (經濟) 不景氣

中高

81. reconcile
[ˋrɛkənˌsaɪl]
v. 調停；調解

 re-「回來」+ con-「一起」+ cile「召喚」

Marie was forced to **reconcile** with Hank for their past differences before teaming up to tackle the Davis Tower project.

在合作進行戴維斯塔計劃之前，Marie 被迫得和 Hank 針對過去歧見進行調解。

補充
reconcile sth. with sb. 和某人針對某事進行調解
be reconciled with sb. 和某人和解

中級

82. reflect
[rɪˋflɛkt]
v. 反映；顯示

⇨ re-「回來」+ -flect-「折彎」，光線折返就會看到影像

The dropping of the sales volume **reflects** the downturn of the housing market.

銷售量下滑反映了房市衰退。

補充
reflect (well/badly) on sth./sb.
給某事 / 某人帶來 (好的 / 不好的) 影響

reflective adj. 反映的；沉思的、思考的

中高

83. relevant
[ˋrɛləvənt]
adj. 相關的，有關的；適宜的

 re-「一再」+ -lev-「拉高，使變輕」+ -ant「形容詞字尾」

I believe that our magazine content is no longer **relevant**, so we need to scrap it and go with something trendy.

我相信我們的雜誌內容不再切合時宜，所以我們得捨棄它然後做些跟得上流行的內容。

補充
be relevant to N. 與 N. 相關

反 irrelevant adj. 不相關的

中高

84. seminar
[ˋsɛməˌnɑr]
n. (學術) 研討會

The convention center is hosting our largest **seminar** ever this weekend, and we expect every downtown hotel to be filled.

會議中心本週末將主辦我們有史以來最大的研討會，我們預期市中心每間飯店都會客滿。

補充
conduct/hold a seminar 主辦研討會
a web-based seminar = a webinar 線上研討會

85. sequence

中高

[ˈsikwəns]

n. 連續；一連串；次序

⇨ **-sequ-**「跟隨」+ **-ence**「名詞字尾」，一個接一個的就是次序

We noticed that the assembly instructions provided in the packaging for our desks listed an improper **sequence** of steps.

我們注意到包裝裡附的書桌組裝說明書所列出的步驟順序是不對的。

 補充
a sequence of N. 一連串的 N.
in sequence 接續

86. series

中級

[ˈsiriz]

n. 系列；連續

Our retail stores are providing a **series** of workshops regarding kitchen remodeling.

我們的零售商提供一系列和廚房改造有關的研習會。

 補充
a series of steps/actions 一連串的步驟 / 行動
a series of books/articles 系列書 / 文章

87. session

中級

[ˈsɛʃən]

n. 會期、會議期間；開庭期間

⇨ **-sess-**「坐」+ **-ion**「名詞字尾」，坐著開會的期間

When the board went into closed **session**, everyone expressed their confusion with the meeting that had just taken place.

當董事會議進入秘密會議階段時，每個人都對剛才舉行的會議提出自己的疑問。

 補充
be in session 正在會期中、開庭中

88. set up

[sɛt] [ʌp]

phr. 安裝；設立；建立

Can you **set up** a meeting to discuss the new marketing campaign?

你可以安排個會議來討論這個新的行銷活動嗎？

 補充
to set up + 機構 成立某機構
to set sth. up 籌劃某事

 比較
to set sb. up 陷害某人
to set sb. up in business 幫助某人成立事業

同 establish / arrange

中級

89. **settlement**

['sɛtḷmənt]

n. 協議；支付 (帳款)

⇨ **settle**「解決，安排」+ **-ment**「名詞字尾」，安排好了就達成協議了

It took several months of back-and-forth negotiations before the two parties could finally reach a **settlement**.

雙方達成協議前花了數個月的時間來回進行談判。

補充
an out-of-court settlement of N.
庭外和解 (協議支付 N.)
reach a settlement (over N.) (針對 N.) 達成協議
in settlement of N. 針對 N. 支付款項

中級

90. **state**

[stet]

v. 載明；陳述；聲明

n. 情況，狀態；(政府) 州

My ideas about the project were all **stated** in the report.

有關這項計劃的想法我都載明在這份報告中。

The **state** of affairs in our payroll department has never been more dire, with several investigations underway from the **state** government.

我們薪資部門的狀況從沒這麼慘過，州政府正在進行幾項調查。

補充
state-of-the-art 最新穎的
state of affairs = situation 情況，情勢

statement n. 陳述；聲明

同 聲明：announce/declare

中高

91. **straightforward**

[ˌstret'fɔrwəd]

adj. 明確的，直接了當的；簡單的；(人) 坦率的

 straight「直接的」+ **forward**「向前」

My offer is pretty **straightforward**, so it shouldn't take you long to ponder.

我提出的條件非常明確，所以你應該不用花很長的時間考慮。

中級

92. **summit**

['sʌmɪt]

n. 高峰會；山峰

 summ「最高的」+ **-it**「名詞字尾」

All of our regional managers got together for a five-day **summit** in Las Vegas, but they spent little time on business.

我們所有的地區經理齊聚拉斯維加斯進行為期五天的高峰會，但他們幾乎沒花什麼時間在工作上。

93. tentative

中高

['tɛntətɪv]

adj. 暫定的；不確定的

Overall, I was pretty impressed with the candidate, but he gave **tentative** answers to some key questions.
整體來說，我對這位候選人印象很深刻，但他對一些重要問題給了不確定的答案。

| 補充 | a tentative plan/schedule 暫定的計劃 / 時程表
a tentative agreement 暫時性的協議 |

回 provisional / temporary

---

94. turn out

[tɝn] [aʊt]

phr. 出席；參與活動；最後結果是

We need all members to **turn out** to help the charity.
我們希望所有成員都出席來幫助這個慈善機構。

It **turns out** that the phone model we got a glimpse of last week is just a prototype, and it won't be ready for a rollout until next year.
結果是上週我們看到的手機樣式只是個雛形，一直要到明年才會準備問市。

| 補充 | a high/low turnout 出席者眾 / 寡
a + 百分比 + turnout of voters（百分比）的投票率 |

turnout n. 出席人數

回 出席：attend

---

95. unanimous

中高

[juˈnænəməs]

adj. 一致通過的；無異議的

 uni-「單一」+ -anim-「理智，心智」+ -ous「多…的」

It is rare for there to be a **unanimous** decision at any managers' meeting, but giving employees a larger, better cafeteria seemed to be a win-win for everybody.
在任何主管會議中都很少能看到無異議通過的決定，但提供員工更大、更好的自助餐廳對每個人都有利。

| 補充 | be unanimous in N. 在 N. 上一致通過、同意
the unanimous support/approval 一致支持 / 同意
reach a unanimous decision 達成大家都同意的決定 |

---

96. understandable

中高

[ˌʌndɚˈstændəbl]

adj. 可理解的

⇨ understand「理解」+ -able「可…的」

It's **understandable** that you're upset about being demoted to part time, but I assure you it was strictly about the numbers, and nothing personal.
你被降爲兼職人員很生氣這是可以理解的，但我保證這是因爲人數的關係，不是針對個人。

中高

97. uphold

[ʌp`hold]

v. 支持；舉起

⇨ up「向上」+ hold「握住，支撐」

It's likely that the board will **uphold** the CEO's decision at next month's meeting, as it falls within the new direction they are taking the company.

由於執行長的決定符合董事會的公司營運新方向，他們可能在下次月會中支持執行長的決定。

補充 uphold a decision 支持一項決定

同 support

中高

98. verbal

[`vɝbl̩]

adj. 言語上的；口頭的

⇨ - verb -「字」+ - al「形容詞字尾」

Although we have a **verbal** contract, that will never stand up in court.

儘管我們有口頭約定，但在法律上那並不成立。

補充 a verbal agreement　口頭協議
a verbal warning　　口頭警告

同 oral

反 written adj. 書面的

初級

99. vote

[vot]

v. 投票

n. 選票

At the conclusion of the speeches, both pro and con, we came together for a deciding **vote**.

在演說的結尾，針對正反兩方，我們進行了投票表決。

補充 vote for/against　投票贊成 / 反對
vote with sb's feet 出走、以行動表示反對

同 v. = lect / ballot

中級

100. workshop

[`wɝk.ʃɑp]

n. 研習班，研習會；工廠

⇨ work「作品：工作」+ shop「商店」

The entire web development department is required to attend a three-day **workshop** in San Antonio to catch up on the latest software and techniques.

網路發展部全體必須到聖安東尼奧參加為期三天的研習會，以跟上最新的軟體技術。

實力進階

Part 1. 開會常用語詞

安排會議	arrange / set up } a meeting
召集 (部門) 會議	call a meeting of 部門
出席會議	attend / participate in / turn out for } a meeting
分發資料	distribute / hand out / pass out } the materials
做會議紀錄	take { notes / the minutes
討論主題	discuss / talk about } the topics
投票表決	take a vote
會議延後	postpone / adjourn / put off } a meeting
取消會議	cancel / call off } a meeting

Part 2. 不同的會議形態

meeting	通常指一般公司內部或商務洽談的會議，如 monthly meeting（月會）、sales meeting（業務會議）等
presentation	指簡報會議，功能為提出發表事物的報告讓與會者參考或理解
conference	通常為較大型的會議，功能為共同商議某事務或公開新知識及新資訊，如 academic conference 學術會議、news/press conference 記者會
convention	指大會形式的會議，此類會議主要用於探討商業或產業議題，常會針對主題邀請主講人 (keynote speaker) 到場演說或交流意見

Part 3. delay vs. postpone

delay 常指須等待一段時間的「延遲、延誤」，像交通工具延遲，或因不確定因素造成的「延後」，如：be delayed by traffic（受交通因素延誤）。

postpone 則是指刻意將某事物的發生時間「延後」，如：postpone a meeting（將會議延期）、postpone a decision（延後決定）。

隨堂練習

★ 請根據句意，選出最適合的單字

(   ) 1. After hours of negotiation, both sides finally agreed to meet, in the hope of reaching a _____.
(A) compromise   (B) summit
(C) conception   (D) provision

(   ) 2. All the members of the board were _____ in approving the deal.
(A) alternative   (B) legitimate
(C) relevant   (D) unanimous

(   ) 3. Due to recession and inflation, the number of people buying their own homes has _____.
(A) reconciled   (B) conceded
(C) declined   (D) contradicted

(   ) 4. It is predicted that the latest smart phone model will _____ the market like its predecessors did.
(A) condemn   (B) convince
(C) pledge   (D) dominate

(   ) 5. A(n) _____ agreement is very hard to enforce, so it's better to have a written contract.
(A) verbal   (B) objective
(C) attentive   (D) tentative

解答：1. A   2. D   3. C   4. D   5. A

06 買賣交易

07 採購與物流

08 廣告與宣傳

09 業務協調

10 企業經營

Unit 6　買賣交易

中級

1. agreement
[ə`grimənt]
n. 同意；協議

⇨ agree「同意」+ -ment「名詞字尾」

The two organizations had a rather loose **agreement**, and as such there were no hard feelings when the split occurred.

這兩家機構間的合作協議相當鬆散，正因如此，當必須分開時雙方並沒有交惡。

補充
verbal agreement	口頭協議
written agreement	書面協議
non-disclosure agreement	保密協定
reach an agreement on N.	對 N. 達成協議

agree v. 同意

中高

2. alter
[`ɔltɚ]
v. 改變；變更

Altering this contract makes it null and void.
變更這份契約會使其無效。

補充　an alteration to sth. 對某事物做變更

alteration n. 變更；修改

同 change

易混 altar n. 聖壇；祭壇

---

3. approximately
[ə`prɑsəmɪtlɪ]
adv. 大約

⇨ ap-「to」+ proximate「最接近的」+ -ly「副詞字尾」

We have **approximately** thirty million dollars of capital set aside for daily operations.
我們另外有大約三千萬元的資金作為日常營運使用。

approximate adj. 大概的

同 about / around

中級

4. attempt

[ə`tɛmpt]

v. 企圖

n. 嘗試，意圖

⇨ at-「to」＋ tempt「吸引」，有吸引力就會想嘗試

We delved into the results of our trial run in an **attempt** to accurately address the areas where the company was struggling.

為試圖準確找出公司有問題的地方，我們深入研究了試營運的各項結果。

補充	attempt to V.	企圖、嘗試做…
	in an attempt to V.	為了…
	an attempt on sb's life	攻擊某人；意圖取某人性命

同 try

中高

5. auction

[`ɔkʃən]

n./v. 拍賣

 -auc-「增加」＋ -tion「名詞字尾」

The bankrupt company will be liquidated, and everything will go to **auction**.

這間破產公司將進行債務清償，所有的東西都將被拍賣掉。

| 補充 | N. come up for auction | N. 要被拍賣 |
| | an online/internet auction | 線上 / 網路拍賣 |

auctioneer n. 拍賣官

初級

6. avoid

[ə`vɔɪd]

v. 避免

⇨ a-「＝ex-，出去」＋ void「空的」，往外清空避免麻煩

We have done everything in our power to **avoid** layoffs, but it seems inevitable after a twenty percent drop in sales this past year.

雖然我們已盡全力避免裁員，不過在今年營業額掉了 20% 後，這似乎是無可避免的了。

| 補充 | avoid N./V-ing 避免… |

中高

7. behalf

[bɪ`hæf]

n. 代表

 be-「在…旁」＋ half「一半，旁邊」

The attorneys are here on **behalf** of Roland and Sons, Inc. to file a suit for copyright infringement.

這些律師代表 Roland and Sons 股份有限公司提出侵犯著作權的訴訟。

| 補充 | on behalf of N. = to act for N. 代表 N. |

同 representative

易混 behave v. 行為

8. **booth**

[buθ]

n. 有篷子的貨攤、亭子

We need several volunteers to man our **booth** at the convention over the weekend.
我們需要數名自願者來顧週末時大會裡的攤位。

補充	toll booth	收費站
	telephone booth	電話亭
	exhibition booth	展覽攤位

同 stand / stall / kiosk

---

9. **buyer**

[`baɪɚ]

n. 買家、買方

⇨ **buy**「購買」+ -er「做…動作的人」

The **buyer**'s offer is contingent upon his attorney's analysis of the health of our company.
買家提供的金額會視他的律師對本公司健全程度所進行的分析來決定。

| 補充 | possible/potential buyer | 有可能的 / 潛在買家 |
| | a N. buyer = a buyer for N. | N. 的買家 |

同 purchaser / customer / client

---

10. **clearance**

[`klɪrəns]

n. 清除；清倉大拍賣

⇨ **clear**「清掃」+ -ance「表性質」

We need to be out of this retail space in less than one week, so put everything on **clearance**!
我們需要在一週內完全撤離這個銷售點，所以把所有東西都低價出清吧！

補充	a clearance sale	清倉大拍賣
	on clearance	低價出清
	customs clearance	清關（將貨品由海關提領出來）

---

11. **client**

[`klaɪənt]

n. 客戶

⇨ -**cli**-「傾向，彎曲」+ -ent「做動作的人」

The **client** cancelled his contract with us when he found a company that could complete the project faster.
客戶在發現能更快完成這項計畫的公司後取消了與我們簽的合約。

| 典故 | client最早指彎著身子向他人尋求保護或協助的人，後來就衍生出「客戶」的意思。|

補充	a major client	主要客戶
	a potential client	潛在客戶
	a client of N.	N. 的客戶
	client base	客戶群
	client service	客戶服務

同 customer

中高

12. closure

[ˋkloʒɚ]

n. 打烊；結束

⇨ close「關上」+ -ure「表狀態」

The **closure** of our print division comes as no surprise, as most people now get their news from the Internet.

我們的印刷部門裁撤並不令人意外，因為現在大部分的人都在網路上看新聞。

補充　to face closure　面臨關門大吉
temporary/permanent closure　暫時 / 永久歇業

同　end

中高

13. commence

[kəˋmɛns]

v. 開始；著手

Let's **commence** with the proceedings regarding the improper distribution of funds by the executive.

我們開始處理這件關於主管人員不當資金分配的訴訟吧。

補充　commence V-ing　開始進行…

commencement n. 開始；開端；(大學) 畢業典禮

中級

14. commerce

[ˋkɑmɚs]

n. 商業；貿易

⇨ com-「一起」+ -merc-「買賣交易」

Several insurance companies operate out of the **commerce** park located at the end of this street.

數間保險公司在這條街尾的商貿園區裡營運。

補充
e-commerce	電子商務
m-commerce	行動商務
t-commerce	電視購物交易
global commerce	全球貿易
international commerce	國際貿易
chamber of commerce	商會

commercial adj. 商業的；商務的 n. 電視廣告

同　trade / business

中級

15. commitment

[kəˋmɪtmənt]

n. 承諾；許諾

 com-「一起」+ -mit-「送出」+ -ment「名詞字尾」

The company offers a 7-day trial to customers without **commitment** to buy.

這間公司提供顧客無須承諾購買商品的七天試用期。

補充
a commitment letter	（銀行）貸款承諾書
a commitment fee	（銀行）貸款保證金
make a commitment to V.	承諾會做…
have a commitment to N.	對 N. 有所承諾

commit v. 承諾，致力

中高

16. **compact**

['kɑmpækt]
n. 合同；契約
[kəm'pækt]
v. 使簡潔；壓縮；訂契約
adj. 結實的；緊密的；小型的

🗣 **com-**「一起」+ **pact**「條約」

You have to sign this job **compact** before you take the 3-day training courses.
你得在上為期三天的訓練課前先簽署這份工作契約。

Mark was able to **compact** all his daily duties into just four hours in order to free himself up for a special project in the afternoons.
Mark 將他的日常公務壓縮至四小時完成，為的是讓自己有空在下午進行一項特別計劃。

補充
make a compact　簽署合約
a compact disk　光碟片
a compact car　(AmE) 小型車

同 合約：treaty / agreement / contract

中級

17. **conceal**

[kən'sil]
v. 隱藏；隱瞞

⇨ **con-**「一起」+ **-cel-**「藏起來」

Frank was able to **conceal** his embezzling for years by using various accounting tricks.
Frank 用各種會計技巧隱瞞侵占公款多年。

補充
conceal N. from sb.　對某人隱瞞 N.
a concealed security camera　隱藏式監視攝影機

concealment n. 隱瞞

同 hide / cover

反 reveal v. 顯露；揭示
disclose v. 使露出

中級

18. **conduct**

[kən'dʌkt]
v. 指導；進行；實施；舉止；指揮（樂團）
['kɑndʌkt]
n. 管理；行為

⇨ **con-**「一起」+ **-duct-**「引導」，把大家引導在一起就是在做管理、指揮的動作

I have to **conduct** a training session Monday morning, so we'll need to reschedule for Tuesday.
我週一早上必須指導訓練課程，所以我們需要改約星期二的時間。

補充
conduct a poll　進行民意調查
conduct a study　進行研究調查
conduct oneself　自我約束

同 指導：direct / lead

中高

19. confer
[kənˈfɝ]
v. 商談；授予學位

 con- 「一起」+ -fer- 「攜帶」，帶東西來一起商談

The CEO and CFO **conferred** about the ramifications of acquiring such a large company.
執行長和財務長討論了關於併購這麼大間公司會產生的後果。

補充　confer with sb. 和某人商談

conference n. 會議；協商；討論會

中高

20. confession
[kənˈfɛʃən]
n. 坦承，認罪；懺悔

 con- 「一起」+ -fess- 「說」+ -ion 「名詞字尾」，你說我也說，我們一起坦白招認

I have a **confession** to make; I have never completed my weekly reports on time.
我得坦承；我從未準時完成我的每週報告。

補充　make a full confession 完整坦白認罪

confess v. 坦白；供認

中高

21. confidentiality
[ˌkɑnfədɛnʃɪˈælɪtɪ]
n. 機密

confidence 「信任；秘密」+ -ial 「形容詞字尾」+ -ity 「名詞字尾」

Before proceeding with the training, you must sign this **confidentiality** agreement stating that you will not discuss anything you are about to see outside of this room.
在進行訓練前，你必須簽署這份保密合約，聲明你不會在離開這裡後談論你將見到的任何事物。

補充
confidentiality clause	保密條款
confidentiality agreement	保密合約
commercial confidentiality	商業機密
to keep confidential	保密
confidential documents/information	機密文件 / 資訊

confidential adj. 機密的

初級

22. **confirm**

[kənˋfɝm]

v. 確認；證實

⇨ con - 「表加強語氣」+ firm「使堅固」，確認事實堅定不變

I want to **confirm** our appointment for four o'clock on Tuesday.

我想要確認我們在星期二四點的預約。

	confirm a reservation/flight	確認預約／航班
補充	be confirmed in writing	以書面確認
	a verbal confirmation	口頭確認
	official confirmation of N.	對 N. 的官方證實

confirmation n. 確認；證實

中級

23. **consume**

[kənˋsum]

v. 消耗、花費，耗盡

⇨ con - 「表加強語氣」+ -sume - 「拿」，一直拿不停，東西就會消耗殆盡

This office **consumes** twice the electricity of others despite being about the same size.

這間辦公室消耗的電量是其他辦公室的兩倍，儘管它們大小差不多。

補充	time-consuming 耗時的

consumer n. 消費者

同 spend / use up / waste

中高

24. **consumption**

[kənˋsʌmpʃən]

n. 消耗量；消費

⇨ consume「消耗」+ -tion「名詞字尾」

The **consumption** of gasoline per household is quite high in this area as it is out in the suburbs.

因為位於郊區，這附近每一戶的汽油消耗量都相當高。

	energy consumption	能源消耗
補充	personal consumption	個人消費
	consumption tax	消費稅
	increase/reduce the consumption of N.	
	增加／減少 N. 的消費	

consume v. 消耗、花費，耗盡

06 買賣交易

07 採購與物流

08 廣告與宣傳

09 業務協調

10 企業經營

中高

25. **correspond**
[ˌkɔrəˈspɑnd]
v. 相符；通信

⇨ **co -**「彼此，一起」+ **respond**「回應」

I promise you that my actions will **correspond** with my words.
我向你保證我會言行一致。

補充　correspond to/with + N. 與…相符
correspond with sb. 與某人通信

corresponding adj. 對應的

初級

26. **currently**
[ˈkɜntlɪ]
adv. 現在；一般

⇨ **- curr -**「跑」+ **- ent**「形容詞字尾」+ **-ly**「副詞字尾」

I am **currently** working for a nonprofit, but I started my career in the private sector.
目前我正為一家非營利組織工作，不過我開始工作時是在私營部門。

補充　N. be currently available　目前仍有 N.

current adj. 當前的、現行的
同 nowadays adv. 現今

中高

27. **customary**
[ˈkʌstəmˌɛrɪ]
adj. 習慣上的；照慣例的
custom n. 風俗，習慣
同 conventional

⇨ **custom**「風俗習慣」+ **-ary**「關於…的」

It is **customary** to greet our Japanese counterparts with a bow and a firm handshake.
按慣例我們要用鞠躬以及堅定的握手來問候日本同級官員。

初級

28. **deal**
[dil]
v. 處理；交易
n. 交易；數量

As our senior buyer, I **deal** directly with the shipping departments of various clients to make sure everything leaves on time.
身為資深採購員，我直接與我們不同客戶的出貨部門交易以確認所有的貨物準時出貨。

補充	deal with sb./sth.	與某人 / 某公司進行交易
	deal with sth.	處理某事
	deal sth. out	處分、分派（利潤 / 刑責等）
	a cash deal	現金交易
	a package deal	套裝商品
	a good/excellent deal	好交易、價格較行情低的交易

dealer n. 交易商、業者
同 handle v. 處理

中級

29. **deceive**

[dɪˋsiv]

v. 欺騙

⇨ de -「從…分離」＋ -ceive -「拿」，從你那兒拿走東西，就是欺騙你

Many uneducated people have been **deceived** by not reading the fine print on their mortgage contracts with the bank.
許多缺乏教育的民眾因為沒有閱讀與銀行簽訂的貸款契約細項而受騙。

補充　deceive sb. into V-ing　騙某人做…
　　　deceive oneself that...　自己騙自己

deception n. 欺騙；詭計
同 cheat / fool / con

中高

30. **decent**

[ˋdisn̩t]

adj. 正派的；體面的；很好的

易混 descent n. 下降；出身

There is a **decent** chance that this deal will work out.
這樁交易有相當好的機會能成功。

中高

31. **decisive**

[dɪˋsaɪsɪv]

adj. 決定性的，確定的；果決的

⇨ decide「決定」＋ -sive「具…性質的」

Actually, the assistant to the manager plays a **decisive** role in this deal.
事實上，那名經理的助理在這樁交易中扮演了決定性的角色。

補充　play a decisive role　扮演決定性的角色
　　　a decisive victory　決定性的勝利

decide v. 決定
decision n. 決定；決心
反 indecisive adj. 猶豫不決的；憂柔寡斷的

中級

32. **declaration**

[ˌdɛkləˋreʃən]

n. 宣佈；聲明

⇨ de -「徹底地」＋ -clare -「澄清」＋ -ation「名詞字尾」

My supervisor made a **declaration** of her intention to retire at the end of the year.
我的主管宣佈了她年底要退休的想法。

補充　make a public declaration　發表公開聲明
　　　sign a copyright declaration　簽署版權聲明
　　　fill in a customs declaration　填寫海關申報表

declare v. 發表、宣佈
同 announcement / proclamation

中高

33. dedicate

['dɛdə،ket]

v. 奉獻給…

⇨ de - 「分開，散佈」 + -dic - 「說」 + -ate 「使…」

Next Friday, I plan to be present to **dedicate** the groundbreaking of our new facility to Bill Ayers, our founder.

下週五我計畫親自出席新設施的破土儀式，並將它獻給我們的創辦人 Bill Ayers。

典故 dedicate 最早指教會宣佈事情讓大家知道，通常都和敬奉上帝和聖人有關，到 20 世紀時便衍生出「奉獻」的意思。

補充 dedicate oneself to N./V-ing 某人奉獻自身給…

dedication n. 奉獻；專心致力；揭幕儀式

同 devote

中高

34. deficiency

[dɪ'fɪʃənsɪ]

n. 缺乏，不足；缺陷；不足的數額

👩 de - 「向下」 + -fic - 「做」 + -ency 「名詞字尾」

I was very impressed with the customer service department, but the IT department had quite a few **deficiencies**.

我對客服部門印象非常深刻，不過資訊部就有相當多的缺失了。

補充 a deficiency in sth. 某方面的缺陷

deficit n. 赤字

同 shortage

中高

35. degrade

[dɪ'gred]

v. 降級；降低；貶抑

⇨ de - 「向下」 + grade 「等級」

The problem with your ad is that it **degrades** women by showing them only as materialistic consumers.

你的廣告的問題在於它貶低女性，將她們塑造成拜金主義的消費者。

同 downgrade

反 upgrade v. 升級；提升、提高

中級

36. delighted

[dɪ'laɪtɪd]

adj. 高興的、感到愉快的

⇨ delight 「使開心」 + -ed 「形容詞字尾」

I am **delighted** to finally make your acquaintance, as we've only spoken on the phone up to this point.

我很高興終於能見到你，之前我們只有在電話上講過話而已。

delight v. 使開心、高興 n. 快樂，高興

delightful adj. 令人愉快的

中級

37. **demand**

[dɪˋmænd]

n./v. 需求；需要

⇨ de - 「徹底地」＋ -mand - 「命令」，有需求就發出命令

We always try to meet and even exceed customer **demands** while staying within our budget for the project.
我們總是致力在計劃的預算內去符合甚至超越顧客的需求。

supply and demand	供給與需求
be in demand	有需求
on demand	隨時可用的
meet the demands of N.	符合 N. 的需求

demanding adj. 苛求的；吃力的

中級

38. **demonstrate**

[ˋdɛmən‚stret]

v. 示範；證明；顯示

⇨ de - 「徹底地」＋ -monstr - 「顯示」＋ -ate 「使…」

Craig **demonstrates** a high aptitude for learning new procedures quickly.
Craig 展現了能快速學習新程式的天賦。

 demonstrate sth. to sb. 向某人展示某物

demonstration n. 證明；示威
demo n. 展示品；試聽帶

中高

39. **denial**

[dɪˋnaɪəl]

n. 否認；拒絕

⇨ deny 「否認」＋ -al 「名詞字尾」

When presented with the evidence against her, Cathy issued a strong **denial** and vowed to put up a fight in court.
對 Cathy 不利的證據被提出時，她堅決否認並發誓要在法庭上進行抗辯。

 in denial 否認；抗拒

deny v. 否認

中高

40. **differentiate**

[‚dɪfəˋrɛnʃɪet]

v. 區別

⇨ different 「不同的」＋ -ate 「使…」

This call chart helps to **differentiate** between the CSRs because it shows the average number of calls that each takes in one hour.
這張通話表能幫助你區別這些客服人員的差異，因為它顯示了一小時內每位人員接聽的平均通話次數。

★ CSR = Customer Service Representative：客戶服務代表

 differentiate A from B 把 A 從 B 裡區分開來

different adj. 相異的；不同的

中高

41. diminish

[dɪ`mɪnɪʃ]

v. 縮減；遞減，降低

 di-「向下；完全地」**+ -min-**「變少」**+-ish**「使…」

Nothing can **diminish** what Rick accomplished as section leader in such a short time.

沒有任何事情可以減損 Rick 在這麼短的期間內作爲部門領袖所達到的成就。

補充　N. diminish in value　N. 的價值減少

中級

42. disappointed

[ˌdɪsə`pɔɪntɪd]

adj. 失望的；沮喪的

⇨ **dis-**「不」**+ appoint**「指派，任命」**+ -ed**「形容詞字尾」，沒被指派就感到失望

I am **disappointed** to find that although more funds were appropriated for the development of the city center, it is behind schedule.

我很失望的發現雖然撥了更多經費推動城市中心的發展，但它的進度卻仍落後。

補充　be disappointed at/about sth.　對某事感到失望
　　　be disappointed in/with sb.　　對某人感到失望

disappoint v. 使人失望、令人沮喪

反 encouraged adj. 受鼓舞的

中級

43. disclosure

[dɪs`kloʒə]

n. 公開；透露、揭露

 dis-「不」**+ close**「關閉」**+ -ure**「表結果」

If you want to apply for a loan, the bank will need full **disclosure** of your financial situation.

如果你想申請貸款，銀行會需要你完整公佈你的財務狀況。

補充　annual financial disclosure　年度財務披露
　　　NDA = non-disclosure agreement　保密協議

disclose v. 露出；揭發

同 revelation

反 concealment n. 隱瞞

中級

44. display

[dɪ`sple]

n. 展示；展示品

v. 陳列；演出

To attract attention, we need a larger, more colorful **display** at the trade show this year.

爲了吸引注意，我們需要在今年的貿易展中有更大更精采豐富的展出。

補充　a display window　　　展示櫥窗
　　　a display shelf　　　　展示架
　　　N. be put on display　N. 被公開展示

同 展示：show / exhibition / presentation

中級

45. **distribution**
[ˌdɪstrəˈbjuʃən]
n. 分銷；經銷；分配

⇨ **distribute**「發送，分派」+ **-ion**「名詞字尾」
We have no problem producing goods at a high rate, but we have not built up a strong enough **distribution** network.
我們高速生產商品沒有問題，但我們尚未建立好夠強大的經銷網路。

補充		
distribution partner	經銷夥伴
distribution system	經銷系統
distribution fee	經銷費用
dealer	交易商
supplier	供應商

distributor n. 經銷商；批發商

中高

46. **diverse**
[daɪˈvɝs] / [dəˈvɝs]
adj. 不同的；多變化的

 di-「分開」+ **-vers-**「翻轉」
We take pride in the fact that we have an extremely **diverse** work force which makes our employees feel at home.
我們很自豪擁有許多不同種類的勞動力，能讓員工自在展現能力。

補充 diverse cultures 不同的文化

divert v. 使轉向

同 various

中高

47. **diversify**
[daɪˈvɝsəˌfaɪ] /
[dəˈvɝsəˌfaɪ]
v. 使多樣化，增加；多元經營

⇨ **diverse**「不同的」+ **-fy**「使…」
The company's financial advisors recommend that we all **diversify** our portfolios into stocks, bonds, and other investments.
公司的財務顧問建議我們將資產組合增加成股票、債券和其他投資。

補充 公司 + diversify into sth. 公司從事某種多元經營

同 vary

48. diversity
中高

[daɪˋvɝsətɪ] / [dɪˋvɝsətɪ]
n. 差異；多樣性

 ⇨ **diverse**「不同的」+ **-ity**「表性質」

The **diversity** of ideas presented in the meeting impressed me and gave us several good options for where we want to go as a company.
會議中的多樣想法令我印象深刻，也爲我們要成爲什麼樣的公司提供了幾種很好的選擇。

補充
cultural diversity 文化多樣性
work-force diversity 勞動力的多樣性
（指企業組織中工作人員的各種不同背景）

同 variety

49. do business with

[du] [ˋbɪzɪnɪs] [wɪð]
phr. 和…做生意

When **doing business with** unfamiliar parties, always double check their references to make sure you aren't being swindled.
和不熟悉的一方做生意時，一定要仔細查核對方資歷背景以確保你不會被騙。

補充
sb. you can do business with
可以和你做生意、有商業往來的人
be in the... business　做…行業
to set up/start a business 成立…事業

50. elevate
中高

[ˋɛləˌvet]
v. 提高

 ⇨ **e-**「向外」+ **-lev-**「拉起」+ **-ate**「使…」，往外拉起就提高了

You will need to **elevate** your proficiency with the latest design software.
你需要提升對最新設計軟體的熟練度。

補充 be elevated to N. 被擢升爲 N.

elevator n. 電梯
同 raise / promote / advance

51. endeavor
中高

[ɪnˋdɛvɚ]
n./v. 嘗試，努力；盡力

 en-「使…」+ **deavor**「古法文，責任，義務」

You'll need all the energy you can muster for our newest **endeavor** in Chicago, which may require several months of preparation.
你必須積蓄足夠能量好加入我們在芝加哥的最新嘗試，這可能需要花好幾個月的時間準備。

補充
endeavor to V. = make an endeavor to V.
努力做…

同 v. = try one's best / strive

中高

52. **exclusive**

[ɪk`sklusɪv]

adj. 獨有的，獨佔的

 ex-「出去」+ **-clus-**「關閉」+ **-ive**「形容詞字尾」

The problem with Right Soda is that it is **exclusively available** at only one supermarket, so naturally it has a smaller market share.

Right Soda 公司的問題是它只在一間超市專賣，所以理所當然它的市場占有率比較小。

補充	exclusive distribution rights	獨家經銷權
	exclusive interview	獨家訪問

exclusively adv. 專門地
exclude v. 將…排除在外

同 unshared

中級

53. **familiar**

[fə`mɪljə]

adj. 熟悉的；通曉…的

 family「家人」+ **-iar**「具…性質的」，像家人般熟悉

I would like Margaret to get **familiar** with my PowerPoint presentation because she will be filling in for me next Tuesday.

我希望 Margaret 能熟悉我的 PowerPoint 簡報，因為她下週二要幫我代班。

補充	be familiar with N.	熟悉、通曉 N.
	be familiar to sb.	某人感到很熟悉

同 acquainted

初級

54. **figure**

[`fɪgjə]

n. 數字；數據
v. 計算；認為

The latest sales **figures** show that the new marketing strategy does work.

最新的銷售數據顯示新的行銷策略真的奏效了。

補充	official figures	官方數據
	unemployment figures	失業率數字
	the latest figure	最新的數據
	a six-figure salary	六位數的薪水

同 n. = digit / number

徐薇教你背新多益單字（上）

06 買賣交易
07 採購與物流
08 廣告與宣傳
09 業務協調
10 企業經營

中高

55. grocer

[ˈgrosɚ]

n. 食品雜貨商

grocery n. 雜貨

The neighbors all used to flock to the **grocer** who had a stand on this corner, but the big supermarkets moved in and forced him to close.
鄰居們以前都習慣到在角落擺攤的雜貨商這裡，不過大型超市進駐後就逼得他關門大吉了。

中高

56. indispensable

[ˌɪndɪˈspɛnsəbl]

adj. 必需的

 in- 「表否定」+ dis- 「分開」+ -pens- 「稱重」 + -able 「可…的」

The advice that my counsel has given me over the years has been **indispensable**, helping me rake in profits.
我的顧問這些年給我的建議已是不可或缺的，它們幫我賺了不少錢。

同 necessary

反 dispensable adj. 可分配的，非必需的

中級

57. inevitable

[ɪnˈɛvətəbl]

adj. 無可避免的；必然會發生的

⇨ in- 「表否定」+ e- 「出去」+ -vit- 「 = vitare，閃避」 + -able 「可…的」，無法閃避的

A leveling out of sales was **inevitable**, as we now have several direct competitors in the market.
銷售額持平無可避免，因為現在市場上我們有幾個直接的競爭對手。

補充 the inevitable 無可避免的事

同 unavoidable

中高

58. ingenious

[ɪnˈdʒinjəs]

adj. 巧妙的；足智多謀的

⇨ in- 「在裡面」+ -geni- 「產生」+ -ous 「多…的」， 在腦海裡不斷產生巧妙的想法

Combining all our best features into one gadget was an **ingenious** way to create high demand.
將我們所有最棒的特點結合在一台小機器裡，是個能創造大量需求的巧妙方法。

同 clever / smart

初級

59. **instant**

[ˋɪnstənt]

adj. 立即的；緊迫的

n. 片刻，頃刻

⇨ in-「在裡面」+ -sta-「站立」+ -ant「形容詞字尾」，情況緊急所以就立即站到裡面了

We offer **instant** access online to all your accounts, complete with easy-to-read charts.

我們提供線上能即時進入您所有帳戶的服務，並有簡單易懂的圖表完整說明。

補充 instant access to N. 可即時存取 N.

中高

60. **invaluable**

[ɪnˋvæljuəbl]

adj. 無價的；寶貴的

 in-「表否定」+ value「評估」+ -able「可…的」

In addition to supplying us with capital, Harrison has also shared his **invaluable** knowledge of business.

除了提供我們資金援助以外，Harrison 也分享了他寶貴的商業知識。

補充 be invaluable to/for N. 對 N. 來說是無價的
invaluable assets　　　無價的資產

valuable adj. 珍貴的

同 priceless

反 valueless adj. 沒價值的

初級

61. **item**

[ˋaɪtəm]

n. 項目；品項

We tour the country, looking for rare, priceless **items** that we can resell at a huge profit.

我們到該國旅遊以尋找我們能轉售賺取高利潤的珍貴稀有品項。

補充 price for single item　　　產品單價
sales/food/household item 商品／食品／家用品
item by item　　　　　　逐項地

itemize v. 詳細列舉

中高

62. **magnify**

[ˋmægnəˌfaɪ]

v. 放大；誇大

 -magni-「大的」+ -fy「使…」

Since our entire office used the same server, the negative effects were **magnified** when it crashed.

由於我們整間辦公室都使用同一台伺服器，所以當機的時候它的負面影響就更大了。

magnificent adj. 壯麗、宏偉的

同 enlarge v. 放大
exaggerate v. 誇大

初級

63. market
['mɑrkɪt]
n. 市場
v. 行銷；銷售

Compared with the industry leader, the **market** share of this company is microscopic.
與產業龍頭相比，這間公司的市場占有率很微小。

補充

create/open up a market	開創一個市場
break into a market	打入市場
corner the market in N.	主宰 N. 的市場
bull/bear market 牛市 (行情好) / 熊市 (行情差)	
direct marketing	直效行銷 (寄廣告單)
event marketing	事件行銷
integrated marketing	整合行銷

marketing n. 行銷

中高

64. massive
['mæsɪv]
adj. 大量的

⇨ mass「大量」+ -ive「有…性質的」

Fraud was conducted on a **massive** scale throughout that corrupt corporation.
大規模的詐欺行為普遍存在於那間貪腐的公司。

補充　on a massive scale　大規模

mass n. 大量；眾多
 big / large

中高

65. motive
['motɪv]
n. 動機

⇨ -mot-「移動」+ -ive「有…性質的」，使人有動作的就是動機

Oil companies don't have enough **motive** to switch to alternative forms of energy.
石油公司沒有足夠的動機轉換其它的能源選項。

補充　profit motive　以利潤為導向的

motivation n. 刺激；動力
motivate v. 激發，刺激

中高

66. noticeable
['notɪsəbl]
adj. 顯著的

⇨ notice「注意」+ -able「可…的」，可以被注意到就表示明顯的

The ineffectiveness of our security department was not **noticeable** at first, but a deeper investigation found that we are wide open to cyber attacks.
我們保安部門沒有發揮作用的狀況一開始並不明顯，不過深入調查後發現我們對網路攻擊毫無防阻。

補充　a noticeable improvement　明顯的改善、進步

 obvious

中級

67. opponent
[ə`ponənt]
n. 對手；敵手；反對者

⇨ op-「逆著」+ -pon-「放置」+ -ent「…的人」，放到你對面的人就是對手

The visit by both political **opponents** to the downtown arena brought in millions of dollars in extra revenue to local businesses.
兩方政治對手陸續造訪市中心表演場地，爲當地業者帶來了數百萬元的額外收入。

同 rival / competitor

中高

68. outlet
[`aʊtlɛt]
n. 批發商店；出口；插座

⇨ out「向外」+ let「讓」

There are quite a few **outlets** at this office complex.
這個商辦中心有相當多家批發商店。

 典故　原本 outlet 是工廠將瑕疵品或過剩的庫存以低價賣給員工的地方，也就是讓工廠囤積的物品向外流通出去，後來這些地方也讓一般消費者進入購買，因爲價格低，吸引許多消費者，許多工廠也紛紛開設這類批發型商店，而集合許多此類商店的地方就稱爲 outlet mall「暢貨購物中心」。

中級

69. outline
[`aʊtlaɪn]
n. 大綱，概要
v. 概述；略述

⇨ out「向外」+ line「畫線」，畫出外圍的線就能看出事物的輪廓、概要

What you see on the screen is simply a rough **outline** of what our final objective might look like.
你在螢幕上看見的只是我們最終目標可能會呈現的概要。

補充　to outline a plan　提出計劃的概要

中級

70. partial
[`pɑrʃəl]
adj. 部分的；不完全的；局部的

⇨ part「部分」+ -ial「有關…的」

Included in the packaging is a **partial** description of the item.
包裝上包括該品項的部分商品描述。

 補充

partial shipments　分批出貨
partial payments　分次付款
partial ownership　部分持有
be partial to N.　偏愛 N.

partly adv. 在某種程度上；部分地

中高

71. **prevail**

[prɪˋvel]

v. 盛行；勝過，佔優勢

 pre -「在…前」**+ - vail -**「強壯」

Adjusting the flavor of our drink according to the results of our blind taste tests has allowed us to **prevail** over other beverage makers.

以商品盲測的結果來調整我們的飲品口味，讓我們勝過其他飲料製造商。

補充 | A prevail over B　　A 強過於 B
prevail in/among 盛行於…

prevalent adj. 盛行的；普遍的

中高

72. **priceless**

[ˋpraɪsˌləs]

adj. 無價的；貴重的

 price「價格」**+ -less**「缺少」，太珍貴無法標價

The old man was forced to quickly sell his **priceless** antiques when the bank demanded that he immediately repay his loan.

在銀行要求老先生立刻還貸款時，他被迫趕快變賣他的珍貴古董。

補充 | priceless collection of N. 貴重的 N. 收藏

同 invaluable
反 valueless adj. 沒價值的

初級

73. **probably**

[ˋprɑbəblɪ]

adv. 或許

⇨ **probable**「可能的」**+ -ly**「副詞字尾」

Lack of oversight was **probably** the chief cause of the failure of the bank, as financial fraud was discovered far too late.

缺乏監督或許就是銀行倒閉的主因，因為金融詐騙實在太晚才被發現了。

同 possibly

中級

74. **proposal**

[prəˋpozl]

n. 提案

⇨ **pro -**「向前」**+ -pos -**「放置」**+ -al**「表事情」，將提案往前放

Your latest **proposal** does not take into account the real cost of all the materials needed to complete the project.

你最新的提案裡沒有考量到完成這項計畫所需的所有材料的實際成本。

補充 | a proposal for N.　　　有關 N. 的提案
a proposal to V.　　　做…的提案
approve/reject a proposal 核准 / 駁回提案

propose v. 提議；求婚
proposer n. 提議人

中高

75. prospective

[prə`spɛktɪv]

adj. 可能的；可預期的

 pro -「向前」**+ -spect -**「看」**+ -ive**「有…性質的」

There are several **prospective** buyers of this business, but none of them have put up a serious offer.
這樁生意有數名有可能的買家，不過他們當中卻沒人出高價。

★ serious 形容金錢時表示大量的。

補充　a prospective buyer　有可能的買家

同　possible / potential

中高

76. questionnaire

[ˌkwɛstʃən`ɛr]

n. 問卷

⇨ **question**「問題」**+ -aire**「名詞字尾」

We are asking that all customers fill out this short **questionnaire**, and in exchange we will give you a coupon for five dollars off on a twenty-dollar order.
我們請求所有顧客填寫這份小型問卷，而我們會提供消費滿 20 元可折 5 元的優惠券作為交換。

補充　a questionnaire on/about N.　有關 N. 的問卷
　　　fill in/out the questionnaire　填寫問卷

同　question sheet

中高

77. quota

[`kwotə]

n. 配額；定額

It's not enough for us to just meet the daily **quota** because we have a severe shortage of inventory nationwide.
只是達成每日額度對我們來說是不夠的，因為我們全國的存貨嚴重不足。

典故　quota 來自拉丁文的 quotus，表「有多少 (what number...)」，最早指由一地或一城能徵收的物資或是能徵集的士兵的量，後來就衍生出固定額度、所分配的額度的意思，也就是「配額、定額」。

補充　an annual/monthly quota of N.
　　　N. 的年度 / 每月配額
　　　fill/meet a quota　　　達到額度
　　　meet sb's sales quota　達到某人的業績目標

中高

78. ratio

[`reʃɪo]

n. 比率；比例

The United States has the highest **ratio** of cars to people in the world.
美國擁有汽車的人口比例是全球最高的。

補充　cash ratio　　　　　　現金比率
　　　debt ratio　　　　　　債務比率
　　　the ratio of A to B　A 和 B 的比例

複數：ratios

同　percentage / proportion

中級

79. reasonable
[ˈriznəbl]
adj. 合理的；講道理的

⇨ **reason**「理由，推論」+ **-able**「可…的」

I think it's **reasonable** to ask everyone to compromise and accept a pay freeze so that we don't need to let anyone go.
我認為要求大家妥協接受薪水凍漲是合理的，這樣一來我們就不用請任何人走路了。

補充 reasonable prices 合理的價格

反 unreasonable adj. 不合理的；不講理的

中級

80. register
[ˈrɛdʒɪstə]
v. 登記，註冊；掛號郵寄
n. 登記簿；註冊表

⇨ **re-**「回來」+ **-gist-**「攜帶」，帶回來以後做成紀錄、登記表

Companies are asked to **register** at least six months in advance for the trade show due to high demand for booths.
由於擺設攤位的需求量大，要參加貿易展的公司都被要求至少要提早六個月登記。

補充
register a company/trademark/domain name
註冊公司 / 商標 / 網域名稱
a registered letter 掛號信
cash register 收銀機
registration desk 飯店櫃台

registration n. 註冊；登記

中級

81. represent
[ˌrɛprɪˈzɛnt]
v. 代表，代理，代為發言

⇨ **re-**「一再」+ **present**「呈現，提出」，一再代替他人提出意見就是去代理

My attorney will **represent** me during the proceedings, as I will be choosing to remain silent.
我的律師將代表我在訴訟期間發言，因為我將選擇保持沉默。

補充
represent the interest/view of N.
代表 N. 的利益 / 意見

representative n. 代表，代理人
representation n. 代理權

 re-present v. 再提出

01 職稱職務／聘僱面試

02 人事／薪資／福利

03 辦公室／電話傳真

04 文書作業

05 會議

中級

82. **research**

[ˈrisɝtʃ]

n. 研究；調查

⇨ re-「一再」+ search「檢查；搜尋」

My **research** on teen habits shows that teens tend to be the biggest participants in social media web sites.
我的青少年習慣研究顯示出青少年是社交網站的最大用戶。

補充
carry out/do/conduct research 做研究
scientific/medical research 科學 / 醫學研究
market/consumer research 市場 / 消費者調查

researcher n. 研究人員

中高

83. **respective**

[rɪˈspɛktɪv]

adj. 分別的；各自的

 re-「一再，回來」+ -spect-「看」+ -ive「具…性質的」

Each member of our department submitted their **respective** analysis of the business proposal.
我們部門的每位成員都提交了他們各自對這份商業提案的分析報告。

respectively adv. 各別地

同 individual

中高

84. **royalty**

[ˈrɔɪəltɪ]

n. 權利金、版稅

 royal「皇室的」+ -ty「名詞字尾」

My objective is to make enough in **royalties** from my novels so that I can retire early.
我的目標是靠我的小說版稅賺夠錢，我就可以早早退休了。

典故
royalty 原指皇室專有的權力，後引申為專有權，使用專有權就要支付的權利金或版稅也稱為 royalty。

補充
royalty payment 權利金 / 版稅付款
royalty agreement 權利金合約

royal adj. 皇家的；王室的

易混 loyalty n. 忠誠；忠實

85. sales

[selz]

n. 銷售量，銷售額

Although car **sales** were slightly down for the first quarter, we will still need to hire a few people for the huge surge that we get every summer.

雖然第一季的汽車銷售量有些下降，我們還是需要爲每年夏季大量激增的訂單僱用一些人。

 sale 來自字根 -sal- 指「鹽」，因爲鹽在古代可以當貨幣使用，所以和錢或買賣有關的字（salary 薪水、sale 銷售）常有字根 -sal-，銷售、買賣在古英文裡就是 sala，後來漸漸演變成 sale。

sales rise/go up	銷量上升
sales fall/go down	銷量下降
sales volume	銷售量
sales location	銷售據點

sale n. 銷售，販賣
sell v. 銷售
salesperson n. 銷售員

初級

86. service

[ˋsɝvɪs]

n. 服務；工作

⇨ **serve**「服侍」＋**-ice**「名詞字尾，表性質」

America is primarily a **service**-based economy, so I suggest continued investment in restaurant chains.

美國主要是以服務業爲基礎的經濟型態，所以我建議繼續投資餐飲連鎖企業。

offer/provide a service for sb.	爲某人提供服務
out of service	停止服務
in service	上線，開始提供服務
in-service training	在職進修
civil service job	公職
數字 years (of) service	…年的年資

serve v. 服侍；服役；供應某物

中級

87. settle

[ˋsɛtl]

v. 安排；解決（問題、麻煩）；決定

⇨ **set**「著手設置」＋**-le**「動詞字尾，表反覆的動作」

In the end, the famous singer agreed to **settle** the lawsuit out of court for an undisclosed sum.

最後，那位知名歌手同意以一筆保密的金額進行庭外和解。

settle a dispute/argument	調解紛爭
settle for N.	妥協接受 N.
settle out of court	庭外和解

set v. 設置；著手開始

中高

88. **speculate**

[ˋspɛkjəˌlet]

v. 推測；做投機買賣

⇨ **specula**「拉丁文，瞭望台」＋ **-ate**「使…」，在瞭望台上張望猜測

He has made obscene profits from **speculating** on the gold market.

他從黃金市場的投機買賣中謀取了暴利。

補充　speculate on/in sth. 冒險投資某物

speculation n. 推測；投機買賣

中高

89. **strategic**

[strəˋtidʒɪk]

adj. 戰略的、策略的；重要的

⇨ **strategy**「策略」＋**-ic**「形容詞字尾」

We made a **strategic** miscalculation by expanding our operations too quickly.

我們有個策略上的失算就是我們營運擴展的速度過快。

strategy n. 戰略；策略

同 tactical

中級

90. **survey**

[ˋsɝve]

n. 調查；考察

⇨ **sur-**「在上方」＋**-vey-**「=-vid-，看」

The results of the **survey** show that customers believe that great service is more important than having the best products.

調查結果顯示顧客相信優質服務比擁有最棒的商品更為重要。

補充　market/product survey 市場／產品調查
carry out/do/conduct a survey 進行調查

同 study / research

中高

91. **synonym**

[ˋsɪnəˌnɪm]

n. 同義字

⇨ **syn-**「相同」＋**-onym-**「名稱」

It's best to restate your main point using several **synonyms** rather than simply saying the same exact thing over and over.

你最好用一些同義字重新說明你的重點，而不要只是一再重複相同的話。

反 antonym n. 反義字

中級

92. **territory**
['tɛrə.torɪ]
n. 領土；領域；範圍

⇨ **terra**「土地」+**-ory**「表地點」

Miles didn't keep a close eye on his **territory**, so the store managers he was in charge of got away with cutting corners.

Miles 沒有仔細盯他管轄的區域，所以他負責管理的店經理常便宜行事卻沒被罰。

★ cut corners：不按常規而尋找更快更廉價的方法做事。

 selling territory　　　　　銷售地區
a new territory for N.　對 N. 來說是新的領域

同 area

初級

93. **trade**
[tred]
v. 交易，進行貿易
n. 貿易

Shirley **trades** stocks and bonds all day from the comfort of her own home.
Shirley 一整天宅在家裡進行股票跟債券交易。

典故 trade 來自 track 指路徑、路線。最早商人進行貿易都靠坐船，所以 track 這個字和經商很有關係，中世紀荷蘭文出現以 trade 表往來商船的路線，後來就衍生出做買賣、交易和貿易的意思。

 trade-in　折價、舊物抵新品
trade-off　交換，利弊相抵以取得所要之物
trade between A and B　A 與 B 之間的貿易往來
trade in sth.　　　　　進行某物的交易
trade A for B　　　　　賣掉 A 來換 B

 n. = commerce / deal

---

中級

94. **trademark**
['tred.mɑrk]
n. 商標；典型特徵
v. 以…為商標

⇨ **trade**「貿易」+**mark**「標誌」，買賣時用的標誌就是商標

"Coca-Cola" is a registered **trademark**.
可口可樂是一個註冊商標。

Finishing every presentation with a joke is Joe's **trademark**.
以一個笑話來結束報告是 Joe 的標準特徵。

 registered trademark　　　　註冊商標
trademark holder/owner　商標所有人
trademark law　　　　　　商標法

同 hallmark

中高

95. transaction

[trænˈzækʃən]

n. 交易；執行、處置

 trans-「越過，穿越」+ **action**「動作，活動」

I check each and every **transaction** that is wired by our bank customers for security purposes.

基於安全目的，我會檢查每一筆由我們銀行客戶電匯的交易。

補充	online transaction	線上交易
	electronic transaction	電子交易
	make a transaction	進行交易

同 trade / deal

中級

96. treaty

[ˈtritɪ]

n. 條約，協定

⇨ **treat**「處理」+ **-y**「名詞字尾」，處理完成就能簽條約

As a result of the new peace **treaty** between the two nations, commercial ties could finally be established.

因為兩國之間簽訂新的和平條約，商務關係終於能建立了。

補充	commercial treaty	商業協定
	sign a treaty	簽署協定
	under the terms of the treaty	在合約規範內

同 pact / agreement

97. trendy

[ˈtrɛndɪ]

adj. 時髦的；流行的

⇨ **trend**「趨勢，潮流」+ **-y**「有…的」，有跟上潮流的就是時髦的

We need to create the next **trendy** item so we can capture the 18-34 demographic.

我們需要開創下一種時髦商品，這樣我們才能吸引 18 到 34 歲族群的注意。

| 補充 | trendy clothes | 時髦服裝、潮服 |
| | trendy nightclub | 時髦夜店 |

同 fashionable

中級

98. union

[ˈjunjən]

n. 聯盟；工會

⇨ **uni-**「單一的」+ **-ion**「名詞字尾」，眾人結合成的單一組織就是聯盟

Our negotiations with the **union** broke down due to their unreasonable demands for worker benefits.

我們與工會間的談判破裂是由於他們對員工利益的不合理要求。

補充	trade union	貿易聯盟
	labor union	工會 (一般也可稱 union)
	join a union	加入聯盟 / 公會

06 買賣交易

07 採購與物流

08 廣告與宣傳

09 業務協調

10 企業經營

99. **vend**

[vɛnd]

v. 販售

Merchants are only allowed to **vend** in designated areas of the fairgrounds.

商家只能在展場內特定的區域進行販售。

補充　vending machine　自動販賣機

vendor n. 商販，賣方；供應商

同 sell

中高

100. **venue**

[ˈvɛnju]

n. 場地；發生地

 - ven - 「來」＋ -ue「名詞字尾」

We are not going to rent out such a large **venue** because there won't be so many attendees at the conference.

我們不會出租這麼大的場地，因為這個會議並不會有很多參加者。

補充　a venue for N.　進行 N. 的場地
a conference/concert venue 會議 / 演唱會場地

同 location

易混 avenue n. 大街；途徑
revenue n. 稅收；收入

195

實力進階

Part 1. 活用部首記單字 – 常用字首篇

英文單字也是由部首所組成，包括：字首、字根及字尾，熟悉這些單字組成零件，不但理解字義更容易，還能加速擴大單字量。

常用字首有：

字首	意思	變化形	例字
a-	去 (to)，朝向 (toward)	ac-, ad-, af-, ap-, as-, at-	at- + -tempt- (吸引) = attempt 意圖 ap- + point (指向) = appoint 任命 as- + -sume- (拿取) = assume 承擔 af- + firm(堅固的) = affirm 堅稱
co-	一起，共同 (together)，和…(with)	com-, con-	con- + firm(堅固的) = confirm 確認 con- + -duct- (引導) = conduct 指導 com- + promise (承諾) = compromise 妥協 co- + -her- (黏著) + -ent = coherent 一致的
de-	往下 (down)，從…離開 (away from)，徹底地 (completely)	—	de- + -mand- (命令) = demand 需求 de- + -ceive- (拿) = deceive 欺騙 de- + -scribe- (書寫) = describe 描述 de- + grade(等級) = degrade 貶低
dis-	表否定 (not)，分開 (away)	di-	dis- + agree (同意) = disagree 不同意 dis- + appoint (任命) = disappoint 令人失望 di- + -verse- (轉向) = diverse 不同的 dis- + tribute(贈禮) = distribute 分發
ex-	向外 (out)	e-	e- + -lev- (拉) + -ate = elevate 提高 ex- + -clus- (關閉) +-ive = exclusive 獨佔的 ex- + -cept- (拿) = except 除外 ex- + -spect- (看) = expect 期待
in-, im-	進入 (in)，在上 (upon)，或表否定 (not)	em-, en-	in- + -stant- (站立) = instant 立即的 im- + -ply- (摺) = imply 暗示 en- + close(關閉) = enclose 隨信附上 em- + -brace- (雙臂) = embrace 擁抱，接受

字首	意思	變化形	例字
pro-	向前 (forward)， 在前 (before)	—	pro- + -pos- (放置) + -al = proposal 提案 pro- + -spect- (看) = prospect 前景，可能性 pro- + -test- (見證) = protest 抗議 pro- + -mote- (移動) = promote 促銷，升遷
re-	一再 (again)， 向後、返回 (back)， 或加強語氣	—	re- + present (展現) = represent 代表 re- + -flect- (折彎) = reflect 反映 re- + -vise- (看) = revise 修訂 re- + -ply- (摺) = reply 回覆

Part 2. 各種合約

英文中表示合約的單字很多，常見的有：

agreement	協議，指各方都同意的約定，但有時不一定具法律約束效力。
compact	合同，契約，具正式效力的約定，也常指國際間或政黨間的契約。
contract	契約，為兩方或多方簽署的正式合約，有強制履行的效力。
memorandum	備忘錄，為各方將協議內容記錄下來，可做為日後合作或簽約的依據。
letter of intent	意向書，將有合作的意願加以記錄，表示雙方願意就某事物或交易做進一步的溝通和合作。

隨堂練習

★ 請根據句意，選出最適合的單字

( ) 1. After a lengthy discussion, they finally came up with a plan for the marketing and _____ of the new product.
   (A) distribution   (B) deficiency
   (C) disclosure   (D) confession

( ) 2. Conserving natural resources has become a critical mission for all the people in the world and therefore, searching for ways to reduce the _____ of energy is something we can do to help save the earth.
   (A) transaction   (B) consumption
   (C) territory   (D) royalty

( ) 3. The manager was demoted because he violated the commercial _____ agreement and leaked sensitive information to outsiders.
   (A) opponent   (B) declaration
   (C) correspondent   (D) confidentiality

( ) 4. International cooperation is _____ to controlling the outbreak of the deadly Ebola virus in Liberia, Guinea and Sierra Leone.
   (A) prospective   (B) inevitable
   (C) indispensable   (D) ingenious

( ) 5. One goal of this business is to promote _____ in the workplace through education, networking and training.
   (A) diversity   (B) attempt
   (C) endeavor   (D) commitment

解答：1. A   2. B   3. D   4. C   5. A

Unit 7 採購與物流

中級

1. **assure**

[əˋsʊr]

v. 向…保證；擔保

⇨ as-「to」+ sure「確定的」

I want to **assure** you that, although we have fallen behind schedule, the deadline will be met.

我向你保證，雖然我們的進度已經落後了，我們還是會在截止日期前完成。

補充
| assure sb. that... | 向某人保證… |
| please be assured that... | 請對…放心 |

assurance n. 自信

中級

2. **bargain**

[ˋbɑrgɪn]

n./v. 協議交易；講價；
提出…條件

同 v. = haggle

Haggling over price can be annoying, but your efforts can pay off if you manage to strike a **bargain** with the seller.

議價是很麻煩的，但是如果你成功和賣家達成交易的話你的辛苦就值得了。

補充 strike/make a bargain 達成交易、成交

中級

3. **batch**

[bætʃ]

n. 一批（貨，生產量）；
一爐（麵包或餅乾）

Margie sent out a **batch** of invoices just yesterday, but I have no idea if yours was one of them.

Margie 昨天才送出一批出貨單，不過我不知道你的是不是有在其中。

補充
| in batches | 分批 |
| a batch of 數字 | 一批有…的量 |

中高

4. **bazaar**

[bəˋzɑr]

n. 市集

同 market

易混 bizarre adj. 奇異的；不尋常的

Helen bought many of the pieces currently available on her online store at a craft **bazaar** at the local flea market.

Helen 在跳蚤市場裡的手工藝市集買了很多現在在她網路商店裡有販售的物件。

典故 bazaar 來自波斯語 bazar，指有小販商人和一般民眾交易買賣各種物資的場合，也就是市場。

中級

5. **bid**

[bɪd]

v./n. 出價；投標

★ **動詞變化：bid, bid, bid, bidding**

No matter what our **bid** is, the city government always gives the contract to J & W Engineers.

不論我們投標出價多少，市政府總是把合約簽給 J&W 工程公司。

 bid 在古英文中指「所提供的東西 (offer)」或「公告 (announce)」，物品要被售出時要公告它的價格，讓大家決定是否要出價購買，愈多人想要同一件物品就必須經過投標 (bid)。

 to bid 數字 for N. 出價⋯以取得 N.

初級

6. **bill**

[bɪl]

n. 帳單；票據；海報傳單

v. 開帳單，要求付款；宣傳

I would like to know why we were sent two identical **bills** with different invoice numbers for just one job?

我想知道為什麼同一件事我們卻收到兩張內容相同但發票號碼不同的帳單？

 bill 源自古拉丁文 bulla，原指張貼在教堂外公告重要事項、類似海報的文件，後來用以告知價格、要求付款的動作就用 bill 這個字來代表。

pay a bill = foot the bill　　付款
bill sb. for sth.　　　　　　開立某物的帳單給某人
a bill of lading = BOL = B/L　提貨單
a bill of entry　　　　　　　報關單

中級

7. **cashier**

[kæˈʃɪr]

n. 出納員，收銀員

同 teller

⇨ **cash**「現金」+ **-ier**「表人的職業身份」

The **cashier** will ring up your entire order while someone else bags your groceries.

收銀員會替你所有的訂貨結帳，而另一個人會幫你將買的東西裝袋。

中級

8. **catalogue**

[ˈkætəlɔg]

n. 產品目錄；型錄

★ 英：**catalogue** / 美：**catalog**

⇨ **cata-**「向下，徹底地」+ **-logue-**「說」，徹底說出內容物的東西就是目錄

We don't send out a **catalogue** in the mail to customers anymore unless they request one since everything we offer can now be found on our web site.

除非客戶要求，我們不會再以郵寄方式寄產品目錄了，因為我們提供的每項東西可以在我們的網站上找得到。

補充		
mail order catalogue	郵購目錄	
catalogue price	商品目錄價格	
card catalogue	卡片目錄	
（如圖書館或資料庫所使用，有依字母排序的卡片）		

初級

9. **charge**

[tʃɑrdʒ]

n. 費用；負責
v. 收取費用；指控罪名；充電

There was a five-dollar **charge** on your checking account last month because you failed to maintain the minimum balance.

因為你的活期存款戶頭沒有保持在最低餘額，所以上個月多收你五元的費用。

補充	
free of charge	免收費
a charge for N.	針對 N. 收費
on charge	充電中
charge sb. + 錢 + for sth.	
因…向某人收取(…元)的費用	

同 cost / expense n. 費用

---

10. **cling**

[klɪŋ]

v. 緊緊黏住；依附、貼近

★ 動詞變化：**cling, clung, clung, clinging**

My research shows that customers tend to **cling** to trucks for a long time, even though they are expensive to maintain.

我的研究顯示顧客傾向長時間保留著他們的卡車，即使保養卡車很昂貴。

補充	
cling to N.	貼附在 N. 上；保留保存 N.
cling film	保鮮膜

中高

11. **commodity**

[kəˋmɑdətɪ]

n. 商品；日用品

I specialize in investment in certain practical **commodities**, like corn and tomatoes, rather than throwing my money down the drain on stocks.

我專門投資特定的實用性物資，像玉米和番茄，而不是把錢投入股票血本無歸。

補充
basic commodity 基本物資
hard commodity
硬性物資（如：金屬、原油、礦物等）
soft commodity
軟性物資（如：穀物、糖、咖啡或可可豆等）

中級

12. **complaint**

[kəmˋplent]

n. 抱怨；怨言

⇨ com-「表加強語氣」+ -plaint -「擊、打」，捶胸頓足是因為有滿腹的抱怨

Kim filed a **complaint** two weeks ago, but no one has gotten back to her.

Kim 兩週前就提出投訴，但是到現在還沒有人回應她。

補充
make/file/lodge a complaint　提出投訴
receive a complaint　　　　收到抱怨、投訴
letters of complaint　　　　抱怨信函
deal with/handle a complaint 處理投訴

complain v. 抱怨

---

13. **consign**

[kənˋsaɪn]

v. 移送，運送；處置

⇨ con-「一起」+ sign「簽名」，簽完名就可以把貨送出去了

The documents will be **consigned** to your company by Friday.

文件將於本週五前寄送到貴公司。

Plenty of people are now **consigning** their old electronics to get some extra cash due to the recession.

由於經濟不景氣，現在有很多人把他們的舊電器處理掉來多賺點錢。

補充　consign sth. to sb. 將某物運送給某人

consignee n. 收件人；簽收人
consignor n. 貨主；發貨人

14. consolidate

中高

[kən`salə͵det]

v. 結合；整合；鞏固，加強

⇨ con-「一起」+ solid「堅固的」+ -ate「使…」

To save some money, I propose **consolidating** the job duties of the two separate positions so we only need to hire one person.

為了節省開支，我提議將這兩個不同職位的工作整合，這樣我們只需要僱用一個人就好了。

補充 consolidate sb's position 鞏固某人的地位

---

15. contractor

中高

[`kɑntræktə]

n. 立契約人；承包商

⇨ **contract**「簽契約」+ **-or**「做…動作的人」

I need to be at the site of our new building for several hours a day to oversee the work of all our different **contractors**.

我一天得在新大樓的工地待好幾個小時以監督管理我們所有不同承包商的工作進度。

補充 approved contractor 合格包商
building contractor 建築包商

subcontractor n. 轉包商；分包者

---

16. cost-effective

[͵kɑstə`fɛktɪv]

adj. 符合成本效益的；
划算的

 cost「成本」+ effective「有效果的」

Having a room full of CSRs to man the phones isn't very **cost-effective**, so we're making the entire phone system automated.

僱用一整間的客服人員來接電話並不符合成本效益，所以我們要讓整個電話系統自動化。

---

17. coupon

中高

[`kupɑn]

n. 優惠券、折價券；贈獎券

⇨ **coup(er)**「法文，剪」+ **-on**「名詞字尾」

Sir, just remember to give the **coupon** to your service technician when he arrives in order to get that discounted price.

先生，您的維修技師到場時請記得將您的優惠券交給他，這樣您就可用折扣價格了。

典故 coupon 來自法文指「剪下來的東西」，原指可由債券上剪下來兌現的到期付息證明，19 世紀時英國的旅遊業者將這個字放到廣告上，用來指憑此券可得到的優惠，從此 coupon 逐漸用來指「優惠券、折價券」。

補充 cut out a coupon 剪優惠券
money-saving/money-off coupon 折價券

中高

18. **courier**

[ˋkurɪə]

n. 快遞業者，宅配業者；信差

⇨ **- cour -**「跑」+ **- ier**「表人的職業身份」

Due to the power outage in this part of the city, the only way for me to send you the documents is by **courier**.
因為城市這一邊停電的關係，我唯一能把文件寄給你的方式就是用快遞了。

 補充 a courier company 快遞公司

易混 carrier n. 運送人；搬運人

初級

19. **customer**

[ˋkʌstəmə]

n. 客戶；顧客

⇨ **customs**「海關」+ **- er**「表人」

Although we have a small **customer** base presently, we believe we can build on that through clever advertising.
雖然我們現在只有很小的客戶群，不過我們相信我們可以透過聰明的廣告策略將它擴大。

 典故 原本 customer 指的是海關官員，後來引申為與之有交易的人；和某個人有交易，這個人就是我們的顧客。

同 purchaser / buyer / client

中級

20. **delicate**

[ˋdɛləkət]

adj. 易碎的；纖細的；精美的；可口的

⇨ **delic(ious)**「美味的」+ **cate**「佳餚美食」

The trouble with making **delicate** merchandise is that it's difficult to package efficiently.
製造精細商品的麻煩之處就是很難有效率地進行包裝。

 典故 delicious 是美味的，cate 是古英文指佳餚美食，delicate 原指美食不但美味、外觀看起來也很精美，很精美的東西一定很容易破掉或碎裂，所以 delicate 就有「可口的、精美的、纖細的」意思。

中級

21. **delivery**

[dɪˋlɪvərɪ]

n. 配送

⇨ **deliver**「運送」+ **- ry**「名詞字尾」

Will anyone be at your office to take **delivery** next Friday since it's a holiday?
下週五是假日，你公司那裏會有人收件嗎？

補充

same-day/next-day delivery	當日 / 次日送達
cash on delivery	貨到付款
door-to-door/home delivery	宅配
free delivery	免費送貨服務
air delivery	空運
delivery date	到貨日

deliver v. 運送，投遞；發表演說；生產

中高

22. descend

[dɪˋsɛnd]

v. 下降，下傾；為…的後裔

⇨ **di-**「向下」**+ -scend-**「攀爬」

Tell your driver that the exit ramp from the highway is particularly steep, and that he will need to brake immediately once his truck starts to **descend**.

告訴你的司機說高速公路的出口匝道特別斜，一旦他的卡車開始往下走時他就需要立刻煞車。

 descend to sth.　　　向下沉淪為…
be descended from N.　源自 N.，為 N. 的後代

descent n. 下降；出身
descendant n. 子孫；後裔

反 ascend v. 上升

初級

23. difference

[ˋdɪfərəns]

n. 差別；差異

⇨ **differ**「相異」**+ -ence**「名詞字尾」

I realize that premium service will be more expensive than the basic service I now receive, but I am willing to pay the **difference**.

我知道升級服務會比我現在用的基本服務還要貴，不過我願意補差額。

 pay the difference　　　補差額
pocket the difference　賺差價

differentiate v. 使有差異、構成差異；區別

中高

24. discharge

[dɪsˋtʃɑrdʒ]

v. 卸貨；解僱

⇨ **dis-**「表否定」**+ charge**「裝載」

There are various loading and **discharging** methods for different kinds of cargoes.

針對不同種的貨物會有各種裝貨和卸貨的方法。

Have you ever been **discharged** for inappropriate conduct on the job?

你曾經因為工作上的不當行為被解僱嗎？

 discharge sb. for sth. 因某因素將某人解僱
sb. be discharged from the army
某人從軍中退伍
sb. be discharged from the hospital 某人出院

中級

25. discount

[dɪsˈkaʊnt]
v. 打折；看輕
[ˈdɪskaʊnt]
n. 折扣

⇨ dis -「分開」＋ count「計算」，算過的金額拿走一部份就是給折扣

High-end clothing boutiques rarely **discount** their inventory no matter how old it is.
高檔流行服飾店的商品不論款式有多舊都很少打折。

補充	at a discount	在打折，有減價
	get a discount	得到折扣
	offer/give a discount	提供折扣
	a cash discount	現金折扣

同 n. = deduction

中高

26. dispatch

[dɪˈspætʃ]
v. 派遣；迅速處理
n. 派送；急件；新聞報導

My records show that our service tech was **dispatched** twenty minutes ago, so he should be arriving at your location any minute now.
我的紀錄顯示我們 20 分鐘前就派出維修人員了，所以他應該隨時會到達您的所在位置。

補充	a dispatch center	任務分派中心
	dispatch sth. to sb.	派送某物給某人
	with dispatch	快速而有效的

中高

27. disperse

[dɪˈspɝs]
v. 驅散；解散；散開

⇨ di -「分開」＋ -sperse -「使散落」

Every morning, our sales associates are encouraged to **disperse** all over the city in search of prospects.
每天早上業務部同仁會分散到城市各處尋找商機。

| 補充 | disperse A with B | 用 B 來驅離 A |

中高

28. dual

[ˈduəl]
adj. 兩的；雙的
n. 雙倍

⇨ du -「二」＋ -al「形容詞字尾」

Craig serves the **dual** roles of CEO and web developer at this small firm.
Craig 在這間小公司擔任執行長與網頁開發者的雙重身份。

同 adj. = twofold / double

中級

29. duration
[dʊˋreʃən]
n. 持續期間；持久

⇨ -dura-「硬的，堅固的」+ -ation「表狀態或結果」，堅固耐用就可以持續使用很久

The executives spent nearly the entire **duration** of the meeting assessing the various issues from the human resources department.
主管們幾乎整段會議時間都在評估人資部門所提出的各項議題。

補充
for the duration	持續直到結束
a contract of 時期 's duration	為期…的合約

中級

30. earnings
[ˋɝnɪŋz]
n. 薪水；工資；收益

⇨ earn「賺取」+ -ing「名詞字尾」+ -s「複數字尾」

When the **earnings** report comes out on Friday, we will have a clearer picture of the health of this company.
收益報告星期五出來的時候，我們就可以更清楚瞭解這家公司的財務健全程度。

補充　expected earnings 預期收益

earn v. 賺取

中高

31. endorse
[ɪnˋdɔrs]
v. 背書；支持；贊同

I am willing to **endorse** Mitch's plan on the condition that the proposed budget is cut by 20%.
只要預算縮減 20% 我就願意支持 Mitch 的計畫。

補充
endorse a plan/decision	為計劃 / 決定背書
be endorsed by sb.	受到某人的背書肯定
endorse sb. for N.	在 N. 方面為某人背書

endorsement n. 背書；簽署表示贊同

中高

32. equate
[ɪˋkwet]
v. 等同

⇨ -equ-「相等」+ -ate「使…」

At this firm, we **equate** success with earnings, so just making a strong effort is not good enough.
在這間公司，賺錢才叫做成功，所以光是很努力是不夠的。

補充
A equate to B	A 等同於 B
equate A with B	將 A 和 B 同等看待

equal adj. 相等的

中級

33. erect

[ɪˋrɛkt]

v. 建立，豎立

adj. 直立的，豎起的

同 set up　phr. 建立

⇨ e-「向外」+ -rect-「拉直」

Dr. Johnson played a key role in **erecting** the country's economic infrastructure.

Johnson博士在建立國家的經濟基礎結構上扮演了關鍵角色。

中級

34. estimate

[ˋɛstəˏmet]

v./n. 評估；估計，估量

I **estimate** that the state of the economy will continue to improve for the next three quarters.

我估計經濟狀況在接下來的三季將持續改善。

補充		
	It is estimated + that 子句	據估計
	a cost estimate	成本估算
	a rough estimate	粗估
	a conservative estimate	保守估計
	an insurance estimate	保險試算
	make an estimate of N.	做一份關於 N. 的評估

underestimate v. 低估

overestimate v. 高估

中高

35. excess

[ɪkˋsɛs]

n. 超越、超過；過度，無節制

 ex-「向外」+ -cess-「走，前進」

Many in this community live a life of **excess**, purchasing merchandise to their heart's content.

這個社區裡許多人過著揮霍無度、隨心所欲地購物的生活。

補充		
	excess fare	超出的費用 (尤指交通票券的差額)
	excess capacity	過剩產能
	an excess of N.	N. 過剩

exceed v. 超過、超出

excessive adj. 過多的、過度的

初級

36. export

[ˋɛksport]

n. 出口，出口品

[ɪkˋsport]

v. 出口

⇨ ex-「向外」+ -port-「攜帶」

Oil is a major **export** of Venezuela.

石油是委內瑞拉的主要出口商品。

補充		
	export A to B	將 A 出口到 B
	A be exported to B	A 被出口到 B

re-export v./n. 再出口

反 import　v./n. 進口；進口品

中級

37. **extensive**

[ɪkˋstɛnsɪv]

adj. 廣泛的；大量的；
大規模的

extend v. 延伸、延長
extensively adv. 廣泛地

⇨ **ex-**「向外」+ **-tens-**「伸出」+ **-ive**「具…性質的」，
向外伸很遠表示範圍很大

I have done an **extensive** accounting for everything in this office, and the old copier is nowhere to be found.
我已將這間辦公室裡所有東西大量清點出來，不過怎樣都找不到那台舊的影印機。

初級

38. **extra**

[ˋɛkstrə]

adj. 額外的，外加的
n. 附加費用

We don't like to charge customers **extra** fees, but when they overdraft their accounts, there needs to be a substantial penalty.
我們並不希望向顧客收取額外費用，不過當他們的帳戶透支時，還是需要收取一筆罰金。

補充	extra charge/fee	額外收費、額外費用
	a hidden extra	隱藏的額外費用
	optional extra	可選購的額外配備

初級

39. **fee**

[fi]

n. 費用

Sorry, sir, but we must charge a restocking **fee** when customers return a shipment because the items have already been used.
抱歉，先生，由於客戶退貨時商品已被拆封使用過，因此我們必須收取重整上架費。

補充	restocking fee 重整上架費 (將退貨重新包裝上架的費用)	
	an entrance fee	入場費
	a fee on N.	在 N. 上收費
	charge a fee for V-ing/N.	收取做…的費用

中級

40. **feedback**

[ˋfidˌbæk]

n. 回饋；回響，回應

⇨ **feed**「餵食；供給」+ **back**「返回」

We've received some positive **feedback** on our prompt delivery service.
我們收到了一些有關及時交貨服務的正面回饋。

| 補充 | positive/negative feedback 正面 / 負面反應 | |
| | give/receive feedback on N. 給予 / 收到有關 N. 的回饋 | |

feed back phr. 反饋

01 職稱職務／應徵面試

02 人事／薪資／福利

03 辦公室／電話傳真

04 文書作業

05 會議

41. fragile

中高

[ˈfrædʒaɪl] / [ˈfrædʒəl]

adj. 易碎的，脆弱的

⇨ **-frag-**「破裂」+ **-ile**「有⋯性質的」

This package was marked "**Fragile** - Handle with care."
這個包裹上標示了「易碎－小心輕放」。

After such a harsh disagreement, the two colleagues maintain a very **fragile** peace by totally ignoring and avoiding each other.
在如此激烈爭執後，這兩名同事以完全忽視和迴避彼此的方式維持著脆弱的和平。

補充 a fragile relationship 脆弱的關係

fragility n. 易碎性

---

42. freight

[fret]

n.（船運）貨物
v. 裝貨、裝載

同 cargo n. 貨物

Our tractor-trailers have very poor fuel efficiency due to constantly pulling a ton of **freight**.
我們的大貨車因不停拖拉大型貨物所以很耗油。

補充	a freight company	貨運公司
	freight charge	貨運費
	air/sea freight forwarder	航運／海運承攬商

---

43. guarantee

中級

[ˌgærənˈti]

v. 保證；擔保
n. 保證（書）；擔保品

同 warrant v. 保證

No other major appliance manufacturer offers such a hassle-free money-back **guarantee**.
沒有其他家電大廠會提供這麼不麻煩的退款保證。

補充	guarantee sb. sth.	保證提供某人某物
	guarantee N. against sth.	擔保 N. 不會⋯
	a guarantee on N.	N. 的保證
	have/carry/come with a guarantee	有附保證書
	money-back guarantee	退款保證
	be under guarantee	在包退包換保證期內

---

44. guideline

中高

[ˈgaɪdˌlaɪn]

n. 指導方針

⇨ **guide**「指引」+ **line**「準繩」

As a general **guideline**, when foot traffic into our retail store is slow, place several racks of clothes outside the front door to attract attention.
一般的原則是，當顧客進店的速度很緩慢時，就在前門外擺幾排衣服以吸引注意力。

補充 issue guidelines on N. 發佈 N. 的指導方針

45. haggle

['hægl]

v. 討價還價，爭論

Since the item is already discounted, we can't allow customers to **haggle** with you about the price.
既然商品已經是折扣價了，我們就不會讓顧客再跟你議價。

 haggle with sb. 和某人討價還價
haggle over sth. 在某事上討價還價

同 bargain

初級

46. handle

['hændl]

v. 處理

n. 把手

I suppose that you'll only need a week of training till you are able to **handle** taking client calls by yourself.
我認為你只需要一週的訓練就能獨立處理客戶來電。

 handling charge 處理費、手續費
handle pressure/problem 處理、面對壓力/問題
get a handle on N. 瞭解並能處理 N.
fly off the handle = lose one's temper 失控發火

同 v. = manage / deal

初級

47. import

[ɪm`pɔrt]

v. 進口

[`ɪmpɔrt]

n. 進口、輸入

⇨ im- 「進入」+ -port- 「攜帶」
We don't want to **import** too many raw materials for our factory due to our country's high tariffs.
由於我國關稅很高，我們不希望進口太多原物料到工廠來。

 parallel imports 平行輸入品
import A from B 從 B 進口 A
a ban on imports of N. 禁止 N. 的輸入、進口

反 export n./v. 出口

中級

48. inquiry

[ɪn`kwaɪrɪ] / [`ɪnkwərɪ]

n. 探詢，打聽；探究

★ 英：enquiry ／美：inquiry
⇨ in- 「進入」+ -quir- 「詢問」+ -y 「名詞字尾」
Please direct all your **inquiries** to our help line anytime twenty-four hours a day.
所有問題請隨時撥打我們的 24 小時諮詢專線。

 make an inquiry about N. 詢問有關 N. 的事
receive an inquiry from sb. 收到某人的詢問
customer inquiry 顧客詢問，客戶諮詢

inquire v. 詢問、查詢

中高

49. installment
[ɪn'stɔlmənt]
n. 分期付款

★ 英：instalment ／美：installment

 install「安裝」＋ -ment「名詞字尾」

I think that we should advertise **installment** payment plans for even our lower-end model laptops.
我認為即使是較低階的筆電我們都應該要廣告說可分期付款。

補充
pay by/in installments　以分期的方式
an installment plan　分期還款計劃
installment payment　分期付款

install　v. 安裝

中高

50. intact
[ɪn'tækt]
adj. 完好無缺的；原封不動的

⇨ in-「表否定」＋ -tact-「碰觸」，沒碰過就是原封不動
We assure you that all goods will arrive **intact**.
我們向您保證所有商品會完好無損到達。

同 undamaged / untouched

中高

51. inventory
['ɪnvənˌtɔrɪ]
n. 詳細目錄；清單；存貨

 invent「發明，編造」＋ -ory「名詞字尾」

Every Sunday night, the Assistant Manager counts the entire store **inventory** and figures out the profit and loss.
每週日晚上副理都會盤點店內所有存貨並計算盈虧。

補充
make an inventory　盤點庫存
inventory cost　　　庫存成本

---

52. invoice
['ɪnvɔɪs]
n. 請款單；出貨單
v. 開立 (出貨／請款) 單

 in-「＝ en-，在…上」＋ voice「＝ -voy-，道路」

The amount of your original quote doesn't match the amount on this **invoice** you just sent me.
你的原始報價和你剛剛寄給我的請款單金額不一樣。

補充
e-invoice　　　　電子請款單據或系統
export invoice　　出口貨單
invoice price　　　請款價格
issue an invoice　開出請款單
invoice sb. for N.　開立 N. 的請款單給某人

06 買賣交易

07 採購與物流

08 廣告與宣傳

09 業務協調

10 企業經營

53. itemize

[ˈaɪtəmˌaɪz]

v. 詳細列舉；分條列舉

item n. 品項、項目

⇨ item「項目」+ -ize「使…化」

When I asked the cashier to itemize my receipt, I discovered that she had charged me twice for the same thing.

我要求店員把收據明細逐項列出時，發現同一件商品她收了兩次的錢。

中高

54. linger

[ˈlɪŋgɚ]

v. 拖延；徘徊、逗留

同 逗留：stay

We ask that no one linger next to the production line while it is running

我們要求任何人不准在生產線運作時在旁邊逗留。

| 補充 | linger on N. | 停留在 N. 上 |
| | linger for + 時間 + to V. | 逗留 (時間) 以做… |

---

55. logistics

[ləˈdʒɪstɪks]

n. 物流管理；後勤

 logis「暫住所」+ -istic「形容詞字尾」+ -s「名詞字尾」

We're still working out the logistics, but we need to move to a new shop location next month.

我們現在還在制訂物流管理方案，但是下個月我們就要搬到新的店鋪了。

| 補充 | a logistics company | 物流公司 |
| | the logistics of N. | N. 的後勤流程 |

---

56. long-range

[ˈlɔŋˌrendʒ]

adj. 遠距的；長遠的；
大範圍的

⇨ long「長的」+ range「範圍」

Unfortunately, there is no long-range plan to mitigate the secretary's workload since we just can't afford to hire anyone else.

很遺憾地，我們沒有減輕秘書工作量的長遠計劃，因為我們沒有錢再多僱用人了。

補充	long-range benefits	長遠利益
	long-range effects	長遠效果
	long-range goals	長遠目標

易混 long-term adj. 長期的，長時間的

中級

57. lower

[ˈloɚ]
v. 降低；減低
adj. 較低的，較少的

⇨ low「低的」+ -er「形容詞比較級字尾」

I refuse to **lower** my expectations of excellence for every product that goes out of our factory.
從本工廠出產的每件商品品質必須是最優的，這標準不可降低。

補充
lower costs/prices 降低成本／售價
lower greenhouse gas emission
減少溫室氣體排放

---

58. misdirect

[ˌmɪsdəˈrɛkt]
v. 將…送錯地方；錯誤引導；誤用

⇨ mis-「錯誤地」+ direct「指導，引導」

The carefully crafted press release is intended to **misdirect** the public from our company's poor quarterly report.
這份精心打造的新聞稿目的是要將大眾對我們公司單季財報表現不佳的注意力引開來。

中高

59. neon sign

[ˈniɑn] [saɪn]
n. 霓虹燈招牌

Since we are located on a major road, putting up a large, gaudy **neon sign** should attract plenty of business.
我們既然位於主要幹道上，豎立大而華麗的霓虹燈招牌應該會吸引很多生意上門。

典故
neon 是 19 世紀才被發現的一種氣體稱為「氖」，它是一種無色稀有氣體，在放電的情況下會產生橙紅色，之後被大量運用在真空管、螢光管等發光物品中。當時發現的科學家用 -neo- 這個字根來命名這種氣體為 neon，字根 -neo- 意思是「新的(new)」；sign 是標誌或招牌，neon sign 就是霓虹燈招牌。

neon n. 霓虹；氖氣

中級

60. obtain

[əbˈten]
v. 獲得

⇨ ob-「to」+ -tain-「持、握」，去握住就得到了

We need to **obtain** all the necessary licenses before we can open the restaurant for business.
在餐廳能營業之前，我們需取得所有必備的執照。

同 get / gain / acquire

初級

61. **order**

[`ɔrdɚ]

n. 訂單；秩序；順序
v. 訂購；命令、指揮；點菜

Please have everything prepared before you call to place your **order**, such as your customer number, item number, and quantity.
請在來電訂購前準備好您的客戶編號、產品編號以及數量。

purchase order	採購單 (縮寫為 P.O.)
delivery order	提貨單
shipping order	裝貨單
CWO = cash with order	下單即付現
place an order for N.	下訂單訂購 N.
on back order	延遲交貨；缺貨、補貨中
in alphabetical/numerical/date order	
以字母 / 數字 / 日期排序	
out of order	故障
in good order	狀況良好

初級

62. **package**

[`pækɪdʒ]

n. 包裹；一整套
v. 包裝

⇨ **pack**「包裝」+ **-age**「名詞字尾」
The **package** needs to be sent out no later than noon if you want the regional manager to receive it by tomorrow.
如果你想要區經理明天前收到包裹，你要在中午前將它寄出。

a package deal	套裝商品；不可分開的一組
a package tour	套裝旅遊
a package price	套裝價格
be packaged with N.	包裝中附有 N.

同 parcel n. 包裹

中高

63. **patron**

[`petrən]

n. 老主顧；贊助人

We offer a 10% discount to our **patrons**.
我們提供九折優惠給老主顧。

補充 arts patron 藝術贊助者

patronage n. 惠顧；贊助

同 贊助人：sponsor

中高

64. **permissible**

[pəˈmɪsəbl]

adj. 可允許的

⇨ per-「通過」+ -mis-「寄送」+ -ible「可⋯的」，可以通過送出的就是可允許的

Is it **permissible** to cancel the order after the goods are shipped out?

貨物出貨之後才取消訂單是允許的嗎？

 It is permissible to do sth. 做某事是被允許的。

permit v. 允許
permission n. 許可

回 allowed

初級

65. **place**

[ples]

v. 安排；定出(價位、名次)

n. 地方；名次，地位

We decided to **place** an ad on several different job sites to give ourselves a large pool of résumés to choose from.

我們決定在數個不同的求職網站上刊登廣告，好讓我們有大量的履歷表可以從中篩選。

 place an advertisement 登廣告
place an order 下訂單

中高

66. **preference**

[ˈprɛfərəns]

n. 偏好；優惠；優先權

⇨ prefer「較喜歡」+ -ence「名詞字尾」

The department supervisor has a **preference** for receiving all reports before lunch the following day.

這名部門主管偏好在隔天午餐前收到所有的報告。

 have a preference for N. 對 N. 有偏好
give preference to sb./sth. 提供優惠給某人或某單位
customer preference for N. 顧客對 N. 的偏好
a preferential price 優惠價格

prefer v. 偏愛，較喜歡
preferential adj. 優先的；優待的

中高

67. **prolong**

[prəˈlɔŋ]

v. 延長；拉長

⇨ pro-「向前」+ long「長的」

Scheduling regular maintainance for the copy machine will **prolong** its life and save us from costly repairs or a replacement.

定期維修影印機會延長它的壽命，而且我們不用花大錢維修或換新。

回 extend / lengthen

68. purchase

[ˈpɝtʃəs]

n./v. 購買；採購

⇨ **pur -**「向前」**＋ chase**「追逐，獵取」，古人打獵取得物品，今人購買取得東西

Our buyer carefully collects estimates before deciding on a large **purchase**.
我們的買家在決定一筆鉅額採購前會仔細地收集各方估價。

補充		
	make a purchase	購買
	be available for purchase	可供購買
	purchase order	採購訂單
	purchase price for N.	N. 的購買價格
	to purchase sth. for 價格	以…價格購買某物

purchaser n. 買家；購買者

 buy

69. pushcart

[ˈpʊʃˌkɑrt]

n. 手推車；販賣推車

⇨ **push**「推」**＋ cart**「手推車」

We don't have the capital to buy a shop, so we'll start by investing in a **pushcart** and selling our food around campus.
我們沒有資金購買店面，所以我們會從投資手推車在校園附近販賣食物開始。

補充	food cart 食物推車

70. quantity

[ˈkwɑntətɪ]

n. 數量

⇨ **quant**「有多少」**＋ -ity**「表狀態」

Edwards, Inc. always orders large **quantities**, so you need to double-check whether they want 500 or 5,000 units.
Edwards 公司總是訂購很大的量，所以你需要再次查核他們想要的是 500 組還是 5000 組。

補充	a large/small quantity of N.	大量 / 少量的 N.
	in large quantities	大量地

 amount

71. quote

[kwot]

n. 報價單；引號，引文
v. 報價；要價，開價；引述

After getting **quotes** from three companies for the job, we looked closely at each of their reputations for service and reliability.
得到三家公司的報價之後，我們仔細審查了他們每間公司在服務和可信度方面的名聲。

補充	a quote for sth.	某物的報價
	to quote 金額 for sth.	針對某物開出某價格
	to quote sb. as saying	引用某人的話說…

quotation n. 報價；引言

217

中高

72. random

['rændəm]

adj. 隨機的；隨意的；任意的

When we opened a second factory just down the road, there was a **random** selection process to determine which factory workers should be stationed there.

在這條路上開第二間工廠時，我們用隨機選取的方式來決定工廠員工要分到哪一間工廠工作。

補充	a random sample	隨機樣本
	random check	隨機抽查
	at random	隨機地，隨意地

中級

73. receipt

[rɪ`sit]

n. 收據；收款憑證；收到

 ⇨ re-「回來」＋ -ceipt-「拿」，付錢出去拿回收據

For each of your purchases, be sure to get your tax number printed on your **receipt** in order to be reimbursed.

你每次買東西時，要在收據上打上統編以便報帳。

| 補充 | a receipt for N. | N. 的收據 |
| | on receipt of payment | 收到款項時 |

receive v. 接收；接到

中高

74. refund

['rifʌnd]

n. 退費；退還；賠償

[rɪ`fʌnd]

v. 退還

 re-「再次；返回」＋ fund「資金」

Since Angie's purchase was less than thirty days ago, she is entitled to a full **refund** when she presents her receipt, no questions asked.

因 Angie 購買未達 30 天，所以她只要出示收據，不須詢問就可得到全額退費。

補充	a tax refund	退稅
	a cash refund	現金退款
	ask for/claim a refund	要求退費、賠償
	offer a refund	提供退費
	get a refund	獲得退費、賠償
	to refund money	退回費用、賠錢

中級

75. refusal

[rɪ`fjuzl]

n. 拒絕

⇨ refuse「拒絕」＋ -al「名詞字尾」

Our request for terminating the contract received a **refusal**.

我們終止合約的請求被拒絕了。

| 補充 | right of first refusal | 優先購買權 |
| | refusal of sth. | 拒絕某事物 |

refuse v. 拒絕

76. reimburse

[ˌriɪmˈbɝs]

v. 償還、歸還；退款；（公司帳）報銷

reimbursement n. 償還；退款；補償

 re-「返回」＋ im-「在裡面」＋ bursa「拉丁文，錢包」

We will **reimburse** you for the full amount of your loss.
我們會全額補償您的損失。

補充 reimburse sb. for sth. 償還某人某物或支出

中高

77. repay

[rɪˈpe]

v. 償還，報答

★ 動詞變化：**repay, repaid, repaid, repaying**
⇨ re-「返回」＋ pay「支付」，拿回去給對方就是償還

Harry has to **repay** the payday lender within two weeks or his interest rate will shoot up to 250%.
Harry 必須在兩週內還錢給發薪日貸款公司，否則他的利率將會飆高到 250%。

補充 repay a loan 償還貸款
repay a debt 償還債務

中級

78. request

[rɪˈkwɛst]

n./v. 請求；要求

⇨ re-「一再」＋ quest「尋找」，一再尋找表示有需求

Each quarter, management asks us to make our formal **requests** for essential supplies, most of which are denied.
管理人員每季會要我們提出申請必需品的正式請求，雖然大部分都會被否決掉。

補充 make a request for N. 提出 N. 的請求
decline/turn down a request 回絕請求
respond to a request 回應請求

中高

79. retail

[ˈritel]

n./v. 零售

⇨ re-「一再」＋ -tail-「切開」，切開來賣就是零售

While our **retail** shops have done poorly, our online sales have more than made up for it.
雖然我們的零售店生意不好，但我們的網路銷售量不只補足虧損，還有賺錢。

補充 a retail chain/store 零售連鎖／零售店
a retail market 零售市場
a food/clothing retailer 食物／服裝零售商
a local retailer 本地零售商

retailer n. 零售商

反 wholesale n. 批發

01 職稱職務／聘僱面試

02 人事／薪資／福利

03 辦公室／電話傳真

04 文書作業

05 會議

初級

80. **sample**

['sæmpl]

n. 樣本；樣品，試用品
v. 取…樣品；抽樣檢查

Of course, we have no problem sending you a small trial **sample** for ten days, and if you don't like it, just return it quickly.
我們當然可以寄一份試用樣品給您試用十天，如果您不滿意只要盡快退回即可。

 free sample　　免費試用品
a sample of N.　N. 的樣品

中高

81. **shipment**

['ʃɪpmənt]

n. 運送；運輸的貨物

➪ ship「運送」+ -ment「表結果」
On arrival, the **shipment** was damaged, so I want you to demand compensation from the delivery service.
運送的物品在到貨時受損了，所以我要你跟貨運公司求償。

 a shipment of N.　　運送 N.
a notice of shipment 出貨通知
delay in shipment　 延遲出貨
regular shipment　　定期寄送

ship v. 寄送，運送

中高

82. **shipping**

['ʃɪpɪŋ]

n. 運輸；運輸業

➪ ship「運送」+ -ing「名詞字尾」
Our **shipping** department is undergoing a change in software, so bear with us while we inquire about the status of your order.
因出貨部門正在進行軟體更新，在我們查詢您的訂單狀態時還請耐心等候。

補充 a shipping company 運輸公司
a shipping route　 運輸路線
a shipping note　 出貨單
shipping method　 運送方式
shipping date　　 出貨日
overseas shipping 海外寄送

易混 shipment 指運送的貨物本身；shipping 指運送的動作和過程。

83. solicit

[sə`lɪsɪt]

v. 請求；懇求；徵求；
(AmE) 招攬（生意）

 sollus「拉丁文，整個的」+ **-cit-**「喚起」

To help your business stay financially healthy, you need to **solicit** new business.
為了維持你們公司財務健康，你們需要招攬新生意。

補充		
	solicit sth. from sb.	向某人請求要某物
	solicit for N.	徵求 N.
	solicit sb. to V.	請求某人做…

solicitor n. 銷售員；(BrE) 初級律師

同 request / ask for

中高

84. specification

[ˌspɛsəfəˋkeʃən]

n. 規格；明細表；詳述

⇨ **specify**「詳細說明」+ **-ation**「名詞字尾」

In order to properly serve you, Sir, I need the **specifications** from the back of your TV.
先生，我需要您電視機後方的產品規格表，以便正確地為您提供服務。

補充		
	specification for N.	N. 的規格表
	products specifications	產品明細表
	a job specification	職務規範

specify v. 具體說明；詳細指明
specific adj. 特定的，特別的

中級

85. stock

[stɑk]

n. 庫存品；儲存物；股票
v. 儲存；存貨

Our half-off sale applies to in **stock** items only.
我們的半價特惠只適用於庫存商品。

補充		
	in stock	有庫存
	out of stock	缺貨中；無庫存
	dead stock	滯銷品

中高

86. storage

[ˋstorɪdʒ]

n. 儲藏，保管；儲存量；倉庫

⇨ **store**「儲存」+ **-age**「名詞字尾」

After cramming inventory into every nook and cranny, we were forced to rent a separate **storage** unit.
在把存貨塞進每個地方後，我們不得不去租另一個倉庫。

★ nook and cranny：一個空間內的每個小角落

補充		
	a storage device	儲存設備
	computer storage	電腦儲存量
	storage space	儲存空間
	storage capacity	儲存量
	short-term/long-term storage	短期 / 長期儲存
	in storage	存放著

01 聯絡職務／贈僱面試

02 人事／薪資／福利

03 辦公室／電話傳真

04 文書作業

05 會議

中高

87. **substantial**

[səb`stænʃəl]

adj. 實質的；大量的

 sub -「在下方」**+ - stant -**「站立」**+ - al**「有關···的」

Consolidating all of our utility fees into one bill resulted in **substantial** savings.

把我們的水電瓦斯費合併在一張帳單裡可以省下一大筆錢。

補充		
	a substantial increase in N.	N. 有大量的增加
	substantial benefits	實質收益
	substantial costs	可觀的成本
	substantial order	大量訂購

中級

88. **sufficient**

[sə`fɪʃnt]

adj. 充足的；足夠的

⇨ **suf -**「在下方」**+ - fic -**「做」**+ - ent**「形容詞字尾」，
做好放到下面就能充分提供所需

Our labor force is **sufficient** for now, but we expect an upturn in business by this time next year.

目前我們的人力充足，不過我們預期明年這個時候生意會好轉。

補充		
	be sufficient for N.	對 N. 來說是足夠的
	be self-sufficient in N.	在 N. 方面可自給自足

同 ample

反 insufficient adj. 不夠的；不足的

初級

89. **supply**

[sə`plaɪ]

n./v. 供應，供給，提供

⇨ **sup -**「在下方」**+ - ply -**「填滿」，下方有缺就幫你填滿就是供應

Oil is in short **supply** now due to the explosions on the major pipeline running through the Middle East.

現在石油供應短缺是因為流經中東的主要輸油管線發生爆炸。

補充		
	supply and demand	供給和需求
	in short supply	缺乏的，不足的
	supply chain	供應鏈
	supply sth. to sb. = supply sb. with sth.	
	提供某人某物	

同 v. = provide

中高

90. surplus

[`sɝpləs]

n. 過剩的量；盈餘

adj. 過剩的；剩餘的

 sur -「超越」+ plus「更多」

The video game company was so excited about increased sales that they produced a huge **surplus** of game consoles.

這間電玩公司對銷量大增感到非常興奮，以致於他們生產了過多的遊戲機。

> 補充
> a surplus of N. 過剩的 N.
> trade surplus 貿易順差

同 excess n. 過量

中級

91. tag

[tæg]

v. 貼標籤

n. 標籤

I want you to go through the system and **tag** all the orders that have a rush delivery so we can get those done first.

我要你將系統看過一遍，並將所有急需出貨的訂單貼上標籤，這樣我們就能先處理那些訂單。

> 補充
> tag A with B 將 B 標示在 A 上面
> a price tag 價格標籤
> a smart tag 智慧標籤（產品上的電子感應標籤）

中高

92. transition

[træn`zɪʃən]

n. 過渡時期；轉變，轉型

v. 轉型

 trans -「穿越」+ -it -「去」+ -ion「名詞字尾」，穿越過去就會歷經轉變

Until the merger has officially taken place, we will be in a period of **transition**.

在合併正式生效之前，我們會有一段過渡期。

> 補充
> a transition of power 權力轉移
> economy transition 經濟轉型
> transition from A to B 從 A 轉變到 B

中高

93. transmit

[træns`mɪt]

v. 傳達、傳播；遺傳

 trans -「穿越」+ -mit -「送出」，穿越各處送出就是在傳播

It may take some time for the Tokyo office to **transmit** all the requested information back to you.

從東京辦公室將所有需要的資料傳送回來給你可能要花一些時間。

> 補充
> transmit a signal/code 傳送信號 / 密碼
> transmit data/information 傳送數據 / 訊息

中高

94. upright

[`ʌpˌraɪt]

adj. 直立的；正直的
adv. 直立地

⇨ **up**「向上」+ **right**「正確的」，正確朝上的就是直立的

Use these shipping labels to ensure that your packages stay upright.

使用這些出貨標籤以確保你的包裹維持在直立的狀態。

補充　return the seat to an upright position
將座椅放回直立的位置（鐵路或飛機內常用語）

中高

95. utmost

[`ʌtˌmost]

n. 最大限度
adj. 最大的、最多的

The sales department is focused on doing their utmost to upsell on every order to maximize revenue.

為擴大營收，業務部將焦點放在盡最大力量增加每一筆銷售的金額。

補充　to the utmost　　　　　　竭盡所能
　　　do sb's utmost　　　　　盡某人最大的力量

中高

96. verify

[`vɛrəˌfaɪ]

v. 證實

 very「真實的，精確的」+ **-fy**「做，使成為…」

Before I can give you access to the account, I need to ask you a series of questions to verify your identity.

在讓您登入帳戶前，我必須詢問您一些問題以驗證您的身分。

補充　to verify that + 子句 去證實…

verification n. 證實

中高

97. voucher

[`vaʊtʃɚ]

n. 優惠券；折抵券

 vouch「擔保」+ **-er**「做…動作的物品」

The airline was forced to distribute vouchers to all the passengers after the flight was delayed for the third time.

這間航空公司在第三度班機延遲後不得不發送優惠券給所有乘客。

補充　a food/travel voucher 餐券／旅遊券
　　　redeem a voucher
　　　將優惠券兌換成現金（或物品）

vouch n. 擔保；證明

中高

98. **warehouse**

['wɛr,haʊs]

n. 倉庫；大商店

⇨ **ware**「商品」＋ **house**「房子」

Every skid in our **warehouse** is piled high with filled boxes, ready to ship.

我們倉庫裡的每個棧板上都堆滿了已裝貨、準備要送出的箱子。

補充 a warehouse club 會員制大賣場

同 storehouse

中高

99. **warranty**

['wɔrəntɪ]

n. 保固；保證書

The scratches on your vehicle are not covered under your **warranty**.

您車上的刮痕沒有在您的保固範圍內。

補充
under warranty　　　　在保固期限內
an extended warranty　保固延長
warranty period　　　　保固期

同 guarantee

中高

100. **wholesale**

['hol,sel]

adj./adv. 批發的

⇨ **whole**「整個的」＋ **sale**「銷售」

Since I have such a large family, we buy most of our groceries from the **wholesale** club down the street.

因為我有這麼一大家子的人，我們大部分的生活用品都是到這條街上的會員制批發賣場購買。

補充
a wholesale price　　　批發價
a wholesale business　批發業

wholesaler n. 批發商

實力進階

Part 1. 比一比：bill, invoice 和 receipt

bill

一般統稱為帳單，為對出售的商品或提供的服務所列出的請款單據，內含各項商品或服務項目、單價及應付總金額等資訊，並註明應付款日期，功能與 invoice 相似，只是 invoice 較 bill 更為正式。

invoice

一般稱為發票，但實際功能為出貨請款單，上面載明貨品或服務細項及單價和總金額等資訊，也會註明應付款日期，買方收到 invoice 後要在應付款日期前支付款項給賣方，賣方收到款項後則會再開立收款憑證 receipt。

receipt

一般稱為收據，為賣方收到買方付款時所開立的憑證。在台灣，購物或使用服務時所開立的統一發票，因為現場銀貨兩訖，所以我們所稱的發票其實是款項的收付證明，正確英文應為 receipt。

Part 2. dual vs. double：

dual

形容一事物分成的兩個部分、兩種用途或兩個面向

如：dual role（雙重角色）
　　dual career（雙重職涯）
　　dual function（雙重功能）
　　dual citizenship（雙重公民身份）

double

形容一事物內含兩個一模一樣或兩個性質非常相似的東西

如：double bed（雙人床）
　　double standard（雙重標準）
　　double room（雙人房）
　　double pay（雙倍薪水）

Part 3. 採購單這樣看：

Purchase Order

① **Ruby English**

I Can Teach You Better

2F.-3, No.70, Sec. 2, Anhe Rd., Da-an Dist.
Taipei City 10680, Taiwan (R.O.C.)
Phone: (8862)2708-5508, Fax: (8862)2707-1669
www.ruby.com.tw

② P.O. # 2015000015
Date: January 5, 2015

③ Vendor
PS DigiLearning
5888 West Inn Road, Suite 600
Tucson, AZ. 85700, USA
Phone: (520)653-5535, Fax: (520)653-5543

④ Ship to
Joe Blow
Ruby English
2F.-3, No.70, Sec. 2, Anhe Rd., Da-an Dist.
Taipei City 10680, Taiwan (R.O.C.)
Phone: (8862)2708-5508, Fax: (8862)2707-1669

⑤ SHIPPING METHOD	⑥ SHIPPING TERM	⑦ PAYMENT TERM	⑧ DELIVERY DATE
AIR	CFR	Net 30	February 5, 2015

⑨ QTY	⑩ ITEM NUMBER / DESCRIPTION	⑪ UNIT PRICE	⑫ LINE TOTAL
500	Upstar Learning software v 3.1	$100	$50,000
100	CJ03 / Digital Mini-Projector	$50	$5,000

⑬	SUBTOTAL	$55,000
⑭	TAX	$4,400
⑮	H & S	$200
⑯	TOTAL	$59,600

⑰
1. Please send two copies of your invoice.
2. Enter this order in accordance with the prices, terms, delivery methods, and specifications listed above.
3. Please notify us immediately if you are unable to ship as specified.

⑱ *Michael Chiang* 1/5/2015

Authorized by   Date

1. 買方公司名稱	7. 付款條件	13. 小計
2. 訂單編號與訂購日期	8. 到貨日期	14. 稅金
3. 供應商資訊	9. 訂購數量	15. 處理及貨運費用
4. 送貨地址	10. 商品編號與內容敘述	16. 總計
5. 送貨方式	11. 單價	17. 備註欄
6. 貨運條件	12. 單項小計	18. 買方授權人及授權日期

隨堂練習

★ 請根據句意，選出最適合的單字

( ) 1. Mr. Benton was _____ from the committee and replaced by Mr. Smith because of the infamous affair with his secretary.
(A) dispatched (B) reimbursed
(C) discharged (D) estimated

( ) 2. Since Beth is a workaholic, it's not easy for her to _____ from working full-time to retirement.
(A) erect (B) transition
(C) solicit (D) quote

( ) 3. It's common to _____ over the price when you make a purchase at a night market.
(A) haggle (B) assure
(C) linger (D) misdirect

( ) 4. This phone is still under _____, so it can be returned for repair for free.
(A) preference (B) invoice
(C) inventory (D) warranty

( ) 5. This car was manufactured to EU _____, which means you don't need to worry about its quality.
(A) logistics (B) specifications
(C) patrons (D) receipts

解答：1. C　2. B　3. A　4. D　5. B

Unit 8 廣告與宣傳

中級

1. **abstract**

[ˈæbstrækt]

adj. 抽象的

⇨ **abs** - 「從…離開」+ - **tract** - 「抽出」，脫離具體事物就是抽象的

The boss wants an ad that appeals directly to the consumers' desires- nothing **abstract**.

老闆想要一個會直接觸動消費者慾望的廣告 - 不要抽象的東西。

> 補充　abstract concept/knowledge　抽象的概念 / 知識

abstraction n. 抽象概念；心不在焉

反 concrete adj. 具體的

中高

2. **abundance**

[əˈbʌndəns]

n. 豐富；充足

 ab - 「從…分開」+ **unda**「拉丁文，表波浪」+ - **ance**「名詞字尾」

There is an **abundance** of topics you can find in our online magazine archives.

你可以在我們線上雜誌的資料庫裡面找到豐富的主題。

> 補充　in abundance　　　充足地
> an abundance of N.　豐富的 N.

同 plenty

初級

3. **advantage**

[ədˈvæntɪdʒ]

n. 優勢，好處

⇨ **advance**「向前」+ - **age**「名詞字尾」，使人向前進步就是優勢

We have the **advantage** of being appealing to the younger demographic.

我們具有能吸引年輕族群的優勢。

> 補充　a comparative advantage　相對優勢
> a competitive advantage　競爭優勢
> have an advantage in + N.　在 N. 方面有優勢
> take advantage of + N.
> 善加利用 N.；佔 N. 的便宜

advantageous adj. 有利的

反 disadvantage n. 缺點；弱點

初級

4. **advertisement**

[ˌædvɚˈtaɪzmənt]

n. 廣告

⇨ ad-「to」+ -vert-「轉向」+ -ise「使…」+ -ment「名詞字尾」，會使你轉過頭來看的東西就是廣告

We now favor posting our online **advertisements** on the most popular web sites.

我們現在很喜歡在最受歡迎的網站上刊登線上廣告。

補充
run an ad　　　　　　　　刊登廣告
place/put an advertisement 刊登廣告
a full-page advertisement　全版廣告
a television/newspaper advertisement
電視／報紙廣告

advertise v. 刊登廣告
advertiser n. 刊登廣告者

縮 ad

---

5. **affordable**

[əˈfɔrdəbl]

adj. 負擔得起的

⇨ **afford**「買得起」+ -able「可…的」

Our goal is to produce a product that is **affordable** enough for the middle class, but of high quality.

我們的目標是生產高品質、但中產階級可負擔得起的產品。

補充　be affordable for sb. 是某人負擔得起的

afford v. 買得起、足以負擔

中級

6. **appeal**

[əˈpil]

v. 對…有吸引力；呼籲，懇求

n. 懇請；吸引力

The Wednesday night comedy TV lineup at our network **appeals** to almost everyone.

我們電視聯播網週三晚間的連播喜劇吸引了幾乎所有的人。

補充
market appeal　　　市場吸引力
appeal to sb. for N. 向某人呼籲、請其協助提供 N.

appealing adj. 有吸引力的

同 attract v. 吸引

易混 appear v. 出現

230

初級

7. **appear**

[ə'pɪr]

v. 出現；似乎

After several executives have made short speeches, the CEO will **appear** for a motivational pep talk.
在幾位主管發表完簡短演說之後，執行長會出來進行精神喊話。

補充　appear to be adj./N.　看起來像…

appearance n. 外表

同　出現：come out / arise / emerge

反　disappear　v. 消失

中高

8. **authentic**

[ɔ'θɜntɪk]

adj. 可信的；可靠的；真實的

 aut -「自己」+ -hent -「做事的人」+ -ic「形容詞字尾」

Many of the shops on the west side are cheaper because they don't carry **authentic** name brands.
西區很多商店比較便宜是因爲它們不是正宗的名牌。

authenticity n. 可信度；確實性

同　reliable / true

---

9. **awareness**

[ə'wɛrnɪs]

n. 察覺；覺悟、體認

⇨ aware「察覺的」+ -ness「表狀態」

There is plenty of public **awareness** about the issue of sweatshops, but people still buy the clothes that are made there.
雖然有很多大眾認知到血汗工廠的議題，但是人們還是會購買那裏出廠的衣服。

補充

raise public awareness	喚起大眾的認知
brand awareness	品牌認知
customer awareness	顧客認知
gender awareness	性別認知

self-awareness n. 自我意識；自知

中高

10. **banner**

['bænə]

n. 旗幟；(張貼或遊行隊伍用的) 橫幅

We proudly displayed our **banner** in front of our booth at the job fair at the convention center.
我們在會議中心的就業展覽會攤位前盛大地展示我們的號召旗幟。

補充

banner ad	網頁上的橫幅廣告
under the banner of N.	打著…的旗號

中高

11. **beforehand**

[bɪˈforˌhænd]

adv. 事先，預先

同 in advance

⇨ **before**「在…前」+ **hand**「手」，在著手之前就是事先

I always research the contractors we agree to do business with **beforehand**.

我都會預先調查我們同意進行生意往來的承包商。

中級

12. **campaign**

[kæmˈpen]

n. 競選活動；宣傳活動；戰役

I believe that our advertising **campaign** needs to go with a cooler, more relaxed theme.

我覺得我們的廣告宣傳活動需要搭配更酷、更輕鬆的主題。

補充	marketing campaign	行銷活動
	sales campaign	銷售活動
	advertising campaign	廣告活動
	launch a campaign for N.	發起 N. 的活動

同 movement

初級

13. **certainly**

[ˈsɝtənlɪ]

adv. 無疑地；必定、確實

同 definitely / surely

⇨ **certain**「確定的」+ **-ly**「副詞字尾」

There is **certainly** no good reason why we can't cut costs on office supplies and electricity!

我們為何無法減少辦公室用品和電費開銷，這鐵定沒什麼好理由！

補充 Certainly not! 當然不是！

---

14. **characterize**

[ˈkærəktəˌraɪz]

v. 以…為特徵；描繪…的特性

⇨ **character**「性格」+ **-ize**「使…化」

I would **characterize** Chase Manufacturing as shrewd and calculating.

我會說 Chase 製造公司的特色就是精明狡猾且善於算計。

補充 characterize A as B 將 A 描繪成 B

中級

15. circulation

[ˌsɝkjəˈleʃən]

n. 循環，運行；流通；（報刊 等的）發行量

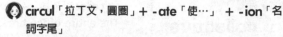 **circul**「拉丁文，圓圈」**+ -ate**「使…」**+ -ion**「名 詞字尾」

A number of magazines in recent years have gone out of **circulation** due to a lack of subscribers.
近年來很多雜誌因訂閱人數不足而停止發行了。

補充
go into circulation 開始流通
out of circulation 停止發行，停止流通

circulate v. 循環，流通，發行

中級

16. classify

[ˈklæsəˌfaɪ]

v. 分類

 class「等級」**+ -fy**「做…」

We only **classify** complaints into two categories: service or product-related.
我們只把客訴分為兩種：服務相關或產品相關。

補充
classified ad　　分類廣告
classify N. into... 將 N. 分類成…

同 categorize

中高

17. cluster

[ˈklʌstɚ]

n. 群、組

There was a **cluster** of people selling cookies on the street.
有一群人在街上販賣餅乾。

補充 to cluster around N. 群集在 N. 附近

同 bunch / group

中高

18. clutch

[klʌtʃ]

v. 抓住；攫取
n. 緊抓；控制

Barbara always **clutches** her reports whenever she tours around the office.
每次 Barbara 巡視辦公室的時候手裡總是緊抓著她的報告。

補充
to clutch at N.　　抓住 N.
clutch performer 在關鍵時刻能漂亮完成工作的人
A drowning man will clutch at a straw.
[諺語] 病急亂投醫。

同 v. = seize / grasp

中高

19. **collective**

[kəˈlɛktɪv]

adj. 集體的；共同的

⇨ **collect**「收集」+ **-ive**「有⋯性質的」

The entire office breathed a **collective** sigh of relief when the company rejected the merger proposal.
當公司回絕了合併提案時，整間辦公室都一同鬆了口氣。

補充
collective decision	共同的決定
collective responsibility	共同的責任

collect v. 收集
collection n. 收集品，收藏

同 united / combined

中級

20. **commercial**

[kəˈmɝʃəl]

n. 商業廣告

adj. 商業的；能賺錢的；商業化的

⇨ **com-**「一起」+ **-merce-**「商品，買賣」+ **-ial**「形容詞字尾」

Why was the TV show interrupted by so many **commercials**?
為什麼那檔電視節目被插進那麼多商業廣告？

補充
commercial film	商業廣告片（簡稱 commercial）
commercial break	廣告時間（電視或電台節目中插播廣告的時間）
commercial property	商業地產，商業大樓
commercial value	商業價值
commercial success/failure	商業上成功／失敗

commerce n. 商業

同 n. = advertisement

中高

21. **comparable**

[ˈkɑmpərəbl]

adj. 比得上的，可比較的

 compare「比較」+ **-able**「可⋯的」

We offer a product that is **comparable** to the big name brands in every way except the high prices.
我們提供的產品在各方面都足以和知名品牌相比，卻又不像它們那麼昂貴。

補充 be comparable to N. 和 N. 是可相比的、比得上的

compare v. 比較
comparasion n. 比較，對照

反 incomparable adj. 無可匹敵的

易混 compatible adj. 可相容的

22. complimentary
[ˌkɑmpləˈmɛntərɪ]
adj. 讚賞的，恭維的；
贈送的，免費的

 comply「順從」+ **-ment**「名詞字尾」+ **-ary**「關於…的」

We offer a **complimentary** tire rotation when you purchase an oil change at regular price.
您以正常價格進行換油，我們會提供免費的輪胎換位服務。

> 補充　complimentary close　書信的結尾敬語

compliment n./v. 恭維，讚美

中級

23. confidence
[ˈkɑnfədəns]
n. 信心；自信，把握

⇨ **con-**「一起」+ **-fid-**「信任」+ **-ence**「名詞字尾」

If you want to be a good salesperson, you have to build up your own self-**confidence** because you'll be rejected often.
如果你想要成為一位好業務，你必須建立好你的自信心，因為你會常被人拒絕。

> 補充
> have confidence in sb.　對某人有信心
> boost sb.'s confidence　提振某人的信心
> consumer confidence　消費者信心
> business confidence　企業信心

confide v. 透露（秘密）；託付
confident adj. 有自信的

中級

24. contemporary
[kənˈtɛmpəˌrɛrɪ]
adj. 當代的、現代的；同時期的
n. 當代的、現代的人事物；同時期的人事物

⇨ **con-**「共同」+ **-tempor-**「時間」+ **-ary**「形容詞字尾」

The interior of this building should be renovated with a more **contemporary** design.
這棟大樓的室內設計應該整修得更具現代感。

> 補充
> contemporary business environment
> 當前的商業環境
> contemporary design　當代設計

中級

25. critic
[ˈkrɪtɪk]
n. 評論家

Most **critics** find the novel pleasurable, but a few believe it is too strongly directed at teenagers.
大部分的評論家都覺得這本小說寫得很好，不過有些人認為它太過於針對青少年了。

> 補充
> a music critic　音樂評論者 = 樂評
> a movie critic　電影評論者 = 影評
> a literary critic　文學評論者

criticism n. 批評，評論
criticize v. 批評、批判，苛求
critical adj. 批評的；至關重要的；危急的

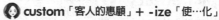

26. customize

[ˈkʌstəmˌaɪz]
v. 客製化；訂做

 custom「客人的惠顧」＋ **-ize**「使⋯化」

We can **customize** the embroidery on your sweatshirt for just a few dollars more.
只要多加一點錢，我們就可以為您客製化長袖運動衫上面的刺繡。

> **補充**
> a customized car/sofa/suit
> 客製化汽車 / 沙發 / 西裝
> customize sth. to N. 根據 N. 客製化某物

customized adj. 客製化的；訂做的
customization n. 客製化服務

中級

27. distinction

[dɪˈstɪŋkʃən]
n. 區別；分清

 dis-「分開」＋ **-stinct-**「刺」＋ **-ion**「名詞字尾」

Marco holds the **distinction** of being the only associate here who has ever made a successful pitch to the CEO.
Marco 不同於別人之處就在於他是這裡唯一曾向執行長提出建言而有被採納的同仁。

★ make a successful pitch：成功投出好球，形容下屬提出的想法能被長官採納。

> **補充** a distinction between A and B A 與 B 之間的區別

distinct adj. 有區別的；明顯的

---

28. effectiveness

[ɪˈfɛktɪvnɪs]
n. 有效用；效力好

⇨ **effect**「效果」＋ **-ive**「有⋯性質的」＋ **-ness**「名詞字尾」

The **effectiveness** of the author's book tour can be seen clearly by the uptick in sales just this past week.
僅從過去這一週上漲的業績來看，就可清楚看出這位作者巡迴簽書會的成效。

> **補充**
> effect 是指「效果、作用」，所有不論是好的效果還是壞的效果都是 effect；effectiveness 指「有效果、有用」，特別指好的方面的效果。

effect n. 效果，效用
effective adj. 有效果的、有作用的

中級

29. endurance
[ɪnˋdjʊrəns]
n. 忍耐力；持久力

⇨ **en-**「在…」+ **-dura-**「硬，堅固」+ **-ance**「表狀態」，在堅固的狀態才耐得住外力

Our new smart phone model provides better battery **endurance**.
我們新型號的智慧型手機提供更好的電池續航力。

補充	human endurance	人體耐力
	endurance test	耐力測試
	beyond endurance	超過忍耐限度

endure v. 容忍，忍耐

初級

30. energy
[ˋɛnɚdʒɪ]
n. 能量，活力；能源

⇨ **en-**「在…」+ **-erg-**「工作」+ **-y**「名詞字尾」，在工作中的狀態就是有活力

The billboard often displays ads for **energy** drinks featuring physically fit youngsters.
廣告招牌上面常常會展示以身材健美的年輕人為特色的機能性飲料廣告。

補充	energy-efficient	節能的
	energy supply	能源供應
	energy waste	能源浪費
	eco-energy = renewable energy	再生能源
	alternative energy	替代性能源

同 活力：vigor / strength

中級

31. ensure
[ɪnˋʃʊr]
v. 保證；擔保

⇨ **en-**「使…」+ **sure**「確定的」

Changing our distributor will **ensure** that the first load of books will arrive on time.
更換我們的經銷商可確保第一批進書準時到貨。

| 補充 | ensure A + B | 確保 A 能有 B |
| | ensure + that 子句 | 確保… |

中級

32. entitle
[ɪnˋtaɪtl̩]
v. 賦予權力或資格

⇨ **en-**「使…」+ **title**「頭銜」，使有頭銜便有資格

The success of our company does not **entitle** us to sit back and relax.
我們公司的成功並不代表我們有資格坐在那裏納涼就好。

| 補充 | entitle sb. to V. | 授權某人去做… |
| | be entitled to V. | 有權做… |

同 authorize / empower

中高

33. essence
[ˈɛsn̩s]
n. 本質；精華

⇨ esse「拉丁文，存在」+ -ence「性質」

The novel is, in essence, about a poor farm boy's journey to manhood.
這本小說本質上是關於一個貧窮的農村男孩長大成人的歷程。

典故 essence 原用來指基督教三位一體的本質，後來字義擴大到指事物的本質、精髓

補充 N. be of the essence　N. 是最重要的、最必要的
in essence　　　　　基本上

essential adj. 本質的、實質的；必要的

同 nature

中級

34. exaggerate
[ɪgˈzædʒəˌret]
v. 誇大；誇張

 ex-「向外」+ ag-「to」+ -ger-「攜帶，運送」+ -ate「使…」

Should a good advertisement exaggerate the benefits of the product?
一則好廣告應該誇大產品的優點嗎？

exaggerated adj. 誇大的；言過其實的
exaggeration n. 誇張；誇大其辭

同 overstate

中高

35. excel
[ɪkˈsɛl]
v. 勝過；優於

⇨ ex-「向外」+ -cel-「拉高」，高人一等就是比較優秀

The motivational speaker claims to excel at selling real estate, but the only thing he can really sell is books.
這位激勵演講人聲稱在賣房地產這方面勝過別人，不過他真正能賣的只有書而已。

補充 excel in/at N. 在 N. 方面優於他人

excellent adj. 優秀的；傑出的
excellence n. 優秀；傑出

中級

36. exceptional
[ɪkˈsɛpʃən̩l]
adj. 卓越的；罕見的；不尋常的

⇨ except「除外」+ -ion「名詞字尾」+ -al「形容詞字尾」

The company claims that their customer service is exceptional.
這間公司聲稱他們的客戶服務十分卓越。

補充 in exceptional circumstances 在特殊情況下

except prep. 除…外
exception n. 例外；除外的人事物

同 unusual adj. 不尋常的
extrodinary adj. 卓越的

中高

37. fad

[fæd]

n. 一時的流行、風尚

I hate to break this to you, but that latest gadget you've been selling is just a passing **fad**.

我很不想告訴你這個壞消息，但你在賣的那個最新款小玩意兒其實早就過時了。

補充	a fad for N.	N. 的流行
	the latest fad	最新的流行
	a passing fad	過時的流行

易混 fade v. 枯萎；褪色

中級

38. favorable

['fevərəbl]

adj. 有利的；適合的；贊同的

⇨ favor「好處，偏坦」＋ -able「可…的」

Although my last novel got **favorable** reviews, the publisher does not want to renew our contract.

雖然我的上一本小說得到不錯的評價，但是出版商並不想續約。

補充	A make a favorable impression on B 使 B 對 A 有好印象
	be favorable to N. 對 N. 有利

favor v. 偏坦；有利於…
favorite adj. 最喜愛的

中級

39. feature

['fitʃɚ]

n. 特色；特徵

v. 以…為特色；由…主演

 feat「功績」＋ -ure「名詞字尾」

A slick logo with neon colors is one of the distinctive **features** of Cracks Soda Company.

有著霓虹色的光滑標誌是 Cracks 汽水公司與眾不同的特徵之一。

補充	additional features 額外的特色
	distinctive/distinguishing feature 與眾不同的 / 顯著的特色
	key feature of N. N. 的主要特色

---

40. flyer

['flaɪɚ]

n. 廣告傳單，宣傳單

⇨ fly「飛」＋ -er「做…動作的人或物品」，宣傳單總是滿天飛

Harry couldn't afford anything more for advertising on his small business budget than printing up a few **flyers**.

以 Harry 的小公司預算，他只負擔得起印一些宣傳單的廣告方式。

補充	distribute/hand out/pass out flyers 散發傳單

fly v. 飛
同 leaflet

中級

41. identification

[aɪˌdɛntəfəˈkeʃən]

n. 識別；身分證明文件

⇨ identity「身分」+ -fic-「做」+ -ation「名詞字尾」，能做出身分的東西就是身分證明

Without proper **identification**, Candy could only inform the front desk security guard that she was there for an interview.

沒有適當的身分證明文件，Candy 只能告知櫃台警衛她是去那裏面試的。

 補充　identification card　身分證
identification number　識別號碼

identity n. 身分
identify v. 表明；認出

初級

42. individual

[ˌɪndəˈvɪdʒəl]

n. 個體
adj. 個體的，個別的

⇨ in-「表否定」+ divide「分開」+ -ual「有關…的」，分到不能再分的就是個體

The small packet of candy was marked 'not for **individual** sale'.

這小包糖果上標示著「不個別銷售」。

 補充　individual income tax　　　　　個人所得稅
individual saving account　　　個人儲蓄帳戶
individual retirement account　個人退休金帳戶

---

43. inexpensive

[ˌɪnɪkˈspɛnsɪv]

adj. 不貴的

⇨ in-「表否定」+ expensive「昂貴的」

With a forty-percent discount, the jewelry was, in fact, quite **inexpensive**.

因爲打了六折，這些珠寶實際上真的不貴。

同 cheap / low-priced
反 expensive adj. 昂貴的

中高

44. infinite

[ˈɪnfənɪt]

adj. 極大的；無限的

⇨ in-「表否定」+ -fin-「結束」+ -ite「形容詞字尾」，沒有結束的就是極大的、無限的

Since we don't have an **infinite** amount of money for advertising, we have to choose the right channels to reach the most potential buyers.

由於我們沒有無限多的錢做廣告，我們得選擇正確的管道好接觸到最有可能的買家。

infinity n. 無限；無窮大

初級

45. **influence**
['ɪnfluəns]
n./v. 影響

⇨ **in-**「進入」+ **-flu-**「流動」+ **-ence**「名詞字尾」，流進來就會影響到原來的東西

Under the **influence** of such a strong mentor, I learned the ropes of the business quickly.
在如此強大的指導者的影響下，我很快就學會了做這門生意的竅門。

補充　expand influence on sth. 拓展在某事物上的影響力
have a strong influence on sb.
對某人產生很強烈的影響

同 v. = affect

---

46. **intercept**
[ˌɪntɚ'sɛpt]
v. 攔截

⇨ **inter-**「在…之間」+ **-cept-**「拿」，從中間拿就是攔截

Our company's cyber security department **intercepted** emails that were being sent out with classified information.
我們公司的網路安全部攔截了幾封正被寄出去、內含機密訊息的電子郵件。

補充　intercept interview　街頭訪問
intercept calls/emails
攔截（監聽、監看）電話／電子郵件

interception n. 攔截

---

47. **introductory**
[ˌɪntrə'dʌktərɪ]
adj. 介紹的；預備的；
新開始的

 intro-「向內」+ **-duc-**「拉」+ **-tory**「形容詞字尾」

Our **introductory** service package includes two hundred minutes of free air time and free text messages.
我們的新用戶服務方案包含兩百分鐘的免費通話時間和免費簡訊。

補充　introductory offer/bonus/discount
試賣（新用戶）優惠／回饋／折扣
an introductory course　入門課程
an introductory price　上市價，試銷優惠價

introduce v. 介紹
introduction n. 介紹，引見；引言
同 opening / starting

48. irresistible

[ˌɪrɪˈzɪstəbḷ]

adj. 富有誘惑力的；無法抗拒的

resist v. 抵抗

⇨ **ir -**「表否定」**＋ resist**「抵抗」**＋ -ible**「可⋯的」

For most people, clearance sales are just **irresistible**.
對大部份的人來說，清倉大拍賣就是令人無法抗拒。

補充　an irresistible offer 誘人的機會、提議

同 resistless

反 resistible adj. 可抵抗的，抵擋得住的

中級

49. issue

[ˈɪʃu]

n. 發行物；議題
v. 發行；發佈；發給

You can read the magazine's previous **issues** on the website.
你可以在網站上看該雜誌的前期內容。

補充
take issue with sb. on/over sth.
就某事和某人進行爭辯，不同意某人對某事的看法
issue shares/bonds 　　發行股票／債券
issue a report/warning 發佈報告／警告
issue sth. to sb. 　　　簽發某物給某人

中級

50. leaflet

[ˈliflɪt]

n. 傳單；廣告單張

⇨ **leaf**「葉片」**＋ -let**「小的東西」，廣告單就像葉片一樣小小一張

I spent all morning sliding **leaflets** under people's doors.
我花了一整個早上把傳單塞進別人家門裡。

補充　distribute/hand out/pass out leaflets
散發、分送廣告單

同 flyer

中高

51. logo

[ˈlogo]

n. 標誌；商標

Rather than hire an outside company, I used the limited design software we had to design our company **logo**.
我沒有請外面的公司，而是用我們有限的設計軟體來設計我們的公司標誌。

典故
logo 為 logotype 的縮寫。logotype 原指將印刷用的活字組裝印製出不連貫的字樣或標誌，最早用於標示物品的所有人。

中級

52. **majority**

[mə`dʒɔrətɪ]

n. 多數；大多數

⇨ **major**「主要的」+ **-ity**「名詞字尾」

A **majority** of those surveyed admitted that our coffee was richer than other brands.

大多數的受訪者承認我們的咖啡比其他牌子的咖啡味道更濃厚。

補充	be in the majority	佔絕大多數
	absolute majority	絕對多數
	the silent majority	沉默的大多數
	the majority of N.	大多數的 N.

major adj. 主要的 n./v. 主修

反 minority n. 少數

初級

53. **match**

[mætʃ]

v. 相符，相配

n. 運動比賽；對手；相配者；火柴

We need to make sure we **match** the right actors together for this commercial so they look like a real family.

我們要確認找到可搭配的演員一起拍這支廣告，這樣他們看起來才會像真正的一家人。

| 補充 | be no match for N. | 無法與 N. 抗衡 |
| | meet sb's match | 棋逢敵手 |

---

54. **maximize**

[`mæksɪ͵maɪz]

v. 使最大化

⇨ **maxim**「最大量」+ **-ize**「使…化」

In order to **maximize** your potential, you can supplement your skills by taking extra classes.

為了將你的潛能發揮到最大，你可以藉由去上額外課程來補強你的技能。

| 補充 | maximize sb's efficiency | 使某人的效率最大化 |
| | maximize profit/sales | 使利益／銷售量最大化 |

反 minimize v. 使減到最少；使縮到最小

中高

55. **merchandise**

[`mɝtʃən͵daɪz]

n. 商品；貨物

v. 促銷；推銷

 merchant「商人」+ **-ise**「使…化」

I no longer shop at that online store because they often ship me the wrong **merchandise**.

我再也不在那間網路商店購物，因為他們常送錯商品給我。

補充	discounted merchandise	折扣商品
	luxury merchandise	奢侈商品
	merchandise mix	商品組合

merchant n. 商人

同 n. = commodity / goods

56. noteworthy

[`notˌwɝðɪ]

adj. 顯著的；值得注意的

➪ note「注意」+ worthy「值得的」

My bad experience with a customer service rep is **noteworthy**, but I still hold an overall positive view of the company.

我和該公司客服代表很明顯有過不愉快的經驗，不過我對該公司整體上還是抱持正面的看法。

| 補充 | A be noteworthy for B　A 以 B 而聞名
It is noteworthy + that 子句　…是值得注意的 |

同 remarkable

中高

57. occurrence

[əˈkɝəns]

n. 發生、出現的事件

同 happening / event

➪ occur「發生」+ -ence「名詞字尾」

Ken missed the deadline again today, and I told him if he has one more **occurrence**, he will be fired.

Ken 今天又再次錯過最後期限了，而我告訴他如果再發生一次他就會被解僱了。

初級

58. offer

[`ɔfɚ]

n. 提議；出價

v. 提供；提議

➪ of-「to」+ -fer-「攜帶」，帶來就是要提供給你的東西

We will have a special **offer** next week - buy one, get one free.

我們下週會有買一送一的特別優惠。

| 補充 | a job offer　工作機會
introductory offer 試賣優惠
make an offer　出價
accept/turn down an offer
接受 / 拒絕工作機會、提議或出價
offer sb. sth. = offer sth. to sb.　提供某物給某人 |

offering n. 所提供的物品、事物

同 v. = provide / supply

中高

59. pamphlet

[`pæmflɪt]

n. 小冊子

 pam-「全面的」+ -phl-「愛」+ -let「小的東西」

This **pamphlet** explains more about our church, our regular activities, and upcoming special events.

這本小冊子對我們教會、我們固定的活動和即將舉辦的特別活動有更詳細的介紹。

| 典故 | pamphlet 原指把所有的愛都裝在裡面的一個小東西，12 世紀時是一首著名情詩的標題，中世紀時廣泛刊載流傳於民間，到今日就是指「把想表達的意思都放進去的小冊子」，也就是宣傳用的「小手冊」。 |

pamphleteer n. 小冊子的作者

中級

60. **pitch**

[pɪtʃ]

n. 廣告詞；(BrE)（街道攤販的）攤位；（街頭藝人的）表演場地

v. 投擲

A good salesperson needs to learn how to deliver a good sales **pitch**.
一個優秀的銷售員必須學會如何傳達強有力的銷售話術。

補充
sales pitch　　　　　推銷詞
make a pitch for N.　努力推動 N.

---

61. **popularity**

[ˌpɑpjəˈlærətɪ]

n. 受歡迎程度，流行，普及

⇨ **popular**「受歡迎的」+ **-ity**「狀態」
The **popularity** of our products is such that we don't even need to advertise.
我們的產品大受歡迎到我們甚至不需要打廣告。

補充
win/lost popularity with/among N.
贏得 / 失去 N. 的歡迎

popular adj. 受歡迎的；流行的

初級

62. **post**

[post]

v. 張貼

n. 職位

If you want to find the right job candidate, you need to **post** your job vacancy on all the top employment sites.
如果你想找到合適的求職人選，你得把你的職缺訊息張貼在所有一流的求職網站上。

補充
post A on B　將 A 貼到 B 上
post N. on the website/Internet
將 N. 公開到網站 / 網路上
Post-It note　便利貼

中高

63. **prevalent**

[ˈprɛvələnt]

adj. 盛行的，流行的；普遍的

同 common / widespread

 pre-「在前」+ **-val-**「有力量」+ **-ent**「形容詞字尾」
Cell phones were not as **prevalent** until the new millennium.
直到西元兩千年手機才開始普及。

補充
be prevalent among N. 在 N. 中很流行、很普遍

中級
64. promotion
[prə`moʃən]
n. 推銷；宣傳；促進；提倡；升職

⇨ promote「宣傳，推動」+ -ion「名詞字尾」

We do product **promotions** using text messages as well as giving out flyers.

我們用發簡訊和傳單來做商品促銷。

 補充

sales promotion	促銷
heavy promotion	大量宣傳
in-pack promotion	套裝促銷
promotion strategy	促銷策略

promote v. 宣傳；推動；擢升
promotional adj. 推銷的；促銷的

中級
65. publicity
[pʌb`lɪsətɪ]
n. 公眾的注意；宣傳，宣傳品

⇨ public「公開的」+ -ity「名詞字尾」

The sexual harassment lawsuit has brought us too much negative **publicity**.

那件性騷擾訴訟已經帶給我們太多負面宣傳了。

 補充

a publicity budget	宣傳預算
a publicity campaign	宣傳活動
a publicity stunt	宣傳噱頭

public adj. 公開的；公眾的
publicize v. 廣告；公布

---

66. publish
[`pʌblɪʃ]
v. 出版、發行；公開

⇨ public「公開的」+ -ish「使變成」

This position requires that candidates have **published** three or more articles in scientific journals.

這個職位的應徵者需具備曾經在科學期刊上發表過三篇以上文章的經驗。

 補充

publish an article/a report	發表一篇文章／報導
publish A in/on B	在 B 上刊出 A

publication n. 出版；出版物

初級
67. regret
[rɪ`grɛt]
v./n. 後悔，遺憾

⇨ re-「一再」+ -gret-「痛哭」，一再痛哭表示後悔

I will never **regret** starting my own advertising agency, no matter how much of a struggle it is.

我不會後悔成立自己的廣告代理公司，不論那是多麼困難的一件事。

 補充

letter of regret 致歉函（寄給未合格求職者的信）

中高

68. **reliance**

[rɪˈlaɪəns]

n. 信賴；依賴

⇨ rely「信賴」+ -ance「性質」

We have reduced our **reliance** on the grid by installing solar panels on our roof.

透過在屋頂上安裝太陽能電板，我們已降低了對一般電力的依賴。

補充 place reliance on N. 依賴或信賴 N.

rely v. 依靠；信賴
reliant adj. 依賴的

同 dependence

中高

69. **revelation**

[ˌrɛvləˈreʃən]

n. 揭示；曝露，顯示

 reveal「曝露」+ -ation「名詞字尾」

The share price of this company plunged 20% after the **revelation** that the CEO was charged with insider trading.

這家公司的執行長被控內線交易消息一出後，公司的股價暴跌了 20%。

補充 come as a revelation 令人大為驚喜

reveal v. 曝露、洩露，揭示

中級

70. **satisfaction**

[ˌsætɪsˈfækʃən]

n. 滿意

⇨ -satis-「足夠的」+ -fac-「做」+ -tion「名詞字尾」，做得夠好使人滿意

We strive for one-hundred percent customer **satisfaction**, but the closest we can get is ninety-five percent.

我們努力要把顧客滿意度做到百分百，但我們最多只達到了 95%。

補充
customer/client satisfaction 顧客滿意度
job satisfaction 工作滿意度
employee satisfaction survey 員工滿意度調查
to the satisfaction of sb.
達到令某人滿意的結果

satisfy v. 使滿意、使滿足
satisfactory adj. 令人滿意的，符合要求的

中級

71. **saving**

['sevɪŋ]

n. 省下的錢；存款

save v. 儲存；節省；拯救

⇨ save「儲存」+ -ing「名詞字尾」

We project that cutting 200 jobs will translate into **savings** of two million dollars.

我們預計縮減兩百個職位將可省下兩百萬元。

 make huge savings 省下一大筆錢

中級

72. **secure**

[sɪ'kjur]

adj. 安全的

v. 使安全；獲得，招致

⇨ se-「分開」+ -cure-「照顧」，分開照顧以確保安全

This manufacturer claims that their latest stroller is the most **secure** model ever.

這家製造商聲稱他們最新款的嬰兒推車是史上最安全的款式。

This saving plan is perfect for **securing** your children's future.

這個儲蓄計劃對保障你們孩子的未來是最完美的。

 make a secure online transaction
進行網路安全交易
a secure network/site 安全網路 / 網站
secure a deal　　　　完成交易

security n. 安全，安全感

同 safe adj. 安全的

反 insecure adj. 不安全的；沒有安全感的

初級

73. **select**

[sə'lɛkt]

v. 挑選

adj. 精選的

selection n. 挑選出來的東西；選拔
selective adj. 有選擇性的

⇨ se-「分開」+ -lect-「收集」，將收集品分類便是挑選

Make sure you **select** the box for "express" delivery, or you may wait up to ten days for your package.

確認你所選的是「快遞」的箱子，不然你可能要等上 10 天才收得到你的包裹。

 select A for B 為 B 選 A
select A as B 選 A 來當 B

同 v. = choose / pick out

74. shortage

中級

[`ʃɔrtɪdʒ]
n. 缺少，不足，匱乏

 ➪ short「短缺」+ -age「名詞字尾」

If sales stay at this level, we will have a major supply **shortage** soon.
如果銷售額維持在這樣的水平，我們很快就會面臨嚴重的供應短缺。

> **補充**
> food/water shortage　食物 / 水源短缺
> staff shortage　　　　人力短缺

short adj. 短缺的

同 deficit

---

75. shortcoming

中級

[`ʃɔrtkʌmɪŋ]
n. 缺點，短處
同 defect / drawback

➪ short「短缺」+ coming「出現」

Despite his **shortcomings**, Robert always makes his best effort.
儘管 Robert 有缺點，但他總是盡他最大的努力。

---

76. slogan

中級

[`sloɡən]
n. 口號；標語

We had our company **slogan** printed on sweatshirts and gave them away to all the marathon participants.
我們將公司標語印在運動衫上面並把它們送給所有參加馬拉松的選手。

> **典故**
> slogan 最早是指戰爭時大聲喊出的口號。18 世紀時，slogan 被用來指不同政治立場族群用以區隔彼此的字句。現在 slogan 則是吸引注意力的標語。

> **補充**
> advertising slogan　廣告標語
> marketing slogan　　行銷標語
> catchy slogan　　　　吸引人的標語

同 catchword

---

77. specimen

中高

[`spɛsəmən]
n. 樣品；樣本

 -speci-「看」+ -men「名詞字尾」

This is a **specimen** of the new fabric. It has better flexibility compared with the old one.
這是新布料的樣品。與舊款相比它的彈性更好。

> **補充**
> specimen signature card
> （銀行）印鑑卡、簽名對照卡

初級

78. spread

[sprɛd]

v. 散播；傳佈

n. 散播；跨頁廣告

Word of our off-Broadway play **spread** quickly, and we sold out for the rest of the month.

有關我們的外百老匯戲劇演出的風聲快速傳遍，我們這個月剩下的票都賣光了。

★off-Broadway play：外百老匯戲劇，指百老匯劇場裡規模較小、製作成本較低的戲劇，若成功的話就能變成正式的百老匯秀。

補充	spread the costs	分攤費用
	spread the risk	分散風險
	spread the load	分攤工作量
	spread the word	將話傳播出去
	a double-page spread	兩頁的跨頁廣告

中高

79. stability

[stə`bɪlətɪ]

n. 安定，穩定性

stable adj. 穩定的；安定的

同 steadiness

⇨ **-sta-**「站立」+ **ability**「能力」

The officials assured the public that they will do their best to maintain the interest rate **stability**.

官員向大眾保證他們會盡力維持利率穩定。

| 補充 | economic/financial stability 經濟／金融安定 |
| | price/rate stability　　　　　價格／利率穩定度 |

中高

80. stereotype

[`stɛrɪə,taɪp]

n. 刻板印象

v. 對…有刻板印象

 stereo「希臘文，堅固的」+ **type**「打字，印刷」

Our office underwent sensitivity training to help prevent workers from having **stereotypes** about those who are different.

我們公司進行了敏感性訓練，以協助員工們避免對與他們不同的人產生刻板印象。

★sensitivity training：敏感性訓練，指透過小團體中的人際互動，使團體裡的成員能學習對其他成員的感受更加敏感、更容易理解別人需求，並進一步覺察自己內在動機的一種訓練。

| 典故 | 打字和印刷都要先在板子上刻好一個個的字母，刻好的字就無法更動，stereotype 就是指腦中的想法就像在硬鋼板刻上的東西一樣無法更改，也就是我們常說的「刻板印象」。 |

中高

81. stylish
[ˋstaɪlɪʃ]
adj. 時髦的；流行的

style n. 風格、類型、式樣
stylishly adv. 時髦地；流行地

同 fashionable / modern

⇨ **style**「風格，類型」＋ **-ish**「具…性質的」

The graphic design of our magazine color is **stylish** enough without having to feature gorgeous models.
我們雜誌色彩的平面設計不需要用漂亮的模特兒就已經夠時髦了。

中高

82. subscribe
[səbˋskraɪb]
v. 訂閱；認捐，認購

 sub-「在下方」＋ **-scribe-**「書寫」

To listen to the show or **subscribe** to our broadcast, visit our website.
要收聽或是訂閱我們的廣播節目請來我們的網站。

補充
subscribe to N.
訂閱 N. / 提供認捐給 N. / 同意，贊許 N.

subscription n. 訂閱；訂閱費；認捐；捐款

中級

83. suitable
[ˋsutəbl̩]
adj. 合適的；適宜的

⇨ **suit**「適合」＋ **-able**「可…的」

Our goal is to provide every customer with the most **suitable** health plan.
我們的宗旨是提供最適合每位顧客的健康計劃。

補充
be suitable for sb. 適合某人
suitable to V. 適合去做某事

suit v. 適合；與…相配

同 acceptable / appropriate / fitting

反 unsuitable adj. 不適合的

---

84. testimonial
[͵tɛstəˋmonɪəl]
n. 證明書；推薦書；證言

⇨ **-test-**「試驗」＋ **-mony**「表功能」＋ **-al**「表事物」

According to customer **testimonials**, our service is second to none.
根據客戶證言，我們的服務是最好的。

補充
customer/product testimonial 客戶 / 產品證言
testimonial from N. N. 的見證說明

testimony n. 見證；證詞、證言

中高

85. **thereafter**

[ðɛr`æftɚ]

adv. 之後，以後

⇨ **there**「那裡」+ **after**「在…後」

Thereafter, all the novels that are released in this series will focus on the romance between the two lead characters.

之後，這系列發行的所有小說會著重在兩個主角之間的愛情故事。

同 after that / then / afterwards

中高

86. **trait**

[tret]

n. 特徵，特點

Mark has all the right **traits** to be a successful manager, but he is choosing to stay at home with his young children.

Mark 具備一個成功經理人該有的所有好特質，但他選擇待在家陪伴他的小孩。

補充 character/personality traits 性格 / 個性特徵

同 characteristic

中高

87. **transparent**

[træns`pɛrənt]

adj. 透明的；清澈的；易懂的

trans-「穿越」+ **-par-**「出現」+ **-ent**「具…性質的」

Our budget must be totally **transparent** to give our entire corporation peace of mind.

我們的預算必須完全透明才能讓整間公司安心。

補充
be transparent about N.
對於某事物很公開、明確
a transparent environment/process
透明的環境 / 過程

同 obvious

反 opaque adj. 不透明的；難理解的

中高

88. **tribute**

[`trɪbjut]

n. 貢品；(表達敬仰的) 禮贈品

The entire ceremony paid **tribute** to our firm's founder, who recently passed away.

這整個典禮是在歌頌我們公司的創辦者，他最近過世了。

 典故 tribute 來自拉丁文 tributus，裡面有個 tribe 指「部落、部族」，以前部落時代小部落要安全存活就需提供強大部落禮贈品以交換保護，而 tributus 就是用來換取保護的貢品，也就是今天英文裡的 tribute。

 補充 pay tribute to N. 對 N. 加以讚揚、歌頌
A be a tribute to B　A 是對 B 最好的證明、讚美

89. **unprecedented**

[ʌnˋprɛsəˌdɛntɪd]

adj. 史無前例的；空前的

⇨ un-「表否定」＋ precedent「前例，先例」＋ -ed「形容詞字尾」

The drop in the stock market is **unprecedented**, and took a lot of people by surprise.

這次股市史無前例的下跌讓很多人大吃一驚。

補充　on an unprecedented scale 以史無前例的規模

precedent adj. 在前的、先前的　n. 前例，先例

---

90. **variable**

[ˋvɛrɪəbl]

adj. 多變的；易變的

n. 可變因素；變數

⇨ -vari-「變化」＋ -able「可…的」

Consumer preferences are always **variable**.

消費者的愛好總是很多變。

There are a lot of **variables** involved in the acquisition of a company, some of which are quite volatile.

併購一家公司會包含很多變數，其中有一些相當不穩定。

補充
variable rate　浮動利率
fixed rate　　固定利率

vary v. 使不同，使變更
variation n. 變動、差異

反 invariable adj. 不變的

---

91. **variety**

[vəˋraɪətɪ]

n. 多樣化

⇨ -vari-「變化」＋ -ety「同 -ity，名詞字尾」

The backpacks are available in a wide **variety** of colors.

後背包有多樣顏色可供選擇。

補充
a variety of N.　各種各樣的 N.
a variety store　雜貨店
a variety show　綜藝節目

various adj. 不同的，各種各樣的

同 diversity

中高

92. **versatile**

[ˈvɝsətaɪl] / [ˈvɝsətl̩]
adj. 多用途的；多才多藝的

 - vers - 「翻轉」＋ - ate 「具…性的」＋ - ile 「可…的」

Natalie is a **versatile** artist who is equally gifted at dancing, acting, and singing.
Natalie 具備跳舞、演戲和歌唱的天賦，是位多才多藝的藝人。

補充	a versatile actor	多才多藝的演員
	a versatile garment	多用途的服裝
	DVD = Digital Versatile Disc	

versatility n. 多才多藝；多功能

中級

93. **version**

[ˈvɝʒən]
n. 版本，說法

➪ - vers - 「翻轉」＋ - ion 「表狀態或結果」，翻轉成另一種狀態就是另一個版本

The software **version** you have is too old for us to run the presentation on.
你的軟體版本太舊了，我們沒辦法打開這份簡報檔。

補充	a trial/demo version	測試／展示版本
	the current/latest version	目前／最新版本
	the amended/updated version	修訂／更新版本

---

94. **visibility**

[ˌvɪzəˈbɪlətɪ]
n. 能見度；明顯性

➪ - vis - 「看」＋ - ible 「可…的」＋ - ity 「表狀態或性質」

With such low **visibility** outside, I would suggest you turn on your brightest headlight setting.
外面的能見度這麼低，我建議你把頭燈調到最亮的模式。

補充	with high visibility	有高能見度
	good/low/zero visibility	能見度很好／低／零
	to increase visibility	增加能見度

visible adj. 可見的，看得見的

中級

95. **vivid**

[ˈvɪvɪd]
adj. 生動的；活潑的

➪ - viv - 「生命」＋ - id 「有…性質的」

The author's **vivid** imagination makes all of her novels page-turners.
這位作者生動的想像力使她所有的小說都令人愛不釋手。

補充	a vivid imagination	生動的想像力
	a vivid personality	鮮明的個性
	a vivid recollection	鮮明的記憶

vividly adv. 生動地；鮮明地
vividness n. 生動；活潑；鮮明

同 lifelike

⇨ **water**「水」**+ -proof**「防…的」

中級
96. waterproof
[ˈwɔtɚˌpruf]
adj. 不透水的；防水的

This high-quality **waterproof** jacket not only keeps you dry, but also looks quite fashionable.
這款高品質防水夾克不只能使你保持乾燥，它看起來也很時髦有型。

fireproof	adj.	防火的
bulletproof	adj.	防彈的
childproof	adj.	防止兒童開啟的
airproof	adj.	密不透氣的
heatproof	adj.	防熱的；隔熱的

同 watertight / water-resistant

⇨ **week**「週」**+ -ly**「形容詞或副詞字尾」

初級
97. weekly
[ˈwiklɪ]
adj./adv. 每週的；每週一次的
n. 週刊；週報

I prefer to read **weekly** news publications to get more complete information.
我比較喜歡讀週報來瞭解更完整的資訊。

weekly earnings/income	週薪
a weekly meeting	週會
a weekly news/magazine	週報 / 週刊

biweekly adj. 雙週的 n. 雙週刊

⇨ **wide**「寬廣的」**+ spread**「散佈」

中級
98. widespread
[ˈwaɪdˌsprɛd]
adj. 廣泛的

There is **widespread** outrage about the car company's lack of concern for meeting vehicle safety standards.
這間汽車公司沒有注意符合汽車安全標準引起了廣泛的憤慨。

補充 receive widespread support 獲得廣泛的支持

⇨ **world**「世界」**+ wide**「寬度為…的」，和世界一樣寬的

中級
99. worldwide
[ˈwɝldˌwaɪd]
adj./adv. 遍及全球的；在世界各個角落的

There is a **worldwide** trend of buying more eco-friendly electronics.
購買更多對生態環境友善的電子產品是全球趨勢。

補充
worldwide sales 全球銷售
a worldwide advertising campaign 全球性廣告活動
a worldwide shortage of N. N. 的全球性短缺
attract worldwide attention 吸引全球的注意

同 adj. = global / international

06 買賣交易
07 採購與物流
08 廣告與宣傳
09 業務協調
10 企業經營

100. **worthy**

[ˋwɝðɪ]

adj. 有價值的；值得的

n. 傑出人物；知名人士

worth adj. 有…的價值；值…的
worthwhile adj. 值得做的

⇨ **worth**「值…的」+ **-y**「多…的」，值很多的就是有價值的

Such an innovative design is **worthy** of the hype it has received.

如此創新的設計值得它所得到的大量宣傳。

| 補充 | worthy of attention/notice | 值得注意 |
| --- | worthy of the name | 名符其實 |

實力進階

Part 1. 活用部首記單字－常用字尾篇

學習英文字尾有助於快速判斷單字的詞性，對理解句意更有幫助。
常用字尾：

名詞字尾	用途與意思	例字
-ance, -ence	加在動詞後，表情況、性質或行為	endure（忍受）+ -ance = endurance 耐力 rely（相信）+ -ance = reliance 信賴
-ment	加在動詞後，表結果、手段或狀態	advertise（做廣告）+ -ment = advertisement 廣告 replace（替代）+ -ment = replacement 代替
-ness	加在形容詞後，表性質、狀態或情況	aware（注意到的）+ -ness = awareness 意識 effective（有效的）+ -ness = effectiveness 有效用
-ion	加在動詞後，表動作的狀態或結果	circulate（流通）+ -ion = circulation 發行量 compensate（賠償）+ -ion = compensation 補貼金

動詞字尾	用途與意思	例字
-ate	使成…	equal（等於）+ -ate = equate 等同 different（不同的）+ -iate = differentiate 區別
-fy	做成…，使…化	class（等級）+ -fy = classify 分類 diverse（不同的）+ -fy = diversify 使多樣化
-ize, -ise	使…化，使變成…狀態	character（個性）+ -ize = characterize 以…為特徵 maxim（最大量）+ -ize = maximize 使最大化

形容詞字尾	用途與意思	例字
-able, -ible	可…的	afford（買得起）+ -able = affordable 負擔得起的 compare（比較）+ -able = comparable 比得上的
-ive	有…性質的	collect（收集）+ -ive = collective 集體的 effect（效果）+ -ive = effective 生效的
-ic	屬於…的	strategy（策略）+ -ic = strategic 策略的 base（基礎）+ -ic = basic 基本的

副詞字尾	用途與意思	例字
-ly	加在形容詞後形成副詞	approximate（大概）+ -ly = approximately 大約 probable（可能）+ -ly = probably 或許

隨堂練習

★ 請根據句意，選出最適合的單字

(　　) 1. This magazine which features the private life of celebrities has a monthly _____ of more than two million.
(A) circulation
(B) version
(C) essence
(D) pamphlet

(　　) 2. We received a(n) _____ bottle of champagne because of the inconvenience of our delayed flight.
(A) authentic
(B) prevalent
(C) complimentary
(D) introductory

(　　) 3. Customer _____, which build customer confidence and help counter consumers' mistrust of the many unknown companies, are often an important part of making a sale.
(A) occurrences
(B) commercials
(C) traits
(D) testimonials

(　　) 4. Although it costs more to _____ a car, the rewards of personal satisfaction and the admiration of fellow drivers are well worth the work.
(A) customize
(B) regret
(C) maximize
(D) exaggerate

(　　) 5. The goal of this event is to attract media coverage; in other words, it is a _____ stunt.
(A) stability
(B) publicity
(C) visibility
(D) reliance

解答：1. A　2. C　3. D　4. A　5. B

01 職稱職務／聘僱面試

02 人事／薪資／福利

03 辦公室／電話傳真

04 文書作業

05 會議

Unit 9 業務協調

中高

1. abide

[ə`baɪd]
v. 容忍；等待；停留

 a- 「表加強語氣」+ bide「等待；停留」

We are forced to **abide** by the policies outlined in our agreement with Smith Bank.

我們必須得遵守和 Smith 銀行簽屬的協議裡面列出的規定。

> 補充　abide by 遵守
> (= follow = obey = comply with = conform to)

bide v. 等待；停留
abiding adj. 持續的，持久的；不變的

中級

2. accommodate

[ə`kɑmə͵det]
v. 給方便，迎合；使適應，調節

 ac- 「to」+ commod「拉丁文，合適的」+ -ate「動詞字尾」

You must **accommodate** your handicapped employees by installing double-size toilet stalls.

你必須設置加大洗手間以利有身體障礙的員工使用方便。

> 補充　accommodate (oneself) to N. 適應（某環境狀況）
> reach an accommodation
> 在金融事務方面達成協議，和解

accommodation n. 適應；和解
accommodating adj. 迎合的，順應的

中高

3. accordingly

[ə`kɔrdɪŋlɪ]
adv. 相應地，照著；因此

⇨ according「相符，相應的」+ -ly「副詞字尾」

As all the workers possess a different skill set, each of them has been assigned **accordingly** to a particular team.

因為所有的員工都具備不同的技能，每一個人都依照專長被分派到特定的團隊中了。

The budget has been cut by 20%. **Accordingly**, we will have to ask for more sponsors.

預算被刪減了百分之二十。因此，我們將會需要拉更多贊助。

accord v. (與…) 一致，符合，調和
according adj. 相符的；相應的

> 同　因此：therefore / hence / thus / consequently / as a result

4. accountable

[əˋkauntəbḷ]

adj. 應負責的；對…有解釋
　　義務的

⇨ **account**「說明；對…負責」+ **-able**「能夠的」

The car repair shop did shoddy work, and I expect them to be **accountable** for it by fixing the problem this time.
那間汽車維修廠之前的維修品質很差勁，我希望他們這次能把問題修復以示負責。

補充　hold sb. accountable for sth. 認為某人應對某事負責
　　　accountable to sb. 對某人負責

account v. 說明；對…負責
accountability n. 責任，權責
同 responsible

5. acquaint

[əˋkwent]

v. 使熟悉

Please **acquaint** yourself with our guests by properly introducing yourself.
請你跟客戶好好介紹自己，去熟悉客戶。

補充　acquaint sb. with sth. 使某人熟悉某事

acquaintance n. 相識；相識但並不親近的人

6. adviser

[ədˋvaɪzɚ]

n. 顧問；(AmE) 指導教授

★ 英：adviser ／ 美：advisor
⇨ **advise**「建議」+ **-er**「做…動作的人」

Our financial **adviser** suggested that we save over twenty percent of our income each month.
我們的財務顧問建議我們每個月要將收入的百分之二十以上存起來。

補充　adviser to sb./sth. 某人或公司機構的顧問

advise v. 建議；勸告

7. aid

[ed]

n./v. 協助

After the typhoon, we needed to provide **aid** to farmers via a subsidy to compensate them for their destroyed crops.
颱風過後，我們需要透過補助金給予農民協助以補償他們受損的農作物帶來的損失。

補充
enlist /seek the aid of someone 尋求某人協助
go/come to one's aid 前去 / 前來幫助某人
financial aid
財務協助 (常指政府提供給個人或機構的補助)
foreign aid 外援
first aid　急救

aide n. 助手
同 n. = help / assistance

中高

8. **ambiguity**

[æmbɪˋgjʊətɪ]

n. 模稜兩可的話

 amb - 「圍繞」 + **-igu** - 「開車；帶領」 + **-ity** 「名詞字尾」

Dearborn Energy's bankruptcy filing left no room for **ambiguity** about whether the business was in trouble or not.

Dearborn 能源公司申請破產確定了這個企業是有問題的。

ambiguous adj. 模稜兩可的；含糊不清的

中級

9. **approach**

[əˋprotʃ]

v. 著手處理；接近；找某人商量

n. 方法；接近；途徑

My partners and I are wondering how you would like to **approach** this new business venture.

我和我的合夥人想知道你打算如何著手進行這個新的商業冒險。

補充

approach + 地點／數字　靠近某處或某數量
approach sb. about sth. 找某人商量某事
adopt/take/use an approach to N.
採取做某事的方法

approachable adj. 可接近的；易親近的

中高

10. **arbitrary**

[ˋɑrbəˌtrɛrɪ]

adj. 武斷的；任意的，隨機的

⇨ **arbiter** 「仲裁人」 + **-ary** 「與…有關的」，仲裁者說了算就是武斷的

After months of deliberation, the Board's decision was anything but **arbitrary**.

在經過數月商議之後，董事會的決定絕對不會是隨便的。

補充　arbitrary decision-making 隨意武斷地做決定

arbiter n. 仲裁人；公斷人
arbitrarily adv. 任意地；武斷地；反覆無常地

中高

11. **ascertain**

[æsəˋten]

v. 查明，確定，弄清

⇨ **as** - 「表加強語氣」 + **certain** 「確定的」

What information are you able to **ascertain** from the documents the company has made public?

從這家公司公布的文件中你能夠確認的資訊是什麼？

補充　ascertain + that/wh- + S+V 確定／弄清某事

ascertainable adj. 可查明的，可確定的
ascertainment n. 查明，確定，弄清

12. assist

中級

[əˈsɪst]
v. 協助

⇨ as-「to」+ -sist-「站立」，站在一旁協助

I would like you to **assist** me with collecting every employee's emergency contact information.
我想請你協助我收集每位員工的緊急聯絡人資訊。

補充
assist (sb.) with sth. = assist (sb.) in doing sth.
協助某人做某事
with the assistance of sb./sth.
在某人 / 某物的幫助下
technical/legal assistance 技術 / 法律支援
government assistance 政府援助

assistant adj. 協助的 n. 助理
assistance n. 協助

同 aid / help

13. associate

中級

[əˈsoʃɪet] / [əˈsoʃɪɪt]
v. 聯想；使結合；結交
adj. 副的

⇨ as-「to」+ -soci-「聯合」+ -ate「動詞字尾」

Because of the scandal, people **associate** this brand with bad quality now.
因為醜聞的關係，現在人們將這個品牌的東西視為劣質品。

As the **Associate** Editor, I am not able to make the final decision on when the official release date will be.
身為副主編，我不能對正式發行日期會是哪一天做最後決定。

補充
A be associated with B A 和 B 有關聯
associate with sb.   和某人結交為友
associate professor   副教授
associate director   次長

association n. 聯想；結合；交往；協會
associated adj. 有關聯的；聯合的

14. backlog

[ˈbæk͵lɔg]
n. 積壓未辦之事；存貨；儲備

 back「後面」+ log「原木；圓木；木材」

Due to the **backlog** of cases, the soonest you can expect to see the judge is four months from now.
因為堆積了很多訴訟案件未處理，你最快可以見到法官的時間是從現在起算的四個月後。

補充 a backlog of orders 訂單積壓

中高

15. bias

[`baɪəs]

n. 成見；偏見；傾向
adj. 斜的

同 n. = prejudice

I believe that my boss has a **bias** towards men, which is why there is not a single female department head.
我覺得我的老闆偏袒男性，這就是爲什麼我們沒有任何一位女性部門主管的原因。

 bias against... 對…的偏見
gender bias 性別歧視

中級

16. challenge

[`tʃælɪndʒ]

n. 質疑；挑戰
v. 對…提出異議；向…挑戰

Mediating in a conflict between two employees is a **challenge**, but someone has to do it.
在兩名員工衝突當中去調解雖然是一個挑戰，但總是要有一個人去做這件事。

 pose/present a challenge to N. 對…提出質疑
face/take on a challenge of... 接受…的挑戰
meet/rise to a challenge 迎接挑戰

challenging adj. 具挑戰性的

中級

17. circumstance

[`sɝkəm‚stæns]

n. 外在狀況，情況

⇨ circum - 「周圍」＋ -stan - 「站立」＋ -ce 「名詞字尾」，站在外圍的事物就是外在狀況

The **circumstances** of Mr. Hayes' departure were mysterious.
Hayes 先生離職事有蹊蹺。

 under/in ... circumstances 在…情況之下
under no circumstances 絕不
financial circumstances 財務狀況

中高

18. coincide

[‚koɪn`saɪd]

v. 一致；同時發生

co - 「一起」＋ in - 「在上面」＋ -cid - 「掉落」

The data we see now does not **coincide** with the sales figures I saw last week.
我們現在看到的數據和我上週看到的銷售數字並不符合。

coincide with... 和…同時發生；和…相符
by coincidence 巧合地
sheer/pure coincidence 純屬巧合

coincidence n. 巧合；符合
coincident adj. 同時發生的；巧合的

19. collaboration

[kəˌlæbəˈreʃən]
n. 合作

⇨ **col-**「一起」+ **-labor-**「工作」+ **-ation**「名詞字尾」
The photography and video divisions need to have **collaboration** on this project to make it a success.
攝影部和影像部需要在這個企劃中合作才能成功。

 collaborate with... 和…合作

collaborate v. 合作
collaborative adj. 合作的
collaborator n. 合作者
同 cooperation / teamwork

中高

20. collide

[kəˈlaɪd]
v. 相撞；衝突

⇨ **col-**「一起」+ **-lide-**「同 **-led-**，表傷害、打擊」
The CEO has again **collided** with the CFO over the budget plan.
執行長和財務長又再度在預算案上面起衝突了。

 collide with... 和…相撞；和…意見衝突
be on a collision course 發生衝突

collision n. 相撞；衝突

中級

21. communication

[kəˌmjunəˈkeʃən]
n. 溝通，傳達；通訊

⇨ **communicate**「溝通」+ **-ion**「名詞字尾」
Your supervisor and I are currently in **communication** about what measures to take concerning your frequent absences.
我和你的主管正在溝通關於你頻繁缺席一事要如何處理。

communication skills 溝通技巧
a channel of communication 溝通管道
be in communication with... 與…有聯繫
means of communication 傳播通訊工具

communicate v. 溝通；傳達
communicative adj. 有關溝通表達的；健談的

中高

22. compel

[kəmˈpɛl]
v. 強迫；引發

⇨ **com-**「一起」+ **-pel-**「迫使」
The department head was **compelled** to resign because of the big mistake.
該部門的部長因為犯了嚴重錯誤而被迫離職。

 compel sb's attention 引起某人的注意力

compelling adj. 很有說服力的
compelled adj. 被迫的
同 force / coerce

23. **conciliate**

[kən'sɪlɪˌet]

v. 贏得支持；使和好，調解

 con-「一起」+ -cili-「= -cal-，表召集」+ -ate「動詞字尾」

We must attempt to **conciliate** the workers by granting them some benefits.
我們必須試著透過給予員工福利來得到他們的支持。

conciliation n. 和好；調解
conciliatory adj. 和解的

初級

24. **conflict**

['kɑnflɪkt]
n. 衝突

[kən'flɪkt]
v. 衝突

⇨ con-「一起」+ -flict-「打，擊」

If the **conflict** between Jean and George cannot be mitigated, they will both be laid off.
如果 Jean 和 George 之間的衝突無法減緩的話，他們都會被解僱的。

補充

conflict between A and B A 和 B 之間的衝突
be in conflict with sb. over sth.
和某人為某事起衝突
conflict of interest 利益衝突
to conflict with sth. 與某物相矛盾

中級

25. **consult**

[kən'sʌlt]

v. 商量，商議；取得允許

I suggest that you **consult** with a financial planner before selecting your retirement savings plan.
我建議你在選擇你的退休儲蓄計劃之前先跟財務規劃師商量。

補充

consult (with) sb. (about sth.)
與某人商量；向某人諮詢，請教某事
consulting room 診療室

consultation n. 磋商會議；商量；諮詢
consultant n. 顧問
consulting n. 諮詢（顧問）服務

中高

26. **contingent**

[kən'tɪndʒənt]

adj. 以…為條件的，視情況而定的；偶發的

con-「一起」+ -ting-「碰觸」+ -ent「具…性質的」

Our offer to acquire your firm is **contingent** on the health of your financials.
我們是否要併購你們公司要視你們的財務狀況而定。

補充

be contingent on/upon sth. 取決於某事物
contingency plan 應變計劃
contingency fund 應急費用
risk and contingency management
風險和應急管理

contingency n. 可能發生的意外事件，不測事件

中高

27. controversy

[ˈkɑntrəˌvɝsɪ]

n. 爭議

⇨ **contro** - 「相反」+ **- vers** - 「轉向」+ **- y** 「名詞字尾」，
轉變成對立相反的立場表示有爭議

The best way to quiet the **controversy** is to release as much positive PR as possible.

平息這項爭議最好的方式就是盡可能多多釋出正面的公關形象。

★PR = Public Relations：公共關係，公關

 補充

| controversy over/about ... | 關於…的爭議 |
| create/spark/stir/cause controversy | 引發爭議 |

controversial adj. 引起爭議的

同 dispute

中級

28. cooperate

[koˈɑpəˌret]

v. 合作

⇨ **co** - 「一起」+ **- oper** - 「工作」+ **- ate** 「動詞字尾」

It's best that you totally **cooperate** with the auditors to avoid suspicion.

你最好全力配合稽查員以免被懷疑。

 補充

| cooperate with... | 和…合作 |
| cooperate in... | 在…方面合作 |

cooperation n. 合作

cooperative adj. 合作的；樂意合作的 n. 合作社；合作商店

同 collaborate / team up / joint forces

中高

29. coordinate

[koˈɔrdɪnɪt] / [koˈɔrdɪnet]

v. 協調，調整；相配

 co - 「一起」+ - ordin - 「順序」+ - ate 「動詞字尾」

Our Executive Secretary will **coordinate** several schedules to choose the best time for the meeting.

我們的執行秘書會調整時間表選出最適合開會的時間。

補充

| coordinate efforts | 同心協力 |
| coordinate with sb./sth. | 與…協調合作 |

coordinated adj. 協調一致的；動作協調的；相配的

coordination n. 協調，配合

coordinator n. 協調人，統籌者

30. **count on**

[kaʊnt] [ɑn]
phr. 仰賴

I can't **count on** people who stab others in the back the first chance they get.
我無法仰賴一有機會就在別人背後說壞話的人。

補充
count on sb. for sth.　　指望某人給予某物
count on sb. to do sth.　指望某人去做某事
You can count on me.　　包在我身上。

count v. 計算；有價值

同 depend on / rely on / bank on / lean on

31. **deal with**

[dil] [wɪθ]
phr. 應付；處理

Sooner or later, we will need to **deal with** the accusations brought forth by the whistleblower.
我們遲早要處理因爲有人告密而產生的那些指控。

補充
deal with sb.　　　　　與某人相處打交道／做生意
deal with + 待處理事物　　　對事情做處置
deal with problems　　　　　處理解決問題
deal with + 工作內容　　　　負責從事某業務
文章／計畫 + deal with + 主題　與某主題相關

deal v. 處理；交易

同 handle / cope with / take care of

32. **debate**

[dɪˈbet]
v./n. 辯論，討論

⇨ **de -**「往下」+ **bate**「源自拉丁文，表打」，辯論就是為了打倒對方
The Board of Directors is **debating** about how to spin the recent drop in the stock price.
董事會正在討論要如何針對最近股市下跌的情況給出一套對公司有利的說詞。
★ 動詞 spin 表示將事實用另一種說法陳述以達利己的目的。

補充
debate sth. with sb.　和某人辯論某事
debate over/on/about sth.　關於某主題的辯論
(a) lively/heated/intense/fierce debate
激烈的辯論
open to debate　可議的

debater n. 辯論者
debatable adj. 可爭論的；有爭議的

06 買賣交易

07 採購與物流

08 廣告與宣傳

09 業務協調

10 企業經營

中高

33. deliberate
[dɪˈlɪbərɪt]
adj. 故意的；慎重的；從容的
[dɪˈlɪbəret]
v. 考慮；商議

 de - 「表加強語氣」+ - liber - 「秤重；權衡」+ - ate「動詞字尾」

The commentator made a **deliberate** swipe at our company with his biased editorial.
那位評論家用他存有偏見的社論故意公開抨擊我們公司。

> 補充
> deliberate attempt 蓄意
> deliberate on/about/over 仔細考慮

deliberation n. 深思熟慮；慎重；從容
deliberately adv. 故意地；慎重地；從容地

中高

34. despise
[dɪˈspaɪz]
v. 鄙視

 de - 「往下」+ - spise - 「看」

Although these two employees **despise** each other, they must complete the project together.
雖然這兩名員工互相看不起彼此，但是他們還是必須一起完成這項企劃。

> 補充
> despise sb./sth. for...
> 因為某緣故而鄙視某人某物

同 disdain / scorn / look down on / hold ... in contempt

中高

35. displace
[dɪsˈples]
v. 取代；迫使離開

 dis - 「離開，遠離」+ place 「放置；安置」

Whether immigrants will **displace** native workers in the labor market is always a debate.
移民者是否會在勞工市場取代本國人一直是個被討論的議題。

The family was **displaced** when their house was foreclosed on.
當這家人貸款的房子被銀行收回時，他們被迫離開了家園。

> 補充
> displaced worker/employee
> 轉業人士，被解僱的工人

displacement n. 取代；撤換；免職

同 取代：replace / substitute / take place of

中高

36. dispose

[dɪˋspoz]

v. 處置；安排，支配

 dis-「分開」**＋ -pos-**「放置；安置」

The company **disposed** of three hundred kilograms of shredded paper to hide evidence of corruption.

這家公司為了隱藏貪汙的證據處理掉了三百公斤的碎紙。

| 補充 | dispose of 處置；解決；捨棄
Man proposes, God disposes.
[諺語] 謀事在人，成事在天。 |

disposal n. 處理；配置；丟棄
disposable adj. 可任意處理的；可自由使用的

中高

37. dissident

[ˋdɪsədənt]

n. 意見不同的人
adj. 意見不同的

⇨ **dis-**「分開」**＋ -sid-**「坐」**＋ -ent**「具⋯性質的」，意見不同所以分開坐

Wayne is the lone **dissident** of the group, believing it best to do things the old way.

Wayne 是這群人裡面唯一一個意見不同的人，他相信以老方法做事是最好的。

dissidence n. 異議

中級

38. district

[ˋdɪstrɪkt]

n. 區域；行政區

⇨ **di-**「分開」**＋ -strict-**「拉緊」，拉繩索將外來者隔開的範圍就成為一個區域

Downtown used to be a bustling financial **district**, but now the buildings need to be renovated.

市中心曾是繁忙的金融區，不過現在那裏的大樓需要更新翻修。

| 補充 | financial/business/shopping district
金融區 / 商業區 / 購物區
district sales manager 區域銷售經理 |

初級

39. divide

[dɪˋvaɪd]

v. 劃分；分配；(數學)除

The remnants of the bankrupt corporation were **divided** up among the creditors.

這間破產公司剩下的東西都被這些債權人瓜分掉了。

| 補充 | divide A into B 將 A 分成 B |

divided adj. 被分割的；分裂的
division n. 分開；分配；分裂；部門；部分

同 separate v. 分開

中高

40. embrace

[ɪm'bres]

v. 欣然接受；擁抱；包含
n. 擁抱

⇨ em-「裡面」+ -brace-「雙臂」，擁抱在雙臂裡

Rather than fear the stress that comes with a new position, **embrace** the opportunity.

與其懼怕伴隨新職務而來的壓力，不如擁抱這個機會吧。

補充	embrace an idea	接受一個想法
	embrace an opportunity	把握機會
	embrace a challenge	迎接挑戰

同 accept v. 接受

41. expedite

['ɛkspɪˌdaɪt]

v. 迅速執行；促進

 ex-「向外」+ -ped-「腳」

As Mr. Henderson's order is already late, let's **expedite** it at our expense.

因為 Henderson 先生的訂單已經遲了，我們自掏腰包趕工吧。

expeditious adj. 迅速的；敏捷的

同 speed up

初級

42. explain

[ɪk'splen]

v. 解釋

⇨ ex-「向外」+ plain「清楚的」，向外解釋清楚

Explain to the seller of this house that he must make certain repairs.

向這棟房屋的賣家解釋說他必須進行某些維修吧。

補充	explain sth. to sb. 向某人解釋某事
	explain oneself 向某人解釋清楚自己做某事的理由

explanation n. 解釋；說明
explanatory adj. 解釋的
self-explanatory adj. 不辯自明的

同 clarify / interpret / get across

中高

43. explicit

[ɪk'splɪsɪt]

adj. 明確的；清楚的；直率的

 ex-「外面」+ -plic-「摺疊」+ -it「形容詞字尾」

The manager left **explicit** instructions for us to update the software tonight after ten o'clock.

經理留下了清楚的指示要我們在今天晚上十點過後更新軟體。

補充	make sth. explicit	使某事物清楚明瞭
	be explicit about sth.	對某事清楚說明

explicitly adv. 明確地；清楚地
explicitness n. 明確性；清晰性

同 definite / clear-cut / unambiguous
反 implicit adj. 隱含其中的；不明言的；含蓄的

44. fall behind
[fɔl] [bɪˋhaɪnd]
phr. 落後

Our R & D department needs to double their efforts to ensure that we don't **fall behind**.
我們的研發部門需要加倍努力以確保我們不會落後。

補充
fall behind with sth. 某事進度落後
fall behind by + 時間 落後了多少時間
fall behind schedule 比預定時間要晚

中高

45. feasible
[ˋfizəbḷ]
adj. 可行的；可能的

⇨ -feas- 「做」＋ -ible 「可以…的」
Expecting us to double our market share in two months is not a **feasible** goal.
期待我們在兩個月內將市場擴張兩倍並不是個可行的目標。

補充
It is feasible for N. to V. 對 N. 來說做某事是可行的
the feasibility of N. 某事物的可行性

feasibly adv. 可行地
feasibility n. 可行性

同 可行的：achievable / viable / workable
可能的：possible

中高

46. gathering
[ˋgæðərɪŋ]
n. 聚集；集會

⇨ gather 「聚集；召集」＋ -ing 「名詞字尾」
There will be an informal **gathering** at the tavern down the street, but it's still a good chance to butter up clients.
街上的小酒館那裏會有一個非正式的聚會，這是一個能討好客戶的好機會。

gather v. 聚集；召集

同 assembly

初級

47. general
[ˋdʒɛnərəl]
adj. 一般的；普遍的；全體的

⇨ -gener- 「同 -gen- ，種族」＋ -al 「與…有關的」，
和整個族群都有關表示普遍常見
In **general**, never lowball a seller or he might cut off any further negotiations.
一般來說，不要向賣方低報價格，否則他可能會拒絕任何進一步洽談的機會。

補充
in general = as a general rule
在一般情況下，通常；大體上來說
in general terms 大概地，籠統地
general manager 總經理

generally adv. 一般地；普遍地；通常

同 common / generic

48. immediately

[ɪˈmidɪtlɪ]
adv. 立即

immediate adj. 立即的

⇨ **immediate**「立即的」+ **-ly**「副詞字尾」

Always try to close a deal **immediately** with the buyer, especially when he has cash in hand.
切記要立即跟買方達成交易，特別是對方手頭有現金的時候。

同 promptly / instantaneously / at once / without delay

49. imminent

[ˈɪmənənt]
adj. 逼近的

 im -「上面」+ **-min -**「突出，突起」+ **-ent**「具…性質的」

Cable news shows report that a deal between the two software giants is **imminent**, and will become official this week.
有線新聞報導兩大軟體巨頭之間的一筆交易即將發生，而且在這一週就會正式生效。

補充 **imminent peril** 迫在眉睫的危險

imminence n. 迫切
imminently adj. 迫切地

同 impending / pending

50. impending

[ɪmˈpɛndɪŋ]
adj. 即將發生的

⇨ **im -**「上面」+ **-pend -**「懸掛」+ **-ing**「形容詞字尾」，掛在上面表示距離很近

If accounting is not able to balance our books, there will be **impending** financial disaster.
如果做會計帳務無法使我們的帳目收支平衡，很快就會有金融災難了。

補充 **impending disaster/doom**
即將降臨的災難／厄運

impend v. 即將發生；逼近；懸置

51. implication

[ˌɪmplɪˈkeʃən]
n. 暗示；含意；可能影響；牽連

⇨ **imply**「暗示」+ **-ation**「名詞字尾」

It seems the **implication** made by the senator is that the CEO clearly knew that his company was in trouble before he resigned.
這位參議員似乎在暗示說執行長在請辭之前早就清楚地知道他的公司有麻煩了。

補充 **by implication** 暗示地

imply v. 暗示

52. **in conjunction with**

[ɪn] [kənˈdʒʌŋkʃən] [wɪθ]
phr. 和…一起配合

We worked on the building plans **in conjunction with** our offices on the west coast.
我們和西岸分公司一起配合著手進行建設計畫。

conjunction n. 連結；連接詞

中高

53. **incur**

[ɪnˈkɝ]
v. 招致

⇨ **in-**「往裡面」＋ **-cur-**「跑；流」，跑進去會招來麻煩
If we leave the car parked in this lot any longer, we will **incur** additional fees.
如果我們把車停在這個停車場更久的話，我們就會有額外花費。

 incur costs/expenses 導致花費
incur losses/debts 虧損／負債

初級

54. **indicate**

[ˈɪndəˌket]
v. 指出；表明

⇨ **in-**「to」＋ **-dic-**「宣佈，說」＋ **-ate**「動詞字尾」，說出事物的情況
Your extra effort **indicates** a company that is willing to do whatever it takes to make the customer happy.
你們的額外努力就說明了你們是一間願意盡其所能滿足顧客的公司。

indication n. 指示；表示；徵兆
indicative adj. 指示的；象徵的；暗示的
indicator n. (儀器上的) 指針或指示器；指標

中級

55. **infer**

[ɪnˈfɝ]
v. 推論；意味著，暗示

⇨ **in-**「裡面」＋ **-fer-**「運載」，將想法往裡送就會推論出結果
From the boss's upset face, we can **infer** his disgust at our marketing strategy.
從老闆煩惱的表情可以知道他不喜歡我們的行銷策略。

 infer A from B 從 B 中推論出 A
infer that S. V... 推論出…

inferable adj. 可推論的
inference n. 推論

中級

56. informative

[ɪnˈfɔrmətɪv]
adj. 資訊豐富的

⇨ **inform**「通知」+ **-ative**「具…性質的」

The slide show was **informative**, but it needs better graphics to make it pop.

這份投影片的資訊很豐富，不過還是需要有更好的圖表使它更加突出。

補充　highly informative 資訊非常豐富的

inform v. 通知；告知
information n. 情報；資訊
informatively adv. 提供大量資訊地

 中級

57. intention

[ɪnˈtɛnʃən]
n. 意圖

⇨ **in-**「to」+ **-tent-**「伸出」+ **-ion**「名詞字尾」，伸出手表示有想要的意圖

I have no **intention** of selling this company no matter how good the offer is.

不論出價多高，我都沒有要賣掉公司的打算。

補充　with the intention of...　　　目的是…
have no intention of doing sth. 沒有做某事的打算
It is one's intention to do sth.
某人的目的是要做某事。

intend v. 意欲；打算
intentional adj. 故意的
intentionally adv. 故意地

 中級

58. interfere

[ˌɪntəˈfɪr]
v. 干涉；妨礙

⇨ **inter-**「在…之間，彼此」+ **-fere-**「打、擊」，彼此對打就是互相妨礙

The vice president **interfered** with negotiations by making several cultural faux pas.

副總裁做出一些不合文化的失禮舉動妨礙了協商的進行。

補充　interfere in sth.　　　干涉某事
interfere with sth.　妨礙某事進行

interference n. 干涉；妨礙

初級

59. **interrupt**

[ˌɪntəˈrʌpt]

v. 中斷；打斷

⇨ **inter-**「在…之間」＋ **-rupt-**「破裂」，從中間破裂開就是打斷了

It's easy to **interrupt** others during a conference call because you can't see whether they've finished speaking or not.

電話會議中打斷別人的情形很容易發生，因為你看不到他們是否結束談話了。

 補充

interrupt sb. 打斷某人說話
business interruption insurance 營業中斷保險

interruption n. 中斷；打斷
interrupted adj. 被打斷的
interruptive adj. 阻礙的

中級

60. **involve**

[ɪnˈvɑlv]

v. 涉及；投入；包含

⇨ **in-**「在裡面」＋ **-volve-**「捲；滾」，被捲進去就是涉入其中了

This case **involves** the illegal sale of trade secrets.

這個案件涉及非法販賣商業機密。

 補充

involve sb. in (V-ing) sth. 使某人參與某事
be/get involved in sth. 牽涉或參與某事

involved adj. 有關聯的，被牽涉的
involvement n. 牽涉；包含

中級

61. **manage**

[ˈmænɪdʒ]

v. 管理；經營

Did you **manage** to finally debug all those lines of code as I asked you to?

你有照我交代的設法去除那些程式碼錯誤嗎？

 補充 manage to V. 設法去做…

management n. 管理，經營；管理層
manageable adj. 可管理的；可控制的
managerial adj. 管理的

初級

62. **means**

[minz]

n. 方法；財產；財力

Before finding our current distributor, we had no **means** of transporting such large quantities in such a short time.

在找到我們現在的批發商之前，我們沒有辦法在這麼短的時間內運送如此大的數量。

補充
by means of sth. 以某種方法
by no means 絕不
private means（來自投資等的非工資性）私人收入
independent means 投資收入
live beyond one's means 入不敷出

mean v. 意思是 adj. 惡劣的

同 method n. 方法

中高

63. **mediate**

[`midɪˌet]

v. 調解，調停

⇨ -medi-「中間」+ -ate「動詞字尾」，在兩者中間調解

Ronda was assigned to **mediate** the terms of the deal between the two corporations.

Ronda 被指派去調解兩家公司之間的交易條款。

補充
mediate between A and B 在 A 和 B 之間調停
mediate a dispute　　　　調停解決紛爭

mediation n. 調解，調停
mediator n. 調停者

初級

64. **method**

[`mɛθəd]

n. 方法；條理；秩序

⇨ meta-「在後面」+ hodos「希臘文，道路」，可以跟在後面走的路就是途徑、方法

There are several **methods** to successfully prospect for possible life insurance customers.

有一些方法可以成功找出會購買壽險的潛在客戶。

補充
method for sb. to do sth. 某人做某事的方法
find/develop/employ a method
找到 / 研發 / 使用方法

methodical adj. 有條理的；井然有序的；辦事講究方法的
methodology n. 方法論；一套方法；教學法

中級

65. mutual
[`mjutʃuəl]
adj. 互相的，彼此的；共有的

⇨ -mut- 「改變」+ -al「有…屬性的」，做改變才能適應彼此

The beverage makers made a **mutual** agreement to dissolve their partnership due to their distrust of each other.

那兩間飲料製造商因為對彼此的不信任雙方同意拆夥。

補充
by mutual agreement/consent	經雙方同意
mutual interest/friends	共同的興趣／朋友
mutual understanding/respect	相互理解／尊重

mutually adv. 互相地
mutuality n. 相互關係

中高

66. notify
[`notəˌfaɪ]
v. 通知

⇨ -not- 「知道」+ -ify「使…」

You were expected to **notify** us of any conflicts of interest you may have with other business that you do on the side.

你應該要告知我們你私自跟其他人做生意可能會有的任何利益衝突。

補充
notify sb. of sth.　通知某人某事
notify sb. that...　通知某人某事

notification n. 通知

同 inform

初級

67. object
[əb`dʒɛkt]
v. 反對

⇨ ob- 「反著」+ -ject- 「丟、擲」，往回丟以示反對

I **object** to your use of the word "unstable" to describe the status of my company.

我反對你用「不穩定」一詞來描述我的公司狀態。

補充　object to N./V-ing 反對某事

objection n. 反對；異議
objector n. 反對者

中級

68. obstacle
[`ɑbstəkl̩]
n. 障礙

⇨ ob- 「反著」+ -sta- 「站」+ -cle「名詞字尾」，對著你站相反方向就成了你的障礙

There were many legal **obstacles** to overcome when we set up this LLC.

我們在建立這間有限公司的時候有許多法規上的障礙要克服。

★ LLC= Limited Liability Company 有限責任公司

補充
obstacle to N./V-ing　…的障礙
overcome an obstacle　克服障礙

同 barrier / hindrance

中級

69. oppose

[ə`poz]

v. 反對；反抗

 op - 「反著」+ -pose - 「放置」，反著放以示反抗

I don't **oppose** colleagues socializing outside of the office as long as they keep it under control.
我不反對同事們在辦公室以外互相熱絡交往，只要他們注意分寸就好。

補充 fiercely/bitterly/strongly oppose N./V-ing
強烈反對某事
be opposed to N./V-ing 反對某事

中級

70. outward

[`autwəd]

adj. 向外的

outwards adv. 向外

反 inward adj. 向內的

 out 「外面」+ - ward 「朝…方向」

Mark showed no **outward** signs of being malcontent at the meeting.
Mark 在會議中沒有表現出他的不滿。

補充 outward investment 對外投資

中級

71. overall

[`ovɔɔl]

adj. 全部的
adv. 大體上
n. (BrE) 罩衫；工作褲

同 大體上：as a whole

 over 「遍及」+ all 「所有」

Overall, I have never had much of an interest in the accounting side of the business.
大體上，我從來沒對商業會計的部分有太多興趣。

補充 overall situation/performance 整體的狀況 / 表現
overall market　　　　　　整體市場

72. pertinent

[`pɝtnənt]

adj. 直接相關的；恰當的，中肯的

pertinently adv. 相關地
pertinence n. 恰當；中肯；切題

同 relevant adj. 相關的

反 irrelevant adj. 不相關的

 per - 「完全地」+ -tin - 「握著」+ -ent 「具…性質的」

Tom's failure as a manager thirty years ago is not **pertinent** to his present ability.
Tom 三十年前當經理時失職與他現在的能力並沒有直接相關。

補充 pertinent to... 和…相關
a pertinent question / remark
高度相關的問題 / 評論

中高

73. precedent

[ˈprɛsədənt]

n. 先例；慣例

adj. 在先的

➩ pre-「前面」+ -cede-「走」+ -ent「具…性質的」

Our professional handling of the Reeves project set the **precedent** for the behavior we should exhibit on all future projects.

我們在 Reeves 專案上的專業處理為我們在未來所有專案上應該有的表現設下了先例。

補充 set/create a precedent 開先例
break with precedent 打破慣例

precedence n. 居先；優先權
precede v. 在前
unprecedented adj. 史無前例的

74. pressing

[ˈprɛsɪŋ]

adj. 緊迫的；迫切的

➩ press「催促，催逼」+ -ing「形容詞字尾」

Unless there are any **pressing** matters, we will adjourn the meeting early.

除非有任何緊急事項要討論，我們將會早早中止會議。

補充 a pressing problem 迫切的問題

press v. 催促，催逼

同 urgent

中高

75. priority

[praɪˈɔrətɪ]

n. 優先；優先權

 prior「在先的；優先的」+ -ity「名詞字尾」

Our number-one **priority** is the speed with which customers receive their goods.

我們的首要之務是在於顧客收到商品的速度。

補充 a top priority 當務之急
give priority to... 優先考慮…
prior to 在…之前；先於…

prior adj. 在先的；優先的
prioritize v. 給予優先權；按優先順序處理

中高

76. propel

[prəˈpɛl]

v. 推動

➩ pro-「向前」+ -pel-「驅使」

Positive encouragement should **propel** employees towards making more sales.

正向的鼓勵應該會推動員工有更好的業績。

補充 propel sb. to/into/towards sth.
推動某人做某事；將某人推向某一境地

propellant n. 推進者
propeller n. 螺旋槳

06 買賣交易

07 採購與物流

08 廣告與宣傳

09 業務協調

10 企業經營

初級

77. regularly

[ˈrɛgjələlɪ]

adv. 定期地

regular adj. 有規律的
regularity n. 規律
regularize v. 使有規則

⇨ **regula**「拉丁文，規則」+ **-ar**「具…性質的」+ **-ly**「副詞字尾」

All accounting procedures should be **regularly** monitored to guard against corruption.
所有的會計程序都應該要定期控管以避免貪汙。

中級

78. representative

[ˌrɛprɪˈzɛntətɪv]

adj. 代表的，代理的；代表性的，典型的
n. 代表，代理人；典型；代表物

represent v. 代表
representation n. 代表

⇨ **represent**「代表」+ **-ive**「具…性質的」

The recent delay of shipments is not **representative** of how we normally operate.
近日延遲送貨的情形並不能代表我們正常運作的狀況。

 補充
be representative of sth.	具有某物的代表性質
sales representative	銷售代表；推銷員
service representative	服務專員

中級

79. resolve

[rɪˈzɑlv]

v. 解決；決定

resolution n. 解決；決心
resolved adj. 下定決心的

 re-「回到」+ **-solv-**「鬆開」

I need you to **resolve** the issue that this customer is having immediately to keep him satisfied.
我需要你立即解決這位顧客現在有的問題讓他滿意。

補充
resolve a dispute/problem/conflict
解決紛爭／問題／衝突
resolve differences 解決差異

初級

80. respect

[rɪˈspɛkt]

v./n. 尊敬

respectable adj. 可敬的
respectful adj. 恭敬的

⇨ **re-**「回來」+ **-spec-**「看」，回頭看表示景仰、尊敬

We should take this opportunity to stand and clap to show our **respect** for our founder and his hard work.
我們應該要利用這個機會起立鼓掌向我們的創辦人以及他的努力致敬。

 補充
gain sb's respect	得到某人的尊敬
lose sb's respect	失去某人的尊敬
treat sb. with respect	尊敬地對待某人

中高

81. **segment**

['sɛgmənt]

n. 部分，區隔；部門
v. 分割

⇨ **-seg-**「切開」**+ -ment**「名詞字尾」

I want each of you to focus on appealing to a different market **segment** and produce a commercial for that group only.

我要你們每個人將焦點放在吸引一個不同的市場區隔族群，並為該特定族群製作一支廣告。

★ market segment 市場區隔：將個人或機構客戶按照一個或幾個特點分類，使每類具有相似的產品服務需求。

segmentation n. 分割；細胞分裂
segmented adj. 分割的

中高

82. **simplicity**

[sɪm'plɪsəti]

n. 簡明；單純；無知

⇨ **simple**「簡單的」**+ -ity**「名詞字尾」

The **simplicity** of your plan means that less time will be required for training.

你的計畫很簡單也就表示說需要訓練的時間會比較少。

 be simplicity itself 非常簡單

simple adj. 簡單的
simplify v. 簡化

中級

83. **situation**

[ˌsɪtʃu'eʃən]

n. 立場；處境；(建築物)位置

⇨ **situate**「使位於」**+ -ion**「名詞字尾」

To deal with the difficult financial **situation**, we need to ask for more sponsors.

要解決財務困難的狀況，我們需要拉更多贊助。

 a win-win situation 雙贏的局面
a situation comedy 情境喜劇 (= a sitcom)

situate v. 使位於；將…置於某環境中
situated adj. 位於…的，坐落在…的
situational adj. 情境式的

中級

84. **solid**

['sɑlɪd]

adj. 固體的；實在明確的；
穩固的；全體一致的
n. 固體

⇨ **-sol-**「獨特、完整的」**+ -id**「具…性質的」

Your business plan is **solid**, but things just haven't worked out in your favor.

你的商業計劃雖然很具體，但是事情就是沒有變的對你有利。

 solid evidence　　可靠的證據
solid earnings　　穩定的盈利
solid foundation　穩固的基礎

solidify v. 固化；使鞏固；使確定
solidity n. 固體；體積，容積；穩固、可靠
solidly adv. 堅固地，牢靠地；團結一致地

282

85. **specific**

[spɪˋsɪfɪk]

adj. 明確的，具體的；特定的

⇨ **species**「物種；種類」+ **-fic**「產生…的」，每個物種產生的特性都很明確

You need to mention **specific** cases where this method has worked before.
你需要提出幾個明確例子來說明這個方法是有效的。

補充　special「特別的」與 specific 的差別在於 specific 還有明確具體的意思。

specifically adv. 特地；明確具體地
specification n. 載明；詳述；規格

---

86. **speed up**

[spid] [ʌp]

phr. 加速

The customer service center will need to **speed up** their turnaround time for resolving complaints.
客服中心會需要加速他們解決客訴問題的來回時間。

speed n. 速度 v. 迅速前進

反 slow down 減速

---

87. **strife**

[straɪf]

n. 衝突

Spreading rumors about colleagues causes all sorts of **strife**.
散播同事的謠言會導致各種衝突。

補充　industrial strife　勞資衝突
boardroom strife　董事會的明爭暗鬥

同 conflict

---

88. **subjective**

[səbˋdʒɛktɪv]

adj. 主觀的

⇨ **subject**「主題；主詞」+ **-ive**「有關的」

Because of my strong **subjective** opinions, I need some volunteers to help me judge which innovation is truly the best one.
因為我的主觀看法很強烈，我需要有一些自願者幫助我判斷哪一項革新才是真正最好的。

補充　subjective judgment　主觀判斷
subjective opinion　主觀看法

subject n. 主題；主詞；v. 使隸屬；使服從
subjectively adv. 主觀地
subjectivity n. 主觀；主觀性

反 objective adj. 客觀的

中高

89. subsequent

[`sʌbsɪˌkwənt]

adj. 隨後的；繼…之後的

⇨ sub -「靠近」+ -sequ -「跟隨」+ -ent「有…性質的」，緊跟著的就是隨後的

The bad review of the restaurant by the Health Department led to the **subsequent** firing of the general manager.
衛生署對這家餐廳的負評導致之後總經理遭到解僱。

補充　subsequent to... 繼…之後

subsequently adv. 隨後；接著
subsequence n. 後繼的事件；後果

中級

90. suggestion

[sə`dʒɛstʃən]

n. 建議；暗示

⇨ suggest「建議；暗示」+ -ion「名詞字尾」

I am open to **suggestions** about what to do with all the old inventory.
我願意傾聽關於該怎麼處理老舊存貨的建議。
★ be open to suggestions：願意傾聽建議

補充　suggestion for/about/on + sth.　對某事的建議
　　　suggestion of + sth.　　　　　某件事情的暗示

suggest v. 建議；暗示
suggestive adj. 暗示的

中級

91. superb

[su`pɝb]

adj. 極好的；一流的

Beth is a **superb** public speaker, so she will be out on the road promoting our products.
Beth 是位一流的演講者，所以她會去各處巡迴推廣我們的產品。

superbly adv. 極好地；上等地
super adj. 極度的，過度的；[口語] 特級的，特佳的

中高

92. supplement

[`sʌpləmənt]

v. 增補，補充；為…補編附錄

n. 補充；補給品；副刊

⇨ sup -「由下往上」+ -ple -「填滿」+ -ment「名詞字尾」，向上填滿空缺就是做補充

It's best to **supplement** your claims with real scientific studies.
用真實的科學研究來補充你的論點是最好的。

補充　supplement to sth. 某物的補充物

supplementary adj. 補充的

初級

93. **support**

[sə`pɔrt]

n./v. 支持

⇨ **sup -**「由下往上」**＋ -port -**「運送」，向上送出我們的支持

Tell customers that if they have any further questions, they should call the **support** hotline for help.

告訴顧客如果他們還有其他問題的話，他們應該打到支援專線求助。

[補充] support sb. in (V-ing) sth. 支持某人做某事

supporter n. 支持者
supportive adj. 支持的；支援的

中級

94. **suppose**

[sə`poz]

v. 認定；以為

⇨ **sup -**「在下面」**＋ -pos -**「放置」，放在腦子下面的是既有想法

The system is **supposed** to be up and running already, but it will be delayed by another week.

這個系統應該已經要上線營運了，但是它還要再延遲一週。

[補充] be supposed to do sth.
被期望做某事；應該做某事

supposed adj. 所謂的，據說的

---

95. **tactic**

[`tæktɪk]

n. 策略，手段；戰術

Few **tactics** will work when trying to pitch a veteran businessman.

在和商場老手推銷的時候，很少有策略會成功。

[典故] 源自希臘文 taktike 表示「安排」。引申為戰術、策略的意思。

[補充] marketing tactics 行銷策略
a delaying tactic 拖延戰術

tactical adj. 戰術的；策略上的
tactician n. 戰術家

---

96. **teamwork**

[`tim͵wɝk]

n. 團隊合作

⇨ **team**「團隊」**＋ work**「工作」

I realize that not all of you are fans of **teamwork**, but this project is too big to be completed individually.

我了解你們不是所有人都喜歡團隊合作，不過這個專案規模太大無法靠個人力量完成。

[補充] teamwork skills 協作技巧

teammate n. 隊友

97. **tension**

[ˈtɛnʃən]

n. 緊張氣氛

⇨ **-tens-**「拉緊」+ **-ion**「名詞字尾」

You could cut the **tension** in the negotiating room with a knife.

協商室裏頭的氣氛十分緊繃。

★ cut the tension with a knife：形容氣氛非常緊繃凝重到像是可以用刀子切開一樣。

> reduce/relieve/ease tension 舒緩緊張
> tension between A and B
> A 和 B 之間的緊張氣氛

tense adj. 緊繃的；緊張的

同 strain

中高

98. **ultimate**

[ˈʌltəmɪt]

adj. 最終的，首要的；(決定責任) 最大的

n. 最終的事物；極限；基本原則

⇨ **-ultim-**「最後」+ **-ate**「有…性質的」

The **ultimate** goal is to let Sandy handle most of her accounts on her own.

終極目標是讓 Sandy 能獨立處理她大部分的客戶。

> the ultimate decision 最後的決定
> the ultimate goal/aim 最終目標
> ultimate consumer 最終消費者

ultimately adv. 最終

---

99. **unrealistic**

[ˌʌnrɪəˈlɪstɪk]

adj. 不切實際的

⇨ **un-**「表否定」+ **realistic**「實際可行的」

We have struggled to successfully meet Mr. Edwards' **unrealistic** expectations for progress.

我們很奮力地想要成功達到 Edwards 先生對於進步不切實際的期望。

> It's unrealistic to... 做某事是不切實際的。

unrealistically adv. 不切實際地
realistic adj. 實際可行的
realist n. 現實主義者，注重實際的人

100. **vague**

[veg]
adj. 模糊的

You can't provide such a **vague** set of instructions about how to navigate our website.
關於如何瀏覽我們的網站，你不可以提供這麼模糊的使用說明。

 補充

vague about...	對於⋯很模糊
vague notion	模糊的概念
vague memory/recollection	模糊的記憶

vaguely adv. 模糊地

實力進階

Part 1. area / district / region / zone 比較

area, district, region, zone 都有區域的意思，在單純表示「某個區域」的時候差別不大，不過每個字還是有個別含意與用法區別。

	字義	例字
area	通常用於面積可測量或計算的地區，界限明確，是日常生活中用得最廣的字，表示的地區可大可小，但通常不指行政分區。	smoking area 吸菸區 residential area 住宅區 penalty area ［足球］罰球區
district	指相對於 region 稍小的地區，通常指一個國家或城市的行政分區，有時也指非行政分區。	a postal district 郵政區 District of Columbia 哥倫比亞特區
region	通常指較大的地區，常指地理上有天然界限或具有某種特色（如氣候、自然條件）自成一個單位的地區。還可以用來表示身體部位。	tropical region 熱帶地區 coastal region 沿海地區 abdominal regions 腹部區域
zone	通常指地理上的（地）帶，尤指圖表上的環形地帶。	time zone 時區 Frigid Zone 寒帶 buffer zone 中立地區

Part 2. intention / purpose / object / objective 比較

這些字都表示計畫去做、去完成的一件事，常常被翻譯成「目的」或「目標」。

	區別	例句
intention	指一個人想做某行為時的意圖、計畫或打算，單純指出想做的事情。	He announced the intention of buying that company. 他公布了要買下那間公司的想法。
purpose	表示目的之外，還強調做事的決心；也表示用途，或是生活目標。	His purpose was to become the top salesperson in Asia. 他的目的是要成為亞洲頂尖的業務員。
object	當名詞有目標、宗旨的意思，指某個行為或活動的目標。	The object of the game is to score 1000 points. 這個遊戲的目標就是要拿到一千分。
objective	指可達成，可實現的目標，常指經濟上的目標，是較正式的用字。	The team tried hard to pursue their business objectives. 這支團隊努力地追求他們的經營目標。

隨堂練習

★ 請根據句意，選出最適合的單字

( ) 1. Since you are a newcomer, I suggest that you spend some time _____ yourself with the regulations.
(A) acquainting
(B) accommodating
(C) resolving
(D) involving

( ) 2. Whether the policy will work out or not depends on the _____ between the ruling party and the opposition party.
(A) controversy
(B) implication
(C) collaboration
(D) obstacle

( ) 3. _____ respect is essential to any relationship; it helps make a relationship healthier.
(A) Vague
(B) Explicit
(C) Subjective
(D) Mutual

( ) 4. The tension is becoming unbearable; we need someone to _____ between staff and management.
(A) oppose
(B) mediate
(C) segment
(D) coincide

( ) 5. David is such a creative person that he always comes up with _____ solutions to any problem.
(A) feasible
(B) accountable
(C) arbitrary
(D) dissident

解答：1. A　2. C　3. D　4. B　5. A

Unit 10 企業經營

中高

1. abolish

[ə'bɑlɪʃ]

v. 廢除

abolition n. 廢除

同 cancel / destroy

反 establish v. 建造

The new CEO **abolished** some of the overly generous benefits the workers enjoyed.
新任執行長廢除了一些員工所享有的過於豐厚的福利。

中級

2. acquire

[ə'kwaɪr]

v. 獲得；併購

⇨ ac-「額外的」+ -quir-「尋找」，尋找額外的好處以獲得更多

The firm's goal is to **acquire** companies that might grow to be major competitors.
這間公司的目標是併購有可能成為主要競爭者的公司。

補充
acquire control/ownership of sth.
取得某物的控制權 / 所有權
be acquired by...　　被⋯併購
acquire rights to sth. 獲得使用某物的合法權

acquisition n. 獲得；併購
acquisitive adj. 想獲得的

中級

3. adapt

[ə'dæpt]

v. 使適應；使適合；改編

⇨ ad-「to」+ apt「適合的」

We have had to **adapt** to our growing technological needs by constantly experimenting with new software.
我們必需持續用新軟體測試以順應不斷成長的科技需求。

補充　adapt to N./V-ing 適應⋯

adaptation n. 適應；適合；改編
adaptable adj. 能適應的；可改編的

4. **affiliate**

[əˋfɪlɪˌet]

v. 使緊密聯繫；使隸屬於

⇨ af-「to」+ -fili-「兒子」+ -ate「使…」，使你成為兒子表示有隸屬關係

This organization is not **affiliated** to any government departments or political parties.

這個組織不隸屬於任何政府部門或政黨。

 be affiliated to/with... 與…有關係；隸屬於…
affiliate marketing 聯盟行銷

affiliation n. 隸屬關係
affiliated adj. 附屬的；相關的

中高

5. **amplify**

[ˋæmpləˌfaɪ]

v. 放大；加強；擴展；詳述

⇨ ample「大量的」+ -ify「使…」

When Doug trained one clerk the wrong way, his mistake was **amplified** when the other clerks copied the first one.

Doug 以錯誤的方式訓練一名員工，結果當其他員工仿效該名員工時，Doug 錯誤的效應就被擴大了。

ample adj. 大量的；豐富的；寬敞的
amplifier n. 擴音器；放大器
amplification n. 擴大；詳述

中級

6. **association**

[əˌsosɪˋeʃən]

n. 協會；聯合；交往

⇨ associate「關聯；交往」+ -ion「名詞字尾」，有關聯的人聚在一起形成協會

Joining a trade **association** may help you boost your business.

加入貿易協會可能會幫助你增加生意。

John's past **associations** with high-ranking members of the community helped him get a job.

John 過去和社群高層的往來關係幫助他找到了工作。

 association 當協會時縮寫為 Assoc.
in association with... 和…聯合

中級

7. **authority**

[əˋθɔrətɪ]

n. 權威；官方機構；當局

 author「著作者；創始者」+ -ity「名詞字尾」

You need to consult the proper **authorities** on this matter before beginning your project.

在開始你的企劃之前，你需要先諮詢相關單位有關的事項。

 a person in authority 有實權者
have the authority to do sth. 有權利去做某事

authentic adj. 可信的，真實的，可靠的
authorize v. 授權給…；批准，委託

8. benchmark
[ˈbɛntʃˌmark]
n. 基準；水準點；標準

➡ **bench**「長椅；法官席」＋ **mark**「標示」，法官標示的就是判決的標準

Although your test results meet the minimum **benchmark**, we have hired a more qualified candidate.
雖然你的測驗結果有達到最低標準，但我們已經僱用了一名更符合資格的應徵者。

 set the benchmark for ... 為…樹立典範
benchmark test　　　　基準測試；評定測試

同 standard / criterion

初級
9. branch
[bræntʃ]
n. 分公司

Angie will be moving from the **branch** office to our downtown headquarters.
Angie 將會從分公司調到我們市中心的總部。

 close/open a branch 關閉 / 開設分公司
a domestic branch　　國內分公司
an overseas branch　　海外分公司
a branch manager　　　分公司經理

中級
10. bureau
[ˈbjuro]
n. (政府機構的) 局

Wayne Corporation has a long record of complaints on file at the Better Business **Bureau**.
Wayne 公司在商業改進局裡有一長串的顧客抱怨檔案紀錄。

★ Better Business Bureau：美國商業改進局，專責收集公布訊息以促進消費者與企業間的信任，並監控有客訴的不良企業，在有糾紛時做為消費者與企業間的協調媒介，相當於台灣的消基會。

典故 bureau 來自古法文的 burel，原指蓋在寫字桌上的一種布，因為辦公室內有很多這樣的桌子，所以 bureau 後來便引申為「政府機構的局、司、處、署等」。

 employment bureau 職業介紹所
service bureau　　　服務局；維修處

中級

11. **coalition**

[ˌkoəˈlɪʃən]

n. 結合；聯合；結盟

⇨ **co-**「共同」+ **alit**「源自拉丁文，表成長」+ **-ion**「名詞字尾」，結合以共同成長

We will assemble a safety **coalition** with the Nigerian oil company to inspect the work site.
我們會和奈及利亞石油公司召集一個安全聯盟以視察工地。

補充	a coalition government	聯合政府
	form/build/assemble a coalition	結成聯盟
	in coalition with...	和…聯合

中級

12. **combine**

[kəmˈbaɪn]

v. 結合

⇨ **com-**「一起」+ **-bin-**「兩個」，兩個放一起就結合了

Local businesses should **combine** their efforts to maintain beautiful city streets.
當地企業應該一起努力來維持美麗的城市街道。

補充	combine forces	合作；協力
	combine A with B	結合 A 和 B
	combined with...	加上…

combination n. 結合；聯盟；密碼鎖
combined adj. 聯合的

初級

13. **company**

[ˈkʌmpənɪ]

n. 公司；同伴；陪伴

⇨ **com-**「一起」+ **panis**「拉丁文，麵包」+ **-y**「名詞字尾」

I founded this **company** with the intention of bringing a reliable service to the community.
我創辦這家公司是為了要提供社會大眾值得信賴的服務。

| 典故 | company 原指軍隊中同伙食、一起吃麵包的士兵，後引申為一群人組成的群體或組織。 |

| 補充 | set up/found/establish a company | 創立公司 |
| | run a company | 經營一家公司 |

中級

14. **compete**

[kəmˈpit]

v. 競爭

⇨ **com-**「一起」+ **-pete-**「苦幹，鬥爭」

It's difficult for us to **compete** since all the bigger businesses get tax breaks.
因為所有較大型的企業都有減稅優惠，我們要與他們競爭是很困難的。

| 補充 | compete with/against... | 和…競爭 |
| | compete for... | 爭奪… |

competition n. 競爭
competitor n. 競爭者
competitive adj. 競爭的；好競爭的；有競爭力的

中高

15. conform
[kənˈfɔrm]
v. 遵守；符合

⇨ con-「一起」+ form「塑造」，一起塑造大家共同遵守的規範

All the business owners on this street must **conform** to a specific type of building theme.
這條街上所有的商家都必須遵守某個特定的建築主題。

| 補充 | conform to/with... 服從…；遵守…
conform to... 符合… |

conformation n. 符合；型態
conformity n. 遵從；符合

同 遵守：obey / observe / abide by

中高

16. confront
[kənˈfrʌnt]
v. 面臨；遭遇；面對；對抗

⇨ con-「一起」+ -front-「額頭」，額頭碰在一起表示遇到了

On arriving at the office, I was **confronted** with an overload of angry customer emails.
我一到辦公室就面臨大批憤怒顧客的來信。

| 補充 | be confronted with... 面臨…
confront sb. with sth. 跟某人當面對質 |

confrontation n. 對抗
confrontational adj. 對抗的

17. conglomerate
[kənˈglɑmərɪt]
n. 企業集團
v. 聚成一團

⇨ con-「一起」+ glomer「拉丁文，線團」+ -ate「動詞字尾」，線團捲在一起就成一團

After years of acquisitions, the multi-industry **conglomerate** now branches into twenty countries.
經過數年的併購，這間綜合企業集團現在分公司已遍佈 20 個國家。

| 補充 | a financial conglomerate 金融企業集團
an industrial conglomerate 工業企業集團 |

conglomeration n. 聚集；團塊

18. consent
[kənˈsɛnt]
n./v. 同意

⚫ con-「一起」+ -sent-「感覺」

We are awaiting the **consent** of the property owner to begin the highway extension.
我們在等待地主同意以開始公路延伸增建工程。

| 補充 | with sb's consent 得到某人的同意
without sb's consent 未經某人同意
by common consent 普遍認可；大多數人同意 |

中高

19. **constituent**

[kən`stɪtʃuənt]

adj. 組成的；選舉的

n. 成分；選民

⇨ **con-**「一起」+ **-stitu-**「建立」+ **-ent**「形容詞字尾」，一起建立的就是組成份子

There are three **constituent** companies proposing to participate in a merger.

有三間子公司提議參與合併計畫。

補充　**constituent company** 子公司，附屬公司

constitute v. 組成
constitution n. 構造；組成；憲法

中高

20. **copyright**

[`kɑpɪˌraɪt]

n. 著作權

v. 為…取得著作權

adj. 受著作權保護的

 copy「副本；本；冊」+ **right**「權利」

We are suing Harris Productions for **copyright** infringement after they made a logo similar to ours.

在 Harris 製作公司做了一個和我們公司相似的商標後，我們就控告他們侵害著作權。

補充　break/breach/infringe copyright　侵害版權
own/hold the copyright on/to sth.
擁有某物的版權
copyright piracy　盜版

中高

21. **corporate**

[`kɔrpərɪt]

adj. 公司的；法人的；共同的，全體的

A small group of **corporate** raiders cornered the market on our stocks and now have a controlling interest in the company.

有一小群企業狙擊手壟斷市場大量買進我們的股票，現在擁有我們公司的控制股權。

★ corporate raider：企業狙擊手，透過大量購買目標公司股票以握有足以影響股東會的票數，進而取得公司主導權的個人或組織，也可指「敵意收購人 (hostile bidder)」。

補充　corporate image　　公司形象
a corporate body　　法人團體

corporation n. 大型公司，大企業

中級

22. critical

['krɪtɪk!]

adj. 批評的；關鍵的

 critic「評論家」+ **-al**「有關…的」

Although my business partner is overly **critical** of me, it keeps me on my toes and sharp.

雖然我的生意夥伴非常會批評我，但這也讓我時時保持戰戰兢兢的態度。

補充
be critical of N.	批評 N.
be critical to N.	對 N. 至關重要
critical path	關鍵路徑

criticize v. 批評
criticism n. 批評
critically adv. 批判性地；危急地

初級

23. develop

[dɪ'vɛləp]

v. 發展；開發；沖洗相片

⇨ **de-**「表相反動作」+ **-velop-**「包裹」，不包起來表示讓事物發展成長

I want you to work with our software engineers to **develop** your programming skills.

我要你跟我們的軟體工程師合作以發展你程式設計的技能。

development n. 發展；開發
developed adj. (國家)已開發的；先進的
developing adj. 發展中的

中高

24. dilemma

[də'lɛmə]

n. 進退兩難；困境

 di-「二」+ **lemma**「希臘文，假設」

The glitch in our program has caused a huge **dilemma** for users that are trying to log in.

我們程式故障讓要登入的使用者面臨很大的困境。

The president is now facing a **dilemma** of doubling the cost or losing the contract.

董事長現正面臨要使成本倍增或失去合約的兩難困境。

補充　in a dilemma 陷入困境

中高

25. discreet

[dɪ'skrit]

adj. 言行審慎的；謹慎小心的

⇨ **dis-**「分開」+ **-cret-**「區別」，區別開來小心處理

In planning the boss's 60th birthday party secretly, be **discreet** when you walk around the office.

為祕密計劃老闆 60 歲的生日派對，在辦公室裡走動時要謹言慎行。

補充　discreet enquiries 審慎的查詢

discreetly adv. 謹慎地

同 careful

反 indiscreet adj. 輕率的

易混 discrete adj. 分開的；各別的；互不相關的

26. distort

[dɪsˋtɔrt]

v. 扭曲

⇨ dis-「分開」+ -tort-「扭轉」

Your description **distorts** the truth about the environment in our board meetings.
你的描述扭曲了關於我們董事會議環境的真實狀況。

distortion n. 扭曲
distorted adj. 扭曲的

中高

27. doctrine

[ˋdɑktrɪn]

n. 原理；(宗教) 教義

⇨ doctor「教師」+ -ine「名詞字尾」，老師教的事就是事物的原理

My partners and I follow a certain **doctrine** to make money at any cost.
我和我的夥伴遵循著不計一切代價賺錢的原則。

doctrinal adj. 教義的；教誨的

中高

28. donor

[ˋdonɚ]

n. 贈送人；捐贈者

⇨ -don-「給予」+ -or「做…動作的人」

The company is sponsoring a blood drive, and **donors** of all shapes and sizes are welcome.
這家公司贊助一場捐血活動，各種血型的捐贈者都歡迎。

 補充

corporate donor	企業捐贈方
donor card	器官捐贈卡
a blood donor	捐血人

donate v. 捐贈
donation n. 捐贈

---

29. downsize

[ˋdaʊnˏsaɪz]

v. 縮編

⇨ down「往下」+ size「尺寸」

We have no choice but to **downsize** after the terrible downturn in the economy.
在經歷嚴重的經濟不景氣之後我們不得不進行縮編。

downsizing n. 縮編

中級

30. dramatic

[drəˋmætɪk]

adj. 急劇的，引人注目的

⇨ drama「戲劇」+ -ic「形容詞字尾」

The announcement had a **dramatic** impact on stock prices.
該項宣布對股價造成了巨大的影響。

 補充

a dramatic change　顯著的改變
at a dramatic rate　以驚人的速度

drama n. 戲劇
dramatically adv. 戲劇性地；引人注目地

31. drastic

[`dræstɪk]

adj. 激烈的；嚴厲的

It's time for a **drastic** change in our company's direction after years of lagging behind our competitors.

在落後我們的競爭者好幾年後，該是我們針對公司方向做出大幅度改變的時機了。

> 補充
> drastic measures　激烈的措施
> drastic cuts　　　大幅度的減少

drastically adv. 激烈地；大大地

32. eliminate

[ɪ`lɪmə͵net]

v. 淘汰；消除

⇨ **e-**「向外」＋ **limin**「拉丁文，門檻」＋ **-ate**「使…」，放到門檻外的就是不要的

I'm going to **eliminate** most of our customer service positions in favor of a mostly automated system.

我將要淘汰掉我們大部分客服的職位，改用一個幾乎全自動的系統。

> 補充
> eliminate someone from your inquiries
> 相信某人是清白的
> eliminate A from B　將 A 從 B 中去除

elimination n. 淘汰；消除

同 get rid of

33. embezzle

[ɪm`bɛzl]

v. 盜用；挪用；侵占公款

⇨ **em-**「使成為」＋ **bezzle**「源自法文，表折磨破壞」

Anita's security clearance allowed her to **embezzle** funds for years without getting caught.

Anita 的安全許可證使她能夠盜用公款數年而沒有被抓。

★ security clearance：美國政府機關或私人機構為確保資訊隱密性對內部成員所進行的背景調查，通過調查者即有權進入管制區域或取得有分級權限的訊息。可指安全審查，或是取得的安全許可證。

> 補充
> embezzle N. from sb.　侵吞某人的東西

embezzlement n. 盜用；挪用；侵占
embezzler n. 盜用公款犯

34. emphasis
[ˋɛmfəsɪs]
n. 強調

⇨ em-「在內」＋ -pha-「顯現」，由內顯現出來就是要強調的重點

I want to put **emphasis** on the fact that our new system needs to be operational in just one week!
我要強調我們的新系統得在一週內實際運作！

補充 place/put/lay emphasis on... 強調…

emphasize v. 強調
emphatic adj. 強調的；加強語氣的
同 stress

中高
35. enlightening
[ɪnˋlaɪtnɪŋ]
adj. 啓發的

⇨ en-「進入」＋ light「光線」＋ -en「使變成」＋ -ing「形容詞字尾」，將光線放入黑暗就消失了，蒙蔽的心智就被啓發了

The past few days of training have been **enlightening**, and I feel far more capable.
過去幾天的受訓很有啟發性，我覺得我更加幹練了。

enlighten v. 啓發；啓迪
enlightenment n. 啓蒙

---

36. enterprise
[ˋɛntɚˏpraɪz]
n. 企業；進取心；事業心

 enter-「彼此」＋ -pris-「＝ -prend-，表抓住」

It has been difficult obtaining capital for my own **enterprise**.
爲我的企業募集資金一向很困難。

補充
private enterprise　　私人企業
enterprise culture　　企業文化
enterprise zone　　　企業振興區

entrepreneur n. 企業家

---

37. environment
[ɪnˋvaɪrənmənt]
n. 環境

⇨ en-「在內」＋ viron「古法文，環繞」＋ -ment「名詞字尾」

We will be moving the website over to a new **environment** temporarily while we fix some bugs.
在我們修正一些程式錯誤時會暫時將網站搬到新的環境去。

補充
marketing environment　　　　市場行銷環境
economic environment　　　　經濟環境
office/workplace environment　辦公環境
business environment　　　　企業環境

environmental adj. 環境的
environmentally adv. 有關環境方面地

38. **establish**

[ə`stæblɪʃ]

v. 創立

⇨ **establir**「古法文，穩定的」+ **-ish**「動詞字尾」，建造使其穩定

It took years for the company to **establish** a good business reputation.

這間公司花了好幾年才建立起良好的商譽。

 establish oneself 經過一段時間得到成功地位

establishment n. 創立；建立的機構，公司
established adj. 已建立的

39. **expand**

[ɪk`spænd]

v. 擴張；擴展；增加

⇨ **ex-**「向外」+ **-pand-**「散開，伸出去」

I would like to **expand** the user options at our online store.

我想要增加我們網路商店的使用者選項。

expand a business/company/program
擴展事業 / 公司 / 企劃
expand the range/scope/capacity
擴張範圍 / 領域 / 容量

expansion n. 擴張；擴展
expandable adj. 可擴展的

40. **far-fetched**

[`far`fɛtʃt]

adj. 遙不可及的；牽強的

⇨ **far**「遙遠地」+ **fetch**「取；去拿」+ **-ed**「形容詞字尾」

What I'm proposing seems **far-fetched** right now, but I am convinced that it can come to pass.

我所追求的東西現在也許看起來很遙不可及，不過我有信心它一定會實現。

a far-fetched idea 牽強的意見
a far-fetched story 令人難以置信的故事

中級

41. **fierce**

[fɪrs]

adj. 激烈的，猛烈的；極度的

The two soda companies have **fierce** marketing campaigns attacking each other.

這兩間汽水公司舉辦了激烈的行銷活動彼此攻擊。

fierce competition 激烈的競爭
fierce opposition 強烈的反對

fiercely adv. 激烈地
fierceness n. 兇猛；猛烈

中高

42. flourish

[`flɝɪʃ]

v. 繁茂；誇耀

n. 誇張華麗的動作或言語

flourishing adj. 繁盛的

同 繁茂：thrive / prosper

⇨ -flour- 「花」+ -ish「動詞字尾」，像花開一樣茂盛

After recruiting Oliver as the new chef, his business soon flourished.

把 Oliver 挖來擔任新主廚之後，他的生意很快就蓬勃發展了。

中級

43. found

[faʊnd]

v. 創立；建造；創辦

Although he **founded** the company, Eric was voted out as the CEO by the board.

雖然 Eric 創辦了這間公司，他卻被董事會辭去執行長的職務。

補充		
	be founded on...	建立在⋯基礎上
	a solid/firm foundation	有力根基
	lay/provide the foundation for...	為⋯打下基礎

foundation n. 創立；基金會；基礎
founder n. 創辦人

同 establish

中高

44. franchise

[`fræntʃaɪz]

n. 經銷權；加盟權

v. 給予特權或經銷權

Let's do a thorough assessment of the new fast food chain before agreeing to sign a **franchise** agreement.

我們在同意簽屬特許加盟協議之前先針對新的速食連鎖店做一個徹底的評估吧。

 典故 franchise 這個字和 frank「坦白直接的」來自相同的法文字 franc；franc 原意是自由的。因為自由，就可以直接坦白的說話，更可以直接給別人權利賣自己的商品。所以 franchise 就是指「政府給予個人、公司或社團經營某種事業的特權，或製造廠商授予聯營業者的經銷權或公司名稱使用權等。」

補充		
	work under franchise	根據特許經營工作
	franchise agreement	特許協議；特許加盟合同
	franchise chain	加盟連鎖店
	rail/fast food franchise	鐵路／速食專營權

franchisee n. 特許經營人；加盟被授權者
franchisor n. 特許經營商；加盟業主
franchising n. 特許經營；連鎖加盟

06 買賣交易

07 採購與物流

08 廣告與宣傳

09 業務協調

10 企業經營

中級

45. gradual

[`grædʒuəl]

adj. 逐漸的

⇨ **gradus**「拉丁文，步伐」+ **-al**「有…性質的」，有一步一步走的性質就是逐漸的

A **gradual** increase in customer dissatisfaction led to the sacking of our department chief.

顧客的不滿逐漸增加導致我們部長被解僱了。

補充　a gradual improvement in sales
銷售額逐步提升

gradually adv. 逐漸地

中級

46. grant

[grænt]

n. 政府補助金

v. 授予

Our staff is feverishly pursuing a **grant** to continue the operation of our non-profit organization.

我們員工為了我們非營利組織的營運正拚了命申請補助。

補充
a student grant	助學金
a research grant	研究撥款
a government grant	政府補助金

中級

47. harvest

[`hɑrvɪst]

n. 收穫

v. 收穫；收割

This year's poor **harvest** led to a rise in coffee prices worldwide.

今年歉收導致全球性的咖啡漲價。

補充
harvest festival	收穫節，豐年祭
poor/bad harvest	歉收
good harvest	豐收

harvester n. 收穫者；收割者；收割機

中級

48. headquarters

[`hɛd`kwɔrtəz]

n. 總部

⇨ **head**「首長；頭目」+ **quarters**「區域」，首領所在區域就是總部

We feel building a new company **headquarters** in a location more towards the center of the country would be advantageous for logistical purposes.

我們覺得在更靠近國家的中心點設置一個新的公司總部有利於物流安排。

headquarter v. 將總部設在…

縮　HQ

中級

49. heir

[ɛr]

n. 繼承人；接班人

Ten years as the vice president makes Mr. Collins the **heir** apparent to succeed Mr. Jones.
擔任副總裁 10 年的資歷使 Collins 先生儼然成為 Jones 先生的接班人。

補充
heir to sth. 某物的繼承者
heir to sb. 某人的接班人

heirless adj. 無繼承人的
heirship n. 繼承權；繼承人的地位

中高

50. imperative

[ɪm`pɛrətɪv]

adj. 重要迫切的；命令式的
n. 命令；規則；必要的事情

⇨ imperare「拉丁文，命令」+ -ive「形容詞字尾」，命令都是重要的

Clear thinking is **imperative** when a snap decision must be made on whether or not to send out a shipment.
當必須快速決定是否寄出貨物時，思路清晰是必要的。

補充
It is imperative that + S. + should + V...
做某事是迫切的
It is imperative for someone to do sth.
對某人而言做某事是迫切的

imperatively adv. 命令式地

同 必要的：compulsory / obligatory

中級

51. imperial

[ɪm`pɪrɪəl]

adj. 帝國的；專橫的

Hewlett Incorporated's takeover of the diamond mines is considered to be an aggressive, **imperial** act by the local people.
Hewlett 股份有限公司收購鑽石礦坑的行為被當地人民視為侵略、專橫的舉動。

補充 imperial expansion 帝國擴張

imperialism n. 帝國主義

初級

52. improve

[ɪm`pruv]

v. 改進，改善

⇨ im-「使成為」+ prove「同古法文 prou，表利益」，使產生利潤，狀況就改善了

Our manufacturing plant has set a goal of **improving** total production time by fifteen percent next quarter.
我們的製造工廠制定目標要在下一季改善整體生產時程達 15%。

補充 improve considerably/dramatically/significantly
大大地改善

improvement n. 改善
improved adj. 改進過的

53. inaugural

[ɪnˋɔgjərəl]

adj. 就任的；創始的

⇨ in-「進入」+ augur「占卜官」+ -al「形容詞字尾」

It is truly an honor to be asked to attend the President's **inaugural** ball.

受邀參加總統就職舞會真的是一件很光榮的事。

典故 古時國王登基需請占卜官算好良辰吉時才可進行。

補充
an inaugural speech/lecture/address	就職演說
an inaugural meeting	首次會議

inaugurate v. 使正式就任；為…舉行就職典禮；為…舉行開幕式或落成典禮
inauguration n. 就職典禮；落成典禮；開始；創始

54. incorporated

[ɪnˋkɔrpəˏretɪd]

adj. 法人／公司組織的；合併的

⇨ in-「進入」+ -corpor-「主體」+ -ate「動詞字尾」
+ -ed「形容詞字尾」，成為一體表示組成公司

I spent years running a small business as a sole proprietor before being **incorporated**.

在被合併成為公司之前，我花了好幾年以獨資企業形式經營我的小型事業。

incorporate v. 組成公司／社團；把…合併，使併入
incorporation n. 合併；法人組織；公司

縮 Inc.

55. initial

中級

[ɪˋnɪʃəl]

adj. 最初的；開始的
n. 首字母

 in-「進入」+ -it-「去」+ -ial「形容詞字尾」

Although many borrowers can afford the **initial** interest rate on the home mortgage loan, the adjusted rate takes them by surprise.

雖然很多借款人負擔得起房屋抵押貸款的首期利率，但是調整後的利率還是使他們大吃一驚。

補充
initial estimate	初步的估計
initial stage/phase/period	初期階段
initial charge/cost/fee	原價／購置成本／首期費用

initially adv. 最初，開頭
initiation n. 開始；創始；入會

中高

56. initiative

[ɪˈnɪʃətɪv]
n. 主動的行動；倡議；計劃
adj. 開始的；初步的

⇨ **initiate**「開始；創始」＋ **-ive**「形容詞字尾」

I'm happy to see that you took the initiative to pick up some of the extra workload in the payroll department.
我很高興看到你主動擔負一些薪資部門的額外工作。

補充	a marketing initiative	行銷計劃
	take the initiative	採取主動；帶頭
	on one's own initiative	主動地

initiate v. 開始，創始 n. 新加入者

中級

57. institution

[ˌɪnstəˈtjuʃən]
n. 公共團體或機構；建立；制定

 in-「在內」＋ **-stitut-**「站立」＋ **-ion**「名詞字尾」

The Johnstown City Bank has been a community institution since it was founded in 1855.
Johnstown 城市銀行自從 1855 年創立以來就一直是一家社區型的機構。

補充	a financial institution	金融機構
	an educational institution	教育機構
	a medical institution	醫療機構

institute v. 建立；制定 n. 協會；學會
institutional adj. 制度的；學會的；公共團體的

中高

58. integrate

[ˈɪntəˌgret]
v. 統合；整合；使完整

⇨ **in-**「表否定」＋ **-tegr-**「同 -tang-，觸摸」＋ **-ate**「使…」，不去觸摸就能保持完整

We were directed to integrate our department more closely with IT to ensure more accurate data processing.
我們被指示要和資訊部門密切整合以確保更精確的資料處理。

補充	integrate A with/into B	使 A 和 B 融合在一起
	racial integration	種族融合
	cultural integration	文化融合

integration n. 整合

中高

59. integrity

[ɪnˈtɛgrətɪ]
n. 正直；完善；完整

⇨ **in-**「表否定」＋ **-tegr-**「同 -tang-，觸摸」＋ **-ity**「表狀態」，性格完整無瑕就是正直

By standing behind our money-back guarantee, we showed a lot of integrity.
我們以堅守退款保證展現了很大程度的誠信。

補充	professional integrity 職業操守

中高

60. **interior**

[ɪn'tɪrɪə]

adj. 內部的；內側的；內政的；
內心的

n. 內部；內政；內心

⇨ **inter -** 「在內部」＋ **-ior** 「比較級字尾」

I would prefer to hire an **interior** designer to modernize our depressing office environment.
我比較想僱用一名室內設計師來將我們充滿煩悶感的辦公環境變得現代化。

interior design	室內設計
interior designer	室內設計師
the Ministry of the Interior	內政部

中級

61. **internal**

[ɪn'tɜnl]

adj. 內部的；內在的；國內的；
體內的

⇨ **inter -** 「在中間」＋ **-al** 「形容詞字尾」，在中間的就是內部的

An **internal** investigation cleared the accountant of all wrongdoing, but federal officials were not convinced.
雖然內部調查證明了這名會計師的清白，但聯邦官員並不採信。

internal communications	內部溝通
internal investigations	內部調查
internal reviews	內部審查
internal affairs	內政

同 domestic adj. 國內的
inner adj. 內部的

中級

62. **launch**

[lɔntʃ]

v. 開辦；展開；發起；開始；
發射

n. 發射；新產品上市

Mars Technologies has **launched** a new app capable of tracking your average daily heart rate.
Mars 科技公司發表了一種新的應用程式可以追蹤紀錄你的每日平均心跳速度。

launch a campaign	發起活動
launch a company	成立公司
launch an assault/attack	發動攻擊
launch a product	發表產品

launcher n. 發射器

63. limited

[ˋlɪmɪtɪd]

adj. 有限的；(公司) 負有限責任的

⇨ **limit**「限制」+ **-ed**「形容詞字尾」

We are trying our best to develop better products with the **limited** resources available.

我們正盡力以有限的資源開發出更好的產品。

 補充 a limited company 有限公司 (縮寫 Ltd)

反 unlimited adj. 無限制的，無數的

初級

64. main

[men]

adj. 主要的

The **main** reason for rejecting the buyout offer is that we feel we still have a chance to rebuild the company ourselves.

拒絕收購的主要原因是我們覺得我們還有機會自己重建公司。

 補充

main office	總公司
the main problem	主要的問題
the main reason	主要的原因
the main objective	主要目的

同 chief / principal / leading

中高

65. merge

[mɝdʒ]

v. 合併；併吞

The company decided it best to **merge** with our closest competitor to grab a sixty percent market share.

公司決定和我們最接近的競爭者合併以取得 60% 的市占率是最好的。

 補充

merge A with B	將 A 和 B 合併
merge A into B	將 A 融入 B
mail merge	電腦郵件合併 (程式)

merger n. (公司的) 合併

中高

66. milestone

[ˋmaɪlˌston]

n. 里程碑；劃時代的事件

⇨ **mile**「哩；英里」+ **stone**「石頭」

We decided to host a banquet to celebrate our **milestone** of serving our one millionth customer.

我們決定舉辦一場宴會來慶祝我們來客數達一百萬人次的里程碑。

 補充

a milestone in N.	N. 的里程碑
milestone payment	階段性付款

同 milepost

中高

67. **monopoly**

[mə`nɑplɪ]

n. 壟斷；獨佔；專賣；
壟斷企業

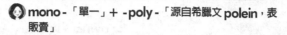 **mono -**「單一」**＋ -poly -**「源自希臘文 **polein**，表販賣」

Although not technically a **monopoly**, we have a nearly seventy percent share of the housewares market.
雖然嚴格來說我們並沒有壟斷，但在居家用品市場中我們有將近 70% 的市占率。

補充
| a monopoly of N. | N. 的壟斷 |
| government monopolies | 政府壟斷的企業 |

monopolize v. 壟斷；擁有⋯的專賣權
monopolistic adj. 獨佔的

中高

68. **odds**

[ɑdz]

n. 機會；可能性

The **odds** are that the stock market will be very volatile this year.
今年股市有可能會非常動盪不穩定。

補充
against all odds	儘管困難重重
be at odds with...	和⋯不合；和⋯相矛盾
The odds are that...	某事可能會發生
The odds are against sth.	某事發生的機會很低

初級

69. **organization**

[ˌɔrgənə`zeʃən]

n. 組織；團體

⇨ **organize**「組織」**＋ -ation**「名詞字尾」

Our **organization** specializes in services for the handicapped.
我們的組織專門為身障人士服務。

補充
organizational skills	組織才能
a nonprofit organization	非營利組織
a charitable organization	慈善組織

organizer n. 組織者
organizational adj. 組織的

中高

70. **originate**

[ə`rɪdʒəˌnet]

v. 發源，產生；創始

⇨ **origin**「起源」**＋ -ate**「使成為⋯」

The financial error **originated** from the CFO, but it got worse in the accounting department.
這個財務錯誤是在財務長那邊產生的，但到了會計部卻變得更加嚴重了。

補充
| originate in/from N. | 起源於 N. |
| originate sth. | 創造，開創某物 |

original adj. 有獨創性的；最初的 n. 原著；原畫；原版
originality n. 創造力；新穎
originally adv. 獨創地；起初

01 職稱職務／聘僱面試

02 人事／薪資／福利

03 辦公室／電話傳真

04 文書作業

05 會議

中級

71. ownership

[`onɚ͵ʃɪp]
n. 所有權

 owner「擁有者」+ -ship「名詞字尾，表狀態或權限」

After years of joint **ownership**, Hank bought out Cindy and she left to form a separate company.

共同持有公司所有權數年後，Hank 買下了 Cindy 的股份，而她離開去創立一間獨立的公司。

補充		
	ownership of sth.	擁有某物
	be under sb's ownership	隸屬某人所有
	share/stock ownership	持股；股權
	joint ownership	共同所有權

中高

72. pending

[`pɛndɪŋ]
adj. 未決定的，待決定的；迫近的

 -pend-「懸掛」+ -ing「形容詞字尾」

The contract with Riley, Inc. is still **pending** due to a disagreement about a certain clause.

和 Riley 公司的合約仍未簽定是因為針對某一條款雙方的意見不一。

補充		
	a pending case	懸案；未決案件
	a pending deal	尚未完成的交易
	pending file	待辦事項檔案夾

中高

73. phase

[fez]
n. 階段
v. 分階段實行

We are now only in the beta-testing **phase**, so please refrain from harsh criticism.

我們現在還是只在 Beta 測試階段，所以請不要嚴厲批評。

典故	
	phase 來自希臘文 phainein，原表「出現」，用來指月相盈虧的不同階段 (phase of the moon)，後來引申為「事物發展或變化的階段、時期」。

補充		
	the initial phase	初期階段
	phase... out	階段性廢除
	phase... in	逐步採用

同 stage n. 階段

中高

74. preliminary
[prɪˋlɪməˌnɛrɪ]

adj. 初步的；開始的；預備的

n. 初步，開端；初步行動、準備工作；預賽，預試

⇨ pre-「在之前」+ -limin-「門檻」+ -ary「形容詞字尾」，站在門檻前就是要準備開始的

We are in the **preliminary** stages of negotiation with Harris & Jones.
我們還在與 Harris & Jones 協商的初步階段。

補充
preliminary data/numbers/statistics
初步數據 / 資料
preliminary approval 初步核准；初步同意
preliminary investigation/inquiry 初步調查
preliminary estimate 初步估計

75. premises
[ˋprɛmɪsɪz]

n. (包含房屋及土地的) 商業經營場所

 pre-「在之前」+ -mise-「送出」+ -s「複數字尾」

No smoking is allowed anywhere on the **premises**, even outdoors.
本場所內任何地方都不准吸菸，甚至戶外也一樣。

補充 on the premises 在公司經營的場所中

premise n. 前提 v. 以…為前提

中級

76. productive
[prəˋdʌktɪv]

adj. 有生產力的；多產的

⇨ pro-「向前」+ -duct-「帶領」+ -ive「形容詞字尾」，向前帶出產品表示生產

The boss monitors the computer activity of all employees to make sure they are being **productive**.
老闆監控所有員工的電腦使用以確保他們是有產能、有在為公司做事的。

補充
productive employee/worker
工作效能很好的員工
a productive meeting 有成效的會議

productivity n. 生產力
productively adv. 有成果地

77. prospectus
[prəˋspɛktəs]

n. 創辦計劃書；內容說明書

 pro-「向前」+ -spect-「看」+ -us「名詞字尾」

Skim through this life insurance **prospectus** and decide whether what I'm offering is right for you.
瀏覽這份壽險說明書，看看我所提供的是否適合你。

補充
a company prospectus
公司行號上市前的公開說明書

prospect n. 前景；展望
prospective adj. 未來的；期望的

中級

78. **prosperity**

[prɑsˈpɛrətɪ]

n. 繁榮；興隆

prosper v. 繁榮；興盛
prosperous adj. 繁榮的

⇨ **pro -**「向前」+ **-sper -**「希望」+ **-ity**「名詞字尾」

I wish you **prosperity** in all your endeavors.
祝福你萬事亨通。

 economic prosperity　經濟繁榮

中高

79. **quest**

[kwɛst]

v./n. 追求

 n. = pursuit / search

My **quest** is to give each employee the highest quality, most up-to-date software.
我所追求的是要給每位員工最高品質、最先進的軟體。

 quest for sth.　追求某事物
in quest of sth.　追求某事物

中高

80. **rally**

[ˈrælɪ]

n. 重振，恢復；集會
v. 價格反彈；集結

The stock market **rally** had no effect on the energy sector.
股市反彈對能源產業並沒有影響。

 a market/stock rally　市場／股市反彈
a rally in N.　　　　N. 的好轉或恢復

中高

81. **reap**

[rip]

v. 收穫；收割；獲得

reaper n. 收割者；收割機

 harvest

After years of hard work, we are finally **reaping** the rewards.
經過幾年的努力，我們終於得到報酬了。

 reap benefits　得到益處
reap rewards　得到報酬
reap profits　　得到利潤

中高

82. redundancy

[rɪˋdʌndənsɪ]

n. 多餘；重複；(BrE) 被解僱，
失業

⇨ re-「再次」+ unda「拉丁文，表波浪」+ -ancy「名詞字尾」，波浪不斷打來水就多出來了，就是多餘了

Double-check the content in your presentation for **redundancy** as it tends to annoy the boss.

仔細檢查你的報告內容有沒有贅字，那很容易惹惱老闆。

redundancy payment	遣散費
voluntary redundancy	自願遣散
compulsory redundancy	強制裁員
a redundancy notice	解僱通知

redundant adj. 多餘的

同 surplus n. 過剩

中級

83. regulate

[ˋrɛgjəˌlet]

v. 控制；管理；調節；
制定規章

⇨ regula「拉丁文，規則」+ -ate「使…」，使有規律就是在調節、管理

The government just passed a law further **regulating** transactions involving stocks.

政府才剛通過一項法令以進一步規範涉及股票的交易。

environmental/safety/import regulations
環境 / 安全 / 進口規定
rules and regulations 規章制度

regulation n. 管理；調整；規章
regulator n. 管理者；調節器
regulatory adj. 管理的；控制的；調整的

中高

84. reign

[ren]

n. 統治時期，支配期
v. 統治；支配

Mr. Hobbs had the second-longest **reign** as the CEO in the company's history.

Hobbs 先生擔任該公司執行長的任期是有史以來第二長的。

reign over 統治

中級

85. reputation

[ˌrɛpjəˈteʃən]
n. 聲望

⇨ re - 「一再」+ -put - 「認為」+ -ation「名詞字尾」，一再認可就有好聲望

Mike has the **reputation** of being a reliable salesperson.
Mike 有可靠銷售員的名聲。

補充	a good/bad reputation	聲望良好 / 不好
	earn a reputation as N.	贏得…的聲望
	spoil/blacken sb's reputation	破壞某人的名聲
	spotless reputation	沒有污點的名聲

repute n. 名聲
reputable adj. 有聲望的

---

86. reshape

[riˈʃep]
v. 改造；重新塑造

⇨ re - 「再次」+ shape「塑造」

My completely unique restaurant can **reshape** the way people think about eating out.
我這間絕對獨一無二的餐廳會重塑人們對於外食的想法。

shape v. 塑造
reshaping n. 改造

中級

87. resist

[rɪˈzɪst]
v. 抗拒；抵抗

⇨ re - 「反向，對抗」+ -sist - 「站立」

It's difficult to **resist** surfing the web when the boss is not in the office.
老闆不在辦公室的時候很難抗拒不到處瀏覽網站。

補充	resist the temptation	抗拒誘惑
	cannot resist N./V-ing	無法抗拒…

resistant adj. 抵抗的；抗…的
resistance n. 抵抗；反抗

中級

88. resource

[ˈrisɔrs] / [rɪˈsɔrs]
n. 資源；機智；財力（常用複數形）
v. 向…提供資源

⇨ re - 「一再」+ source「源頭，來源」，一再提供來源就有資源

Our senior analysts are a great **resource** to consult before making our final decisions.
我們的資深分析師是我們做最後決定前能諮詢的最佳智庫。

補充	human resources department = HR	人力資源部
	natural resources	天然資源
	limited resources	有限的資源

resourceful adj. 資源豐富的；富有機智的
resourced adj. (BrE)（資金、設備）充實的
under-resourced adj.（資金、設備等）供應不足的

中級

89. rival
[ˋraɪvl]
n. 競爭者；對手；匹敵者
v. 與…競爭；與…匹敵
adj. 競爭的

⇨ **-riv-**「小河」＋ **-al**「名詞字尾」，使用同一條河的人會競逐同一資源

Zach and Mary are two **rivals** who are both vying for the chance to become the next regional manager.
Zach 和 Mary 兩人是角逐下一任區經理的競爭對手。

closest/nearest rival	實力最接近的對手
one's main rival	某人的主要對手
a rival company/firm	競爭對手公司
rival products	對手的產品

rivalry n. 競爭；競爭的行為
arch-rival n. 主要競爭對手，勁敵

同 competitor n. 競爭者

中級

90. scheme
[skim]
n. 計劃；方案；詭計
v. 計畫，設計；策劃；密謀

Harry started his embezzling **scheme** years ago, but only recently got caught.
Harry 幾年前就開始盜用公款的計畫了，但是他最近才被抓到。

| a training scheme | 訓練方案 |
| a pension scheme | 養老金計畫 |

同 n. = program / plan

中高

91. shareholder
[ˋʃɛrˌholdə]
n. 股東

⇨ **share**「股份」＋ **holder**「持有人」

The **shareholders** all made clear that they wanted a bigger dividend.
所有股東都清楚表明他們想要更多分紅。

minority shareholder	小股東
majority shareholder	大股東
controlling shareholder	控股股東
shareholder value	股東利益
shareholder rebellion	股東抗爭

同 (AmE) stockholder

中級

92. **significant**

[sɪɡˋnɪfəkənt]

adj. 重要的；重大的；顯著的；
有意義的

 sign「標誌；記號」+ **-fic-**「做」+ **-ant**「形容詞字尾」

I suggest making some **significant** adjustments to this commercial as some may find it offensive.

我建議針對這個廣告做一些重大的調整，因爲有些人可能會覺得它很令人不舒服。

補充
be significant for sth.	對某事來說很重要
highly significant	非常重要的
it is significant that...	某事相當重要
a significant other	
重要的夥伴（如配偶、生意搭檔等）	

significance n. 重要；意義
significantly adv. 意味深長地；值得注目地

中級

93. **sponsor**

[ˋspɑnsɚ]

n. 贊助者；保證人
v. 贊助；爲…做保證人

 sponsus「拉丁文，承諾、保證」+ **-or**「做…動作的人」

We have lost several **sponsors** due to the scandal with our spokesman.

因爲我們發言人的醜聞，我們已經失去了一些贊助商了。

sponsorship n. 保證人的地位；資助；贊助

中級

94. **statement**

[ˋstetmənt]

n. 聲明；陳述；銀行對帳單

state「陳述，聲明」+ **-ment**「名詞字尾」

Our newest tablet has to make a **statement** if we want our sales to spike.

如果我們想要銷售大增的話，我們最新的平板電腦必須要能展現特色。

補充
make/issue a statement	做出聲明；展現主張
bank statement	銀行對帳單
a joint statement	聯合聲明
a written statement	書面聲明
a public statement	公開聲明

state v. 陳述；聲明

95. **streamline**

['strim.laɪn]

v. 精簡（企業組織等），簡化使效率更高；使…成流線型

n. 流線型

 stream「溪流」+ **line**「線」

I believe our website should be **streamlined**, so let's cut out all the extra options.

我認為我們的網站應該要精簡，所以我們把所有多餘的選項刪掉吧。

> 補充
> streamline operations/procedures/processes
> 簡化操作 / 步驟 / 流程
> a streamlined structure/system 精簡架構 / 系統

streamlined adj. 流線型的；有效率的

中高

96. **subsidiary**

[səb'sɪdɪ.ɛrɪ]

n. 子公司；輔助物；輔助者

adj. 輔助的

⇨ **sub-**「向下」+ **-sidi-**「坐」+ **-ary**「形容詞字尾」，坐下來提供協助

Thomas Films is just a **subsidiary** of Hughes Media, but they are allowed some degree of independence.

Thomas 電影公司雖然只是 Hughes 媒體公司的一個子公司，不過他們有某些程度的獨立性。

> 補充
> sales subsidiary 銷售子公司

中高

97. **takeover**

['tek.ovə]

n. 接管；收購

 take「拿」+ **over**「從一方至另一方」

It was not a surprise when there was a government **takeover** of our country's biggest bank.

政府接管我們國內最大的銀行這件事並不令人意外。

> 補充
> make a takeover bid for... 競價收購…
> friendly takeover 善意收購
> hostile takeover 惡意收購
> takeover offer 收購條件

take over phr. 接收；併購

中高

98. **thrive**

[θraɪv]

v. 茂盛；興旺；繁榮

Being assigned a mentor helped me to truly **thrive** in my new position due to great training.
因為有前輩的訓練，我才得以在新職位上真正成長茁壯。

補充　thrive on something 在…下茁壯成長
a thriving economy 繁榮的經濟

thriving adj. 繁榮的；興旺的；成功的

中高

99. **turmoil**

[ˈtɜˋmɔɪl]

n. 騷動；混亂

⇨ **turn**「使變得…」＋ **moil**「辛苦」，混亂使一切變得辛苦

All business operations were thrown into **turmoil** after the terrorist attacks.
恐怖攻擊發生後所有的企業運作都處於混亂狀態中。

補充　in turmoil 處於混亂狀態
in a state of political turmoil 處於政治動盪中

同 unrest / commotion

中高

100. **yield**

[jild]

n. 產量

v. 產生；屈服；讓與

Using more efficient machines to separate the fruit from the stem will result in a higher **yield**.
使用效能更佳的機器將水果從莖上面分開來將產生更高的產量。

補充　yield to N. 服從…；屈服於…
yield... results 產生…結果
yield... profits 產生…利潤

實力進階

Part 1. 比一比：coalition vs. combination

coalition	combination
指兩個以上人或團體的「聯合」	指兩個以上事物的「結合」
in coalition with 人／團體 例：The CEO decided to work in coalition with some non-profit organizations. 執行長決定要和一些非營利組織合作。	in combination with 事物 例：A traditional wooden tub in combination with the new technologies is the selling point of the state-of-the-art Jacuzzi. 結合新科技的傳統木製浴缸是此先進按摩浴缸的賣點。

Part 2. 易混字：expand, expend, extend

expand

expand = ex- + -pand- (展開)，向外展開就是「擴大、擴張」

如：expand a business 擴張生意
　　expand a company 擴大公司

expend

expend = ex- + -pend- (稱重，付錢)，付錢出去的動作就是「花費」

如：expend the money/time 花費金錢／時間
　　expend the efforts 花費力氣

extend

extend = ex- + -tend- (伸出)，向外伸出去也就是「延伸、延長」

如：extend the deadline 延長截止日
　　extend a contract 延長合約

隨堂練習

★ 請根據句意，選出最適合的單字

(   ) 1. Due to the economic slump worldwide, many small companies are _____ by large conglomerates.
       (A) reaped   (B) acquired
       (C) originated   (D) adapted

(   ) 2. The secretary was arrested for _____ of company funds.
       (A) embezzlement   (B) redundancy
       (C) dilemma   (D) coalition

(   ) 3. This company has _____ its workforce by 20% in order to pull itself out of a bad financial position.
       (A) resisted   (B) thrived
       (C) sponsored   (D) downsized

(   ) 4. The proposal of merging the two companies into one was strongly _____ by the board of directors.
       (A) resisted   (B) conformed
       (C) launched   (D) flourished

(   ) 5. The government's _____ of this bank is inevitable because of its economic plight.
       (A) emphasis   (B) quest
       (C) takeover   (D) milestone

解答：1. B   2. A   3. D   4. A   5. C

職場必學－實用詞彙

1. RSVP

RSVP是法文「Répondez s'il vous plaît」的縮寫，翻譯成中文就是「請回覆」的意思。常用在邀請函或書信中，要收件人回覆確認是否參加其邀約。要注意的是 RSVP 已經包含了「請 please」的意思，因此使用時只要寫 RSVP 就好，不要再加上 please，不然就變成贅字囉！

2. attn

attn（或 attn.）是 attention 一字的簡寫，通常會標示成「attn: 某人 / 某部門」，表示要某人或某部門注意，要他來處理這份文件的意思。發送傳真、公文、信件的時候都很常用。在發出的文件上加註 attn 是為了讓發出去的文件能快速準確的被送到該去的地方。同樣的，收到加註了 attn 的文件就可以馬上知道東西要交給誰囉！

3. acct.

acct.（或 a/c.）是 account 一字的簡寫，可以指銀行的帳戶，也可以指商業上往來的客戶，如：廣告業中替客戶執行廣告行銷規劃的廣告 AE，就是 Account Executive。

4. e.g.

e.g.（或 eg）是拉丁文「exempli gratia」的縮寫，就是「例如 for example」。因此出現 e.g. 的時候直接讀 e.g.，或是讀成 for example 都可以。書寫英文要舉例的時候要注意用的是 e.g.，千萬不要直接把 example 一字簡化成 ex，那樣可是錯誤的用法喔！

5. c/o

c/o 是 care of 的縮寫，表示轉交的意思。通常會標示成「XXX c/o 某人或某機構」表示「由某人或某機構轉交給 XXX」。除了工作場合，其實日常生活中也用的到 c/o。比如說收件者沒有自己私人的住址，或是住在別人家的時候，就可以在信封上標註 c/o 表示要請誰將信轉交給收件者。

6. w/o

w/o 是 without 的簡寫；相反地，「w/」就是指 with。

7. N/A

N/A 是英語 Not applicable「不適用」的縮寫。

N/A 較常用在填寫表格，用來表示「本欄目（對我）不適用」。在沒有東西可填寫，但空格也不允許此項留白的時候，可以寫 N/A。在英語國家，也會用 n/a 或者 n.a. 來表達，都是同一個意思。

不過 N/A 也可以代表 not available「不提供」；通常用來表示不提供某種服務。

8. net

商務情境中，net 最常表示「淨值」。如：net income 淨收入、net weight 淨重等，net weight 一詞也可以縮寫成「N.W.」。而採購單或出貨單上通常會標註付款條件如：net 10、net 30 等，其實就是指 net 10 days 或 net 30 days，意思是指在出貨或服務完成後 10 天或 30 天內需支付款項給賣方，這也是 net 常見的用法。

9. C/P 值

C/P 值源自英文 Cost/Performance ratio「性價比」，即價格對於性能的比值。常改寫成 cost-performance ratio 或直接稱為 cost-performance。也有人會把 C/P 值用 Capability/Price 解釋。

由 C/P 值一字還衍生出了 C/V 值（Cost-Value 值價比）一詞。

10. SWOT

SWOT 指的是 SWOT Analysis「強弱危機分析」。SWOT 四個字母分別表示：Strengths（優勢）、Weaknesses（劣勢）、Opportunities（機會）和 Threats（威脅）。

SWOT 是一種企業競爭態勢分析方法，也是市場行銷的基礎分析方法之一，通過評價企業的 strengths 和 weaknesses、競爭市場上的 opportunities 和 threats，用以在制定企業的發展戰略前對企業進行深入全面的分析以及競爭優勢的定位。現在 SWOT 分析的用途非常廣，除了用在企業中，也用在分析個人職涯規劃上。

字彙索引

字彙索引

字彙索引

字彙索引

字彙索引

字彙索引

國家圖書館出版品預行編目（CIP）資料

徐薇教你背新多益單字 / 徐薇編著 . -- 臺北市：
碩英，2015.02
　　冊；　公分. --
　　　ISBN 978-986-90662-1-1（上冊：平裝附光碟片）

1. 多益測驗 2. 詞彙

805.1895　　　　　　　　　　104001171

徐薇教你背新多益單字（上）

發行人：江正明

發行公司：碩英出版社

編著者：徐薇

責任編輯：賴依寬、黃怡欣、黃思瑜、王歆

英文編輯：Jon Turner、Paul Deacon、Sherry Wen

美術編輯：陳爾筠

錄音製作：風華錄音室

地址：106 台北市大安區安和路二段 70 號 2 樓之 3

電話：02-2708-5508

傳真：02-2707-1669

出版日期：2015 年 06 月

定價：NT$450